*continued . . .*

# SHADOW GAME

"Having fast made a name for herself in the vampire romance realm, Feehan now turns her attention to other supernatural powers in this swift, sensational offering . . . The sultry, spine-tingling kind of read that [Feehan's] fans will adore."
—*Publishers Weekly*

"One of the best current voices in the darker paranormal romance subgenre, Feehan has begun another series that, while lacking the fantasy feel of her Carpathian romances, is equally intense, sensual, and mesmerizing and might appeal especially to fans of futuristic romances. Known for her vampire tales, Feehan is a rising star in paranormal romance."
—*Library Journal*

"Sizzling sex scenes both physical and telepathic pave the road to true love . . . Action, suspense, and smart characters make this erotically charged romance an entertaining read."
—*Booklist*

"Feehan packs such a punch . . . it will leave one gasping for breath . . . [She] wields the suspense blade with ease, keeping readers enthralled and teetering on the edge . . . Guaranteed not to disappoint, and will leave one begging for more. A must-read book, only cementing Ms. Feehan's position as a genre favorite for yet another round."
—*The Best Reviews*

"A very fast-paced, action-packed thriller/love story all wrapped up into one . . . I highly recommend this book and will be adding it to my keeper's shelf."
—EscapeToRomance.com

...and more praise for the novels of
Christine Feehan

"Just as I begin to think the romance genre has nowhere else to run, I get to read something that takes another giant leap down a totally unknown road. Romance, suspense, and intrigue, and the paranormal . . . combined to make one of the most delicious journeys I have had the pleasure of taking in a long, long time . . . Definitely something for everyone."

—*Romance and Friends*

"Feehan's newest is a skillful blend of supernatural thrills and romance that is sure to entice readers."

—*Publishers Weekly*

"If you are looking for something that is fun and different, pick up a copy of this book."    —*All About Romance*

"This one is a keeper . . . I had a hard time putting [it] down . . . Don't miss this book!"    —*New-Age Bookshelf*

"Vibrant characters, suspense-filled plot . . . and just the right touch of the supernatural . . . a must-read, especially on those dark rainy nights, when the wind howls its anger at the world. Kudos, Ms. Feehan, you have penned a page-turner—good to the last drop."    —*Romance Reviews Today*

"Christine Feehan is a magnificent storyteller."

—*Romantic Times*

# DEADLY GAME

# CHRISTINE FEEHAN

JOVE BOOKS, NEW YORK

**THE BERKLEY PUBLISHING GROUP**
**Published by the Penguin Group**
**Penguin Group (USA) Inc.**
**375 Hudson Street, New York, New York 10014, USA**
Penguin Group (Canada), 90 Eglinton Avenue East, Suite 700, Toronto, Ontario M4P 2Y3, Canada
(a division of Pearson Penguin Canada Inc.)
Penguin Books Ltd., 80 Strand, London WC2R 0RL, England
Penguin Group Ireland, 25 St. Stephen's Green, Dublin 2, Ireland (a division of Penguin Books Ltd.)
Penguin Group (Australia), 250 Camberwell Road, Camberwell, Victoria 3124, Australia
(a division of Pearson Australia Group Pty. Ltd.)
Penguin Books India Pvt. Ltd., 11 Community Centre, Panchsheel Park, New Delhi—110 017, India
Penguin Group (NZ), 67 Apollo Drive, Mairangi Bay, Auckland 1311, New Zealand
(a division of Pearson New Zealand Ltd.)
Penguin Books (South Africa) (Pty.) Ltd., 24 Sturdee Avenue, Rosebank, Johannesburg 2196,
South Africa

Penguin Books Ltd., Registered Offices: 80 Strand, London WC2R 0RL, England

This is a work of fiction. Names, characters, places, and incidents either are the product of the author's imagination or are used fictitiously, and any resemblance to actual persons, living or dead, business establishments, events, or locales is entirely coincidental. The publisher does not have any control over and does not assume any responsibility for author or third-party websites or their content.

DEADLY GAME

A Jove Book / published by arrangement with the author

ISBN-13: 978-0-7394-7947-6

JOVE®
Jove Books are published by The Berkley Publishing Group,
a division of Penguin Group (USA) Inc.,
375 Hudson Street, New York, New York 10014.
JOVE is a registered trademark of Penguin Group (USA) Inc.
The "J" design is a trademark belonging to Penguin Group (USA) Inc.

PRINTED IN THE UNITED STATES OF AMERICA

*For Val Philips, a treasured friend*
*who doesn't like alligator ponds with alligators in them*
*(who would have known?)*
*or terribly alpha males,*
*this one's for you.*

# For My Readers

Be sure to write to Christine at Christine@christine
feehan.com to get a FREE exclusive screen saver and
join the PRIVATE e-mail list to receive an announce-
ment when Christine's books are released.

# Acknowledgments

I want to thank Domini Stottsberry for her help in the tremendous amount of research necessary to make this book possible. Brian Feehan and J&L deserve much gratitude for talking about rescues and action, and answering endless questions! As always, Cheryl, you are incredible!

# The GhostWalker Symbol Details

SIGNIFIES
shadow

SIGNIFIES
protection against
evil forces

SIGNIFIES
the Greek letter *psi,* which
is used by parapsychology
researchers to signify ESP or
other psychic abilities

SIGNIFIES
qualities of a knight—
loyalty, generosity,
courage, and honor

SIGNIFIES
shadow knights who protect
against evil forces using
psychic powers, courage,
and honor

nox noctis est nostri

# The GhostWalker Creed

*We are the GhostWalkers, we live in the shadows*
*The sea, the earth, and the air are our domain*
*No fallen comrade will be left behind*
*We are loyalty and honor bound*
*We are invisible to our enemies*
*and we destroy them where we find them*
*We believe in justice and we protect our country*
*and those unable to protect themselves*
*What goes unseen, unheard, and unknown*
*are GhostWalkers*
*There is honor in the shadows and it is us*
*We move in complete silence whether*
*in jungle or desert*
*We walk among our enemy unseen and unheard*
*Striking without sound and scatter to the winds*
*before they have knowledge of our existence*
*We gather information and wait with endless patience*
*for that perfect moment to deliver swift justice*
*We are both merciful and merciless*
*We are relentless and implacable in our resolve*
*We are the GhostWalkers and the night is ours*

# CHAPTER 1

Ken Norton glanced up at the swirling dark clouds obscuring the stars and casting an ominous charcoal veil across the moon. He noted the shadows of the trees, closer to the hulking building, checking them constantly for any alteration, any sign of someone slipping through the darkness out of sight of the cameras, but his gaze kept straying back to the large hunting cabin and two carcasses swaying from meat hooks on the porch. The smell of blood and death assailed his nostrils and he wanted to gag, a stupid reaction to the two skinned deer hanging from hooks on the porch when he was a sniper and had done more than his share of killing.

His skin color changed to better blend with his surroundings, and his specially designed clothes reflected the colors around him, allowing him the effect of disappearing completely into the surrounding foliage, hidden from prying eyes. For the thousandth time he looked away from the swaying carcasses still dripping blood.

"So who the hell orders a hit on a senator of the United States?" he asked, his steel gray eyes turning to turbulent mercury. "And not just any senator, a senator being considered as a vice-presidential candidate. I don't like this. I haven't liked it from the moment they told us who the target was."

"Hell, Ken. This is no innocent man," his twin, Jack, replied, easing forward to get into a better position to cover the cabin. "You know that better than anyone else. I don't know why the hell we're protecting the son of a bitch. I want to kill him myself. This is the bastard who was the bait to lure you into the Congo. He got out and you were left there to be cut into little pieces and skinned alive." The words were bitter, but Jack's voice was utterly calm. "Don't tell me you don't think he was in on it. Any number of people might have ordered it. The senator set you up, Ken, handed you over to the rebel leader and Ekabela nearly killed you. I could whack him a hundred times and never lose sleep over it—or stand by and let him get whacked."

"*Exactly.*" Ken rolled over, using care to keep the bushes surrounding him still. He hoped the darkness had hidden his slight wince when his twin brought up the past. He didn't think about the torture much—being cut into tiny pieces, his back skinned—or how the knife felt slicing through his skin. But he had nightmares every time he closed his eyes. He remembered it all then. Every cut. Every slice. The agony that never stopped. He woke choking, covered in sweat, his own screams echoing deep inside where no one could ever hear. The deer hanging from meat hooks brought it all back in sharp, vivid detail. He couldn't help but wonder if that was all part of a much larger plan.

He held out his hand, checking for tremors. The scars were rigid and tight, but his hand was rock steady. "Why do you think we were chosen to protect him? We have a grudge against this man. We know he's more than everyone thinks, so who better to take him out without questions? Who better to blame it on? Something's not right."

"What's not right is protecting this bastard. Let them kill him."

Ken glanced at his twin. "Do you hear yourself? We aren't the only ones who know Senator Freeman isn't squeaky clean like the public has been led to believe. We were all debriefed when we came back from the Congo, both teams, and both teams came to the same conclusion—that the senator was dirty—yet he was never questioned, never reprimanded or exposed. And now we've been ordered to protect him from an assassination threat."

Jack was silent for a moment. "And you think we're being set up to take the fall if they get to him."

"Hell yeah I think that. Did the order come down directly from the admiral? Did the admiral actually tell Logan himself? Because, if they have dirt on this guy, why didn't they arrest him? And we just turned down a job to get rid of General Ekabela, another old enemy of ours—one connected to the senator here. It's looking a bit like a pattern to me."

"Ekabela was taken out anyway. They just brought in another shooter and I didn't get the pleasure of putting the guy in the ground."

Ken frowned at his twin. "You're making it personal."

"The senator made it personal when he delivered you to Ekabela so that sadist could torture you. I'm not going to pretend. I want the senator dead, Ken. I don't mind looking the other way if someone wants to slit his throat. If he lives and continues the way he is, he's bound to become president, or at least vice president, and then where are we going to be? He knows we know he's dirty. The first thing he'll do is send us on a suicide mission."

"Like when they wanted to send us back to the Congo to kill Ekabela?" He had to stop looking at those carcasses. He was going to get sick, his stomach churning in protest. He could almost hear the steady drip of blood even though he was yards away. It ran like a small stream down through the boards and collected in a dark, shiny pool. He tried to shut off the sound of his own screaming in his head, but his skin was crawling and each scar throbbed as if every nerve remembered the steady slice of the relentless knife.

"Ekabela deserved to die," Jack said. "He more than deserved it and you know it. He leveled villages, committed genocide, ran the drug industry, and stole from the UN when they tried to get food and medicine to the area."

"That's right, but look who stepped into his shoes. General Armine, more feared and hated than Ekabela, and how strange that the transition of power went so smoothly."

"What the hell are you trying to say, Ken?"

Ken looked up at the clouds obscuring the sliver of moon, watching them spin slowly and lazily, a dark veil with nowhere to go. He remembered the pattern of the clouds in the jungle, the sway of the canopy and the smell of his own sweat and blood. "I'm saying we never make things personal, but someone has been doing just that for us. I don't like it and I like this job even less. I think we're being set up again. I just don't believe in coincidences, and this is a huge one."

Jack swore under his breath and fit his eye to the scope, carefully surveying the mountain cabin several hundred yards away. "He's in there with his wife. I could take him out and we could just walk away clean; no one would be the wiser."

"Just our entire team."

Jack flashed a small, humorless grin at his brother. "They'd help me and you know it. They detest the man nearly as much as I do."

"Someone wanted Armine in a position of power. Someone here, in the United States. I've thought a lot about this, Jack. Every assignment we've been sent on in the past year has created a void, a hole for some other lowlife to step into. From Colombian drug lords to General Ekabela in the Congo, we're creating a vacancy in those positions of power and someone is manipulating that. I just don't happen to think it's the president of the United States." He cast his brother a quick glance. "Do you?"

Jack swore again. "No. I think we're screwed."

"I can't ask Logan if the admiral gave him the order face-to-face, because Jesse Calhoun contacted him, said it was urgent, and Logan went to see him. Jesse's been conducting an investigation into the Ekabela-Senator tie. That's why Kadan Montague took his place on the team."

"I thought Jesse was still in a wheelchair," Jack said. "The last I heard he was inactive and doing physical therapy."

"Well, apparently he's working again. He's one of the more powerful psychics on our team and he's got brains. The admiral wasn't about to give him up. It was a hell of a thing what they did to him. Between enhancement and the psychic experiments and Jesse's legs, he got the short end of the stick."

"We all did. When we volunteered for the psychic testing," Jack said, "we had no idea we were pointing a gun at our heads.

We're screwed, Ken. We're in so deep, hell, all the GhostWalkers are. What have we gotten ourselves into?"

At least they had volunteered for the experimentation. All Special Forces, all military trained. The women had been babies, orphans Whitney had adopted from foreign countries, children he bought and paid for, experimenting on them without thought to their lives.

Ken shook his head. "I don't know, but we have to find out. Colonel Higgens tried to take out Ryland Miller's team. He murdered a couple of them before they got away and exposed him. Maybe they didn't get the head of the snake."

"We know the head is Dr. Whitney. He's the brains. He came up with the experiments, had the contacts, money, and security clearance to get the green light, and he faked his own murder. We find Whitney, we kill the snake."

"Maybe." There was doubt in Ken's voice. "First we all believed Whitney was murdered. Then we believed he faked his own death to get out from under the illegal experiments he was conducting right along with his military experiments. Now . . ." He trailed off, once again staring at the clouds. The steady drip of blood seemed overly loud in the night. Never before had his past consumed him to the point of endangering a mission, but for the first time, he was beginning to doubt his ability to stay focused.

"You think someone was after Whitney to kill him for real and he *had* to fake his own death, not to hide from exposure and us, but to keep from being targeted?" Jack rubbed his temples. "How the hell did we ever get into this mess?"

"We didn't give a damn at the time," Ken said. "Now you've got a wife and twins on the way and you've got something to live for. Let's pull back, regroup with our team, and ask a few hard questions. We can have Logan contact Ryland Miller's team, and between us, we ought to have enough brains to figure out what's going on."

Jack frowned, rolled back over, and using elbows and toes, inched his way forward through heavy foliage. "We can't leave the bastard an open target, can we? If someone else wants him dead, we should probably find out why and how it affects us."

Ken wiggled his way along a rabbit path, belly down, gun cradled out of the dirt. He'd had a bad feeling for a while now.

"Hold it, Jack," Ken whispered, eye to the scope. *Something is wrong.* He reached out to telepathically communicate with his twin brother. It was a handy ability when they wanted to remain unseen. They'd been talking back and forth like this for as long as Ken could remember, never needing to communicate verbally with each other when telepathy was so handy. Consequently, they had a strong bond that had stood them in good stead over the years. The psychic experiment they'd agreed to after SEAL training had only added to that already powerful tool.

*I feel it too. Kadan sent out the alert. They're going to come in hard and fast. We're going to have to protect the bastard. Whoever wants him dead is already here.*

Ken kept his eye on the senator through the window. *The senator's young and beautiful trophy wife is aware they have company too. Look at her.*

Jack peered through the scope. Through the window of the cabin a blonde leaned down to give her husband's cheek a peck. She said something, smiled, showing a lot of teeth, and the senator answered her, touching her chin. She turned away, toward the window, giving them a look at her face.

*Oh yeah, she knows. And she didn't say a word to him about it,* Jack said.

A lot of good men might go down this night. Ken could barely resist the urge to slide into the house and save them all the trouble by slitting the bastard's throat. The senator had betrayed his country for money, or power, or a combination of both. Ken didn't really give a damn what his motives were; he'd sold out. And he'd been the bait that had sent Ken into the Congo on a rescue mission—a mission that had sent him straight into hell—and his brother after him. And now, ironically, they were protecting the traitor.

"What the hell is his wife's name?" Jack asked. "You don't suppose she's one of us? A GhostWalker?"

They both studied the tall blonde carefully. She had walked away from the senator into the next room, where she caught up several weapons, handling them as if she knew what she was doing.

Ken took a deep breath and let it out. The senator's wife? A GhostWalker? What was her name? Violet Smythe. Little had been in the report about her life before marrying the senator. Violet. The name of a flower. When they'd been briefed on Whitney's psycho experiments with children, the orphans he worked on had all been female and he'd given them the names of flowers. "Violet," he said aloud.

Where did she fit into all of this? How could a Ghost-Walker betray her fellow soldiers? She knew what they'd all been through. He peered through his scope again, taking a bead on the senator's left eye. All he had to do was pull the trigger and it would be over. No one else would get killed. One shot and the man who had delivered him into the hands of a madman would be dead.

*I know what you're thinking,* Jack said. *God knows that if anyone has the right to kill the son of bitch, it's you. If you want it done, Ken, say the word and I'll take him out now.*

Jack would do it in a heartbeat. Ken touched his scarred jaw. There was little sensation on any part of his skin, and little that remained of a once-handsome face or body. A tremor went through that body, and for one moment, rage boiled over, hot and pure and not covered up by the glacier of ice he usually wore. He hesitated, knowing he could just nod his head and Jack would pull the trigger. Or, better yet, he could do it himself and have the satisfaction of knowing he'd removed a traitor. He inhaled deeply and breathed away all emotion. That way lay insanity, and he refused to follow the legacy he was born into.

He felt Jack's relief and realized just how close a watch his brother had had on him lately. *I'm fine.* Of course Jack knew he was sweating bullets and hearing screams. Jack and Ken lived in each other's mind. Jack knew. And the knowledge ate away at him that he hadn't been able to get to Ken before Ekabela tortured him. Never mind that, in the end, Jack had pulled him out and been taken prisoner. Jack believed he should have prevented it. *I'm fine,* Ken repeated.

*I know.*

But he wasn't fine. He hadn't been born fine, hadn't been fine as a child, or in his early military career. He was worse after his capture and torture in the Congo, demons riding him hard, day and night. And now, with the senator needing protection—probably from the very man who had been paying him for years—Ken knew the dangerous shadow inside him had grown into an all-too-real threat to his sanity. *We have company,* Kadan announced telepathically. *Be alert. I'm hustling the senator into a safety room. Kadan. Watch the wife,* Ken warned. *We think she may be one of us. She's armed to the teeth and she felt the presence of intruders the moment we did.* Kadan never expressed surprise. No one was ever really sure if he felt emotions at all. He seemed a machine, matter-of-fact, simply doing the job. And he was good at it. *Copy that.*

Ken settled into position. Kadan's life would depend on him. Jack would keep the senator alive. If Violet made a move against Kadan, she was a dead woman. He kept his focus on his primary objective. Kadan moved through the shadows. It was nearly impossible to see him. A blurred edge sometimes, a perception of movement, only because Ken knew where he was going to be. They'd gone over his route several times. Ken kept it clear, sweeping the surrounding area with heightened awareness.

An assassination squad was moving into place, and they would be trying to reduce any numbers against them. Neil Campbell and Trace Aikens were impossible to spot, but they were out there. Martin Howard had fallen back to help Kadan secure the senator.

Kadan gained the porch, moving past the swaying carcasses to enter the cabin. He spoke briefly to Violet and they both hurried into the room with the senator, pushing him back toward the kitchen where the "safe room" was. The fireproof room was beneath the main floor.

The macabrely swinging carcasses drew Ken's attention again. Blood dripped. The odor carried on the night breeze. He swallowed bile, wiped the beads of sweat from his forehead, and put his eye to the scope again. Something about the deer nagged at him—just wouldn't let him go. A shadow seemed to grow out of the deer on the far side, emerging from the top near the meat hook.

Ken squeezed the trigger and the shadow fell with a heavy thud, one arm stretched out as if in entreaty. Even as Ken took the shot, Jack's gun went off, and a second body fell simultaneously, that one from the far side of the roof.

A third shot rang out as Jack scooted back into the bushes for cover, the bullet hitting where his head had been. Ken was already targeting the brief flash. Taking his time, he tightened his finger on the trigger just as his quarry shifted position. The bullet slammed home, driving the sniper backward, the rifle still in his hands. Ken followed with a second round, but his target was dropping through tree branches. He knew that neither bullet had killed his target, a rare occurrence. Eye to the scope, he followed the path of the sniper as he tumbled down the slope, crashing through trees and brush.

Instant awareness rippled through Ken's mind, as if all members of the GhostWalkers and the assassination squad were connected in some way to the sniper.

*Stand down, Ken!* Kadan issued the command. *They're backing off to protect that man. Get to him first. Whoever he is—he's more important than the primary target. Secure the sniper immediately. We'll hold his team here while you make a run for it.*

*I've got his back,* Jack said unnecessarily. Every member of the GhostWalker team knew that where Ken went, so did Jack, and vice versa.

There was an instant of stillness, and then an electrical current sizzled through the air, snapping and crackling, so real that the edges of the clouds lit up with answering current. Power surged. There was no mistaking the sudden anxiety in the environment. It shimmered on the night breeze, a sudden alarm the other members in the sniper's unit couldn't control.

Ken shouldered his rifle and double-timed it. He knew the location of the body, and judging by the way the sniper had free-fallen, he'd been unconscious going down. That didn't mean he'd stay unconscious. Just like the others, he was a supersoldier, enhanced physically as well as psychically. And that meant containing him as quickly as possible.

Ken planned every move as he ran, trusting Jack to keep the enemy off of him. Two gunshots rang out almost simultaneously. A bullet zinged off to Ken's right, shaving the bark from a tree close to where he veered. The shooter had anticipated him leaping over a fallen trunk and onto another one to gain the far hill. Jack had no doubt been more successful with his bullet, because no one else shot at Ken despite the itch between his shoulder blades.

*We've got them pinned down.* Kadan's voice was ultra-calm. *I'm keeping them from communicating, but I can't hold them forever. Take the sniper, get out of here, and for God's sake, keep him alive so we can extract information. The rest of us will take the senator and his wife out of here. I've called for a second helicopter. We'll take the secondary escape route. You rendezvous with Nico and get to a safe house.*

*Copy that,* Jack sent back. They'd be on their own once they determined a location to hold the prisoner, at least until Kadan and the rest of the team made certain the senator was safe.

Ken scrambled through loose dirt and leaves, uncaring of leaving a trail. Speed was of the essence. Jack fired twice more.

*They're taking chances, Ken. They don't want you to get ahold of that man. I'm right behind you, so don't shoot me.* Jack reloaded as he ran, keeping to the heavier foliage as he swept the region for any sign of the enemy, protecting Ken as he zigzagged his way through the heavy timber and brush to reach the fallen enemy.

Ken slowed as he closed in on his prey. If the man was still alive, as Ken believed him to be, he could very well be armed and ready for trouble. There was a buzzing in Ken's head, the pressure that accompanied telepathic communication. Someone not from their own team was trying to talk, but Kadan was a strong shield and he was successfully jamming all psychic interaction. Few enhanced soldiers could do what Kadan could, and it was probably a shock to the assassination team. But it also was clear that the other team was enhanced not only physically, but psychically as well—which meant they were GhostWalkers.

It had to be Whitney coming after the senator. Did that mean they'd had a falling out? Ken proceeded with more stealth, careful to move with the wind, to avoid stepping on branches when he could. The sniper would know he was coming, but he'd hesitate to shoot, afraid of hitting one of his own. He was calling for help though, the buzzing frantic and continuous in Ken's head. There were no words—Kadan saw to that—but everyone open to extrasensory interaction would know the sniper was alive and seeking help. Ken had to close down all psychic contact immediately before the combined efforts of the other team overpowered him.

He pushed aside foliage and saw the sniper lying just below him, facing away. The first bullet had taken him in the chest, and he was wearing at least one, possibly two vests, making his chest appear barrel-like beneath his reflective clothing. The body armor had saved his life, but the second bullet had sliced through his leg. Blood splattered the leaves and grass in huge black splotches. Sometimes Ken thought he would never see blood as red again. In the jungle his blood had appeared black, pooling around him like a river. He slung his rifle around his neck and drew his gun, careful now as he approached the sniper.

The man's weapon should have been tangled in the bushes, but the sniper had held on, and that told Ken that the man wasn't unconscious. He wasn't moving and he didn't have the gun in a firing position, although it was in his hand, finger on the trigger.

Ken came up on the sniper out of the his line of vision, making certain the wounded man would have to turn at an awkward angle. And it just wasn't going to happen with that leg the way it was. The man was utterly silent, coiled like a rattler, waiting for friend or foe to explode into action.

Ken moved fast, snagging the rifle and flinging it a distance away before the sniper was aware he was on top of him. The sniper didn't fight for the gun; instead, his free hand moved like lightning, a smooth draw of a hold-out pistol from the bloody boot, the hand sliding just as fast, finger on the trigger, up toward his own head.

Ken's heart nearly stopped. He reacted without thought, kicking hard, driving the toe of his boot into the hand, sending the gun flying and hearing the satisfying crack of bones.

Still the sniper made no sound, but his other hand went for a hidden knife. Just as smooth. Just as fast. The sniper was going to kill himself to avoid capture. What kind of fanatics were they dealing with? The sniper used his broken hand, not even flinching as he drew the knife, but this time he screamed when Ken stomped on the hand, pinning the knife to the ground. The scream was high-pitched and sent chills down Ken's spine.

He crouched beside the wounded man and stared into the large, heavily lashed eyes. Eyes he recognized. Eyes he'd seen staring back at him with laughter and affection. His belly muscles clenched, and he swore softly under his breath as he jerked the cap off the man's head. He wasn't looking at a man, and damn it all, he knew *exactly* who she was.

That small millisecond of recognition was enough for her. She slammed her elbow into his throat, going for a death blow, trying to drive through his trachea and crush his airway. She was definitely physically enhanced. She had the speed and the strength in spite of her injuries, but Ken slipped the blow and pulled out his med kit, then leaned his weight into her, pinned her down, and prepared the needle. Using his teeth, he pulled off the cap and slammed it home, injecting her fast, praying she wasn't allergic and he could do a fast medical on her and make a run for it.

Jack came up behind him, taking a position facing away from them, making a sweep with his rifle to keep back any of the sniper's squad that might slip through their team's net.

"Hurry up," Jack growled. "Knock him out and stop being so gentle about it."

"It's Mari, Jack," Ken whispered, needing to say it aloud.

"What?" Jack jerked around, staring at the sniper as the eyes fluttered closed. "Are you certain?"

Ken pulled the woman's belt loose and buckled it around her leg. "Either that or your wife is playing sniper for the other team. It has to be Mari. She looks exactly like Briony."

Jack backed up until he had a good look at the woman's face. There was dirt and scratches and blood, but the sight of her lying pale, platinum and gold hair spilling around her face, nearly stopped his heart. "Is she going to make it?"

"I'm trying. She's lost some blood. We've got to get out of here, Jack. Kadan and the others aren't going to be able to hold them for long. Who's our medic?"

"Nico is the closest. He's with the helicopter, about an hour out."

"Tell him to rendezvous at the point. We'll hump it out of here and hope she doesn't bleed out while we make a run for it." Ken reached over the top of the woman to grab her arm. He inhaled as he did so. He'd been holding his breath without realizing it, afraid to take in her scent. Whitney had done a lot of experimenting, everything from genetic enhancement to pheromones. Ken wanted no part of that. He already had enough to contend with.

Mari was small and shapely beneath the vests, camouflage clothing, and regulation boots. The moment Ken drew her scent into his lungs, he knew he was in trouble. It mattered little that they were surrounded by the enemy, or that she smelled of sweat and blood; her natural scent acted like a powerful drug, an aphrodisiac, and he found his body reacting in spite of the dangerous situation. He clenched his teeth and brought her up to his shoulders, then moved quickly through the heavy brush toward the rendezvous point with the helicopter.

Jack retrieved her weapon, slinging it around his neck and falling in behind his brother, forcing his attention on keeping them alive, and not worrying about what might happen to his wife's sister.

Kadan and the rest of the team would get the senator and his wife to safety, utilizing the vehicles. Kadan had already arranged for another helicopter pickup at an opposite location. Ken and Jack were fairly certain the assassination team was going to be charging after them and their prisoner, or at least dividing. In any case, Kadan needed to question the senator's wife. At the very least they needed to take a much closer look at her.

Ken ran, feeling with every step he took the weight of the knowledge that he was the one who had shot the woman. If she died, he would never be able to face Briony, Jack's wife. He loved Briony. She accepted him with his ugly face and body, never flinching away or averting her eyes. But more than her acceptance, she'd changed Jack's life. She'd brought happiness and hope to both of them when their world had been bleak and unforgiving.

Briony and her twin sister had been two of the orphans Whitney had experimented on, and he had separated the twins, keeping Marigold and giving Briony up for adoption. Briony was frantic to find Mari, and if Ken had killed her, he had no idea what that would do to their family. He sent up a silent prayer as he jogged, trying to ignore the smell of blood and the feel of it soaking into his shirt.

They had been looking for Marigold, unraveling the clues leading to her for weeks now. They'd started with the premise that Whitney still had her locked away in one of his many compounds. The locations were secret and difficult to find, as he had a high security clearance and someone very high up was helping him cover his tracks. But they had the name and registration number of the private jet that had gone down in the Congo carrying the senator. And there had been a private jet carrying the team of men who had chased Briony across the country.

The jets were owned by two different corporations. The company in Nevada had a secretary who simply stated that the owner, an Earl Thomas Barlett, was not available. He signed all the documents and owned a home, yet there was no public document on him, not even a driver's license. Strangely enough, the company in Wyoming mirrored the one in Nevada. Both consulting companies were represented by the same attorney, who had purchased the jets for each.

The corporation in Wyoming owned a great deal of wilderness in the Cascades, inaccessible by anything but small planes landing on the very expensive airstrip or by a rapid and dangerous river. The senator just happened to own a hunting cabin on the adjacent land and have landing privileges given by the Wyoming consulting company. The same attorney had been used to acquire those privileges.

Jack and Ken had been on their way to do a little recon when the orders came down to protect the senator. Their team had taken a helicopter into the remote area and set up surveillance and an exit plan. The senator had insisted he and his wife should continue their hunting trip in spite of the danger, and she had concurred, turning down the team's recommendation to move to a more secure area.

Ken tried not to think about the woman slung around his shoulders, or how her body felt against his. He didn't want to touch her skin or feel for a pulse, or acknowledge the slide of silky hair along his jaw where her head bounced. She seemed to envelop him, and the scent of her soaked into him through his pores, his lungs, deep into his tissues and bones where he knew he'd never eradicate her.

He wanted to stay numb for the rest of his life. He didn't

want to have to face another trial by fire. He wasn't certain he was strong enough to overcome the rage living and breathing inside of him. He couldn't afford to feel. He couldn't afford to want or need. He lived for the job. He lived to keep Jack safe, and now Briony and the twins she carried. Life for him had stopped almost before he was born, and it was much safer for everyone that way.

This unknown woman, already the enemy, could destroy not only him, but his family. It was through no fault of her own, but he didn't dare allow compassion to sway his course. He was not going to become more of a monster than he already was. Inch by slow inch, his life had been compromised, until his outside skin reflected the dark shadows inside him where no one could see.

*The hounds have been unleashed,* Kadan warned. *Not one stayed to go after the senator. They're coming after you. I don't dare leave the senator, just in case this is a setup, but watch yourself. I'm not certain who your sniper is, or why he's so important, but get the hell out of there. You're in enemy territory. And he'll be able to communicate with them if you don't get him out of range.*

*Copy that,* Jack said. He'd dropped back even farther to protect them as they raced toward safety. *And our him is a her.*

Ken didn't bother to acknowledge. He splashed through three narrow streams and up a steep embankment, grateful for the fact that he was genetically enhanced. He could run long distances without fighting for air, and carrying the woman, as small as she was, was no problem. But soldiers coming up behind them were enhanced as well, and they carried guns. He tried to stay to the heavier foliage when at all possible, deep in the trees, careful not to expose his body as he ran toward the rendezvous point.

The sound of the helicopter reached him. It was flying in low and fast. Kadan had held the other team off to give them the break they needed.

*They might double back on you out of sheer frustration,* Ken warned Kadan.

*Nico flew over that stretch of land the corporation you were talking about owns. It's a military training facility,* Kadan announced. *Watch yourself, they may track you in the air.*

Ken swore softly and moved into position just on the edge of the clearing, where he could stay covered by the foliage. Jack came up behind him, but faced back toward the way they'd come.

"You need to get out of this, Jack," Ken said. "I'll have Nico drop me at a safe house and you get home to Briony. This most likely isn't going to end well."

"I'm not running out and leaving you in a hornet's nest."

"And what if we have to kill her? What then? Just go home and you're out of it. You never have to tell her we found her sister."

"Lie to Briony? Live a lie with her? That's what everyone else did to her all those years. I'm damned if I do. I promised her I'd always tell her the truth, and no matter how messy this gets, she gets told everything just the way it happened."

"You don't have to be in it."

"We don't change things at this late date. Briony wouldn't want that and neither do I. Whatever you're thinking, Ken, forget about it. If there's a chance to pull Briony's sister out clean, we'll do it. If we can't recover her, then we have no choice here and we'll accept that."

"Briony won't."

"She's stronger than you think she is. She doesn't want Whitney to get his hands on our children any more than I do. I'm not leaving, so drop it."

Ken kept his gaze on the helicopter as it dropped into the clearing. Nico was in the doorway, hands steady, eye to the scope to cover them as they ran.

# CHAPTER 2

Marigold Smith seemed to be floating in a sea of pain. It wasn't entirely unusual to wake up that way, but this time her heart was pounding in utter and total fear. She'd botched her mission. She hadn't managed to speak to the senator and plead their case. She hadn't protected him, and when she was captured, she hadn't managed to end her own life. She had no idea if the senator was safe, or if he'd been murdered. It wouldn't be so easy for anyone to get through Violet to him, but then Marigold hadn't considered that she herself be unsuccessful either. Briefly she let that failure shake her confidence in herself. She wanted to keep her eyes closed tight and just wallow in misery. She had been taken prisoner by the enemy, and it was too late to end her life and save the others. That left her one option—she had to escape.

Her leg, her back, her chest, and even her hand throbbed and burned. Worst of all, she didn't have an anchor to keep the psychic overload from frying her brain. She was wide open to assault, and that was more frightening than all the physical wounds in the world. She felt rather than heard movement near her and kept her eyes closed, her breathing even. There was no sound of footsteps, but she had the impression of someone large and very powerful leaning over her.

She wanted to hold her breath, self-preservation rising sharply, but then he would know she was awake. She drew in her breath and took him into her lungs. He smelled of death and blood and spice and outdoors. He smelled dangerous and like everything she didn't want—everything she feared. But her heart accelerated and her womb clenched and her stomach did a frightening little flip. Her eyes flew open, in spite of all her resolve. In spite of the danger. In spite of her years of training and discipline. Her gaze collided with his.

His eyes were the most frightening she'd ever seen. Cold steel. A glacier, so frozen she felt as if the cold burned her skin everywhere his gaze touched. There was no mercy. No compassion. A killer's eyes. Hard and watchful and utterly without emotion. They appeared gray, but were light enough to be silver. His lashes were jet black like his hair. His face should have been beautiful—it was constructed with care and attention to detail and bone structure—but several shiny, rigid scars crisscrossed his skin, running from under both eyes to his jaw and across his cheeks and up into his forehead. One scar dissected his lips, nearly cutting them in half. The scars ran down his neck and disappeared into his shirt, creating an unrelenting mask, a Frankenstein effect. The cuts were precise and cold and had obviously been inflicted with great care.

"Have you looked your fill, or do you need a little more time?"

His voice made her toes want to curl. Her reaction to him was disturbing and not at all that of a soldier—she was reacting entirely as a woman, and she hadn't even known that was possible. She couldn't tear her gaze from his, and before she could stop herself, the pads of her fingers traced one rigid scar down the length of his cheek. She braced herself for the psychic backlash—the onslaught of his thoughts and emotions, the shards of glass tearing into her skull that always accompanied touch, or even close proximity to others—but she could only feel the heat of his skin and the hard ridges that had been sliced into it.

He caught her wrist, the sound of flesh slapping flesh loud.

His grip was vise-like, but for all that, surprisingly gentle. "What are you doing?"

She swallowed the lump in her throat threatening to choke her. What *was* she doing? This man was her enemy. More importantly, he was a man, and she detested men and everything they stood for. She could respect and admire soldiers, but not relate to them at all when they were off duty. Men were brutes without loyalty, in spite of the camaraderie among the soldiers. She was *not* going to feel compassion for an enemy, especially one who obviously couldn't feel sympathy for others. He was probably the interrogator, a sadist bent on hurting others the way he'd been hurt.

She should have pulled her arm away, but she felt helpless to do anything but soothe him. His mask was just that, a layer over the strange masculine beauty of his face. He seemed so alone. So cut off and distant. "Does it still hurt?" Her thumb slid in a small caress over his arm where the ridges continued. Her voice was unnaturally husky and she had no idea what she was doing—only that when she touched him, the pain in her body receded and everything feminine inside her reached out to this one man.

He blinked. His only reaction. There was no change of expression. No smile. Nothing but that one small downward drift of his lashes. She thought he might have swallowed, but he turned his head slightly, his peculiar light eyes drifting over her face, seeing inside of her, seeing how vulnerable she felt, more woman than soldier, half-ashamed, half-mesmerized.

He hadn't pulled his arm away from her, she realized. It was like touching a tiger, a wild, exhilarating experience. She coaxed his cooperation with that small caress, the pad of her thumb brushing gently back and forth over those terrible, relentless scars, keeping him from whirling around and perhaps killing her with one stroke, or bolting into the underbrush, forever lost before she could uncover his secrets and know the man behind the mask. He trembled, the smallest of reactions, but she felt it, rather like a great untamed predator shuddering beneath a first touch.

He turned his hand over, wrapping his fingers around hers, effectively stilling her efforts. Again, she was struck by the gentleness of his touch. She hadn't known gentleness in her life. She'd never touched another human being the way she had him. She looked down at their joined hands and saw the scars running up his arm and into his sleeve. The moment seemed somehow surreal and distant from her. Her life had been filled with training and exercise, a narrow tunnel of expertise and little else other than duty. His life seemed exotic and mysterious. There was a wealth of knowledge behind those cold eyes. There was something hot and dangerous burning beneath the glacier of ice that called to her.

His thumb slid over the sensitive skin of her inner wrist. A single stroke. Feather-light. She felt her womb spasm. His touch was electric. The smooth silk of her skin in contrast to the violent scars of his. She wasn't without flaws, but that small touch made her feel flawless and beautiful when she'd never felt that way. She wasn't whole or complete, but he made her feel it when nothing else ever had.

Where the pad of his thumb passed over her skin, tiny flames licked and spread until she felt the burn rushing up to her breasts and down lower to the junction between her legs. One touch. That was all it took and she was utterly aware of him as a man and herself as a woman. She pulled her hand away, stricken at the break in contact, but afraid of giving too much of herself away.

Her gaze remained locked with his as if he held her there mercilessly, in the bright spotlight. She tried not to flinch, tried not to moisten suddenly dry lips. She'd been interrogated a hundred times—more, even—and she'd never felt so nervous.

"Why did you want to kill the senator?" His voice was mild, not accusing, the inflection almost gentle.

The question shocked her. She stared at him wide-eyed, frowning a little, trying to assimilate why he would ask such a thing. "*You* were there to kill the senator. We were protecting him."

"If you were there to protect him, why did your entire team leave him behind when we acquired you?"

She bit down on her lip. She didn't know how he could be genetically enhanced without being part of their unit, a special unit of the military designed for covert operations, but she'd never seen him before. And he *was* enhanced. She could feel the strength and power in him even without physical contact.

"I can't answer that," she said truthfully.

"You weren't there to assassinate the senator?"

"No, of course not. We were his protection team."

"A protection team doesn't pull out and leave the client when one of their team goes down or is captured. Your unit did just that."

"I can't answer for my unit."

"Why did you think we were there to kill the senator?"

Without his touch, pain was closing in again. Her leg hurt bad enough to bring tears burning behind her eyes. She risked a look at it. The leg was swollen, but it had been worked on. Her clothes had been cut off, which meant no hidden weapons. She wore only a long T-shirt. "Am I going to lose the leg?"

"No. Nico worked on you before the doc got here. You'll be fine. Your hand is broken too. You didn't give me much of a choice. Why would you try to kill yourself if you were there to protect the senator?"

"I can't answer that."

No flicker of impatience crossed his face. He didn't blink, watching her intently with glacier-cold eyes. She wasn't afraid of him in the way she knew she should be.

"Let me help you sit up. We've given you fluids, but you should try to drink on your own. You lost a lot of blood." Before she could protest, he slipped his arm underneath her back and helped her to sit, arranging pillows behind her.

She breathed him in and felt an instant electric current run between them. She swore little sparks danced over her skin. His gentleness disarmed her. He was a straight-up killer. She'd been a soldier all of her life and she recognized a lethal predator when she saw one, but when he touched her, there was no sign of aggression or the need to brutalize or dominate. He simply helped her, when he could have stood back and watched her struggle.

"Ken?" The voice came from the other room and her captor half-turned to face the doorway. "Briony says to bring her sister home and she sends her love."

She looked past the man standing by the bed and her heart nearly stopped. The face of the man standing in the doorway was everything Ken's should have been. Strong. Handsome.

Classically beautiful. It was the face she imagined on an aveng-ing angel—the bone structure, the lines and masculine perfec-tion. The stranger had the same eyes, the same mouth. She had avoided looking too much at Ken's mouth because she might have fixated on it. The scar that marred the soft fullness of his lips ran from the top lip to the bottom and down his chin in a straight line, and had the same precise symmetry that the other scars had.

The man in the doorway stopped. "I didn't realize she was awake."

Ken turned back to her, his arm still cradling her body, as he picked up a glass of water. "Can you manage with one hand?"

She could shoot a gun or throw a knife with one hand. She certainly could drink water, but having Ken close to her was intoxicating. She'd never been intoxicated before either. She allowed him to hold the glass to her lips. His hands were rock steady. She was trembling. Whatever was affecting her cer-tainly wasn't doing the same to him.

Mari hesitated, staring at the clear liquid with a sudden thought that she was a prisoner and they wanted information. As if reading her mind, Ken brought the glass to his lips and took a long drink. She watched the glass slide against his mouth, the way his throat worked as he swallowed, and she couldn't help noticing those same horrific scars on his neck and, lower still, reaching under the shirt. Where else did they go?

She let him put the glass to her lips, astonished at how good water could taste. She hadn't realized she was so thirsty. All the while she drank, she had to force her mind from stray-ing to Ken. She tasted him on the glass, felt him through the thin material of the T-shirt—or maybe it was his T-shirt. Maybe that was why she felt him imprinted deep in her bones.

She held the glass to her forehead, fighting for air. With every breath she drew into her lungs, a sharp pain stabbed through her chest.

"You're lucky to be alive," Ken said, taking the glass and setting it on a table beside the bed. "If you hadn't been wear-ing two vests, you'd be dead right now."

Cami had insisted she wear two vests. She'd have to re-member to thank her friend for that. She touched the painful spot. "Was it you?"

"I was aiming for your eye. You moved as I pulled the trigger."

"I figured you would fire as soon as you knew where I was. I kept rolling, but you hit me with both shots."

"I didn't kill you," he pointed out, his voice mild. "And that's a rare thing."

She blinked up at him, seeing the beauty of his face when he wanted her to see his mask. She knew he hid behind that mask of complete indifference. He hid himself away where no one could get to him—and why it mattered, she had no idea. She had obligations and she had to escape as quickly as possible. She just knew she didn't want to add to this man's scars.

"Lucky me. I didn't kill you, and that might be even rarer."

He quirked an eyebrow at her, the one without a scar slashing white through the black hairs. "Actually, it was Jack you nearly hit. Do you need a painkiller?"

Mari shook her head. "You've given me something. I'm already floating. How bad is the leg?"

"Let's just say, you're going to have to put off your escape plans for a little while."

Was he reading her mind? It was possible. She was a strong telepath; maybe he was too. Maybe touching her allowed him entrance to her mind. Panic swirled in her belly, her stomach churning. Dr. Whitney had experimented on the soldiers with the idea of creating a unique black ops team capable of slipping in and out of situations, and handling any problem that might crop up, including interrogation. With the right psychic ability, just touching another might be all that was necessary to extract the information wanted.

"I'm not."

"Not what?"

"I'm not reading your mind."

She blinked up at him. "If you're not, how did you know what I was thinking?"

"You don't have a poker face and I know your sister very well." His gaze locked on hers—held hers. "She has a lot of the same expressions."

The punch took her breath away, robbed her of every bit of air left in her lungs. How did he know she had a sister? Who was he? She felt sick, bile rising so fast she pressed the back of her hand to her mouth. Had she talked when she was unconscious? She would not be used to capture her sister. *Never.* "My sister?" Even as she echoed his words, she remembered Jack calling out to his brother. *Briony says to bring her sister home.* Briony was not a common name. How did they know? She hadn't even told Cami about Briony. She kept her memories of Briony close, afraid Whitney might take them away.

She stayed very still, making herself smaller in the bed. She might be at their mercy right this moment, but they would underestimate her, especially with the way she was acting around Ken. There would be one moment when they would grow complacent, when they would forget she was a trained soldier, and she would be able to escape.

She reached out telepathically, calling on the other members of her unit, hoping someone was in range. Sometimes, when they were all connected, they could reach far, miles even, but most of the time they had to be fairly close.

Ken pressed several fingers to his temples, rubbing them as if they ached. "Stop it. When you're reaching out to your friends, it sounds like bees buzzing in my head. Not only is it distracting, but it can be painful."

She flushed, unable to keep the color from rising in her cheeks. "I'm sorry. I didn't mean to hurt you." She glanced at Jack. He was watching his brother, his expression wary—why, she couldn't tell. "I was checking in."

"I'll bet you were," Jack said. "Ken, why don't you take a break and I'll have a little chat with our guest?"

The tension in the room shot up perceptibly. Ken turned slowly, hands out away from his sides. There was nothing overtly threatening in his manner, but Marigold's heart began to pound in alarm. She reached out without thinking, her fingers sliding down Ken's arm. She felt his muscles rippling beneath the thin material of his shirt and then the pads of her fingers slid over warm skin and settled there. She could feel his scars against her smooth palm. Once again heightened awareness of him as a man and her as a woman shot through her.

Ken stopped moving, leaving her fingers wrapped halfway around his wrist, but he didn't turn around. He faced his brother, and Mari glanced at the window, trying to see his expression. In the glass, his scars didn't show and she could see the same masculine beauty that was carved so exquisitely in his brother's face. Her heart gave off a curious melting sensation. She had a strange desire to frame that face with her hands, to kiss every single scar and tell him none of them mattered. But she knew they did. Something deadly lay beneath that surface of destruction, and somehow it was tied up in each of those terrible slices made into his flesh and bone.

Jack spread his hands out in front of him, held his right palm up. "It was just a suggestion."

"I can handle things here, no problem," Ken said.

Jack shrugged and stepped out of the room.

"What was that?" Mari asked.

Ken turned back to her, his face as expressionless as ever. "You don't know?"

Did she? Mari was so confused with her reaction to him, with her behavior and the fact that she wasn't in terrible pain as long as she was close to him that she couldn't seem to think with a clear head. He had admitted he'd given her painkillers; maybe they were making her thinking fuzzy, because nothing was making sense.

Unless . . . It couldn't be. She would know, wouldn't she? Her mouth went dry at the thought that Whitney had somehow paired her with this man. Her fingers tightened around his wrist. "Come closer to me." Whitney had many, many experiments, and his worst was combining couples—his breeding program. It was why she had convinced the others in her unit to allow her to join them one more time so she could personally speak to the senator.

Violet knew her. Violet would vouch for her. Speaking to the senator and asking—begging—him to intervene was the only way she and the other women could continue to do their duty as soldiers. And if she didn't get back to the compound fast, too many people were going to get hurt.

"You know," he said, his voice soft.

She closed her eyes and looked away from him. She'd been trained as a soldier almost since the day she was born, and she was proud of her abilities. But suddenly, Whitney had pulled the women off the units and brought them to a new location, a new training center, and they'd become virtual prisoners. Whitney had paired some of the men with the women using some kind of scent compatibility. It was more complicated than that, but she had seen the results and they weren't very nice. The men were obsessed, whether or not the women responded to them. And it didn't seem to matter to most of them one way or the other. She and the other women had conspired to get one of them out of the compound to approach Senator Freeman and Violet in the hopes that he would shut down Whitney's operation and return them to their units.

Mari had never been attracted to any of the men she knew and respected, yet she was fascinated by a total stranger, her enemy, a man who would have killed her. She was not just attracted; the feeling was all-encompassing. She wanted to soothe away his hurts. She needed to find a way to take away the stark loneliness she saw in him.

Somehow Whitney had paired her with this man. He didn't act as if he reciprocated, and Mari was ashamed of herself. She detested the men in the breeding program for their lack of discipline and control, and yet she was acting nearly as bad. This was a horrible situation and one that wasn't going to be easily overcome.

What did she want anyway? To sleep with him, just as the men did with her? Did she think he was going to fall madly in love with her? There was no such thing. Love was an illusion. According to Whitney, it was their duty to sleep with their partner in order to have a child. So far, she had resisted, and she'd been punished numerous times, but the idea of intimacy with Brett, of all men—a vicious brute of a man who enjoyed inflicting punishments—was a little too much for her stubborn streak.

Ken hadn't pulled away from her, and she let him go, the heat of his skin burning into her palm. He refused to look away. She could feel his gaze on her, and she shook her head.

"You know Whitney," he said.

"So do you. Why don't we know each other?" Her lashes lifted, and she silently prayed she was wrong, that he wasn't going to have any effect on her. His eyes met hers, and her stomach did that stupid flip she was beginning to hate. The tingle of awareness spread, becoming a rush of heat that made her breasts tighten. She wanted to cry. It was wrong to manipulate anyone sexually—even soldiers raised on duty and discipline.

"Whitney has several experiments going. We're just beginning to understand how many. He adopted female babies from foreign countries and experimented on them. Regardless of his security clearance, no one was going to authorize that, so he kept the girls hidden using various means. Briony was adopted out to a family, but he kept tabs on her, insisting on mapping out her education and training as well as sending his private doctor to monitor her health. I met her a few weeks ago."

She tried not to react. It could be a trick—a setup. Another test. Whitney often tested them, and if they failed, the consequences were dire. She said nothing, just stared up at his face. The mask gave nothing away. She was good at reading people, but not him. Even touching him gave her no information, only a strange, soothing peace. And she shouldn't feel peaceful; she should feel alert. Could it be a new kind of interrogation drug? She almost wished it were. She feared it was the beginning of an addiction to a man, and that was simply not acceptable.

"You're identical twins, obviously. She looks just like you."

Mari turned her face away from him, knowing she couldn't hide her expression. She had longed for information on her sister for years. Now, here it was, if she could believe it. Dropped straight into her lap, and how big of a coincidence was that? She bit her lip to keep from a sarcastic reply. It had to be a setup. There was no way she could casually meet this man and have him know her long-lost sister. But even if he was lying, she was so starved for news of Briony she wanted him to keep talking, and that was just plain pathetic.

"Are you listening?"

Of course she was listening. "I like fairy tales."

"I can stop then. I wouldn't want to bore you." He stepped away from her, back toward the shadows, away from the light. It was the first restless move she'd seen him make, when he was so in control. The movement reminded her of a great caged tiger, pacing with impatience and frustration. He needed to be outside, in the mountains, away from civilization. He was too wild, too much of a predator to be caged in a house.

"I was enjoying the story." Had she revealed too much, or had she managed to sound as if that was all it was to her—a fairy tale? She wanted him back, wanted him closer. As soon as he retreated, pain engulfed her. "You're an anchor," she said.

Without an anchor to draw psychic backlash, she was always wide open to assault. Much like someone born with autism, she no longer had the necessary filters to keep her brain from being under constant attack by all the stimulation around her. He was controlling that for her, she realized.

"Yes. So is Jack."

Jack. The beautiful one. The one who had Ken's face. How did it feel to stand beside his brother every day, to look into the face he should have had? It had to hurt. No matter how stoic he was, no matter how much he loved his brother, he had to look at that face and hurt.

Mari studied him as he leaned one hip lazily against the far wall, there in the shadows. She was certain it was a place he was far more comfortable. Did he realize the scars weren't as obvious as in the glare of light? That when darkness touched him, his face was nearly as handsome as Jack's? She doubted it. He favored the shadows simply because he could disappear into them.

"And Jack knows this Briony you claim is my sister?"

He sighed. "We're going to play games?"

"You're a soldier, probably black ops. How much are you willing to give up? Not even your name, rank, and serial number. You don't exist in the military, do you?"

"I know your name. It's Marigold. Your sister told me. She suffers tremendous pain when she tries to remember you, because Whitney manipulated her memories. She's been frantic to find you. Whitney had her adopted parents killed when they refused to allow her to go to Colombia. You know why he was so determined she go there?" He didn't wait for an answer. "He wanted her to run into Jack. He wanted her to meet him so he could continue his latest experiment. He wants their child."

Her heart slammed hard in her chest and the bile rose again. This time she couldn't stop it. "I'm going to be sick."

He was there in an instant, handing her a small pan. It was humiliating to lie in bed throwing her guts up under his piercing gaze. She wanted to scream at him to go away and leave her so she could rage at the unfairness—at the betrayal. She had sacrificed everything to keep Briony safe. *Everything.* She had endured her sterile life, living without a home or family, never seeing the outside of the compound unless she was running a mission, the punishing training, the discipline and experiments—all of it. She endured it without protest so Briony could have a life somewhere. That was the bargain she'd made as a child, with the devil. He'd promised her that if she cooperated, Briony could live a dream life. She could have the fairy tale. Love. Laughter. Family. Briony was supposed to have it all.

Ken handed her a wet cloth to wipe her mouth. She didn't meet those glittering eyes. She couldn't. If he was telling the truth—and she suddenly suspected he was—her entire life had been a lie, and if Ken saw her face right then, he would know.

Whitney cared nothing for the soldiers he housed in his compounds. She had watched him as he made his observations on them all, his cold snake eyes excited and fanatical when he got his results, and angry and malevolent when he didn't. They weren't real to him—not people—only test subjects.

"Did they meet in Colombia?" Her voice was a whisper, a strangled sound that was too close to tears. Tears were a weakness—one soldiers didn't indulge in. How often had she heard that as a child? Soldiers didn't play. Soldiers were about duty and hardship and skill.

"No. Her parents refused to allow her to go and he had them murdered. She walked in right after and found them." His voice was gentle, as if he knew he was hurting her with the telling. "She has brothers, but like you she needs an anchor. Living in close proximity without one was hell on her at times. Particularly as a child, before she was strong enough to build some small protections."

Mari nodded. She knew what it was like to be bombarded with too much emotion, and a child living in a household with parents and brothers would have headaches and blackouts, maybe even brain bleeds. "He did it on purpose to see how tough she would be, didn't he? I was in a controlled, sterile environment and she was put out in a chaotic, busy household. He wanted to compare how we handled it."

"That's what we believe."

"And he wanted her to have your brother's baby because he's genetically enhanced, isn't he?"

Ken nodded. "Yes. We think he wanted you pregnant at the same time."

Again there was no inflection in his voice, no change in expression, his glacier-cold eyes completely unfathomable, yet she winced, sensing extreme danger. It was odd that he never stirred, not even the ripple of a muscle, but the aura of danger, the tension in the room, seemed to build at times so that she could barely breathe, waiting for disaster. She had been around genetically altered soldiers for most of her life—was one herself—and some, like Brett, were cruel; others were men she respected, but all of them were dangerous. She just sensed something more in Ken. She couldn't put her finger exactly on what it was—but she knew she never wanted to go into combat against him again. She'd been lucky.

"Mari?" The way he said her name shook her. A caress. A stroke of velvet. He created intimacy when there was none. He always sounded so gentle. Men weren't gentle. Soldiers weren't gentle. Men like Ken, predators, hunters, they weren't gentle. How could he make her feel so vulnerable with just his voice?

"What do you want me to say? Yes, you're right?" She should have kept her mouth shut. Anyone would have heard the stress, the anger, the repressed fear and hurt. Her life had been hell since Whitney had decided to pair the genetically altered women with soldiers. He didn't care if the women wanted the men; in fact he seemed to delight in seeing how far the men were willing to go to get the cooperation of the women. Everything was meticulously detailed and reported. And men like Brett didn't like failure.

"He tried to force cooperation from the women?"

She suppressed a small hysterical laugh. That was a gentle way of saying it. "Whitney wouldn't put it that way. He creates a situation and sits back and observes. He isn't messy enough to force us. He leaves that to the men." She pressed her lips together and turned away from him. How could she be giving up information? Personal, vital, information. She had to be drugged.

"Whitney is a first-class bastard." Ken moved, a rippling of muscle, a gliding of silent steps across the room until he was once more beside her and she could breathe him into her lungs. His palm was cool on her forehead as he brushed back strands of her hair. "He faked his own death and has gone underground. Someone high up is helping him. After Jack met Briony—"

"How? This all seems too big of a coincidence for me to swallow. You just happened to be the shooter when we were supposed to protect the senator. You miss when you've probably never missed in your life."

"I didn't miss."

"You missed."

A ghost of a smile pulled at his mouth. His even white teeth flashed. The effect was breathtaking. Her stomach somersaulted. Even her broken fingers tingled—fingers he had crushed. She remembered the swift attack, so fast he seemed a blur of movement. Even as she'd tried to fulfill her promises to the other women, she had admired his efficiency.

"Tell me," she urged.

"It started with Senator Freeman. He was flying over the Congo, over rebel territory, and his plane went down. Mysteriously, General Ekabela, who was renowned for torturing prisoners, didn't touch the senator, the pilot, or anyone traveling on that plane. At the very least, the pilot should have been killed." He waited a moment, letting the implications of that sink in. "Jack was supposed to lead a rescue mission and pull the senator out. The orders came down, but Jack was still in Colombia. He'd run into a snag there, so I took his place."

"You led a team into rebel territory to get the senator and his people out, but things didn't go well." Her gaze drifted over the terrible scars.

"They were waiting for us. We were ambushed and I was cut off from my unit. They were definitely after me, singling me out and sending in so many soldiers I didn't have a chance. My men got the prisoners out and I was captured."

Again, she was struck by the complete lack of inflection in his voice. He showed no emotion, when she felt the emotion like a raging volcano churning beneath the tranquil surface. She couldn't imagine what the pain had been like—or the fear.

"How long did he have you?"

"An eternity. I knew Jack would come for me. Later I found

out three rescue attempts had been made, but the rebels moved me constantly from camp to camp. By the time Jack found me, I was in pretty bad shape. I don't remember anything but seeing his face. There wasn't a whole lot of me left."

"Ekabela had you cut like that?"

"Sliced into little pieces and then he skinned my back. Peeled it right off, like those deer on the senator's porch."

"So you had every reason to want Senator Freeman dead." She made the statement quietly, watching his face for a reaction.

"I still want him dead."

# CHAPTER 3

"Well at least you aren't lying to me." Mari held her breath, afraid to move. She'd gone from suspicion to belief and now she had to backtrack. Why would anyone be stupid enough to send in a skilled sniper to protect the senator when he clearly had a reason to see him dead? It made no sense.

Ken shrugged his broad shoulders. "Why would I deny it? I thought about killing him and saving everyone the trouble. So did Jack. But it smelled too much like a setup to me. If someone managed to kill him, we were right there, patsies to take the fall. Why would anyone order us to protect that man?"

"It doesn't make sense," she agreed, noncommittal.

"Out of curiosity, how can you be trained as a sniper when you're not an anchor? Briony can't use a gun against anyone without terrible repercussions."

"I have an anchor. He draws the aftermath of violence away from me."

"Your spotter."

She nodded, watching his face. Shadows flickered in his silver eyes, turning them charcoal gray, giving them a smoldering appearance, as if any moment they might shoot flames.

A muscle ticked in his jaw. He wasn't quite made out of stone, as he would have her believe.

"Is your spotter paired with you?"

Was there an edge to his voice? Not really, but there was a heightened alertness in him. "No, he's a friend. Was any of my unit killed back there?"

"I didn't ask. I can have Jack find out for you. It was odd that the moment you were shot, everyone in your unit backed off the senator and fell back to try to protect you. Why would they do that?"

Sean had to have been injured. He had been closest to her and should have gotten to her position before the enemy. She sent up a silent prayer that he was still alive. He was a good soldier and the closest thing to a male friend she had. "I can't answer that."

"I seem to be giving you a lot of information, but you aren't giving me anything in return."

She was giving more than she should have, and both of them knew it. "If it was just my life I was risking, I might tell you what you want to know. I don't have any loyalty to Whitney, or I wouldn't have gone AWOL and tried to get to the senator."

"You're protecting the others, the women, aren't you?" Now there was an edge to his voice, the ice cracking just a bit, enough to let out a wave of heat. "He's going to hurt them if you don't return."

She said nothing, her heart pounding. Was she that transparent? Whitney would kill one of them. He'd started with seven, all raised together in that miserable compound, a life of duty and discipline where few things from the outside world were permitted and everything was recorded. They'd learned to move in the shadows and time the cameras to avoid detection. They'd learned to talk late at night, congregating in the bathroom with water running and signing their conversations, until Marigold had discovered she could build a telepathic bridge and they could all communicate that way. Those women were her family. She'd accepted her life and had pride in her abilities, until Whitney had changed everything.

Cami had protested and tried to escape. She'd been caught and Whitney had ordered a name drawn. One of the other women, Ivy, had been taken away, and a few minutes later they heard shots. There was blood on the walls, but no one had seen the body. They tried to tell themselves he hadn't really killed her, but no one tried to escape after that.

"That's why you tried to kill yourself. If you were dead, he wouldn't have a reason to punish the others. And your unit knew he might kill one of the other women, a woman they might be paired with." He swore softly under his breath. "Someone has to kill that son of a bitch and fast. Why would you think the senator would help you? He's friends with Whitney. He's been helping him."

She raised an eyebrow. "You don't know anything about the senator."

Ken studied her face. He'd given her a lot of shocks very fast. She was doped up, her eyes unfocused, and the news of her sister had thrown her completely off guard. The revelations about Whitney garnered him a little trust. He knew his guesses about the threats to the other women had been right on. Whitney didn't care about his human subjects—they were all expendable. He frowned. Maybe not the women. He could make more supersoldiers, but it would be difficult to find women he had data on almost from birth. "Tell me about Senator Freeman."

"He isn't friends with Whitney. They don't like each other. I think Whitney went to school with his father, but the senator's father and Jacob Abrams are best friends. The two of them have tried to keep Whitney from doing so many experiments. They've talked to him countless times. I've heard them. They told him he had to stop, that he was jeopardizing everything.

"Senator Freeman violently objects to the things Whitney has done," she continued. "In front of Whitney, he chastised his father for making them a part of the experiments. There's no way the senator would betray our men and our country for Whitney. If his plane went down in the Congo, and there's any kind of a tie between Ekabela and Whitney, then it was probably because Whitney wanted the senator dead. Jacob Abrams probably gave the order for you to go in and rescue the senator, not Whitney."

*You heard of Jacob Abrams?* Ken reached out to his brother.

*Big banker. Loaded. Maybe more than Whitney. Definitely a billionaire and has a lot to do with the world money market. Considered a genius. Don't know much else about him, but I'll run him by Lily. She'd know. Why?*

*Mari dropped his name, said he's a friend of the senator's and both aren't too happy with Whitney, that he's going to jeopardize everything. Have Lily check to see if the senator's father, Whitney, and Abrams all attended a school at the same time.*

"You're talking to someone," Mari said, pressing a hand to her temple. There was accusation in her voice and a reprimand in her eyes.

"My brother. Didn't you always talk to your sister when you were together?"

Mari frowned, thinking about it. It had been so long ago. Telepathy had been strong between them. Of course they'd talked, hardly thinking about it, sharing every thought. Was she jealous of his brother and that strong bond? Or was she leery because he was the enemy? She should know, but if she were honest with herself, she had no idea what the answer was. She suspected jealousy.

Frustrated and embarrassed at her lack of discipline, she attempted to shift her leg. Gut-wrenching agony slid through her. She choked back a sound by shoving her fist in her mouth and biting down hard on her hand. She turned her face away from Ken, unable to stop the tears burning in her eyes.

His hand was there instantly to steady her. "Take a breath. You're probably due for your meds again. You've been shot. We had a surgeon work on you after Nico, and being genetically altered, you're bound to heal at an exceptionally fast rate, but you're going to have to give yourself time." *Jack, we need meds in here now. She's so pale she looks like she's going to faint.*

*I'm coming. Hold your pants on.*

"I don't have time. Didn't you hear me?" She couldn't remember what she'd told him about the other women. If she didn't get back, Whitney might harm them. She couldn't take any chances; she had to go back. The pain was growing, moving through her system, making her unable to focus properly. There was something about the genetically enhanced system that allowed them to clear drugs much more quickly, and this time, it wasn't a benefit.

"By now Whitney knows you were shot. He'll try to go through the chain of command to find you. Whoever runs our teams is going to get slammed with questions and demands. Whitney won't touch the other women because he can't replace them. The men are expendable—not the women."

"Whitney had my friend killed when Cami tried to escape."

He was silent a moment. "Did you witness it; anyone see him?"

She shook her head. "Only the blood after."

"You didn't see a body and Whitney is a master of illusion. My guess is she was taken to another of his facilities."

"But you don't know that."

"No, but we've had a lot of time to study Whitney."

"Really?" Her voice dripped with sarcasm. "I lived my life in his compounds, with his experiments. He's a megalomaniac. He believes rules don't apply to him and that he's smarter than everyone else. He believes everyone else is a sheep and that he can manipulate them with ease. And he can—and does all the time."

"He's one man, Mari," he said gently.

"If men like the senator and Jacob Abrams can't keep him under control, how can we? If he ordered a hit on either one of them, he has the means to get it done."

"Maybe," Ken conceded. *What the hell is the holdup, Jack? She's shaking and beginning to sweat.*

Jack hurried into the room. "I'm sorry. Kadan called."

"He could have waited." Ken's voice was gruff. He pushed the needle into the IV. "You'll feel better in a few minutes," he assured Mari, his thumb sliding over her skin as if it were an accident. "If not, we'll bring in the doc."

There was real concern in his voice, but his face was as expressionless as ever. She couldn't help looking at his brother's face. Jack had a couple of scars running down one side of his face, as if Ekabela had gotten his hands on him and just gotten started. They only served to add to his good looks. It gave him a rough edge that was intriguing. Ken's face was a grid of scars, giving him the appearance of someone very frightening. A child might run from him.

She felt his eyes on her and turned her head to catch him staring at her with glittering eyes. She flashed a small smile. "You two look amazingly alike. He has that stubborn set to his jaw that you do."

He dipped a cloth in cool water and sponged the beads of sweat from her forehead. "How long do you think we have before they find this place?"

"With Whitney's connections? If you used a helicopter and any aid at all from military or black ops personnel, he'll have the information in hours."

"That's what I thought too. We moved you once after the surgery, but we had to use a helicopter. We're going to have to move you again."

"Let them take me back."

"No." His voice was soft, a hiss of sound, low and mean, sending chills through her body. "We've already called the helicopter. When you wake up, we'll be in another safe house."

"And it will be a matter of hours before he has that information. Eventually he'll catch up with us and someone will get killed."

"We'll keep moving until they can take you off the IV. Doc says another twenty-four hours. We can buy that much time."

It hit her then what he'd said. *When you wake up.* "You drugged me."

"I'm not stupid. The minute you thought your people were anywhere near, you would use telepathy to call them. Of course I drugged you. Do you think I didn't see your body when they cut your clothes off? Somebody beat the hell out of you with a cane." His voice was so low she could barely catch the flashes of repressed rage. He dragged his shirt up to show the crisscross of scars, long and deep, making a patchwork quilt of his body. "I know what it feels like to have someone cut and skin you like an animal—to treat you like you have no rights and no feelings—that you're nothing at all."

"Stop it."

He swung around so she could see the mess that was his back, the numerous skin grafts and the terrible scars that remained of a once beautiful man. He spun back around, his face close to hers, his silver eyes, fierce and steady and totally implacable. "I saw what they did to you and you're not going back there."

"Stop it." Her voice came out in a whisper. "Don't say anything else." He had reduced her to that helpless creature, crawling across the floor, determined she'd never beg for mercy, never give what was demanded of her. She saw herself through those silver eyes—not the soldier who commanded respect, but that animal, half-mad with pain and despair, torn and bleeding and without hope.

Of all the people in the world, it had to be Ken who saw the mess Brett had made of her body. *I can keep this up all night, Mari; eventually you'll give me what I want. It will just hurt a lot more, but I don't mind that.* Ashamed, she pulled the blanket closer around her as Brett's words echoed in her mind. Of course he hadn't touched her face. Whitney would have killed him, but sooner or later, Whitney's threats wouldn't be enough to deter Brett. In a way she felt sorry for him. Whitney had programmed him, turned him into an animal who no longer thought about right or wrong, only what he wanted—and he wanted Mari. He would be on the team that came for her, and he would kill anyone who stood in his way.

She reached down to touch her hip. There was a bandage there. They'd found and removed the tracking device Whitney had implanted. She should have known they would find it. She had been certain her team would be able to find her quickly, using that tracking system, but now they would have to rely on Whitney—or Abrams and his military contacts—and that would take some time. There were few trails leading to the GhostWalkers and no one carried identification. If they died during a mission, they were buried quietly, without public fanfare, because no one knew they existed.

Ken jerked down his shirt, covering the scars running down his belly, disappearing even lower into his jeans. He leaned over her, his hand spanning her throat, fingers stroking a caress over her silken skin. His whisper was soft, lips against her ear so that his breath was warm, fanning curls of heat through her body. "I don't live by anybody else's rules. I make up my own."

She wrapped her fingers around his wrist, a bracelet that went halfway around, but her fingers dug into his skin, into the

ridges of his scars as her lashes drifted down. "Don't let anyone else see me. Especially not Briony."

Ken closed his eyes and pressed his forehead against hers.
It was sheer hell to be so close to her and not touch her. Even
with blood and sweat and the drugs, her scent drove him
crazy. Whitney's experiment into pairing through scent was
more than a success. But even more than the physical need, he
felt the urge to protect her. Maybe it had been the sight of her
broken and battered body when they'd cut off her clothes.
Maybe it had been the sound of Nico and the surgeon swearing, or Jack's hiss of rage. All he could remember was feeling
the impact like a punch to his gut, and then later, when they'd
rolled her over to examine her back, he felt his heart being
ripped from his body.

He had known there were monsters in the world—he'd met
a few, destroyed a few—but who would want to do this to a
woman? *Someone like his father.* Abruptly he pulled his mind
from going in that direction.

"Are you all right, Ken?" Jack asked, touching his arm.

"I swear, Jack, this is like going through it all again. First
the deer and then Mari. I don't think I'll ever close my eyes
again."

"We've got to get out of here. We don't dare stay any
longer."

"I'll stay behind. You take her to a safe place and get some
rest. I'll make certain they can't come looking."

"You can't kill them all, Ken. And in any case, we don't
know who the bad guys are. She said they weren't there to kill
the senator—that they were supposed to protect him. If the order came down that way, they're no different than we are.
They want her back because we don't leave a GhostWalker
behind."

"One of them did this to her."

"We don't know which one."

Ken straightened slowly and turned to face his brother.
"She doesn't want Briony to know."

"Briony's not a child. I don't lie to her, not even for you,
and you can't ask me to, Ken." Jack spread out his hands.
"Let's get her on the helicopter and we can sort all this out
later. We'll take her to the small house Lily rented for us and

stay there a few hours. The van will meet us there and we can disappear with her."

"Are you bringing Briony in?"

Jack shook his head. "It's too dangerous. She's pregnant and Whitney wants her. I'm not willing to risk her life, although she wants to see her sister. She's staying with Lily now at the big house, and Kadan and Ryland's team is guarding her while we make a run for it."

"You mean while we figure out how best to use Mari in our little game with Whitney."

Jack pushed the gurney toward the door, ignoring the bite in his brother's voice. "She'll go back the first chance she gets, Ken. You can't trust her. You heard her. You saw her. She's not Briony, as much as they look alike. This one is tough as nails and could rip your heart out if you take your eyes off of her. Don't you forget that. At this point I wouldn't trust her with Briony's life, let alone yours."

"I haven't forgotten." Ken slung his rifle around his neck and checked his guns and ammunition belt. "I just am not willing to turn her back over to whoever hurt her like that."

"Don't identify with her. She's our prisoner. And she could easily cut your throat—or mine. We don't know anything about her. She's capable of running a con just like we are. She was trained as a soldier, so her first duty is to escape."

"Copy that, Daddy," Ken said.

Jack halted so abruptly Ken ran into the bed. Their eyes met, a slash of steel swords clashing over Mari's head. "I'm going to look out for you, Ken, whether you like it or not. You think I don't know how shook up you were looking at the deer carcasses? You're identifying with them."

"Maybe, but I'm not letting anyone take this woman back to Whitney."

"If she goes back, we can follow her, rescue the others, and cap Whitney's ass," Jack pointed out. "It all sounds good to me."

"Has anyone ever told you that you're a bloodthirsty son of a bitch?" Ken asked.

"Yes," Jack assented. "More than once."

"Well, it's true." Ken lifted Mari into his arms while Jack steadied her leg and took the medical rigging. The helicopter was a few yards away, Nico waiting, rifle ready as he searched the area around them for an enemy. "You always think in terms of killing, Jack. I thought once you were with Briony, you'd get out of that habit."

Jack shrugged. "It's easier than jawing at everyone the way you do. By the time you finish talking to them, we realize we have to kill them anyway. I just save you all that trouble."

Ken scowled at his brother. "You do realize everyone thinks you're the pretty boy, now that my face is scarred. It doesn't go well with your Dr. Death image."

"*Pretty* boy!" Jack glared at him. "If I didn't have my hands full, I'd shoot you for that comment."

"You mean to tell me Briony doesn't tell you how pretty you are late at night when the two of you are all alone?"

"Don't think I won't take you out," Jack threatened.

Ken flashed a sudden grin, genuine this time. "She does, doesn't she?"

"She thinks I look rough and tough," Jack corrected.

"Hey, Nico," Ken called out as they boarded the helicopter, no easy feat with trying to keep Mari's leg from being jarred. "Don't you think Jack here is a pretty boy?"

Nico glanced at Jack's face and grinned. "Yeah, he's a hot babe, all right. Must make all the women folks crazy."

"You can both go to hell," Jack said.

Ken turned away, depositing Mari carefully on the small gurney locked in place. Jack secured the medical gear and Nico took the pilot's seat. They waited for the doctor, who hurried after them carrying the rest of the supplies they needed. Eric Lambert was a good doctor and often aided the GhostWalker teams, although he wasn't physically or psychically enhanced. He knew a lot about gene therapy and was interested in Whitney's experiments and had a high clearance, so he was often the man Lily sent out into the field to protect the GhostWalkers. He was the surgeon who had saved Jesse Calhoun's life when he'd been shot several times deliberately in both his legs, and Jack and Ken had a soft spot for him, simply because Jesse was their friend and they had few real friends in the world.

Ken moved over to make room for him. "Are you up for some excitement, Doc?"

"No. Don't shoot anybody."

Jack snorted. "See, it isn't just me. He knows you talk a lot of bull and in the end you shoot them anyway."

Ken narrowed his eyes as Eric got up to check his patient. "Her pulse is stronger than I thought it would be with the dose we gave her. I'd like to take some more blood samples. I think she heals a lot faster than we anticipated. Whitney included an extra pair of chromosomes when he was altering all of you and that gives him a lot of genetic code to work with. The more I study all of you, the more I realize we don't know a third of what you can do."

"You took enough of her blood," Ken objected. "She's been used as a guinea pig for Whitney's experiments all of her life. I don't think it's necessary for us to do the same to her."

As always, Ken sounded mild, but Eric heard the warning note in his voice and glanced at Jack, who simply shook his head. Eric settled back in his seat. "We need to really understand what's going on with all of you," he pointed out. "If she heals faster and can push drugs through her system faster, we need to know. We wouldn't want to be in the middle of a complex operation and have one of you wake up on us."

Eric sank down onto the bench and gripped the seat as the helicopter took off. He'd never liked flying, Ken remembered, and they should be grateful that he was always willing to come when one of them was injured, but instead, Ken felt an unreasonable wash of emotions he couldn't quite identify.

He clenched his teeth at the unbidden images that rose the moment Eric planted the idea of waking up in the middle of an operation. Was that the kind of experiment Whitney conducted on a regular basis? From all accounts he loved science and lived for little else. Was his mind so twisted that he might subject a human being to that kind of torment again and again just to see the results? Ken had been tortured—he knew what it was like to feel the slice of a knife going through his skin while he was wide awake and unable to fight back. The idea that Whitney might have done the same thing to another human being in the name of science made him ill.

A tremor went through him and he had to fight back a wave of nausea. Why was it all coming back after all these months? His belly throbbed, and lower, much lower, he could feel the mind-numbing pain, an agony crawling through his body, hear laughter echoing insanely through his head. Was he finally losing his mind? The rage inside of him, kept so carefully bottled up, surged up through his belly and into his throat until he wanted to scream and tear someone apart with his bare hands. Beads of sweat dropped from his forehead onto his arm. He never saw blood as red anymore, so he couldn't tell whether the droplets were sweat, simply an illusion, or real blood the way his mind wanted to see it.

"Ken." Jack said his name sharply.

Their eyes met across the gurney as the helicopter vibrated, shaking them as they flew through the air, just skimming the treetops. Ken could hardly bear to see the knowledge and compassion in his brother's eyes. His mouth went dry, but he managed to pull off his slight grin, the one that he kept in reserve for moments like this. He was all right. He was just fine. They'd taken his skin, his looks, even his manhood, and made his body into something out of a horror movie, but he was just fine. No nightmares, no screaming, just a flash of a grin, telling the world a monster didn't live and breathe inside of him, raking him with claws, demanding to get out and annihilate everyone around him.

Sometimes Ken thought that monster would rip open his belly from the inside out. Jack thought he wanted to talk everyone to death. He was the good twin. The easygoing twin, the one that got along with everybody. His fingers curled into two tight fists and then, aware of what he was giving away to his sharp-eyed brother, he spread his fingers out in front of him. Steady as a rock. He could always count on that. His hand might be scarred, his fingers not as flexible as they should be, but Ekabela and his sadist friends had made the mistake of mutilating them but not taking away his ability to shoot. They were too eager to get down to the real pleasure of cutting him in other, much more painful and frightening places.

He shifted his gaze away from his brother. Jack could read his mind. Hell, they'd been slipping in and out of each other's mind since they were toddlers. Even then it had been self-preservation. They learned at an early age to count only on each other. Jack knew him too well. He knew that the monster that lived inside of both of them was all too close to the surface these days. Jack had to be worried that Ken was not going to able to keep it contained. Insanity was a very real possibility he had to face.

Dr. Peter Whitney was a man with far too much money and power. He didn't believe the rules were for someone like him, and unfortunately he had the backing of some very powerful men. Jack and Ken, like several other men in the military, had fallen for his enthusiasm over his psychic experiments. It made perfect sense at the time—to take men from all branches of the service with Special Forces training and test them to see if they had potential to use psychic abilities. The doctor would enhance the inherent talent and create a unit of men who could save lives with their abilities.

Whitney hadn't said a word about gene therapy and genetic enhancement. He hadn't mentioned cancer or brain bleeds or strokes either. He certainly had never admitted he would pit the men unknowingly against one another. And never once had he mentioned a breeding program, using pheromones to pair a supersoldier with a woman.

Ken rubbed his pounding temples. Whitney hadn't screened them very carefully—or maybe he had. Maybe he knew about Jack and Ken's father and how he was so jealous and obsessed with their mother he couldn't bear to share her with his own children. Obsession was a very ugly word, and Whitney had certainly compounded the demon the twins fought on a daily basis. They had vowed they would never chance becoming the man their father had been, yet they had both been chosen, without their knowledge, to participate in Whitney's breeding experiment.

*Of course he knew about the old man,* Jack said. *He's the reason Whitney chose us. We're twins. He's paired us with twins and he's kicking back waiting to see the results.*

*You're fishing, bro,* Ken replied. *You want to know if I'm somehow affected by Mari's scent.*

*Aren't you?*

Ken glanced at his brother. He couldn't tell—and that meant neither could Mari. She had a chance then, a slim one, but still a chance when he'd thought they were all lost. He didn't watch tragic movies and he sure as hell wasn't going to live a tragic life, nor was he going to allow Jack and Briony and certainly

not Mari to live one either. Whitney be damned and his experiments too. If necessary, Ken would go hunting the man.

*Aren't you?* Jack repeated.

*You'd know it if I was, wouldn't you?*

Jack swore under his breath. *That's not an answer and you
know it.*

Ken shrugged, making it as casual as he could. *Evidently,
my genes are not quite as in demand as yours.*

Jack narrowed his eyes and frowned at his twin. Suspicion
pushed at Ken's mind. Jack was not in the least bit satisfied
with his answer.

*You're acting possessive of her.*

*I shot her. She's Briony's sister. Not just a sister, her twin
sister. If this doesn't end in a good way, do you really think
Briony's going to be okay with that? You can't get anywhere
near Mari, because if she dies, Briony will blame you whether
she wants to or not; it's human nature. You can't, Jack. You
have to let me handle this one.*

Jack shoved his fingers through his hair, a rare moment of
agitation. *It's not right. Because you're looking out for me,
you'll destroy your own relationship with Briony.*

*I'm not married to her. And that's what we do. We look out
for one another.*

*Keep that in mind if you decide to take any unnecessary
risks just to protect me with my wife.*

*I didn't know there was such a thing as an unnecessary
risk.* Ken flashed a small, cocky grin at his brother and was re-
lieved to see him relax.

Nico set the helicopter down on a small pad just above the
house Lily Whitney-Miller had rented for them. A brilliant
woman, she was the only orphan Peter Whitney had raised as
his own daughter, and the betrayal of all that she had known
and believed had been devastating. Married to a GhostWalker,
Ryland Miller, she'd opened her home, a huge estate, and her
resources, to the GhostWalkers. It was Lily who had found
ways for them to build shields to protect their brains from
continual assault. And it was Lily who had put Flame's cancer
into remission. And it was always Lily who stayed one step
ahead of her father to keep the GhostWalker teams safe. When
they didn't know who else to turn to, they called on her.

As the helicopter settled to earth and Nico shut it down, Eric slipped from his seat and once more bent over his patient, stethoscope to her heart. His hand slid down her arm until he found her wrist, searching for her pulse.

Ken's gaze jumped to the palm sliding over Mari's bare flesh, and a roar of protest started deep in his belly. Primitive and ugly, the monster inside gnashed its teeth and clawed for freedom.

"Didn't you just listen to her heart rate?" Ken asked, keeping his voice even. "Is something wrong that you're not telling us?"

Eric turned his head with a small frown. "She lost a great deal of blood and we could only give her—"

His voice broke off abruptly as Mari caught his hair, jerking his head back and down toward her. Her hand slid from his hair to his belt, extracting the knife there and whipping it around his throat.

Jack already had his gun out, aimed between her eyes. "I'll fuckin' put a bullet in your head if you don't drop that knife right now." His voice was low and frightening and he meant every word.

Mari tightened her hold on the knife, pushing it against the doctor's throat. "Take out the IV. You shoot me and I'll still have enough time to cut his throat."

"Maybe, but I don't think so," Jack said. "And either way you're still dead."

"Let's all calm down here." Ken moved into her sight. His eyes were pure mercury, a slash of liquid steel. "This can only end badly, Mari, and no one wants that." He was gliding across the helicopter, a silent, graceful flow of muscle and sinew that was as intimidating as hell.

"Stop moving," she bit out between clenched teeth, tightening her grip on the knife until her knuckles turned white.

*Stay the hell away from her, Ken. Don't you damn well get between us. I'll kill her right now,* Jack warned.

*There's no need for this; she can't go anywhere.*

"I fuckin' mean it, Ken. I'll take her out."

"Just be calm and think about this," Ken said. He didn't look at his brother or acknowledge the warning, and he didn't stop moving. "You still have a catheter in. How far do you think you're going to get with that?"

"The doctor is going to tell you how to take it out. I mean it, Doc, rip the IV out and do it now."

"Jack isn't a nice man, sweetheart," Ken said. "He looks handsome and talks soft, so people sometimes get the wrong impression about him. Remember when I was telling you how he pulled me out of Ekabela's camp? He was captured and escaped. Now, anyone in their right mind just keeps running, especially when they're in the middle of rebel territory, but not Jack." His voice was low and conversational, as if they were sitting across a table from each other, not staring down death.

He kept coming, a silent stalker, making her feel small and vulnerable. Was he within striking distance? He didn't appear to have a weapon, yet she was suddenly terrified. Not of the fact that she might cut a man's throat, or that Jack would shoot her, but of those glittering eyes that never left hers, eyes so cold she shivered.

"Stay away from me," she said, her voice choking.

"Jack went back into that camp and rigged everything to blow. He stole weapons and sat up in the trees and picked them off one by one. He killed over—" Ken exploded into action, moving so fast he was a blur, his elbow slamming into her head as his hands locked hers around the knife, jerking it down and away from the doctor, his enormous strength pinning her wrist to the gurney. For a moment everything went black and a million stars danced in front of her eyes. His thumb jabbed hard into her pressure point and her fingers jerked open in reflex.

Ken removed the knife and tossed it to Eric, but retained possession of her wrist. "Stay the hell away from her."

Jack swore aloud, a long and creative curse that was anatomically impossible. Ken glanced at him. "Watch your mouth."

"Don't you fuckin' tell me to watch my mouth. What the hell were you thinking? You walked right in front of my gun and you did it on purpose, you son of a bitch."

"I was thinking I'd defuse the situation," Ken replied, his tone as mild as ever. "She's supposed to escape, Jack. That's what we do when we're captured. I figured she'd try it eventually. I just didn't think it would be this soon." He glanced at Eric, who was still rubbing his throat and looking horrified. "There's no doubt she can push drugs through her system with remarkable speed, is there? You got your answer without taking more blood."

Ken was touching her, his fingers a vise around her wrist, so she felt the anger in him, a river of it running deep and fierce, when on the outside he appeared as cool—as cold—as ice.

# CHAPTER 4

Ken leaned toward Mari, creating an intimacy between them, as if they were the only two people in the helicopter. "Are you all right?"

Mari closed her eyes against the sound of his voice. So concerned. So incredibly gentle. He wasn't gentle. There was nothing gentle about him. His hands still clamped her wrist to the gurney and her head felt like a bomb had gone off inside of it. She turned her face away from his, determined not to be taken in by his false concern.

He shifted even closer; she could tell by his scent. It was suddenly everywhere, all around her, inside of her. She felt the warmth of his breath on her temple, the feather-light touch of his lips. His lips were soft except for one slight rasp over her skin, making her aware of the knife scar running across his mouth. That light rasp sent heat curling through her body. Her womb actually spasmed. She didn't want to respond to him. She didn't want to feel anything at all other than the need to escape. She didn't want to feel guilty for having used a razor-sharp blade, reminding him of the way his body had been so mutilated.

"It's all right, Mari. No one blames you for making a try.

It's what we all do, what we're trained to do. At least wait until you're a little stronger and we sort this entire mess out. You wouldn't get very far the way you are right now."

If she waited until she was stronger, they'd have the time to make certain there was no chance of escape. As for being stronger, her body was repairing itself faster than they guessed. The leg was bad—she might not be able to use it—but there were ways . . .

His lips brushed her ear this time. "I'm reading your mind, you know."

She jerked her hand in reaction. Ivy, before Whitney had killed her, had been able to read people as well as objects, simply by touching them. It was more than possible that Ken had that talent. *And then he would know how she felt when he touched her.*

Humiliation rose and mixed with anger. She whipped up her broken hand without thinking, aiming for his nose, wanting to smash it into his skull. He was her enemy and she would not buy into the attraction between them again. Or maybe she was just mortified because there was no mutual attraction between them; it was entirely one-sided.

He caught her wrist with almost casual strength, slamming both arms above her head and pinning them there, bringing his body nearly over the top of hers in a much more dominant position. It made her seethe with anger. She had to fight back the impulse to lunge forward and bite him like a rabid animal—or maybe claw the clothes from his chest to see if the web of scars she was certain covered his chest and belly disappeared lower into the narrow hips and across his groin.

"Stop struggling."

"Get off of me."

"Calm down first. I just saved your life, you ungrateful little wretch."

He was laughing at her. Damn him to hell, he was laughing at her. She could see a glint of humor in his eyes. He didn't smile or change expression, but she *felt* his laughter, and it made her want to explode—or maybe press her mouth to the softness of his, just to feel the caress of that heated rasp once more.

Furious with herself, she nearly came up off the bed, adrenaline pouring through her body, but there was no give in him.

She remained pressed against the gurney as if he didn't notice her struggles. "You. Get. Off. Me." She bit out each word from between clenched teeth. "I swear I'll tear out your heart with my bare hands."

His brilliant gaze drifted slowly, almost possessively over her face. "You don't want to be talking to me that way; you're turning me on."

Her heart accelerated and her breasts tingled with anticipation. His chest was so close. A breath away from her aching nipples. It was perverted to feel like this, to be a man's captive, to have him slam his elbow into her head and still have her body react like a cat's in heat. In that moment she hated herself, hated the way she despised Brett and the other men. She understood now, understood how desire could take over every sense and push aside discipline and training, until all one could think about was assuaging a chemical need.

Did he know? Was he feeding the addiction deliberately with his nearness? If so, he was playing a very deadly game. She forced her body to relax and looked up at him, frowning, hoping she looked intimidating. "Black widows eat their lovers."

He released her wrists and drew a finger down her cheek, the pad of his finger sliding over her lips, lingering as if he belonged there. When she looked at him, when he touched her, she felt the anger slide away before she could catch and hold on to it. He did something to her, made her feel whole and at peace. Maybe it was a psychic talent peculiar to him. Could Whitney do that to a person? Could he make it so that she trembled with need and yet felt whole inside just by touching this one man?

"I don't think I'd mind all that much if you ate me," he returned, his voice almost a purr.

Once more she felt the electric current running between them, sparking along her skin and heating her blood into a thick, molten stream. A shiver of need went down her spine. She could only stare at him, feeling vulnerable and feminine instead of like the soldier she knew herself to be. She'd never felt like this, so female she couldn't relate in any other way to him then seeing him wholly as a man. She didn't dare speak, afraid he would realize she was trembling from his touch, not from fear or anger.

He caught her chin in his hand and tipped her head to one side to examine her temple. "You're going to have a bruise. I'd let the doc look at it, but I think we can manage without him. Do you need more pain medication?" His fingers moved over her throbbing temple, taking some of the sting away.

"No." It was a blatant lie, but she looked him right in the eye, because she couldn't handle this man when she was on drugs. She needed her wits about her if she was going to survive.

"We're going to move you, Mari, and it's going to hurt."

"I've been hurt before."

A flash of something crossed his expressionless face, a quick glimpse of an emotion she knew was important, but she didn't get a good enough look to identify it. But he wasn't made of stone—that was for certain. "Are you ready?"

Mari noticed that it was the doctor, not Jack, who took up the position at the foot of the gurney. Jack looked grim and held a gun in his hand. There was no question in her mind that he intended to use it on her if she made one wrong move toward his brother. A part of her admired that; another part filed the information away for future use. She was a solider and it was her duty to escape. She no longer had loyalty to her job, but she did to her unit, and she was determined that Whitney wouldn't catch her in a trap, no matter how addicting the bait—because this had to be another Whitney sadistic setup.

Mari nodded and touched her tongue to her dry lips. She'd rather be tortured than feel this way, confused and helpless and so feminine she ached with need. She understood torture and duty and discipline. There was no way to understand the heat in her body or the blood pounding in her veins. Her awareness of Ken was incredible, as if her every sense—every cell in her body—were tuned to him.

She tried to steel herself as they lifted her, but nothing could prepare her for the pain ripping through her, driving out everything else, robbing her of breath and thought and for one moment clearing her head so she could be who she was—strong and stoic and in control. She was the one the other women looked up to, the rebel refusing to give in to Whitney's latest demands. She was the one encouraging the idea of escape—if that was all that was left to them—and she was the one who promised that if they all helped her get a chance to see the senator, she'd convince him to free them.

The other women believed in her and she had let them down by being captured. It was possible Whitney had already killed one of them, but he'd been away from the compound, and as long as no one told him she was gone, they would all be safe. The men would be frantically looking for her—not wanting Whitney's wrath to fall on one of them. His punishments were sometimes lethal.

Now that she knew what it was like to be so absorbed in another human being, to need to feel his touch, hear his voice, while he seemed to be indifferent to her other than as a prisoner, she wanted to take back everything she'd said and done the past couple of years regarding the men helping Whitney with his breeding program.

The men were prisoners as much as the women, they just didn't realize it—but Whitney's experiment couldn't continue. She knew it with a certainty. It wasn't natural and it was fundamentally wrong to take away choice. Even if she fell in love—and she wasn't certain that was possible with the way she felt about men—she would never get over wanting Ken. It gave her understanding and compassion that she'd never had before for the men unnaturally paired with the women. How could any of them find happiness?

Ken watched the conflicting emotions flit across her face as he helped carry her into the small house where they would wait for ground transportation while Nico threw off the hunters. He'd continue his flight plan to another location, a house Lily had also rented. When Mari's team got there, it would be empty and Nico would already have the helicopter back on the base where it belonged. He'd lay low for a while in case they decided to grab him to extract the information. Nico wasn't a man easily found. He was only waiting for the doctor to get moving so there would be little time to realize he'd made a stop somewhere.

Ken found it difficult to watch the beads of sweat break out on Mari's face with each step they took. She had refused more pain medication because she wanted to be alert. He could read

her confusion and humiliation. She was undeniably attracted
to him, with the same frightening addictive rush he felt each
time he inhaled her scent. He understood now what had driven
Jack to go to such lengths to keep Briony. Jack had managed
to walk away from the woman who was everything to him
once, but he couldn't do it twice. Ken wasn't certain how his
twin had managed the first time, but he knew he had to find the
same strength.

He couldn't have her. It didn't matter that she wanted him,
or that he could persuade her—*he couldn't have her.* He didn't
dare. Jack had come through it, but he was different. Jack
hadn't believed he was a good man, but Ken had always known
that Jack was. Ken had watched him carefully for any signs of
the legacy of madness their father left them. He had stayed
close to Jack and smoothed his way in every situation, making
certain Jack didn't have to do any of the things he preferred not
to do, so there would be no reason for him to feel the burning
rage—rage so deep it burned cold, not hot. Rage so ugly, it was
beyond madness and as relentless as hell.

Jack had the same ice in his veins, the same ability to turn
off emotion with the click of a switch, a trait that was dangerous but manageable, but Jack knew how to protect others. He
watched out for the men in his unit, for the one woman who
had saved them so many years ago when they were still raw
teens out for blood and revenge on the world, and he watched
out for anyone else they stumbled across in their lives that
needed protection. He looked out for everyone, including Ken.

Ken hid his rage behind a ready smile and a quick joke,
and he guarded his brother with his life. He looked out for one
person, and that was Jack. He loved his twin fiercely, protectively, and was determined that Jack would have a good life
with Briony and their children. Ken would keep his brother
and his family safe—even from him and the certain knowledge he had that their father's insanity lived inside of him. It
was a monster he dealt with every day, knew intimately, and
could barely conceal or control.

"You're frowning."

Mari's voice startled him out of his introspection.

At once his smooth mask slid into place. It was ironic to him
that the very mask people now saw revealed what was beneath

the skin as well, but no one bought it. "I don't frown." He would have to be more careful. If she caught him slipping, so would Jack, and that wouldn't do.

"The doctor is going to examine you one more time, and if he can, he'll remove the catheter and the IV." Jack's voice was ultra-calm. He had his gun out, his hands rock steady and his eyes cold. "If you so much as twitch, I'll kill you."

She turned to look at him, forcing a smile when she wanted to scream with pain. "Maybe you'll be doing me a favor."

Something dangerous flickered in Jack's eyes. "You don't want to play games with me, Mari. I don't know anything at all about you. Briony is my world, and if you are in any way a threat to her, you're gone."

Briony. She couldn't think about Briony. Her twin was somewhere in the world, far away from all of this insanity. She was safe and happy and had a husband who adored her, not a stone-cold killer with silver slashing eyes and without a single shred of mercy in him.

The doctor moved in close to her. It took a moment before she realized just how humiliated she was going to be. He was removing the catheter with both men in the room. She wore little beneath the thin cover.

"Take a breath," Ken advised. "We don't exactly have a choice here, and in any case, we'll be seeing to your needs until you can walk again."

"How long did you have someone helping you with bodily functions after they chopped you into little pieces? Did they remove all of you or just parts?"

The soft snick of the gun was loud in the suddenly quiet room. The doctor gasped and studiously avoided looking at Ken. It wasn't hard for anyone to imagine just what body part she was asking about.

Mari would have given anything to be able to take back the words the moment they left her mouth. She was lashing out in embarrassment, trying to hurt him, trying to get some reaction from him. It was petty and beneath her. She didn't care about his scars, although she had to admit she did wonder if they had cut him everywhere. She couldn't imagine a sadist like Ekabela—a man capable of genocide—not doing as much damage as possible to another man he hated and feared.

That drove out every other thought—*Ekabela had feared this man*—yet she was deliberately provoking him, prodding a coiled viper with a stick, digging into a predator's wounds just to cover her own humiliation. She looked up at him, uncaring that the room seethed with tension and his brother *wanted* to pull the trigger. The two men were very connected. Jack must feel a stab of pain cutting as savagely as the knife that had cut his twin each time he looked at Ken. She would feel it if someone had tortured Briony and left visible evidence behind.

"Take the catheter out, Doc," Ken said, his tone mild. "And don't you think it's a little dramatic to hold a gun on her, Jack?" He sighed and brushed more stray strands of hair from her face. "Jack likes to shoot first and ask questions later. I've sent him to a couple of psychiatrists, but they always send him back and tell me there's no help for him."

She couldn't apologize, couldn't say the words in front of the others. She could only look up at his carefully expressionless face and wish Jack would pull the trigger. She doubted Ken allowed himself to be hurt by much, but her barb had gotten to him. He didn't show it at all, but Jack had and that seemed worse. As if her thoughtless comment had gone so deep Ken couldn't show his reaction.

He was her enemy. She repeated the words over and over as the doctor removed the IV and catheter. All the while she kept her gaze locked with Ken's, seeing every detail, the perfect bone structure, the heavy dark lashes in contrast to his gleaming silver eyes. There was latent sensuality there, but she knew those grid patterns on his face were all most people were ever going to see.

"What did my sister say when she saw you?" She whispered the words aloud, needing to know, knowing the question would be misconstrued, but it would tell her the truth, tell her things she needed to know in order to keep going on her course. She had to be right about Briony's character.

"Damn you," Jack hissed, taking an aggressive step forward. "Shut the hell up, before I do it for you."

Ken cut him off with one smooth step, blocking his twin's path to the bed, the only reason, she was fairly certain, Jack hadn't knocked her out with the gun butt.

"Briony never seems to notice unless someone else does,

and then she turns protective like a mama tiger," Ken answered. "Does it bother you so much?"

She should have said yes. She desperately needed protection, some kind of armor, some distance between them, but the lie wouldn't come. "No."

Jack took a breath and let it out, shoving the gun out of sight and turning away. "Doc, you're out of time. Stay low until you're contacted that it's safe. You know the drill. Thanks for all your help and I apologize for the knife. I underestimated her abilities." His gaze bored into her. "It won't happen again."

She flicked him a glance. "Sure it will. You're a big caveman and I'm just the little woman, too stupid to know how to fend for myself."

Jack left the room, following the doctor out to the helicopter, leaving her alone with Ken. Instantly the room felt too small, too intimate.

"Stop baiting the tiger," Ken said. He slipped his arm around her back and gave her another drink of cold water. "We're only going to be here an hour or so, just enough time for you to rest."

"He only thinks he's the tiger. That's what you make everyone think, isn't it?" She made it a guess, but she knew it was the truth.

"Don't think for one moment that Jack wouldn't pull that trigger. He's no kitty cat," Ken said.

"Maybe not." Jack might be the quiet one, the no-nonsense one, but Ken lured the enemy into a false sense of security. He smiled more often than Jack, but it never reached his eyes. There was something inside of him, still and watchful and so full of danger it made her heart beat hard in her chest. "But neither are you."

Ken watched the way her throat worked as she swallowed the water. He could barely keep from leaning down and touching his tongue and teeth and fingers to that fragile expanse of skin. He longed to taste her. To put a mark of ownership on her. To brand her his to the rest of the world. And that need disgusted him. He had faced danger his entire life, but this one woman held more threat to him personally than a thousand rifles had ever done. She would take his honor and his self-respect and expose his deepest, ugliest secret to the world.

"Why wouldn't Briony come to see me, if you really know her?"

"Jack doesn't trust you."

"That wouldn't stop me." She was inexplicably hurt. If she found out where her sister was, she would move heaven and earth to catch a glimpse of her—as long as she could be certain Whitney would never find out.

Ken allowed her to lie back, and he straightened, once again giving her a feeling of loss. "You said you were there to protect the senator. Do you know who gave your team that order? I'm assuming someone said there was going to be an assassination attempt on him."

He looked so remote—so utterly alone. She felt that way inside, where no one ever saw who she was. No one ever cared who she was. She was a soldier. It was everything and yet nothing at all. She sometimes felt, especially recently, as if she had no humanity left—as if it had been stomped or trained out of her. She wasn't certain which, but it was gone. *Do you feel that way?* She asked it silently, wanting to reach out to him, needing to connect after she'd raked at him with her claws. *Do you feel as if you have no humanity left in you? That they stamped it out and made you into something you don't even recognize anymore?*

His gaze moved over her face, seeing too much. For one moment she felt connected, as if he had managed to crawl into her skin and share it with her. *I was born without humanity so I have never had it to lose.*

The words were harsh, but his voice, moving through her mind, was a caress, stroking at her insides, raising her temperature and setting her on fire. She was struck by the utter honesty in him, when what he was saying was impossible. Ken obviously believed what he was saying, and that confused her. What kinds of monsters were hidden behind that mask of scars? He'd once had a face of masculine beauty. Had that been a mask as well?

She studied him, trying to be objective, trying to really see him when the chemicals in her body were reacting and rushing through her bloodstream in wild abandon. Whitney was fond of experiments. He had a way of twisting everything good into something that left a bad taste in one's mouth. She had been raised with discipline and control, but to her orderly mind, everything Whitney did seemed to be chaotic and wrong—a subtle or not-so-subtle form of torture.

Mari shook her head. "Whitney has no humanity. He's cruel and callous and hasn't an ounce of kindness or compassion in him. You aren't like that."

"Don't kid yourself, I'm *exactly* like that."

"You do kind things."

Ken shrugged his shoulders. Most of the time he felt nothing at all, but when he did, it was an icy rage that burned so deep it terrified him. Now his emotions were all out of whack and he wished he could go back to the familiar. He did kind things because he had to do them—it was necessary to keep Jack safe. And above all else, Ken wanted Jack in the world, happy and healthy and living his life. One of them had to survive, and Jack was extraordinary.

Ken bent down once more, his breath stirring tendrils of hair from her face, his expression harsh. "It gets results."

She studied the scars up close. The torture had been recent. She should have been intimidated, but Mari didn't scare easily. She knew soldiers, and she recognized control when she saw it. Ken had discipline and restraint down to an art. She reached up and brushed his face with her fingertips, needing the tactile experience, the flood of information that could accompany a single touch of skin to skin.

Everything inside Ken went still as her fingers traced the pattern of his scars. She left tiny pinpoints of fire burning on his face, when he couldn't feel his own touch. He didn't have sensation on most of his body, yet he could feel her *beneath* his skin, sparking damaged nerve endings to jump and sizzle with electric current. The sensation spread from his face to his chest, a heat so thick it felt like lava pouring through his veins and tissue, gliding like hot silk over muscle to burn him from the inside out. The fire settled in his groin, bringing him to hard, painful life.

He had always been a large man, well endowed, and Ekabela's men had had a field day with him. One had been a master of torture, and he had inflicted those small, deep cuts in a precise pattern over every inch of Ken's body. He had lovingly called it art, and the men around him admired and encouraged those neat cuts, cuts designed to inflict the most pain while never allowing the victim to lose consciousness. Cuts designed to ruin a man should he happen to escape. They had skinned his back, but it hadn't been as bad—*nothing* had been as bad as that knife slicing into his most intimate, private part.

He could still feel agony flooding his body, the urge to beg them to kill him. The need to mete out justice to someone—anyone. He had known when he woke up in the hospital and saw the nurses' faces that the monster living and breathing inside of him had been revealed. And he had known he would never function as a normal man again. The raised ridges left him with little sensation, and if he wanted to feel again, feel any pleasure at all, stimulation would have to be rough enough to reach beyond the damage.

"Son of a bitch." He bit the curse out between his teeth, his voice harsh.

His pounding blood flowed hotly to settle in his groin, and he clenched his teeth against the inevitable pain as rigid tissue reluctantly stretched, swelling into a long, thick bulge he hadn't known still possible. His breath rushed from his lungs and sweat beaded on his forehead. He gripped the edge of the bed and forced himself to breathe through the pain. All the while his gaze never once left hers. She'd done, with one stroke of her fingers *on his face*, what he thought no one could ever do for him again.

"Son of a bitch," he repeated, fighting for air, fighting not to let the pain and pleasure, now mingling together, become the same.

"Ken?" Mari tried to push herself into a sitting position. "What is it?"

He was hunched over, and whether he wanted to admit it or not, he needed help. She couldn't sit up; her leg was held tight, and movement threatened her precarious control, so she did the only thing she could think of. "Jack! Jack! Get in here!"

Ken's hand clapped tightly over her mouth, and he bent closer until his lips were directly over hers, with only his hand separating them. "I don't need him."

The sound of the helicopter was loud outside, and she was fairly certain Jack hadn't heard her call. Ken had been so fast he'd muffled most of what she'd said.

A drop of sweat fell on her face and her eyes widened. She caught his wrist with her one good hand and tugged. When he reluctantly lifted his hand only inches from her mouth, she touched the droplet. "Tell me what's wrong with you."

"Every now and then I feel a few residuals from my little vacation in the Congo." He shrugged. "It's nothing to worry Jack over."

"You don't worry Jack much at all, do you?" she guessed.

"There's no need. Stop squirming around before you hurt yourself." He tested himself, straightening his body just a little, trying to ignore the way her lips had been so soft against his palm. He could feel sensation with her, every sense heightened beyond normal until he could almost taste her in his mouth. "How well do you know Whitney?"

"No one knows Whitney, not even his friends. He's like a chameleon; he changes his skin when he feels like it. He presents one face, one personality, one day, and the next he's totally different. Personally I think he's a lunatic, drunk on his own power. The government gave him too much authority without anyone to answer to, and he has too much money, so he's like the number one megalomaniac of the world. And I told him so on several occasions recently."

"Are you aware he does very accurate profiling? I mean dead-on, Mari."

She knew he was leading up to something, and she was already there. "He has to have some kind of psychic ability. Otherwise, how could he have managed to choose the right infants in an orphanage? He knew we all had talents. He touched us, or was drawn in some way to us, because of our psychic abilities. That would have been impossible unless he was psychic himself. It's how he knows things about us."

Ken swallowed the sudden bile rising in his throat. He'd had a bad feeling, ever since he'd taken Jack's mission in the Congo and been captured, that it had all been orchestrated. Even down to Jack's delay in Colombia so he couldn't lead the rescue team when the senator's plane went down.

He cleared his throat. "You said Whitney wasn't exactly friends with the senator. Did Whitney know the senator's plane had been shot down in the Congo by the rebels a few months back?"

"Yes. We were told."

"And did you know the first rescue mission was successful but that a man was left behind? Did Whitney know?"

"I overheard Sean telling him the news."

"And how did Whitney react?" His chest hurt. His lungs burned for air.

"He seemed excited. I thought he was excited the senator was rescued, but then he said something about it being too bad that Freeman had to survive."

Ken kept his face carefully blank as his world crashed around him. He should have known. Dr. Peter Whitney found great joy in using human beings in his experiments. He went to extraordinary lengths to manipulate people into position so he could record the events and trigger reactions he had predicted. He had done so with Jack and Briony, and now, Ken was certain, he was doing so by sending out Mari to guard the senator.

"Who gave the order for you to protect Senator Freeman?"

Mari hesitated, but it was clear to her that Ken was on to something—and it was entirely possible that they were on the same side. What could it hurt? As he probed her for information, she was collecting data of her own. "I was no longer part of the protection team. I'd been moved over to another program. Whitney was gone, and with a little help from some others, I convinced my old team to let me go so I could get the opportunity to speak to the senator on another matter."

Ken inhaled sharply. "Is Whitney enhanced?"

She shook her head. She had loyalty to her unit, but certainly not to Whitney, and if this was a trap set by Whitney, he already knew her views on him and his despicable experiments. "I tested him a couple of times, just to see. His bodyguards had to pull me off of him. I'm sure he isn't. Probably too chicken."

"You attacked him?"

"I was hoping I'd get lucky and break his neck, but he has one guard, Sean, who is really, really good."

The admiration in her voice triggered something vicious and ugly deep inside of him that he always took great pains to keep hidden. He turned away from her abruptly, keeping his back to her until he could bring himself back under control.

His fingers curled into two tight fists and his gut clenched hard. A black shadow moved in his mind.

"How did he react when you attacked him?"

"He smiled. He likes to smile just before he does something really nasty. That's when I was pulled off of my unit and moved to another program."

"His breeding program."

She forced herself to maintain control, neither flinching nor looking away. "He sent Brett to me."

Ken's gut knotted and the shadow in his mind grew larger. He could hear the thud of his heart pounding in his ears like the roar of a wounded animal. "And just what did Brett do?"

"Brett is part of his new breeding program, and he's paired with me."

The roaring reached a crescendo. His sight went to heat imaging, glowing shades of yellow and red, flashing like a warning signal as he spun back to her, his hand spanning her throat. "What exactly did Brett do you? Touch you like this?" His palm slid from her throat to the swell of her breasts, stroking caresses. He shoved the blanket back, exposing her body, the smooth firm lines and the lush curves. "This?" He bent his head to flick her nipple with his tongue.

Mari went rigid as sensations burst through her. She should be screaming, fighting, doing anything but what she wanted to do. She knew what this was. She knew he was taking advantage of her injuries and that he was deliberately using sex against her, but she had never felt the bright burst of pleasure that the mere touch of his tongue had brought her. Her fingers fisted in his hair, but instead of jerking him away, she held him to her, closing her eyes and savoring the feel of his tongue, his teeth, the heat of his mouth as he suckled.

He wasn't gentle; she could feel that the scrape of his teeth and his mouth was more ruthless than sensual, as if he was angry with her, but her body reacted with such urgency she nearly sobbed. One of his hands traveled across her stomach, slid lower, stroking once, twice, and then his finger was deep inside her welcoming body, her muscles clenching around it, wanting to hold him to her. Her body threatened to implode, the orgasm rushing over her when there was no reason for it other than that one single plunge of his finger. She cried out as the sensations overtook her, shaking her, shaking her faith in herself and her ability to resist anything he did to her.

"Fuck." Ken spat the word at her, jerking his finger from her body, his hand wrapping around her throat a second time. "Did he make you feel like this? Did you get wet for him? Did you come for him like that? Damn you, did he make you come apart for him?"

"Ken! What the fuck are you doing?" Jack demanded.

Ken went rigid, his face going completely white, eyes wide with shock and horror. He stumbled away from her, looking helplessly at his twin, one hand reaching out to him. There was utter and complete despair on his face, in the bleakness of his eyes, in the way he wiped his mouth with the back of his hand as if her taste disgusted him.

Jack took a step toward his brother, shaking his head.

Time slowed. Mari knew. She saw it all happening in her head as if somehow, that brief moment of connection had left part of her inside of Ken to read his mind. She knew exactly, as if the entire scene had been rehearsed.

Ken pulled his weapon in one smooth movement and turned to her. "I'm sorry, Mari," he said quietly and put the gun to his head.

# CHAPTER 5

The thunder in Ken's head grew louder. He would never get Mari's taste or scent out of his mind; he would never stop needing to reach for her, touch her, *own* her. Eventually, as surely as he lived and breathed, he would go to her, take her, make her his own. And once that happened, both of them would be lost. He had shown her—and himself—he could not be trusted. He would destroy her the way his father had destroyed his mother. First the jealousy and then the punishments, and finally madness would overcome love, and murder would be swift and brutal. And then Jack would be forced to hunt and kill him.

He sent his brother a small, sad smile and lifted his other hand to shield Mari's eyes. *I've always loved you, Jack. I don't want you to have to do this.* His finger tightened on the trigger.

"No!" There was fear, agony, in Jack's voice. "Damn you, no, Ken!" He leapt forward, a hundred years too late; even with his enhanced strength and speed, he could never get there in time.

The way Ken had drawn the gun was smooth and practiced. There was no hesitation, only resolve, as if he had known someday he would have to use that last line of defense for his brother. Even as he lifted the gun, Mari was already in motion. She threw herself off the bed, every move carefully calculated. Her head rammed Ken's arm. She felt the heat of the explosion as the bullet left the gun, far too close to her face. The sound was deafening next to her ear, but she latched on to his wrist and took both of them to the floor. She landed hard, unable to protect her leg.

She heard herself scream, the cry torn from her throat, but she hung on grimly to Ken's arm, pinning it with her body weight when she was seeing stars, afraid she'd pass out before Jack got to his twin.

Ken didn't struggle. Instead he wrapped his arm around her and put his mouth against her ear. "I tried to save you. Whitney has my profile too. He knows me inside, where no one else does, and he thought it would be fun to pair you with the devil."

She turned her head to stare into his strange-colored eyes. "The devil wouldn't have tried to take his own life in order to keep me safe."

There was a moment, one small heartbeat, when she glimpsed raw emotion in those silver eyes and her heart jumped in response.

"You'll never be safe again, Mari, not while I'm alive."

Jack kicked the gun across the floor away from Ken and sank down beside them, his trembling hand going to his brother's shoulder. Mari hadn't thought he could be so shaken.

"What were you thinking? Ken, you should have let me help you."

Ken shook his head, gathering Mari closer to him, reaching for the sheet to once again cover her body. His hands were impersonal, as if his mouth had never tasted her flesh, brought her to a fever pitch of sensual pleasure without even trying. "There's no way to help me, Jack, and you know it. You can only help her. You know what you have to do to keep her safe."

"This is bullshit, Ken. I can put a bullet in her head and be done with it."

Mari raised her hand. "Do I get a vote?"

"You're bleeding all over the place again," Ken said. He stood, lifting her into his arms, the pain driving the air from her lungs. "You can't kill her, Jack. You have to protect her from everyone—even me."

Mari tried desperately to cling to consciousness. The movement wrenched her leg, made her stomach protest with a violent heave, but she refused to faint, needing to hear every word.

Jack shook his head. "It doesn't have to be like this."

"What? You didn't see me acting like an animal? You know exactly what it's going to be like—a long drop into hell. I'm not doing that. I refuse to be *him*. I'd rather be dead." Ken placed Mari back on the gurney, careful to avoid jarring her leg. "Take a look, Jack, see how much damage she did." He stepped away from her side, not looking at her, not touching her, his voice as empty as his expression.

"You look." Jack reached down and snagged the gun. "Are you going to be stupid again?"

Ken refused to answer. Jack stepped closer to the gurney and suddenly jammed the weapon against Mari's head. "I swear to you, on our mother, if you even think about doing that again, I'll blow her brains out."

Ken instantly came to life, his face darkening, eyes narrowing to slashing silver slits. "Get the fuck away from her or we're going to have trouble, Jack."

"She can bleed out for all I care, Ken. Anything happens to you, *anything*, by your hand or someone else's, she's dead. You got that? I give you my fuckin' word on that. She's dead. You know me. You know I don't ever stop. You think long and hard about that before you try this shit with me again." Jack withdrew the weapon, threw it to Ken, and shoved past him to stalk over to the doorway.

Ken stood for a moment just holding the gun, staring after his twin. He said nothing, just stood in silence, his knuckles white where he gripped the butt of the gun. Finally, he shoved it inside the holster under his arm and took a deep, calming breath before looking at the blood seeping into the sheet.

Mari inhaled sharply, trying to find a way to ease the tension. "Well, that went well. I can see that he does have a bad habit of wanting to shoot people. He wasn't kidding."

"No, he wasn't." Ken pushed the sheet off her leg. "Did you have to land so hard? You really made a mess."

"It hurts," she admitted and reached out to catch his arm.

"You didn't hurt me. I participated. It wasn't all your fault, you know. I could have said no."

He shook his head and she felt the tremor that ran through his body. "You have no way of understanding what's going on here."

"I have more understanding than you think I do," Mari said.

Jack leaned his hip in the doorway, glaring at both of them. "Then tell us."

She flicked him a quick glance. "This is about Whitney's breeding program of course. We're all caught up in it. This is one big experiment. Is Briony pregnant?"

Jack stiffened. "Why would you think that?"

"Because Whitney was desperate for me to get pregnant. He was furious with Brett for not getting the job done. Once I found out she was with you, it wasn't all that hard to realize he wanted her in the same condition."

Ken shook his head. "It's far more than that."

"We already knew what he was doing, Ken," Jack said. "We've known since he sent his team to retrieve Briony. He wants the babies."

"He did what?" Mari pushed at Ken, demanding an answer.

He ignored her, shaking his head at his brother. "Don't you understand? He knows. He did this. He knows about me."

"You aren't making sense," Jack said.

"He means Whitney," Mari interpreted.

Ken nodded, brushing his face with his hand, smearing Mari's blood along his jaw. "I've always suspected he was psychic. He knows about me. He knows what I'm like and he set this up. It can't be anything else, Jack. He knew if he sent her to me what I'd do."

"He *thinks* he knows you, just like he thought he knew me. I still have Briony. And I'm fine with her. You see us together; I might get a little jealous now and then, but I'm not like *him* and you aren't either."

Mari looked from one to the other. "Who is *him*? You're no longer talking about Whitney."

"I am," Ken said to Jack. His voice was a low, soft whisper of sound, but the impact it carried was lethal. "I am *exactly* like him."

"That isn't true, Ken," Jack denied.

"The hell it isn't," Ken snapped. "Do you know what I wanted to do to her when I knew another man had been inside of her? Touching her? Hell, Jack. I don't even know her. I don't know the first thing about her. I'm not in love. She's not in love with me; how could she be? But it didn't matter. I wanted to pound into her, make her forget anyone else, punish her for daring—*daring*—to allow another man to touch her that way. I wasn't gentle with her; I didn't want to be. I wanted her to know who she was with."

Jack hit the back of his head against the doorjamb. "This is insane."

"I've always known he was alive, living in me. I've always known it. And that son of a bitch Whitney knew it too. He wants to see what will happen to us. How his little game will destroy our family. Fast. Slow. A big explosion, a quiet bullet to the head. He's just sitting back and watching us, Jack. The bastard is wired to us some way. He wants to force the issue to see if you're up to the job of putting a bullet in me."

"And what good will that do him?" Jack asked.

"He wants to see what it does to Briony, to see if both of you are strong enough and worthy enough for your kids to be his supersoldiers. Mari is expendable to him; she always has been. Why do you think he tried to get a baby out of her by someone else? He didn't want his work to be a total loss."

Mari turned her head away from both of them. She could hear the anguish in Ken's voice, and it ripped her up inside. He didn't love her. How could he? She didn't know whatever was in Ken and Jack's past, but she heard the ring of truth in Ken's voice and things were making sense. Whitney detested her because he couldn't control her very well. He had to use threats against the other women to keep her in line. And she was strong, always a threat to him and his programs. She asked too many questions. Whitney had been furious when Brett was unable to get her pregnant.

She tried to separate herself from what he was saying. It was all happening to someone else. A woman she didn't know. She was a soldier and needed to get back to her unit. It's where she belonged—what she understood. She wasn't the type to lie helpless, tears burning in her eyes, while a man used her body, but she'd done just that, helpless to resist Ken's mouth and hands.

With Brett, it was a fight every single time he came near her. She was committed to defending herself and her right as a person to choose whom she wanted to be with. With Ken, she desperately needed him near. Every moment she spent in his company worsened the addiction to him, until she felt frantic with wanting his touch.

"Could Whitney do that?" she asked, searching her memory for an unguarded moment he might have let something slip. "What's your last name?"

"Norton." It was Jack who answered, his eyes still locked on his brother.

Again her heart jumped. She recognized the name and she should have known. Snipers. Not just any snipers. The elite.

Ken wiped the blood from her leg, all the while avoiding touching her skin. Pride should have kept her from looking, but she was fascinated by the way his body moved, by the glide of his hands, always so careful to keep from contact. The memory came out of nowhere, triggered by the mesmerizing ripple of muscle beneath skin. Whitney's face contorted with anger.

*Damn the Nortons anyway. How did you let them slip away from you, Sean? I made it easy and you still blew it.*

*It won't happen again, Doctor.*

Sean had been standing close to her while Whitney jabbed her with a needle right before one of their missions. She remembered the surreptitious brush of his hand to encourage her. She'd always hated needles, and only Sean had known that little weakness.

Ken stiffened, his fingers circling her foot like a vise. "Who is he?"

Mari blinked, glanced at Jack and back to Ken. "I don't know what you're asking me. And you're hurting me."

Ken let go of her as if she'd burned him, wiping his palm along his thigh. "The man you were just thinking about. I caught the impression of him. Big man, standing by Whitney. You like him."

"You caught all that just by touching me?"

"Damn it, answer me," Ken ordered.

"Ken, back off," Jack warned.

"You had your chance, Jack." Ken shot him a hard glare. "Now we all have to live with the consequences."

Mari laid her head on the blanket stuffed under her head, her eyes narrowing on his face, lending her a kind of tunnel vision. She recognized the familiar signs of her temper kicking in. "Wait a minute. I have a horrible feeling I'm beginning to understand what's going on here. Call me slow, but for some reason, although you're men, I expected you to act with intelligence."

"Mari . . ."

"You don't know me well enough to use my name. You don't know the first thing about me or my life. I'm your prisoner, remember? You shot me." Her voice was tinged with fury, so she kept it ultra-low, but it was too late to rein her temper in. She was already looking for something to smash over his head. "Don't you dare Mari me. I don't care if I have a broken leg. If you want to torture me, get on with it, but I'll be damned if you sit there being smug and acting like a jealous lover because of *Brett*. *Brett*, of all people. That's what set you off. I get it now. The 'did he touch you like this' and then losing your mind. What a complete ass."

"Mari . . ."

"What a moron. Don't talk to me. Don't touch my leg." Adrenaline poured through her body, so that she found herself shaking. "Do you have any idea what that man is like? What it's like for a woman to have someone who repulses her touch her? Go to hell, Ken. Next time you want to put a gun to your head, I'll help you pull the trigger."

"You don't understand," Jack said.

"Are you kidding me? I'm the one who has to endure Brett—or anyone else—at Whitney's whim. Not you, not Ken. And catching a glimpse of a soldier who has treated me with decency and respect—one I admire—is cause for jealousy as well?"

Ken remained very still, his fingers still circling her foot, the physical contact sending electric sparks zinging along her nerve endings, adding to the flood of anger building like a volcano.

"Who is he?" Ken repeated.

She was already in pain. What the hell? She used her good

leg, snapping it up and out, straight at his face, using enhanced strength, needing the satisfaction of scoring just once against him. He was messing with her mind and Mari found that un-acceptable.

He blocked the blow with one arm, hard enough to make her leg go numb, never letting go of her other foot, not even loosening his hold, as if her attack had been so inconsequential he almost hadn't noticed it.

"It was Sean, wasn't it?"

"Go to hell."

"You don't understand," Jack repeated. "Whitney didn't do this."

Mari pressed her lips tightly together, studying their faces. Ken hadn't moved a muscle, his hand still around her toes. She could feel the warmth of his palm, was all too aware of him as a man—not a captor—not an enemy.

"Fill me in."

"The old man managed to leave his legacy with one of us," Ken said, his tone matter-of-fact.

But he was shaken. He covered it well, so well she doubted Jack could see past his mask—that false emotionless mask Ken showed to the world. But when he touched her, when they were skin to skin, she saw more, felt more, knew more than he ever intended—and he was definitely shaken.

"I was the lucky one our father handed down his legacy to, and Whitney knew all along. I thought I had buried it deep where no one would ever know, but he's psychic and he read me like an open book, and all this time he's been waiting his chance."

Jack cleared his throat. "You think he wants to see your re-action to her when he's paired her with other men?"

"He thinks I'll kill them—or her."

Mari's stomach did a somersault. There was quiet truth in Ken's voice. She moistened her suddenly dry lips. "Someone really needs to fill me in here, because, quite frankly, I don't like the sound of that. Whitney has a way of manipulating people into doing exactly what he wants them to do and I'm not exactly his favorite person."

"Ken." Jack ignored her. "He isn't reading *you*. He has no idea of your character. You think the old man is lurking around inside of you. Hell, I thought the same thing, but it isn't true. We were investigated. Whitney has a high security clearance and he read everything in our files."

"What is everything?" Mari asked, trying desperately to ignore the way Ken's individual fingertips were bringing points of fire to her ankle.

"Jack, it has nothing to do with that. He probably did read the files, but he knows. He set this up because he wants to see how I'll react and how Mari will react, and now that you have Briony to protect, he wants to see how you'll react." Ken's fingers dug into Mari's ankle, and he suddenly turned his glacier-cold gaze on her. "My father was an insanely jealous man. He brutally murdered our mother and tried to kill both of us. Whitney knows it and he set this up. You. Me. Jack. Briony. It's all one big game to him."

"Well he's playing a deadly game then," Jack said. "Because no one controls us, Ken. We do what we've always done; we make our own rules and we stick together."

"What about her?" Ken's reply was so low Mari barely caught the words.

Jack sighed. "You know it's impossible to leave her behind, so we're going to have to work through it. It wasn't that easy for me with Briony, but we managed."

"I'm not you, Jack. I'm telling you, I'm like he was."

"No, you're not." Mari was firm, startling both men into noticing her. "If Whitney saw that information in a file somewhere, yes, he'd use it against you. He's very good at twisting people into knots, exploring their weaknesses, but if he has psychic abilities and he touched you, he didn't read that in you."

"How do you know that?" Ken's fingers continued that gentle brushing along her toes, his grip as strong as ever, but the touch had lost its warning and had become an involuntary caress.

"Because I touched you."

Ken blinked. It was his only movement. There was no change of expression on his face, but she knew he'd reacted.

Jack edged closer. "You have that kind of ability? To read people when you touch them?"

"She doesn't," Ken denied. "She's lying to try to ease my mind."

"You wish. I don't even like you. Why would I want to ease your mind? The worse you feel, the happier I am." His eyes had gone to cold steel, but she held his gaze and shrugged with feigned casualness. "I couldn't care less whether you believe me or not."

"Do you?" Jack asked.

Mari studied their faces. There were definite chinks in their armor, whether they wanted to admit it or not. "Not strong, but strong enough to know Ken isn't a flat-out murderer, especially not of women. He would carry out an order, but he wouldn't just go around killing someone for no real reason."

"Good to know." Ken let go of her foot and took away the warmth. "If you're so good at all of this, why don't you tell me who this man is and we can let it go?"

She frowned. "You know it was Sean."

"And he'll come after you."

"Whitney will send him, yes, but if you're right that this is an experiment, why would he do that? Why would he send someone to bring me back to him? Wouldn't he want to see what happens between us?"

"He's sending Brett first," Ken replied. "That's all part of his happy little plan. And then he'll send the other one because there's a bond between you, and Whitney knows it—and he knows I know it and he knows I'll kill them."

There was an edge to his voice that alarmed her, his tone low and mean and without mercy. She wanted to say it shouldn't matter, but she already knew the power of Whitney's experiments, and she had enhanced scent, just as Ken did, just as Jack did. That made the pheromone response all the more potent. Whitney had created a powerful sexual attraction that transcended common restraint and threatened the discipline of even the strongest soldier—just as the doctor had planned.

If Ken was really like his father, as he evidently feared, she could be in more trouble than she'd ever dreamed. She doubted if she could resist Ken Norton if he made sexual advances toward her, but she would try. What she hadn't counted on was caring one way or the other about the man. She was drawn to him, not just sexually, but emotionally, and that made no sense to her and almost scared her more than the physical attraction.

"My leg hurts and this conversation is making me feel sick. I shouldn't be giving out information to you. We're enemies."

Jack shook his head. "I don't think we are. If you were really ordered to protect the senator, as we were, then we're on the same side. You have the GhostWalker crest tattooed on your upper back." He shoved up his sleeve. "We're a member of an elite unit of the Special Forces and we all work for the United States. We're on the same side, Mari. I don't know how the wires are getting crossed, but I suspect Whitney has something to do with it."

"You think Whitney has gone rogue."

"We all thought he was dead—murdered," Jack replied. "He disappeared about eighteen months ago, and his daughter 'saw' his death, saw him murdered."

"I can assure you, he's very much alive."

"No one has seen or heard from him. Only recently, we began to suspect he faked his own death."

Mari frowned, shifting slightly to ease the soreness in her hips. Nothing could stop the pain in her leg, so she ignored it, the way she'd been taught. It bothered her that Jack was doing all the talking, as if Ken was still dwelling on other things—things she didn't want him to be thinking about. "It's possible he faked his own death so he wouldn't be killed. If the government, or his friends, decided he was a liability, or a lunatic, they might have decided to get rid of him, or at the least have him locked up in an institution." She risked a quick glance at Ken, but he was looking at her leg.

"What friends?" Jack asked.

"He has a couple of people visit every now and then. The compound is under heavy guard when they come, and they're surrounded by bodyguards. Most of the time we're moved to the back of the compound and only catch glimpses of them. Sean works with Whitney now, so a few times he's told us about the arguments between them."

Ken stepped away from her, folding his arms across his chest and regarding her with cold eyes. "It didn't occur to you that killing a woman because someone didn't return might be a little out of the ordinary?"

Mari noticed his body was still slightly between hers and his brother. Something about his deceptively casual stance and his tone sent a chill down her spine. "What's ordinary? I was raised in the barracks with other girls. We were soldiers, trained as soldiers, ran missions even as young as twelve. None of us have ever been away except on a mission or training exercise. Normal was whatever Whitney told us it was."

"And now?" Jack prompted, shooting his twin a warning glance.

Mari shrugged. "Whitney is getting worse. When I was a child, he just seemed mean, and remote, but over the years, he's really deteriorated, especially the last year or two. For a while, he seemed like he had a human side. I thought maybe his daughter, Lily, was keeping him grounded, but—"

"You know about Lily?" Jack interrupted.

Mari nodded, trying not to flinch as Ken cleaned her leg. More blood had seeped out. "He talked about her often, and it seemed like he really might love her, although, to be honest, I couldn't imagine that he was capable of real love. He didn't see any of us as human beings. Over the last two years he's become fanatical. Even his friends seem to be having trouble holding him in check."

"Tell us about his friends," Jack encouraged, taking another step forward.

Mari tried to keep her gaze from straying to the gun at his waist, or the two other weapons in the twin harnesses beneath his arms. He was close enough that she might be able to snag one of the guns if she was fast—very fast.

"Is there something about my brother's face you find fascinating?" Ken asked.

The low tone made her shiver. He could sound so utterly menacing at times. "Actually, no," she brazened, determined not to be intimidated. "I was wondering if he was deliberately tempting me to make a try for his guns or whether he was so into the conversation he forgot I was his prisoner."

"Do you really think you're that fast?" Jack asked.

"Ordinarily, but I'm hurting a little bit right now, so my timing might be off. In any case, you're double-teaming me. Ken is waiting for me to jump you, and frankly, it's a really uninspiring trap. Neither of you put much thought into it."

"Sorry, it was spur of the moment, just to see where we stood," Jack said. "You thought about going for a gun."

"I have to escape. I don't have a choice. As much as I'm enjoying your company, I really, really have to get back—everyone's waiting for me."

"And all this time I thought we were getting to be friends. Didn't we agree we were on the same side?"

Ken ignored both of them and once more took up a position by her head. He wiped her face with a cool cloth. "Put off trying to escape just a little longer. Your leg isn't up to it yet."

"I wish I could, but even if we were on the same side, they're going to come looking for me and someone will end up hurt. I may be able to sneak back into the compound before Whitney realizes I've ever been gone. My people are going to try to make that happen."

"Just give us the location of the compound, and we'll be happy to escort you home," Jack suggested.

"And you'd bring a few of your friends just to make it fun," Mari said. She waved him away. "I'm tired. You can interrogate me later, okay?"

"Take another drink of water." Ken slipped his arm behind her back again. "We can't risk you getting dehydrated."

"Did she do much damage to her leg?" Jack asked.

Mari closed her eyes and turned her face away from them. She liked them. She even understood them. They were soldiers. She respected that. They were doing their job and they very well could be on the same side—she was fairly certain they were—but she couldn't chance risking everyone's life to find out.

She inhaled, dragging Ken's masculine scent into her lungs. She'd been more stimulated, more humiliated, and more exhilarated than she'd ever been in her life. She *had* to escape. Nothing she said or did was going to convince them to let her go.

"Mari, drink the water."

The steel in Ken's voice set her teeth on edge. She knew the ripple of anger going through her body tipped him off. She had a stubborn streak a mile wide, and it was the one thing that had gotten her through her separation from Briony—through her unusual childhood—and through the degradation of Whitney's insane breeding program.

Ken tightened his arm around her and lowered his face

until his warm breath fanned her cheek—until she was enveloped in his scent and her body began to respond. She tried desperately to focus on the pain in her leg, on her dire situation, on anything but the feel of the muscles in his arm, the heat of his skin so close to hers.

*Are you doing this on purpose? Because it's low.*

*Don't defy me just to prove some silly point. You need the water to keep you healthy. Drink it.*

She turned her head to glare at him, her lips inches from his, her gaze locked with his. It was a good thing she was telepathic, because she had no air left in her lungs to breathe—or talk. *Has anyone ever mentioned to you that you're a complete ass?*

*I believe my brother has done so on many occasions.*

She nodded her head. *Well. Okay then. As long as someone has.*

She took a small sip of the water and let it trickle down her throat, surprised at how parched she was. The drugs were beginning to leave her system, and things were much more sharply in focus. Time had passed. She understood why they had kept her knocked out as they moved her from place to place, probably one step ahead of her unit, but she had no idea if it had been hours or days.

Panic gripped her for a moment and she fought it down. The five women left in the compound were her only real family. Well, there was Sean and a couple of the other men who had not been caught in Whitney's web of deceit. But she'd been raised with the other women. They were all close, sisters. They had no parents, no other friends, so the bond between them was strong. In the end it didn't matter if she was on the same side with Ken and Jack, because she had to go back. She couldn't leave the others to face possible death at Whitney's hands.

She was absolutely convinced Whitney had begun a descent into madness. He might have started out a brilliant scientist, but somewhere along the way he had become convinced he was far smarter than anyone else and his ends justified his means. Rules weren't for him. He had too much power and too little accountability.

Mari drank more water. She had to regain her strength. "How long did you keep me out?"

"A couple of days," Jack answered. "We can't have you calling in your unit, and they've been hard on our heels."

She flashed him a brief smile, deliberately leaning back against Ken's arm, determined to show him—and herself—that she could be in control of her physical feelings. "They're good."

"Not that good," Jack disagreed. "They don't have you and we do. Had we been looking for you, we would have found you."

"You're so arrogant."

Jack's eyebrow shot up. "That isn't being arrogant. It's a fact."

"I'm tired and my head hurts." She glared up at Ken. "Probably from where you slammed your elbow into me."

"I remember. And you didn't even thank me for saving your life."

"I would have preferred you being a lot gentler about it." She was joking, trying to lighten the situation—or stall for time, she wasn't certain which—but a shadow crossed Ken's face. Up so close to him, she caught that fleeting reaction to her words.

Ken laid her back on the pillows. "You've been out a couple of days. We've been leading your unit away from anyone who could get caught in the cross fire."

Mari glanced at Jack. They had a plan. Whatever they were doing, she couldn't be a part of it. "I have to get back. You don't understand. If I don't go back, Whitney is going to hurt one of the others. I can't let that happen."

"Give us the location and we'll go in and bring them out," Ken said.

She pushed at his chest. "You know I can't do that. I won't sell them out. I have no idea who you really are."

His glittering eyes met hers like the slash of a sword. Cold. Possessive. Very frightening. Her pulse began a frantic rhythm. He showed little emotion, and that had been frightening, but this seemed worse. Behind his mask, his mind was working fast, calculating, formulating, processing data every bit as fast—or faster—than hers did. What other attributes had Whitney brought out in him? What other genetic code had Whitney slipped into his body—because right at that moment he looked more predator than man.

The throbbing in her head increased. She caught the exchange between Jack and Ken. A single look, no more, but it was enough. She took a deep calming breath and relaxed her mind and body. *Sean? Anyone? Are you out there?* Her head was hurting not because of the elbow, but because someone was out there, calling, using telepathy, and the Nortons had been alerted.

Ken's hand slipped around her neck, his fingers sliding to her pressure point. She tried to stop him, but it was a lifetime too late. She could feel the waves of dizziness, the room spinning away from her, and everything went black.

# CHAPTER 6

"They're coming, Ken, let's get the hell out of here," Jack said. He snapped open his radio. "What the hell is taking you so long, Logan? Another couple of minutes and we're going to be in a firefight. Nico's trying to lead them away, but if you don't get here, all this is for nothing."

"I'm about five minutes out, running without lights."

Ken had already plunged the room into darkness before taking up a position beside Mari. He felt for her pulse, his fingertips sliding in a caress over her smooth skin. He was sick with fear for his brother and Mari. Ever since he had inhaled her scent, the monster so carefully locked away had grown stronger with each moment spent in her company. He was jealous of those men, Brett and Sean. It was ugly and sharp and cut with as much pain as the slice of the knife into his skin.

He knew Jack, knew Jack would do exactly as he warned and kill her should Ken try to take himself out of the equation. Jack had effectively removed Ken's choices. And it was impossible to be alive in the world and know another man was holding Mari, kissing her, touching her. He nearly groaned aloud. She had brought his body painfully to life when Ken and the doctors had been certain he had been ruined. But even if she had, what did that mean for both of them? Hell, just because his cock was hard didn't mean the damned thing could work anymore.

Jack pressed a hand to his head. "They're calling for her and they aren't being quiet about it."

"They must be searching in grids and using more than one helicopter or they couldn't cover so much territory so fast," Ken added.

Telepathy could be quiet. Jack and Ken had been using it since they were toddlers, and they could send easily to each other without a lot of energy spilling over to give them away. The GhostWalkers trained in sending precise waves when communicating, because anyone familiar with the strange buzzing and head pounding recognized it for what it was, but it wasn't an easy talent to master. Right now it didn't appear as if Mari's GhostWalker team cared one way or the other that anyone else might hear them. They were frantic to find her and being loud about calling her.

Her team wanted her back. Ken understood the creed of the GhostWalkers. They never left a man behind. If one was captured, they kept coming for him—or her. But he couldn't help wonder if Brett or Sean were leading the rescue mission and if it was entirely personal. The team had been pressing them hard for two days, and they were definitely following Nico's flight plans, filed with only a high security clearance access.

He swore softly to himself. There seemed to be no controlling jealousy. He had never allowed himself to care about anything or anyone other than Jack, so it had never come up. When Briony had entered their lives and Jack had fallen so hard for her, Ken had only worried about Jack losing the one good thing that had ever happened to him.

Ken touched Mari's face, tracing her bone structure, imprinting it forever on his mind and into his skin and organs. He wanted her for himself. It was unexpected and shocking to him, even frightening, that he could want something so much, but he did. She was there. Inside of him. All the while she talked, he watched every expression, every gesture, and he had rested his palm on her body, absorbing what he could of her nature and character. It wasn't one of his strongest gifts, but he caught impressions of her life, stark, sterile, and often unpleasant. She was the kind of woman he would have been drawn to without Whitney's interference.

She was strong and opinionated, not easily intimidated. She was beautiful. He knew she wouldn't think so; women never did. They always wanted to be thinner, or have a different hair color, or be taller or shorter, but he'd been the one to undress her, and her body was perfect for him. He wanted her with an almost savage, primitive need, and now that she'd awakened his cock, that too, had become a monster, raging for attention.

He'd always had tremendous stamina, a strong sex drive, and now that it was back, and he knew she was naked and receptive, it bordered on obsession. And what would it take to satisfy him? To stimulate him? He was fairly certain it would take a lot to stimulate him to orgasm, and a woman who had endured the kind of things Mari had would want no part of rough sex. He swore under his breath and turned away from her.

What the hell was he thinking? He couldn't have her. He couldn't think with his dick; he had to think with his brain—and he couldn't have her. It was that simple. He couldn't think about the way her eyes lit up when she smiled, or the sexy curve of her lips and how she would look ... He groaned softly and rubbed the front of his jeans, swearing again when he had to use a hard pressure to even feel the wave of pleasure that edged far too close to pain.

"They're two minutes out, Ken."

Jack's voice startled him, never a good sign when he had to be alert. It had just been so long since he'd felt sexual pleasure, and being close to her, feeling his body harden and fill with pounding need was a miracle—and a curse—he hadn't expected.

"Are you certain she's unconscious? We can't chance her warning anyone. If they don't follow Nico, we can't get her to Lily's. And you and I both know Whitney has something else up his sleeve that insures she'll go home. I want Lily to check her over thoroughly before she ever gets near Briony."

"She's out. We cut that one a little too close. They were an hour behind us. Nico could be in trouble." The buzzing in his head was fading, indicating that the team was moving away from them.

"We wanted them to think they were gaining on us. They had to follow him. Nico knows what he's doing. Logan will be here any minute, Ken. I need to ask you . . ."

"Don't. I tried to tell you and now it's too late."

"We have to talk about it. I had to face it when Briony came to me asking for shelter. There was every possibility our father lived inside of me."

"There was never that possibility. We made a pact, Jack, that we'd never get close enough to a woman to fall in love, but I always knew you would be fine if it happened."

"How? I didn't know. I feel nothing at all when I take the shot, Ken, you know that. I didn't feel remorse when I killed our father."

"When you finished what I started," Ken reminded. "Mom was already dead when I walked in on him. I should have run, but all I could think about was killing him." He could still remember in vivid detail tearing the baseball bat from his father's grip and swinging it hard. There was absolute pleasure when the bat connected with a satisfying crack and his father screamed. For the first time in his life, Ken had felt powerful and in control. He wasn't even a teenager, and yet he'd planned his father's death a million times, and when he'd found his father with his mother's blood all over him, something cold and ugly, vicious and merciless, had sprung to life and taken hold.

"You think I didn't have those same feelings, Ken? He made our lives a living hell. He beat the crap out of us, out of Mom; he ridiculed and embarrassed us. He wanted us dead, and he punished her every day of her life for loving us. Of course you wanted him dead. That has nothing to do with her." Jack stepped closer, gesturing toward Mari.

"It has everything to do with her and you know it." Ken was too ashamed to admit his feelings to his brother, the one person he loved and respected the most in the world. It was bad enough that he knew his own fatal flaw, that he had to stare into the mirror every day and see his father looking back at him, but he sure as hell didn't want Jack to see what he did. "I would feel like that, not wanting to share her with anyone.

I'm not taking the chance that we might have children and I'd lose my mind completely. When I heard about Brett . . ." He could hardly say the name and a wealth of disgust and anger was in his voice. "I should have been thinking what she went through, but all I could think about was that he'd touched her, been inside her, that I wanted him dead."

"I had the impression she despised him. If he forced her, he deserves to die. Hell, I'd want to kill him."

"The point is, I wasn't thinking about her—I was thinking about my own feelings, and they weren't exactly noble. And I wanted to be inside of her, driving any memory of him out of her." There was shame in his voice.

"Ken," Jack said, keeping his voice low, "we're both different. We have to be careful, but it doesn't make us like him. So we're a little more dominant . . ."

Ken snorted. "A little?"

"And a little more jealous than the average man . . ."

"A little?" Ken repeated. "Hell, Jack, Briony's too sweet and lets you get away with going all badass on her; she thinks you're cute or something. Who knows what goes through her head. And you don't lose your mind when she's around other men."

"It disturbs me," Jack admitted. "I handle it."

"And what if you couldn't? What would that eventually do to your relationship with Briony? How do you think it would make her feel every time some man smiled and you were instantly angry?"

"I'd have the good sense to keep it to myself. I trust her. You don't even know this woman, Ken. She doesn't love you; you don't love her. Why do you expect to be able to handle something like jealousy when you haven't even built a relationship with her yet? If you trusted her, and loved her, it would be different."

Ken shook his head. "Logan's here. Let's keep them away from her. We had to ditch her clothes, and the thought of any of the others seeing her naked is enough to set me off. I had a difficult enough time with the doc."

For the first time, Jack's expression was leery, as if it might be sinking in that Ken was telling the absolute truth—that his possessive, dominant nature might be too strong to control, as he feared.

"We'll handle it," Jack said. "We'll do it the way we always do." He indicated the gurney. "Let's get out of here."

Ken lifted his end, but hesitated. "If you had walked out into the backyard first and saw mom dead, and him standing there smiling, covered in her blood, would you have gone after him, or done the sane thing and left?"

Jack sighed. "It was a long time ago, Ken. I saw him beating you; he broke both your arms, and I went after him. I don't know what I would have done had I found him with Mom. Probably exactly what you did. I'm the 'shoot first, ask questions later' kind, remember? You're out front keeping everyone from bothering me, keeping them safe. You aren't our father, Ken, and you'll never convince me you're like he was."

Logan Maxwell, leader of the SEAL GhostWalker team, was riding shotgun and Neil Campbell was driving. Logan opened the doors and stepped back to allow the Nortons to shift the gurney into the Escalade. Ken and Jack climbed in beside Mari, Ken tucking the sheet around her carefully so that no skin showed.

He reached for the medical kit beside Jack's feet. "I'm going to give her another painkiller while she's out. Drugs don't stay with her long, but it will give her some relief on the ride. She'd probably try to take me out if I gave her a shot while she was conscious."

"She's been giving you a hard time?" Logan asked. "She looks on the small side. I thought you two could handle it all by yourselves, but no worries, Daddy is here now." He grinned at Ken, studiously avoiding looking at Jack.

Ken always found it amusing that Jack made everyone, even his fellow GhostWalkers, nervous and Ken was considered friendly. He'd cultivated the image carefully, hiding what he was behind a ready smile and a joke. It eased the way for Jack's more abrasive personality and kept them out of fights— fights Ken knew would turn deadly the moment anyone threatened Jack. While there were plenty of people who should be scared of Jack, it wasn't Jack they should have feared the most. Jack had tremendous control and discipline, but Ken would never hesitate to destroy any threat to Jack. He would do it fast, viciously, and without remorse—and that inner knowledge kept the smile firmly in place and the jokes coming, because no matter what, Jack would back him, just as he had so many years earlier.

Jack always thought that, after discovering their parents, Ken's tears had been from both grief and the pain of two broken arms, but it had been grief for his mother and the terrible knowledge that he had put his twin in the position of having to kill their father. Years later, when he had been tortured by Ekabela's men, Ken had known Jack would come for him. Dead or alive, Jack would come and Ken chose to stay alive to keep Jack from single-handedly trying to wipe out the rebels in the Congo. Ken had always felt responsible for his brother. He knew Jack's personality, the demons that drove him, and he would always feel responsible for bringing out the worst in his brother.

After injecting Mari with the painkiller, he passed a hand over his face. They'd stripped her of her clothing and her dignity. How could she forgive that? He knew what it was like to be stripped, the fear that accompanied the complete vulnerability a prisoner felt. His fingers tangled in her hair, stroking the strands under cover of darkness. He needed to touch her— needed to be close to her—and that was so dangerous to both of them. He'd worked his entire life to stay ahead of the monster and in one brief moment she had brought it roaring to life, all claws and teeth, raking at his gut and his mind.

He'd known the moment he'd inhaled her scent, taken her deep into his lungs, that he had been paired with her by Whitney. Anger had been his first reaction, anger that he could have so easily been made a victim, but then, when Jack had stepped close to her, he felt the sharp knife of jealousy, as ugly and as dangerous as anything his father had ever displayed. It had been a vicious reaction, knotting his guts, sweeping a black, swirling haze through his mind until he could taste it in his mouth. The need for violence had nearly overwhelmed him. And then he'd been afraid—more afraid then when Ekabela's men had stripped him naked, laid him out spread-eagled, and begun their slow, meticulous work on his body.

His mouth went dry just thinking about how he'd wanted to wrap his fingers around Jack's neck to keep him away from Mari when she'd looked at his face—his perfect face. Ken scrubbed a hand over the mask, feeling the ridges and the shiny skin, the edge to his lip. Funny how he'd never really minded before. He'd had pangs, of course, but for the most part he accepted what had been done to his body the way he accepted everything in his life. It was a fact, and one dealt with it. Besides, his face was nothing compared to the damage done to his dick. He closed his eyes briefly, remembering how they cut closer and closer and the bile had risen and the fear—the terrifying moment when they were finally there and made that first gut-wrenching cut.

"Ken," Jack said, his voice low, "are you all right?"

Ken wiped the beads of sweat from his forehead. Jack was far too tuned to him for him to hide any strong emotional reaction. Jack wouldn't willingly lose his twin, but it was only a matter of time before Jack would be forced to accept the truth—and that would endanger Mari's life and Briony's well-being.

Ken held out one hand. As steady as a rock. "I'm fine. Just trying to figure what we're going to do about this situation."

"Lily says she'll be up waiting for her. Flame, Gator's wife, is working on hacking into Whitney's computers," Logan reported. "She's very skilled and doesn't leave any trace, so hopefully Whitney won't catch on that she's able to access his files. So far, Lily has no real data on Mari. No one really remembers much about her before she and Briony were taken away."

Ken knew Gator was out of the original GhostWalker teams. The two teams had become much closer after Nico and his wife Dahlia, both members of the original team, had rescued Jesse Calhoun, a member of the SEAL GhostWalker team, stealing his bullet-ridden body right out from under the protection of his captors. They had combined their resources and fallen back on trusting each other rather than the chain of command.

"Did you speak to the admiral, Logan, to confirm who gave the order for protecting Senator Freeman, and where the threat came from?" Ken asked.

Logan shook his head. "I tried, Ken, but they said he'd

headed for Boston, that he had a meeting and would be contacting me as soon as possible. I've been maintaining silence just in case anything we're doing is monitored. There's definitely activity on all the bases. They want this woman back. Were you able to find out anything?"

"Only that she's a GhostWalker and her team seemed to be there protecting the senator from the same threat we were," Ken answered. "She heals far faster than we do. If Lily can add that in for us, it would be helpful. Her leg was in bad shape and she lost a lot of blood. I can't believe how fast she's healing."

"Actually, Lily noticed that with Flame. She was attacked by an alligator and her arm healed at an amazing rate of speed," Logan replied.

"Has Flame kicked the cancer?"

"It seems to be in remission. Lily is hopeful for a full recovery this time. She's asking everyone who is physically enhanced to come in for tests as soon as possible, just to be on the safe side."

"Whitney deliberately gave her cancer. He didn't like her," Ken said, as his gaze drifted over Mari's face. He knew the moment she regained consciousness. She didn't move, didn't speak, listening to their conversation, but his heightened awareness of her and his enhanced abilities in the dark made him all too aware of her breathing changes, and she was giving off the scent of fear.

He forced back the need to gather her into his arms and hold her, to reassure and protect her, a reaction he hadn't expected when every other reaction connected with her seemed so violent. He knew he should break contact, but he couldn't, not when she was so afraid. Jack glanced at him and knew immediately she was awake. Ken shook his head slightly, and Jack stared out the tinted window, ignoring everyone.

"Whitney has a lot to answer for," Ken said grimly.

"Ryland has been worried Whitney may try to snatch Lily's baby. They've been reinforcing all the security systems so if he makes a try at the house, he'll run into trouble."

"It would be ridiculous for Whitney to try to take down Miller's GhostWalker team, especially there. That house is a fortress."

Ken felt a tremor run through Mari, and he slid his hand along her shoulder and down her uninjured arm until he found her hand. His fingers laced with hers. He half expected her to pull away from him, but she curled her fingers around his and held on.

*You drugged me.*

*I knew the ride would be painful. I'd say I'm sorry, but I'm not, so I won't bother lying about it.* His thumb slid over the back of her hand in a small caress. *No one is going to hurt you, Mari.*

*No thumbscrews?* There was a small note of humor that managed to cut through the fear.

*No. Lily is going to run a few tests though, just to make certain Whitney doesn't have any nasty surprises up his sleeve.* Ken glanced at Logan, who was rubbing his temples. Logan was a powerful talent, and Ken was fairly certain he was well aware they were communicating telepathically, but he didn't allow his expression or his gaze to give him away. *Mari, energy waves like to spread out and keep going through all surfaces, including human beings. We find them disturbing, so people around us often react with headaches. When you talk to me, concentrate only on me. Think of a small stream with precise banks. Send the energy wave straight down that path, from you to me. You're used to sending to a team, not one person.*

*I'll try. Ken? I wanted to tell you something important. I'm a little doped up right now, so I may not be saying it right, but all that stuff about you being like your father, well it just isn't true.*

*You can't know that, Mari. You can't trust me. Hell, I don't trust me.*

*Brett makes my blood freeze every time he gets into the room with me. The other women feel it too. I don't have that reaction with you.*

*Whitney programmed you to have a physical reaction to me; that's all it is, Mari. Don't make anything else out of it.*

Mari kept her eyes closed, not wanting to deal with any of the others. The vehicle was swaying, tires bumping over obstacles occasionally jarring her, but it was still peaceful. She could smell the night, clear and fresh after a recent rain. She had no idea where she was, no way to escape, and she was naked beneath the sheet, feeling entirely too vulnerable, especially now when there were other men close by.

She knew by the scents that there were two men, the driver and one who was closer to her. He was dangerous. She sensed his alertness, the way he held himself still and quiet. They were always the deadliest of the soldiers. Sean was the same. Jack was like that. Ken was like that. Men, coiled and ready, quiet and calm but able to strike so fast no one would ever know what hit them.

She should have been terrified, but Ken made her feel safe and protected, which was silly when he was just as much of a threat—maybe even more so to her—than the others. She lay still, eyes closed, pretending he was holding her hand on a date. She'd never had a date. Never been to a movie that wasn't a training film. She'd never walked down the streets of a city holding hands, and she'd never gone out to dinner in a restaurant. She wouldn't know how to act in a family setting. It was a dream, a silly, foolish dream, but it suited her to pretend—even if it was only for a few minutes.

The compound would be waiting for her when she found a way back to it, and then her "sisters" were going to have to get serious about escaping because she was not putting up with Brett and his punishments for not cooperating with him. She'd thought of a dozen ways to kill him, but she knew Whitney would punish the other women. Ivy was proof of that. Mari had to go back regardless of whether or not the Nortons and their team were on the same side. She had to go back because Whitney was a megalomaniac whack job and he had far-reaching tentacles.

*Do you think Whitney ordered a hit on the senator?* Mari asked Ken.

She loved the sound of his voice. It seemed to move through her, as slow and thick as warm molasses. The sound felt like a caress inside her head, sliding over her skin and into her body to heat her bloodstream. He wasn't trying to seduce her, and it was frightening to think what would happen if he actually set his mind to it. She tightened her fingers on his, uncaring how much of her emotional state she was giving away.

*Why would he, unless the senator was going to give him up? I take it Freeman knows about Whitney's laboratory experiments? After all he married one of them.*

Violet. Violet had been a good friend. Whitney had paired her with the senator. He'd sent her to be his bodyguard, and the next thing anyone knew, Violet was married. Whether or not Whitney still pulled her strings—and Mari couldn't imagine him letting her go—she seemed to love her husband.

*What's the tie between Senator Freeman and Whitney?* Ken asked.

*His father and Whitney went to school together.*

Ken considered her answer. It wasn't the first time he'd heard it. *Logan, contact Lily. Have her find out as quickly as possible who Whitney's friends in school were. He only ran with the very intelligent and very wealthy.*

Marigold jerked her hand away, her eyes flying open, glaring at him, knowing he could see her in the dark—just as her enhanced vision allowed her to see him. *You passed that information on to your friend.*

Ken stared down at her furious face. He didn't spill energy—not ever. She was tapped into him more than just through pheromones. What the hell had Whitney done? And how? When? She was reading his thoughts without benefit of expression, energy spill, or anything else. What kinds of psychic abilities did she have? How dangerous was she? As much as he wanted to protect her, he had to think first of Jack and Briony and the twins Briony carried. Whitney would go to any lengths to get his hands on those children—even sending Briony's own sister.

*Jack. Briony isn't waiting for you at Lily's, is she?*

Jack stirred, a predatory tiger stretching. His gaze was flat and cold as it drifted over Mari. *Yes. It was the only safe place I had to stash her. Ryland and his crew are watching over her. And I thought if she was going to meet her twin for the first time, it was the safest place.* There was a question in his tone, although he didn't voice it.

*Don't!* Mari blinked back sudden tears. He was warning his brother off, sending Briony away. For the first time Mari really let herself think about seeing her sister. Just a quick glimpse, that was all she really needed. Just to know she was alive and happy. Mari desperately needed Briony to be happy.

Mari wasn't touching him, but she knew. Ken could see it on her face, read it in her mind. There was panic, sorrow, anger, all mixed into one, as if Mari couldn't quite make up her mind how to feel about what he'd done. But he had no choice.

*Get her out of there, Jack. Send her to Jesse Calhoun or Nico and Dahlia. We have to have Lily take a look at Mari, and we just can't take the chance without knowing what's going on. She has talents we don't have a clue about.*

Jack swore softly. Briony was anxious to see her sister. He had made her a promise that he would find Marigold, and he meant it. But Ken was right. There were no taking chances with her. Until they knew what Whitney was up to and whether or not Mari was really on their side, they just couldn't take the risk.

*How could you warn him off of me like that? What kind of threat could I possibly be to my sister? That's what you did, isn't it? I'm a prisoner, surrounded by trained GhostWalkers, and I have a broken hand and leg. You must think I'm really good.*

Shaking with anger, she stared up at Ken's expressionless face. He was every bit as cold and unfeeling as she'd first thought him. He'd managed to fool her because Whitney had set it up that way, made her vulnerable to him. Whitney so loved his little jokes. He loved to feel superior, and she'd defied him so often. This was probably his punishment—to make her believe she was close to seeing Briony. She'd been right not to think about her, not to hope.

*Mari, we have to protect her until we know for sure.*

She wouldn't listen to that caressing voice, so velvet soft and playing through her body like a musical instrument. Not again—never again. Her throat felt raw and her eyes burned, but she stared up at Ken defiantly. Let him try to defeat her. Nobody, not even Whitney, with all his humiliations and his tricks, had defeated her.

*Wouldn't you want Briony protected?*

*I don't want you to say her name. She's dead to me. She's not my sister. My sisters are back at the compound waiting for me, and believe me, I'll get back to them. There is no Briony. It was a trick, a fairly vicious one at that. I accepted her death a long time ago.*

He wasn't going to use her sister to hurt her. She had to put everything out of her head except her desire to escape. If she didn't do it soon, before they arrived at their destination, it would be nearly impossible. They were going to a fortress; she'd heard Ken say so.

Ken knew better than to touch her, and yet, even without touching her, he knew what she was thinking. He was catching images, emotions, impressions she wouldn't want him aware of. *Something is happening that I don't understand, Jack. I know what she's thinking and I don't have physical contact. And she can do the same with me. It isn't perfect, but we're picking up the gist of it as if there's some sort of silent transmitter between us. Do you have something similar with Briony?*

Jack shook his head and shifted his weight slightly, leaving his gun in an easier position to pull out should he need it.

Mari shut out everything around her. The swaying vehicle. The pain. The fuzziness in her brain. The men. It was hardest to block out the image of Ken and the mask that was his face. Those eyes that always stared directly into hers. She forced her thoughts down a long, dark tunnel, bringing in waves of water to wash away random thoughts. She needed to focus on only one thing. The steering wheel. It was her only chance. She planned out every step carefully and then locked on to the wheel.

She couldn't actually see it, so she built the image in her mind. She could see it clearly, feel it in her hands, hard and smooth, ready to do her bidding. She tested it just once, a very small little movement to the right. The vehicle jerked to the right and then was back on track, running smoothly down the road. It wasn't a freeway, more of a back road. And that meant there would be foliage.

"Would you mind opening a window? I can't breathe." Not too pitiful, just the right balance of neediness and defiance.

She didn't dare look at any of them; they were too skilled, so she kept her face averted, her fingers gripping the sheet.

Logan hit the button to bring in the night air. She inhaled, taking in the scents of the evening. Trees for certain. Lots of them. Grass. Animals. Oh, yeah, if they were heading for a city, they were taking the back road in. She could so deal with that!

*Whatever you're thinking, Mari, don't.*

She wasn't going to talk telepathically to him again. It was a shade too intimate for her liking. She had to find a way to break the mesmerizing sexual web he'd trapped her in. "I have no way of knowing this isn't one of Whitney's traps. He loves to play with people's minds."

"How so?"

"He knows what I think about his breeding program. It's common knowledge the other women are following my lead and resisting. It would be just like him to pair me with you, use my own body against me, to punish me, to force me to do his bidding." She glanced at him, when she knew it was a bad idea. The night hid the mask covering his beautiful face, leaving him looking too handsome with his brilliant eyes. His eyes were like jewels, diamond hard and so intriguing. One moment so cold she felt burned by their touch, the next alive with some hidden pain she wanted to soothe away.

"I haven't seen Whitney in a couple of years and he certainly isn't pulling my strings." *I know you're upset about Briony, Mari, but if you really care about your sister, you would want to know she was getting the best protection we can give her.*

She wouldn't be swayed by his looks or his voice. She concentrated on the road, utilizing every bit of information the air would provide. There was only the dim light from the moon, partially obscured by clouds. There were no sounds to indicate farms or ranches, or even the occasional house. She didn't even know what state she was in. She couldn't smell the ocean, so they had to be inland.

She focused on the brake, building the shape and feel of it in her mind, the cables and the way it worked. She tapped, just for a moment, and the car lurched and ran smooth. It was just a fraction of a second, barely noticeable, but she heard a man's voice, coming from the driver's seat, swearing. She immediately filled her mind with other things, puzzling out whether Whitney had paid these men to trick her.

It had to be a trap. She remembered Whitney, the last time she'd seen him, furious because not only the women were upset and uncooperative, but some of the men had become reluctant. He had locked them in their rooms, refusing to allow them to interact, blaming Mari for the mutiny. He had promised her retaliation if she didn't do as he wanted. She thought sending Brett had been what he meant, but evidently she was wrong. It was no wonder it had been so easy to convince her unit to allow her to go along to plead their case to Senator Freeman. Whitney had to have virtually orchestrated everything. And that meant these men were his men and her "sisters" back at the compound were in danger.

"Talk to me, Mari."

Her plan had to be carried out with precision and without hesitation. They had made the mistake of not securing her. To keep Ken off balance and from reading her plan, she kept images of Brett in her mind. Brett bent over her. Brett touching her. Brett tying her down to keep her from fighting him.

Ken clenched his teeth, a muscle ticking along his jaw. His fingers curled into fists. His eyes glittered in the night, twin swords of steel piercing through her body, seeing far more than she wanted him to see. He knew she was deliberately taunting him.

*You're playing with fire, Mari.*

He bit the words out between clenched teeth, the sound stabbing at the walls of her mind. Mari turned her face away from him, all too aware he could see clearly in the dark. She stared at the door straight across from her. The vehicle was slowing for a turn. She groaned and pushed herself up, leaning forward to clutch at her leg. The sheet slipped down, exposing her breasts. The men froze, staring at her. Ken growled deep in his throat, adding to their immobility. It gave her the precious second she needed.

She attacked, using her mind, applying pressure to the brake, wrenching the steering wheel from the driver and opening the door in front of her. Using enhanced strength, she dove out, hands in front of her, as if springing off a board, prepared to break her fall in an aikido roll, even as she changed the color of her skin to match her surroundings.

She heard the squeal of the brakes as the driver tried to recover and stop. There was a burst of male voices swearing, but she had already landed, camouflaged by the thick foliage, smashing through a bush, the branches tearing up her hands and arms, as she rolled, trying to protect her leg.

# CHAPTER 7

Fury swept through Ken. She had done it deliberately, exposing her breasts to every man there. Damn her to hell for that. Ken didn't wait for Neil to get the Escalade under control; he dove out after her, breaking his fall the same way, rolling over leaves and fallen branches along the wet ground to lie still, staring up at the night sky. They were in a heavily wooded area. He could hear a stream running off to his left.

*Now you've really pissed me off. I could strangle you for that. You didn't need to give them all a show.*

He was afraid for her. She had a broken hand and leg. She had no weapons and no clothes. And he just might be angrier over the gripping fear for her than for her exposing herself to all the men. What if she had hit one of the trees and broken her neck? It could easily have happened. He couldn't imagine finding her dead body. *Answer me, damn you.*

Was that him? That near panic when he was always so cool under fire. He didn't mind dying, he never had, so it made it easy to run the covert missions all over the world, but this was something altogether different. She had gotten under his skin. He tried to tell himself it was simply Whitney's experiment and that once she was gone, Jack and Briony would be safe and things would be back to normal, but that didn't stop the panic inside of him. Fear had blossomed into full-blown terror for her. She couldn't be dead.

The ground shifted slightly beneath his feet, trees and bushes trembling. He rose to his feet and tried to breathe normally. *Mari. I need to know you're alive.* He should have been humiliated and ashamed that there was pleading in his voice, but he wasn't. He was telling a simple truth. He *needed.* It was that simple and it made no sense. If it was simply physical attraction between them—as powerful and as potent as it was— why would he be feeling such terror that she might be dead?

Of course she wouldn't answer him. He was the enemy. He had to be logical, get past the fear and use his brain. He was far more experienced than she was. He had to go on the premise she was alive. He could track her. Every person shed skin cells, and his sense of smell was phenomenal, thanks to Whitney's genetic enhancing, but there were other, far easier ways than walking around in the dark sniffing the ground. It mattered little if she had been trained since birth; he had years of hard battles beneath his belt, but most of all, Jack and Ken had been using their psychic abilities long before Whitney's experiments, and both were strong talents. With the enrichments, they were able to do things Whitney would kill to know about.

He sank down onto the leaf-covered floor, sinking into the cool, damp earth, drawing his legs tailor fashion and resting his hands on his knees. He let his mind expand to take in the world around him, soaring free, becoming powerful. *Mari, come to me. You have no choice. Come to me. You feel me. I'm inside of you. All around you. Come to me. You need me. You have to be with me. There isn't a choice for us. Come to me.* It became a litany, a mantra, broadcasting the command over and over, oblivious to the men who came and went as they searched for their lost prisoner.

Ken concentrated on Marigold, building the picture of her in his mind. He knew the feel of her satin skin, the lush curves and sexy body. He knew every detail: the injuries on her body, the way her mouth was full and promising, the heavy lashes that curled and framed her large eyes. *Come to me now. Hurry, Mari. You need to come to me. You can find me. We're one, in*

*the same skin; we need to be together.* Most of all, he'd been inside her mind, knew it on a more intimate level. She couldn't
shield herself from him, or ignore him.

His mind shifted, drawing her, calling repeatedly. Her skin
would be shades of green and black and tan, blending in with
the leaves and bushes around them. She wouldn't be able to
stand with her broken leg, so she would crawl, a sensuous slide
through the cover, her bare breasts swaying gently, invitingly.
He imagined sweeping his hand down the curve of her bare
bottom as she moved toward him like a jungle cat, creeping
through the foliage to make her way to him.

There was no sound, but he opened his eyes, knowing she
was there. The first sight of her took his breath away. He'd
never seen anything more sensual. She crawled toward him,
her body perfect in the night, flowing muscle and curves begging for attention. His body flared into life, a savage, painful
reaction, his cock near bursting, pulsing with urgency. He had
a primitive urge to yank down his jeans and mount her like an
animal, rough and dominant, branding her his.

She lifted her face, and he could see tears tracking down
her cheeks. There were several scratches on her shoulders and
across her left breast. His heart turned over, the sensation
strange and very shocking. She kept coming to him, a mixture
of defiance and submission in her eyes. She dragged her leg
behind her, but managed to crawl almost into his lap.

"Is this what you want? Someone mindlessly obeying you?
Is that what you need to get you off?" Her arms circled his
neck before he could stop her, and her mouth found his almost
desperately.

He wanted her submissive, but not due to his mind control.
His fantasies were sexual domination, not taking away her
identity or her free will. If she was submissive, he needed her
to want to give herself to him, to trust him that much, but the
moment her mouth found his, the volcano inside him nearly
exploded.

It had been so long since he'd been able to feel pleasure. He
had thought sex lost to him. His arms came up around her body
to bring her in close to him, so he could feel her breasts pressing into his chest. He took command of the kiss, one fist in her
thick blond hair, forcing her head back while he explored her

mouth, his tongue dueling with hers, taking possession, not giving her a chance to do anything but respond.

He swore an electric current ran through his body and sent fire racing through his bloodstream. For a moment he couldn't think one coherent thought, only feel his raging hard-on, the shock of his body more alive than it had ever been. Her body moved against his like hot silk, her mouth warm and moist and perfect, her lips sensual. His teeth tugged at her full bottom lip, fingers biting into her skin. He wanted her, right there, right then. Nothing could come between them. He needed this more than he needed to breathe.

Her tears registered; a soft sob cut through the heat of hot lust and brought him up short. He felt her face, the tracks of her tears, felt the drops on his neck. Abruptly he jerked away from her, breathing heavily, trying to regain his sanity. "What the fuck have I done?" he asked softly. "I'm sorry, Mari." He knew he was a bastard, but not this—never this—and not with her.

When had his commanding call turned sexual, and why? Why would he do something like that, knowing how powerful the chemistry between them already was? He couldn't re- member changing the command, forcing sexual compliance. Had he done that? What kind of a man was he? "I swear to you, I didn't mean for this to happen."

He wiped the tears from her face. "It will never happen again. I was calling you to me, bringing you back, not trying to make you accept me sexually." He pulled his shirt over his head and tugged it over hers, settling the warmth around her, giving her protection and him a measure of relief. She was so beautiful, and he was destroying any chance that she could ever think well of him.

"You were punishing me." Another sob escaped, although she struggled to hold it back. "Because the other men saw me naked. You were punishing me."

Had he done that? He shook his head. "No. I was calling you to me." Could he really be that despicable? He didn't trust himself with her anymore. He couldn't be around her. She wasn't safe and never would be again. Damn his father. Damn Whitney. Mostly just damn Ken Norton to hell.

*Jack!* It was a sharp command, something he rarely did with his brother, always allowing Jack to take the lead, but this time was different. This time, Mari was involved, and he wasn't going to take any more chances with her. *What if I hadn't stopped?* His body still shuddered with need. His hands wouldn't let her go, needing to keep contact with her. If there was a hell, he was already in it.

Jack burst through the brush, gun in hand. He took in Mari's tear-streaked face, her sobs, and Ken's horrified mask. "What the hell happened here?"

"Find her a pair of jeans. If they're too big, they'll slide over that lightweight thing the doc put on her leg." Ken tried to distance himself from what he'd done. There was no taking it back, no changing it. The monster lived and breathed, was alive and well and clawing for supremacy. *I nearly raped her, Jack.*

*She looks willing enough to me.*

*Shut the fuck up and take care of this. We had a deal. We made a pact. It was all well and good when you thought it was you. You made me promise to put a fuckin' bullet in your head, but now that it's me, you threaten her instead of taking care of me.*

Jack gave him a hard look and stepped forward, deliberately close, so close Mari's body was up against his chest. He wrapped his arms around her as if he might lift her away from Ken, all the while watching his brother carefully. When nothing happened, he buried his face in her neck and inhaled deeply.

Ken went very still, his silver eyes never leaving his brother's face.

"Does my sister know you're a pervert? Get the hell off of me. You're not sharing me." Mari's outrage lessened the stream of tears.

"If you're such a jealous bastard, why aren't you tearing my head off, Ken?" Jack demanded, ignoring Mari's comment as he stepped away from her. "The old man would have pulled his gun and shot us both."

"Get her the jeans and then get her the hell out of here."

Mari held her breath. He was leaving her with the others. She should be happy, thrilled, but instead she was terrified. "No." She shook her head, said it softly, a plea she couldn't stop. "No, you have to stay with me."

He framed her face with both hands. "I can't. You have to understand. I don't trust myself with you."

"It's all right. It is. I threw myself at you. I feel the connection the same as you do. It wasn't just you."

His thumbs brushed at the tearstains almost tenderly. "You didn't throw yourself at me and you know it. Mari, I'm not going to take a chance on hurting you. I'm not a good man."

"Like hell you aren't, Ken," Jack interrupted. "I don't know what's going on, but you've never treated a woman with disrespect in your life."

Ken flashed his brother a warning look, and muttering a curse, Jack swung around to call in the others and to find a pair of jeans for Mari.

Careful of Mari's leg, Ken lifted her into his lap, holding her close to comfort her, rocking her gently back and forth. "I'm sorry, honey, I really am. I drew you to me, but it wasn't supposed to be about sex." He didn't know what happened, couldn't remember changing the command. He rested his forehead against hers, breathing deep to try to quiet the storm of need and the roar of self-hatred.

Her leg was bleeding again, and there was a trickle of blood near her ear. Another at the corner of her mouth. Ken wiped it away with his thumb, a warning going off in his mind. The thin trickle returned.

"I can move *things*, and I can even make suggestions, have a guard look away, that sort of thing, but I've never seen anyone else with the power to control another person's movements. I didn't want to come to you, but I couldn't stop myself," Mari admitted. She shook her head and wiped at the blood staining her mouth. "Whitney can never find out. Never, Ken, not even accidentally. You can't do that in front of anyone who might report it to him." She lifted her head, the color draining from her face. "You didn't report it, did you? It isn't written in a file somewhere?"

"You're really upset. No, there's no file. Jack and I try using various talents on our own. If we have them, we practice until we get good at them. We live quietly and we just try different things."

"If Whitney knew you could control other human beings, take over their minds like that, he'd never rest until he had you.

And he'd definitely want your baby, or . . ." She broke off. "Can Jack do that? Is Briony really pregnant? Is Whitney after her because she's going to have a baby? That's it, isn't it? That's why he sent Brett and was so determined I get pregnant. He knows already. You were telling me the truth."

"Calm down. You're trembling, Mari. Whitney is a jackass. Of course he'd want our children. He's a nutcase and he thinks he can have a superbaby. He doesn't know what I can or can't do, other than what he deliberately enhanced." He used the corner of the shirt she was wearing to wipe at blood dripping steadily from her leg.

*Hurry up, Jack!*

"When he targeted certain psychic talents, he strengthened other ones too, didn't he?" Mari asked. "That's what happened to all of us. We don't tell him everything either, but Ken, this is a major talent. He would want it more than anything else. He'd want a child to have it. He can shape and mold children where he has more trouble with the adults. Adults don't have as many negative side effects, but he can't control them so easily. He can't find out about what you do."

Ken was silent a moment, listening to the sound of his own heartbeat. "If he knew, if it came out, say he had access to a file of mine it was recorded in, he'd make a grab for me, wouldn't he?"

"He'd move heaven and earth to get to you. He'd pull every string he had in the military and with every official who owes him favors to have access to you." She shook her head. "Don't even think about it. I've seen him take apart people to see if their brain is different. You'd spend the rest of your life hooked up to machines so he could study your brain activity."

Ken didn't reply. He knew he was a sick son of a bitch to do the things to Mari that he'd done. In spite of what Mari and Jack believed, Ken was certain Whitney had psychic ability and had already discovered the hidden monster in him. His fingers tunneled into Mari's hair, and he leaned his head to brush a kiss along the top of her head. "You have to stop trying to escape. You could have been killed, you know. You dove out of a moving car without even knowing where you were going to land. You could have hit a tree. As it is, you're bleeding again."

"I didn't. And you would have done the same thing."

"It's different."

"Because I'm a woman?" She snorted. "I'm a soldier first. It's my duty to escape."

He closed his eyes briefly and then opened them to meet her steady gaze. He had to tell the truth, just once. He owed her that much. "Because you're *my* woman. I might not be able to have you, but I don't want you dead." His fingers moved over her injured hand and dropped to her leg. "Or hurt."

Mari looked up at him. "I can't be your woman if you're planning on running away from me. Ken, he's destroying everyone's life. He has to be stopped. It isn't just me. There are others, both men and women, he's got locked up for his stupid breeding program. We can come up with a plan to make this all right."

"I'm not a product of his breeding program, Mari; I wish I was. I wish I had that excuse for my behavior, but I don't. People are born with things wrong with them—little glitches most people ignore or can't ever see. Mine is dangerous. I may be attracted to you physically because Whitney paired us, but it's more than that, and whatever it is, it's growing stronger."

"With me too. The more I'm near you, the more I seem to care about you. The sex and the emotion are all woven together. Whitney's never been able to make me do what I don't want to do. He can't control my mind—or emotions—so he isn't doing this. He tied us together chemically and sexually, but he couldn't make me want to make everything better for you."

"There's no making it better for me, Mari. The sooner we both accept that, the better off we'll be. The only thing I can give you is the certainty there will be no other woman. Whatever happens in your life, and I swear, I can't think about you with another man because it makes me crazy, but whatever happens, wherever you are, you'll always know there's no one else for me."

"There has to be a way to make this right."

"Mari." His voice was low and compelling, washing through her body like the touch of fingers on skin. "You're afraid of me, and you have good reason to be. I don't trust myself and I'm not going to fuck up your life any more than Whitney's already done. The last thing you need is to be tied to a man who could fly into a jealous rage and do you physical harm."

"I'm capable of protecting myself, Ken, and I don't think you're the type of man to be beating women."

"No, just losing my mind and nearly raping one because another man looked at her." He shoved a hand through his hair, leaving it more disheveled then ever.

"I wanted you. I didn't care the circumstances, or the excuse. I wanted you."

"There are things you don't know about me, none of them good. You've been through enough with Whitney and his program. We're taking you to Lily. She'll make certain you're healthy and she'll help you start a new life."

"Lily Whitney, the doc's daughter?"

"Don't say her name like that. She's as much a victim— maybe more—than any of the rest of us."

"You really trust her? I've worked with Whitney on and off for years and I sure don't trust him—or his friends. They know what he's doing; they don't approve, but they don't stop him or even tell someone higher up what's going on."

"Tell us where the compound is, Mari. We'll get the women out."

She shook her head. "You know there'd be a fight. The men would protect the laboratories. Hell. They're under orders. They *have* to protect the base."

"Then we'll have the admiral shut it down."

"The minute the orders came down, Whitney would move everyone. He's got places all over, and he'd never willingly allow anyone to shut him down. He's protected, Ken. You can't just walk in and get him."

"But you thought Senator Freeman might be able to help you."

"We hoped. His father has a lot of influence with Whitney. We thought if I talked to him and explained what was really going on, he would intercede for us. We know his father is already upset by the experiment. Whitney wants babies. He's certain he can produce the perfect weapons, psychically and physically, so that no one would ever suspect a child of being brought into a country and doing whatever needed to be done."

"Whitney wouldn't just give you that information."

"No, but I have friends. Not everyone involved agrees with what he's doing. One of the women is already pregnant, Ken. He's going to take her baby away from her if we don't get her out of there. I have to go back and help them."

"You wouldn't have to if I let Whitney get to me."

"No! He'd never let you near the others. He'd have you in a lab and dissect you so fast you wouldn't know what happened."

Jack returned, handing Mari the jeans, his gaze narrowing when he saw the blood running down her leg.

"He's thinking of allowing Whitney to take him prisoner," Mari said. "You can't let him do that."

"Actually that's one way, but I'm thinking maybe the admiral can get me assigned to the compound. If he's using the military as a cover, and he has soldiers guarding the place, then we should be able to get assigned," Ken said. "Put your arm around my neck. I'm going to lift you a little so we can slide the jeans on. There's no need for you to be nude with a bunch of men around."

"She's bleeding again. Why the hell is she bleeding so much?" Jack asked.

"Be careful," Ken cautioned as he watched Jack clean up the wound. "Did she reinjure it?"

Jack was gentle as he slid the jeans over the light cast on her leg. The doctor had put on more of a splint than an actual cast, because he wanted air to get to the bullet wound. "Doesn't look like it." Other than the excessive bleeding, her body seemed remarkable, healing at such a rapid rate that both men knew it was impossible even with genetic enhancement. "Whitney shot you full of an accelerant, didn't he?" Jack asked, his voice grim. "I should have expected he would do something like this."

Ken's fingers tightened to the point of pain on Mari's shoulders. "He gave you Zenith? Oh, God, baby, tell me you didn't let him shoot you up with that stuff."

"We're always given a shot of it before every mission, just in case we're wounded. Isn't everybody?"

"When?" Ken snapped, jumping to his feet, Mari in his arms. She had to grab his neck and hold on as he took off for the Escalade at a dead run. "Damn it, Mari, when did he give you the shot? Day and time. Tell me now."

Fear put her heart into overdrive. Both of the Nortons were alarmed. "What do you know about Zenith that I don't?"

"It can kill you, Mari. Tell me now, how long has it been in your system?"

Logan held the door open and Ken practically leapt inside, Jack after him. "Tell Lily to send a plane. Not military, private. One of her company planes."

"We can't risk that, Ken," Logan protested. "What's going on?"

"They shot her full of Zenith before they sent her out," Ken replied. "We have to risk it."

Neil put the vehicle in motion, racing down the road. "I can get us there by morning. We're a few hours out. How much time does she have?"

Ken swore bitterly, his silver eyes glittering with far too much menace as he exchanged a long look with his brother.

"Have Lily send the plane, Logan. Tell her to meet us at one of the labs with a medical facility. Tell her we need the antidote for Zenith."

"Ryland isn't going to let her risk her life." But he flipped open his radio and began talking into it.

Mari held herself very still. They weren't joking around. The tension in the Escalade could have been cut with the proverbial knife. Zenith, the drug used to accelerate fast healing, was dangerous, and they all knew it. Why would Whitney pump all of his men full of it before he sent them out on a mission if he knew the drug was dangerous? And if these men knew it was dangerous, Whitney had to know. He was the inventor of Zenith.

"I should have known; you were healing way too fast even for a GhostWalker. Damn it." Ken smashed his fist on the seat in front of him. "What the hell was I thinking?" But he knew. And Jack knew. He could see it in his brother's eyes. He was so fucked up thinking about sex, he hadn't given much thought to anything else.

"There's an airstrip about eighty miles from here. A small farmhouse with a crop-dusting plane. Lily says to make it there and she'll have a pilot waiting, a friend of hers, not military. She'll meet us at the underground laboratory where Ryland and his men were first imprisoned. It isn't far from her house, and no one would think twice about her going there. She works there often. Kadan will be with her to protect her, along with most of Ryland's crew, so no worries on that score," Logan announced.

Ken leaned close to Mari, his breath warm against her ear. "You're forgetting to breathe. We'll get you there in time."

"How long have you known about Zenith?"

"Lily found the compound in the laboratory with all the data on it. It clearly works to regenerate cells, but if left in the body too long, it begins to break down the cells and hemorrhaging occurs. And yes, Whitney is well aware of it. It's his find, his results. Two men died in his laboratory as well as dozens of research animals," Ken said. "We don't even mess with the stuff short-term."

Mari buried her face against Ken's shoulder, uncaring that the others would see it as weakness. She wasn't afraid of being a prisoner. She could endure torture if she had to, but Whitney's continual betrayal was difficult to take. He'd raised her, had been her only source of information. He'd brought in teachers, but ultimately, she had followed his curriculum. She had learned languages, studied and mastered subjects quickly, and followed the training of a soldier. She was disciplined and proficient with weapons and in hand-to-hand combat, as well as being highly skilled in her psychic talents. Whitney should have been proud of her—of all of them—yet he continued to betray them in every way.

He was the closest thing any of them had to a parent, and he was cruel and cold, completely without emotion as he conducted his endless experiments. He had grown worse over the years, and now to find out it wasn't just the women he'd betrayed. The men in the special ops unit had all been given Zenith before they went out.

Ken's fingers tunneled in her hair, a slow massage that seemed more soothing than sexual. She was certain he brushed a kiss on the top of her head. "The unit was given orders to go out Monday evening. Whitney was gone, but he left the Zenith for the men to take before they left. His doctor gave the shot to everyone. Sean stole a syringe-full for me. We thought it was a good thing."

She felt Ken's reaction to the name. He took a deep breath and let it out. "This Sean, was he with the team?"

Mari shook her head. "Not anymore, not usually, but he knew I was going and he didn't try to stop me. He could have. He guards Whitney and he didn't want me to go. He said it was too dangerous, but he went along with it this time to protect me."

"You're a trained soldier, why would he say it's too dangerous?" Ken asked.

She frowned. "I don't know. We're friends. I think he just worries about me."

*This Sean seems to be around her a lot. Do you think Whitney has paired her with him as well as with Brett and with me?*

Jack glanced up sharply at the edge to Ken's voice. *Not unless he wanted Sean and Brett to kill each other. I wouldn't share Briony with some other man, and anyone paired isn't going to want to share either. More likely he's someone she's been around and is a friend.*

*She may think they're friends, but old Sean has the hots for her.*

Jack scowled at his brother. *You could try to get that jealousy under control. I feel it when men look at Briony, but I have in under control.*

*This is me being controlled. I'm not hunting him down to put a fucking bullet in his head, now, am I?* Because very soon he had to let Mari go and he wanted her to be happy.

Brett was going to die, and if he ever touched Mari again, Ken would tear the bastard apart with his bare hands. That was all there was to it. He was going to make certain of that, but Sean—now Sean might be someone Ken could respect— at least enough to let him live, as long as he never thought of Mari and Sean together.

He tried not to groan aloud and give his thoughts away. Mari was so tuned to him now that, like him, she could catch impressions of what he was thinking. He didn't want her thinking worse of him than she already must.

Holding her on his lap was plain stupidity, but he couldn't let her go. He couldn't control his body's reaction, and it was too good to feel alive again. And the more he was around her, the bigger a reaction he got—and the faster. The painful continual erection was part of the pleasure now, but pain was a small price to pay to be able to feel like a man. He had thought that had been taken from him. Holding her, feeling her body so soft and pliant, the way it fit into his, the curve of her bottom nestled in his lap, the brush of her breasts against his arm, robbed him of his breath and most of his sanity.

His body throbbed and burned, his raging hard-on constant. Hell, he hadn't been able to get it up at all after the torture, and now it wouldn't go away, bulging and painfully swollen with need, wedged along the seam of her buttocks. She couldn't fail to feel how much he wanted her. The sway of the Escalade only added to his increasing discomfort, as her bottom rubbed over him.

He was starving to taste every damn inch of her, was desperate for the feel of her bare skin against his—and the heat of his body was affecting her as well. Her breath quickened, her breasts rose and fell beneath the shirt she wore, her body moved restlessly, sliding over his, causing a burst of pleasure throbbing through his cock.

He needed to slide his hands beneath her shirt and feel hot skin, cup her breasts and tease her nipples into hard peaks. He wanted more than that—so much more. He wanted to eat her like candy, take her fast and rough, hearing her soft little cries, her moans, begging him for more. Always more. He had to keep her wanting him—tie her to him sexually. He could do it—he had no doubts about that.

Her mouth was made for kissing, for sex. He could only fantasize about her mouth around his cock, her teeth scraping over the scars, her tongue dancing over him. She would be kneeling in front of him, cupping his sac, her fingernails raking over him, drawing out his pleasure, and all the while her chocolate eyes would be locked with his, while she took him down her tight, hot throat, watching what she did to him— loving what she was doing to him.

He had never lusted after a woman the way he did Mari. His heart thudded so loud he thought it might burst through his chest. His blood heated to boiling, rushing through veins sizzling with fire, and spreading through his body to sensitize every nerve ending. His pulse thundered in his ears, roaring to bury his body into hers.

He would seduce her slowly, teasingly, lick and suck and bite her breasts and nipples. Just an edge of pain. She would stare up at him with her large eyes, a little shocked, but breathless with need, silently begging him for more—and he would oblige. He'd show her who her man was, ruin her for anyone else, make her crave his touch—the hot lick of his tongue over every inch of her body.

He wouldn't be able to be easy when he took her; he'd struggle for control, but she'd be too hot, too tight, her velvet-soft muscles clamping around him as he plunged into her, driving hard, taking possession of not only her body, but her soul. She was his and he was going to make certain she knew it.

Mari could see erotic images dancing in her head. Her stomach muscles clenched hard, her womb spasmed. She couldn't help but react to the desperate hunger in him. His was a dark seduction, rough and edged with violence, the images dominant and filled with raw lust. She swallowed several times, her mouth dry, her heart pounding as she met the sheer intensity of his silver gaze.

Her breath stilled, caught in her lungs as his gaze drifted possessively over her, hot and aroused and filled with naked desire. She could feel fingers stroking over her breasts, almost feel the bite of his teeth, the lap of his tongue teasing her nipples, fingers stroking her inner thighs until her body wept with need.

*Stop it!* Mari circled his neck with her arms, pressing closer so he could feel the hard peaks of her nipples. *You're killing me here. You can't do this with the others here. We aren't alone.*

*I can't do this without them here. If we were alone, I'd strip you naked and eat you alive. God, Mari, do you have any idea how bad I want to lay you down and fuck your brains out? Damn it. That didn't come out right. It's more than that—far more than that.* Because he wanted her to belong to him. He wanted to wake up every morning looking at her face, find ways to make her laugh, take years to know every facet of her personality. He didn't know why, but that need was every bit as strong as the need to be deep inside of her.

He could smell her musky scent, calling to him. She was damp with need, reacting to his graphic fantasy and language. Instead of being afraid or repulsed, she was reacting. A part of him wanted to weep. Any woman should run screaming from his mutilated body. In his fantasy, the images in his head, he had been explicit, his cock scarred with multiple cuts, his balls covered with them. He hadn't held back the need for rough sex, yet she wanted him. Just the thought of her wanting him made him so hard he thought he might burst, and each time her bottom slid seductively over the thick bulge in his lap, his blood pounded savagely.

*Has it ever been like this for you before?*

Ken could hear the sudden shy note in her voice. She was embarrassed to ask him, yet needed to know. He tunneled his fingers through the thick mass of gold- and platinum-colored hair. *No.*

*What are we going to do about it?*

*Nothing. Absolutely nothing. I'm going to put as much distance between us as possible.*

*And I don't have a say in your decision?*

He bent his head to hers, buried his face in her hair and just held her close to him, savoring her scent and the softness of her body. *You don't know what you are, Mari. A gift. Something to treasure, something so precious I don't dare take a chance on being around you. If I had you, even once, I'd never be able to let you go.* He brushed a kiss in her hair, uncaring that his brother was watching. He had only a few more precious hours with her and then she'd be out of his life forever. He was going to take what he could get. *I could never say these things out loud to you. It'd sound corny, and I'd feel like an idiot, but you need to hear them.*

*Maybe I'm not able to let you go,* Mari ventured.

*You have no choice.*

# CHAPTER 8

"She's had two nosebleeds on the plane and we can't get this one stopped," Logan announced, racing to open the door for Lily. "Did you pull her file so we could match her blood type?"

Ken carried Mari in his arms, jogging after the dark-haired woman as she hurried down the hall to the small clinic in the giant laboratory complex.

"Jack or Ken can donate. They're both the same blood type," Lily answered, gesturing toward the beds. "Get her in here fast."

Everything was happening so quickly, Mari didn't have time to think about it. The moment her nose started to bleed, the men were on the radio talking to Lily Whitney, getting instructions and talking to one another in rapid code.

She knew they were worried when she was whisked from the plane and into a heavily armored car with tinted windows and they drove at breakneck speed to a heavily guarded facility. Ken placed her carefully on the bed, and she reluctantly let her arm drop from around his neck. The moment she was no longer in physical contact with him, she felt alone and vulnerable.

Lily Whitney walked with a limp and was very pregnant.

She had dark hair and a worried look on her face. Still—she was Peter Whitney's daughter—the one person the sadist megalomaniac seemed to care about. She sent a distracted smile toward Mari, obviously meant to reassure her. "Which of you is giving blood?"

Ken rolled up his sleeve. "Me."

"Take the bed next to her. I've got to administer the antidote, but she's going to crash and crash hard. I've got a team assembled, so don't panic on me."

"What do you mean crash?" Mari asked. She reached out instinctively to Ken, gripping his hand. "What does she mean?"

"There's no time," Lily snapped. "You've had the drug in your system too long. Your cells are breaking down. I've got to get the IVs in you right now. Don't fight me on this."

"Mari." Ken's voice was low and calm. He wrapped his arm around her shoulders. "I'm going to be right here. Let her put the IVs in and give you the antidote."

Mari tried to quell the panic rising rapidly. They were all afraid—especially Ken. He had that same expressionless mask he normally wore, but his eyes slashed at her in warning. He would force compliance if she didn't stay calm and let them do this.

Terror reigned. She didn't know them. She didn't trust them—especially Peter Whitney's daughter. She had known betrayal most of her life. Could all this be an elaborate plot of some kind?

Ken framed her face with both hands. "If you never trust me again, this one time, I'm asking you to put your life in my safekeeping. You're going to crash as soon as Lily gives you the antidote, but you'll bleed out if you don't get it. We'll bring you back. I swear to you, Mari, this is no trick."

Lily didn't wait for Mari to make up her mind. She was putting the IVs in her arm and one in each leg with astonishing efficiency. "Lie down on the bed beside Mari, Ken." She flashed a small smile in Mari's direction. *It will help to keep her calm. We need her very calm.* "I'm Lily. I'm sure you don't remember me," she said aloud.

"I know of you." Mari tried not to wince when the needle went in. *I hate needles,* she confessed, ashamed. *It's so stupid really. I can break bones and shoot someone at a hundred yards without batting an eye, but I hate needles.* She should be used to them; Whitney was always taking blood for something, or giving her shots, or strapping her to a table and adding to her genetic enhancements. He used her as the guinea pig much more often than the other women because he considered her difficult to control. She asked too many questions, incited the other women to rebellion.

She felt Ken settle in next to her, his weight making her body roll toward his. Their hips touched. His thigh slid along hers. The heat of his body warmed the cold of hers. She was instantly hyperaware of him, of his masculine scent and his sheer strength—of the fact that she was a woman and he was a man.

"Relax, Mari." His fingers tangled with hers.

Lily and another man were working to get bags of something thick and yellow into the IVs while someone else was sticking needles into Ken's arm.

*Tell me what's happening.*

*Don't panic. We'll get you through this. Lily is really good. She's studied this drug, because Zenith obviously can regenerate our cells, but after it's been in our systems for a length of time, it begins to have a negative impact. The cells deteriorate at a very rapid rate, almost the same rate as healing occurs.* He squeezed her hand to reassure her. *Mass hemorrhaging occurs. She's giving you the antidote fast, that's why so many IVs. She'll shoot some of the antidote into your muscles as well.*

*And that's already happening to me. That's why the leg keeps bleeding and now I'm getting nosebleeds.* A frisson of fear crept down her spine. She could deal with anything if she knew what was happening. She would *not* panic. *Why would he continue to give us the drug if he knew it would kill us?*

The pad of Ken's thumb brushed back and forth over her wrist. Blood began to run in a tube from his arm to hers. *If you're captured and can't get to him, you die. It's another protection in place for him. If you come back, he administers an antidote and no one is the wiser. If someone comes back late, he either saves them where no one can see or that person simply disappears. He wins any way you look at it. All of us are disposable.*

*I'll bet Lily isn't.* Mari studied the face of the doctor's daughter. She wore a look of total determination. No one was that good of an actress. Lily Whitney was totally focused on saving Mari's life.

*Has he talked about her lately?*

*No one gets that close to him—well—other than Sean. Sean's a supersoldier, and Whitney keeps him around as a bodyguard.*

There was that name again. *Sean.* Ken often caught glimpses of Sean in Mari's mind. More than that, there was respect—admiration even. His gut twisted into hard knots at the mention of the man, and something dark and shadowy swirled in his brain.

*Could I really die?*

He brought her knuckles to his lips wanting to comfort her, not wanting to answer her, or think about the possibilities. She sounded forlorn, and vulnerable. His heart reacted with a strange shifting. There was more blood at the corner of her mouth. Ken ignored the way air rushed from his lungs, leaving him fighting to breathe. He refused to panic if Mari wasn't. Lily would save her because there was no other choice.

*If something happens to me, tell Briony I thought of her every day—that her happiness mattered more to me than anything else.* Even in his mind, her voice sounded faraway, paper thin, as if she struggled to breathe, to live.

Ken went still, holding her hand tightly against his lips. Her skin was soft, even along the scar that split his lip. "You aren't going to die, Mari. We won't let that happen." He said the words aloud because he wanted Lily to hear. He struggled to keep his voice even, calm, without a threat, when he knew he meant it as a threat—when everyone in the room knew it was a threat. His heart pounded in terror. He couldn't lose her this way. He wouldn't let Whitney win this battle. Mari had to live.

Lily put her hand briefly on his shoulder. "It's okay, Ken. I understand."

Maybe she understood, but he didn't. He felt torn in two. Mari was virtually a stranger, yet he felt as if he knew her intimately. He had known the GhostWalkers for some time, many of them for years, but it was Mari he wanted to protect, Mari he needed to know was safe and alive and well somewhere in the world—even if it couldn't be with him.

"How could he do this?" Ken bit out the question before he could stop himself, glaring at Lily, a sudden flash of anger shaking him.

Ryland, Lily's husband, frowned, straightening slowly from where he was bent over Ken's arm, making certain blood was flowing smoothly from one patient to the other. There was a certain threat in his manner.

Lily shook her head slightly to warn her husband not to interfere. "I don't know, Ken. I've asked myself that question a million times. They say the line between genius and insanity is too fine to measure. And he's deteriorating every day."

"Why do you say he's deteriorating?"

"He's been hacking into our computers right from the day he disappeared. Flame found a way to get a program into his computer so we can spy on him. From his notations I can see that his mental state is slipping more and more with each new project. He's so far from reality, I can't even begin to guess what he might do next. I have no idea how we're going to stop him."

There was utter weariness in her voice. Lines of worry edged her young face. Her eyes held sorrow—too much sorrow and responsibility for a woman her age. Ken reached out to touch Lily's hand. "I do." He said it with conviction, wanting her to believe him, wanting to ease her suffering.

Mari caught his arm and tugged, the gesture weak but insistent. He turned his head toward her. She was glaring at him. *What's wrong?*

She blinked, her expression changing to one of confusion. *I don't know. I didn't like that—you touching her—which is totally absurd. You were only comforting her, and her husband is right there, so it makes no sense to feel upset about it.* She sounded puzzled and unguarded and suddenly very fragile.

Alarm spread through his body. Ken wanted to gather her into his arms and hold her tight, afraid of losing her. The life was already draining out of her. Blood trickled from her mouth and nose. *I'm here, Mari, right beside you. I'll get you through this.*

*I know you will.* She tried to smile at him, but her eyes closed and she went limp.

"Damn it! I need more time. Jack, get over here," Lily ordered. "We didn't get enough of the antidote in."

"Talk to me, Lily," Ken snapped. "Tell me what's happening."

"She's crashing!" Lily's voice was tight. "Jack!"

Jack straddled Mari and began CPR while Lily grabbed a syringe with a very long and wicked-looking needle from the surgical tray.

"Open her shirt, Jack," Lily instructed. She sounded calm and controlled.

She took Jack's place, sitting on top of Mari, driving the needle through the chest wall straight into the heart to administer the stimulant.

Ken's stomach lurched. For a moment there was silence. He heard the ticking of a clock. Lily's breath. Someone shuffling their feet. Beside him, Mari wheezed, drawing in a hard lungful of air, her eyes flying open, terror on her face, her hand gripping his wrist as if her life depended on the contact, and then she went limp again.

Lily bent over her, feeling for her pulse, listening to her heart. "She's back. Get the antidote in her and as much blood as we can. We may need you before this thing is over, Jack."

While she worked on Mari, Lily kept glancing at Ken. "You said you thought you had a way to stop him. As long as he's allowed to keep up his experiments, none of us are safe. Do you really have a plan?"

"I can control people's actions with my mind," Ken said, his gaze shifting toward his brother to catch the look of shock he knew would be there. *Don't admit you can do the same thing. You have Briony and the babies to think about.*

"That's not possible." Lily stepped back, shaking her head, looking at him with sudden fear in her eyes. "He can't have managed to find a way to do that."

"You knew he was trying?" Ryland asked his wife gently. He reached for her, drew her into his arms, and held her, tenderness evident on his face as he tried to comfort her. Cleaning up after her father was taking a terrible toll.

"Of course. That would be the ultimate triumph, wouldn't it?" She pulled away from her husband to go back to working on Mari, although her face was very pale. "There were many arguments on the subject. My father believed mind control was possible and could be used for a multitude of purposes.

He tried to sell the idea that mind control could be used to make foreign leaders see the light, even on troublesome teens when their parents couldn't get them to cooperate."

"You argued often with him about it, or someone else did?" Ken asked.

"I argued against it, but actually, a couple of his friends were adamant that he shouldn't try to develop mind control. Jacob Abrams often argued against it. I think he was worried about my father having control of that kind of power. People would literally be puppets in his control. No one would be able to stand against him. Jacob didn't like the idea at all, and they would often get into a really heated argument if the subject came up. I was terrified he might actually find a way to do it."

"He didn't. I had the ability naturally and developed it myself."

She frowned at Ken. "When did you know you could do that?"

He shrugged and reached over, trying to look casual as he pulled the edges of Mari's shirt closed. He hated her being exposed to everyone. "I've been able to do it as long as I can remember. When I was a kid I used it mostly on teachers and foster parents, but my control wasn't all that reliable." He grimaced. "Eventually I was able to gain control over it, although it requires complete concentration and if used for a prolonged length of time, or for an intricate task, I'm left completely incapacitated. Also I can't use it on more than one person at a time, or anything really significant, without huge repercussions. I can get guards to look the other way, but all of us have that ability to influence. Real mind control leaves me useless for hours."

"Why isn't it in your file? You didn't test out for that ability."

"I figured it best to hold some things back. Put it in my file now as if you've just discovered it. I'm sure Whitney's very interested in both Jack and me right now, and he won't be able to resist looking if he sees you've been pulling us up on the computer. You said he monitors your work, but doesn't realize you're aware of it," Ken said. His knuckles lingered along the swell of Mari's breast as he held the shirt closed. "Put it in there how you've studied both of us and how it's strange that I'm capable of mind control but Jack's not, and you need to further evaluate us. We can figure out a place for him to grab me, without endangering anyone else."

"No." Jack said the single word in a low tone that spoke volumes. "I won't let you set yourself up so this bastard can grab you. It's not happening, Ken."

"We can trap him, Jack. He'll come out into the open for me."

"Lily, don't listen to him," Jack cautioned. "He's a little nutty right now. Meeting Mari has shaken him up and he's in martyr mode. I'm not allowing it, and anyone trying to help him is going to be in trouble."

Lily continued to work on Mari, wiping her face with a cold cloth, adding another bag of the yellow liquid, and checking the amount of blood Ken had given her. Seeing that Ken couldn't let go of Mari's shirt, she tugged up a thin sheet to add to her patient's privacy while Logan removed the needle from Ken's arm.

Ken sat up and let his feet drop to the floor.

"Sit there for a minute and let Ryland get you some juice," Lily cautioned. Her gaze slid to Jack. "You don't need to threaten me, Jack. I have no intention of ever handing anyone over to my father. Whatever Ken's reasons, and I'm certain he has them, nothing is worth that."

"We can find him," Ken insisted. "Right now he's in the shadows. He's got all kinds of protection, layers of coverage we can't break through. His security clearance raises red flags every time we try to hunt him using a computer. If we go through the admiral or the general, they get the same runaround. Someone very high up is protecting him. The only chance we're ever going to have to stop him is to get him out in the open."

"And then what, Ken?" Lily asked. "What do you think is going to happen? If we take him prisoner, whoever is protecting him will simply step in and take him away from us."

There was a small silence. Lily looked from Ken to Jack and then to her husband. She shook her head. "You want to use me to draw my father out into the open so you can kill him? Is that your big plan?"

"Actually no, Lily," Ken replied. "I was planning on using myself as the bait to draw your father out into the open so we could eliminate him."

"By eliminate you mean kill," she persisted.

"What do you think we should do with him? Hand him back over to his friends so they can pat him on the back and give him a bigger budget for his experiments?"

Lily glared at him. "I've done everything I can to help all of you, but I'm not about to lure him to you so you can kill him. I won't." She backed away from the bed and glared up at her husband. "Not that—not for any of you. No matter what he's done, he's still my father. I want to get him help." Even as she said it, she pressed a hand to her rounded belly and shook her head. It was clear she knew what had to be done; she just couldn't accept it yet.

Ryland held out his hand to her. "There is no us or them, Lily. There is only *we*. We're all in this together. We're Ghost-Walkers; we're what your father made us and we stick together. We can only trust each other. That's it. We can't even trust the men who send us out on missions."

Lily opened her mouth to protest, and then closed it again. It was well known that her family had been very close with General Ranier, the man in charge of the special ops team Ryland Miller was responsible for. Whitney and Ranier had been good friends. Lily had grown up practically in Ranier's house. He too had believed Peter Whitney had been murdered, and he seemed to be on the side of the GhostWalkers.

"Someone attempted to have General Ranier murdered," Lily pointed out. "He isn't part of all this."

"His wife wasn't in the house, Lily," Ryland said gently, "and you and I both know she is almost always there. Odd coincidence."

"You don't trust the general, Ryland? We've had dinner at his house several times. How can you sit at his table and at the same time suspect him of conspiring with my father to do these horrible things?"

"What horrible things, Lily?" Jack asked. "Peter Whitney has worked for the government in one capacity or another for years. He's got the highest security clearance, has provided weapons and defense systems as well as drugs and genetic enhancement far before the rest of the world even knew it existed. He's been invaluable. He came up with an idea for supersoldiers, enhancing both physical and psychic abilities, and he has provided both of those things. As far as the people he answers to are concerned, Whitney has delivered."

Ryland nodded. "Colonel Higgens tried to highjack his program and sell the information to other countries, and he was stopped. If Whitney told his people he needed to fake his own murder and disappear, well, it was one more sacrifice for his country. Ranier would view it that way. He would fake grief, promise to look after you, assume command of all of us, and be thankful a man such as Peter Whitney existed in the world."

Lily leaned against the bed as if her legs couldn't hold her up. "Why didn't you tell me this before? You've mentioned it in passing, but no one ever has just come right out and explained why you believe it is a possibility. Put like that, there's every possibility, because that makes my father look a hero, rather than a traitor."

Jack glanced at Ken. *Lily is a brilliant woman when it comes to academics, but she's so blind when it comes to people.* It was a small warning to keep Ken's anger from boiling over. *She's struggling to accept that Whitney needs to die, but she needs more time. The pregnancy also probably makes her more emotional when it comes to her father.*

*When the hell did you get so smart?* Ken demanded.

*I've been reading all the pregnancy books.* Jack sounded a little smug.

"He isn't selling his work to a foreign country. He turns over his work to the government, and as long as no one knows how he got his results, they're all happy," Jack said aloud. "They don't want to know how he does it, only that he gets the job done. And Whitney has a track record of providing results."

"We can screw all that up by exposing him, and that means exposing the government, at least a very elite group of men in the know," Ken said, trying to gentle his voice when he really wanted to yell at her.

"The president?" Lily asked.

"Probably not. My guess is he knows he has supersoldiers and a few special ops teams called GhostWalkers, but I doubt he knows anything more than how we can be used," Ken added. "Someone goes before the committee and gets funding for some of these projects. He has to report the results and sugarcoat it so Whitney's extremes are never brought to the light. I'll bet the breeding program is called something altogether different. The president and the committee of senators are certainly not going to approve anything with the word *breeding* in it."

"Everything we do is classified," Ryland said. "No one knows we do it, and no one is going to admit it. If we take out a drug lord in Colombia, or tip the scales of power in the Congo, the last thing the government wants is for anyone to know we were there. There's the entire point of having us. GhostWalkers don't exist."

"So why are we being pitted against one another?" Jack asked. "Why was Mari's team told about the assassination attempt when our team was already on it? You know the admiral is talking to the general, and whoever is giving orders to Whitney's team has to know what we're doing at all times. How else was Mari's team tracking her?"

"The other thing I think we're going to have to accept," Ken said, "is that Whitney has his own team, men reported dead, men who have, like us, gone through the School of Warfare, special ops training, and had plenty of experience. Whitney tested their psychic abilities and profiled them, just as he did all of us. Something in their profiles appealed to him, so he set out collecting his own little army of supersoldiers. Jack and I ran into them when he sent them after Briony. Jack recognized one of them from when he tested. He was supposedly killed in Colombia right after a mission he went on with Jack."

Lily frowned at them. "What would be different about those soldiers?"

Ryland and Ken exchanged a long look. There was a small silence. Lily straightened. "Don't keep me in the dark. I know my father has lost his grip on reality. I know something has to be done about him. I need to know all the facts."

Ryland stroked a caress down her hair. "The fact is, some soldiers enjoy killing. It doesn't much matter whether it's a soldier or civilian, they like the rush having the power over life or death gives them. We think he's collected a few of them, enhanced both their psychic and physical powers, and now he uses them for his own end. He has to be sinking into paranoia at this point, Lily."

"So you think he has soldiers no one knows about for his own personal use as well as a team considered black ops that he can command when orders come down."

"Yes, that's exactly what we think," Ryland said.

"Where do Mari and the other women come in?"

"They were originally, from childhood, educated and trained as soldiers. He needed them to continue his experiments as well as have women he could study who hadn't been raised in families," Ken said. "When he decided it was too difficult to hook the women up with the men he had intended to pair them with . . ."

"I know that he did choose women and men by their genetic abilities and IQ as well as the strength of their psychic gifts and what those talents were," Lily admitted. "I've been reading quite a lot on it ever since I became pregnant."

"He's gone to plan B," Ken said, keeping his voice flat and calm and nonjudgmental, when he felt his rage cold and utterly deadly, building with a strength that shook him. "He's forcing the women to be with men they aren't paired with—men who are obsessive about them, but who the women have no real feeling for."

Lily's hand went to her throat in a defensive gesture. "What do you mean forcing? Rape? Are you saying he's condoning the rape of women?"

"It's science," Ken said.

"I think I'm going to throw up," Lily said. "He's given children cancer, sent men into jungles to be tortured—I can't take this. I don't know what to do." She began to cry silently. "How can he do these things? I kept thinking if I worked hard enough to make up for the things he did, I could somehow make it better, but I can't. He doesn't stop. He just keeps doing horrible, unforgivable things."

"Sit down for a minute." Ryland took her hand and led her to a chair. "This is too much for you right now, Lily."

She shook her head. "No, I have to know. You can't keep anything like this from me. When I was growing up, I knew he was always pushing boundaries, but I believed he knew right from wrong. When I discovered we'd all been taken from orphanages, that he bought us for experimenting on children, I knew something terrible was going on with him." She pressed both hands protectively to her stomach. "He wants the babies, and if he has the chance, he'll take them. You're all right. I know you are. I know it." She sounded lost, hopeless.

There was a small silence. Lily sighed, her lips firming. "We have to get the women out of there and we have to protect our children from him."

"Lily," Ken said, "I believe he has psychic talent of his own."

"He always said he didn't."

"But no one can read him, and how could he possibly know which infants had psychic talents. He had to have sensed it in some way. There's no other answer. That's probably why he's always been so obsessed with the subject," Ken insisted.

"He would never admit it, not to anyone," Lily said. "He wouldn't want to be considered anything but a man of science. Psychic talent is still considered freaky, and Peter Whitney would never, at any time, want someone to laugh behind his back."

"Anyone laughing at Whitney is at risk to disappear," Ken said. "I understand you're torn about this, Lily, but the truth is, unless Whitney dies, none of us are ever going to be safe, and neither are our children."

"He needs help. We can put him in a hospital."

"He knows too much. You know he's considered one of the smartest men on the planet. He knows secrets and he has powerful friends. He could name names. They'll never leave him in a hospital."

Lily shook her head and remained silent. Ryland kept his hand on her shoulder in an attempt to comfort her. She knew they would have to kill her father. His experiments would never stop until Whitney was dead. She was finally accepting that there was no real way to save him, and Ryland wanted to spare her the inevitable grief.

Ken felt sorry for Ryland. Ken wasn't married to Mari. Mari wasn't carrying his child. He hadn't even had time to get to know her, yet he felt protective. Ken hadn't known he had protective genes in his makeup, or even tenderness. He hadn't known lust could be so sharp and urgent and intense. That it could crawl inside a man and eat him from the inside out. He hadn't known lust could be wrapped up in dark emotions, black jealousy and obsession, the need to control and dominate. He hadn't known softer emotions could cut through everything dark and ugly inside of him and make him want to be a better man—make him *need* to be better so that he was worthy of one woman—the only woman.

Ryland had found those things with Lily, and Jack had managed to discover them with Briony. Ken might want to be a better man, but he wasn't certain he was strong enough to overcome his darker tendencies. Mari wasn't a submissive woman like her sister. She didn't have a soft, sweet nature, willing to compromise and soothe Ken's rougher side. Mari would fight his dominant nature, wanting freedom and control, and he would never be able to concede. The more she fought him, the worse he would get, until he would be like his father, a monster without equal, until their fights were real and it became a clash of wills to see who would win.

*Not if you fall in love with her, Ken.* Jack's telepathic voice interrupted his thoughts. *You haven't figured that into the equation. Briony didn't exactly change me, but she brought out the best in me.*

*And if there is no best?* Ken glanced down at the pale face lying so still beside him. She looked too young for a man like him. It was different when she opened her eyes, and he saw her too-old eyes—where he read the same edgy hunger and need. Then he could imagine himself with her, even if it was only briefly, but not like this, not when she was so small and fragile-looking.

*Then the old man won after all,* Jack replied harshly. *And you let him.*

*Fuck you, Jack.*

*Right back at you. You've never walked away from a fight in your life. This is the biggest, most important battle you'll ever have. You're going to leave her to Brett? Or Sean? Hell, if you do, Ken, you don't deserve her and you're not man enough to have her. She needs someone who will stand up for her.*

*Shut the fuck up.*

*You only swear when you know you're full of shit.*

Ken glared at his brother. *You walked away from Briony.*

*The first time, yes. I wasn't strong enough to give her up the second time, and I had to learn more about myself than I ever wanted to know, and that was a good thing, Ken, because I learned I could control the things that would hurt Briony. I don't want to see her disappointed or hurt by something I say or do.*

*And if you couldn't control it?*

*How do you know if you don't try?*

Ken's eyes glittered with menace. *I know I don't want to take a chance with her life. You saw me acting like an animal. The things I want to do to her scare the hell out of me. If I end up hurting her, don't you think that's a win for the old man?*

*You would never hurt her. I know you better than you know yourself.* Jack suddenly turned his attention to Lily. "What do you know about post-traumatic stress, Lily? Can a child suffer a trauma that would cause the symptoms? What about years of tracking and killing enemies? And torture, Lily, would that bring out the symptoms?"

Logan and Ryland glanced at Ken's face, the gridiron mask of scars disappearing into the neckline of his shirt. For the first time in his life, Ken felt color rising and was utterly aware of his patchwork skin. He looked like a freak show, sewn together to keep his body from falling apart. "Go to hell, Jack." His tone dropped to a low caress, a growling purr of warning.

"Of course a child can suffer trauma," Lily said. "Post-traumatic stress disorder is very common in men who go into life-and-death situations. It's usual to have nightmares and not be able to sleep. Often someone experiencing PTSD has feelings of detachment and a belief that they have no future."

"I don't want to hear this," Ken said.

"I do," Jack persisted, keeping a wary eye on his brother.

Lily took a deep breath and continued. "They can easily become irate and have outbursts of seemingly irrational anger. They might become increasingly vigilant and can become paranoid that a loved one may be in danger, so their reaction is intense to the extreme."

"This is bullshit, Jack," Ken warned. Anger swirled close to the surface, threatening to break through the icy calm he presented to the others in the room. *If you're spoiling for a fight, I'll oblige, but not here, not around the women,* he added.

*Are you listening to either Lily or yourself? You hardly ever sleep. You have nightmares all the time. You pace half the night.*

*So do you.*

*Not anymore. Briony is there now.*

*Yeah, Jack, thanks for the vision. I don't want to hear any more. Leave me the hell alone.*

Beside him, Mari stirred, her hand sliding across the bed until she found his arm.

*You okay? Cuz I'm a little sore here. I feel like someone beat the holy hell out of my chest, but if you need backup, I'm all over it.*

Her voice was soft and carried a tinge of humor and even more determination. His heart did that curious overheating-and-melting-into-a-puddle thing he was beginning to recognize only Mari managed to induce in him.

*Shh, honey. Go back to sleep. Everything is fine.*

*Was I asleep? I thought I was dead, but then I thought maybe you needed me so I came back to you.* Her thoughts were completely unguarded, entirely open to him when she reached out to make the connection. *I think you need me, Ken. I've never actually thought about being needed, or having a home.*

Did she sound wistful? Ken only knew he wished they were alone together. *Go to sleep, Mari. I'll be right here.*

*Don't beat the crap out of your brother. My sister wouldn't like it, and then I'd have to stick up for you and we'd get into a big thing and it would all turn ugly.*

The tension eased in his belly and shoulders. The pounding around his temples lessened. *We wouldn't want that. I'll let it go this time, but he's being a bit of a bastard. Jack can be like that sometimes.*

He was looking down at her face, and even though her eyes were closed, she smiled, her full, sexy lips curving into a smile that made him want to kiss her.

*Jack can be a bastard sometimes? Who would ever have thought? He isn't at all like you, now, is he?*

*Maybe,* he conceded. He slid his hand up her arm to her shoulder, caressed her neck, and tunneled his fingers into her hair. "We're disturbing Mari. She needs to rest." It was a good excuse to shut his brother up.

Lily stood up immediately and once again checked Mari's heart and pulse. "She'll be fine. She does need rest. We can go into the other room and let her be."

"We'll have to lock her down," Logan reminded. "She nearly escaped."

Ken shot him a warning glare. "I'll stay here with her. She's not going anywhere."

"Actually she's going to be very weak. GhostWalkers have a tremendous capacity to heal, but their bodies can only take so many traumas."

Ken tried not to wince at the word. He knew what Jack was trying to say, but if he took a chance and kept Mari, and he was like his father, she would be the one to suffer.

Lily led the others out of the room, leaving Ken alone with her. He knew he should go to. She was temptation and he was weak, but he couldn't bring himself to give her up quite so soon—and she was safe from him in her weakened state, he was fairly certain.

# CHAPTER 9

"So, you're all set to beat up the world for me," Ken whispered, stretching out beside Marigold. He turned toward her, scooping her close to him with one arm, trapping her leg with his thigh.

"Mmm." Her voice was drowsy. "Of course. It's the least I can do. After all, you did save my life when your brother was going to shoot me with that gun of his. He needs help, you know. He can't just go around offing people he doesn't like."

Ken smiled, for the first time in a long time feeling it was genuine. "I've been telling him that for years." He found the drowsy note in her voice unreasonably sexy.

"What did they do to me?"

"A little torture. We tried extracting names, but you held firm." He watched her face, and sure enough, he was rewarded with that same brief, intriguing smile.

"Good for me. I would have sung like a bird if you'd tried to make me eat peas." She gave a little shudder and opened her eyes, blinking up at him. "That's how all the interrogators get information from me."

"I've made a note and we'll go that route next time." He wrapped his arm around her, holding her close to his body heat. "You scared the hell out of me, Mari. That was close. Way too close."

She shifted toward him, wincing a little. "I think the Zenith did the job healing gunshot wounds and broken bones, but I feel like a truck ran over me."

He ran the pads of his fingers down her face in a small caress. "You'll feel better in a couple of days. You need lots of sleep."

Mari's lips tightened and her dark eyes went somber. "You know they'll come for me, Ken. Everyone, including Lily, is in danger with me here."

"We know. We're taking precautions."

"They'd better be darn good precautions. Don't underestimate them."

"We won't," he assured.

She liked having him lying beside her. "I've never lived anywhere but the compound. I've never been away from it except when they sent me on a mission, and we were always closely supervised. I've been on a lot of missions, and actually it was a relief to go somewhere and get away from there. Funny how this feels so different to me when it should feel the same. It's a research facility, isn't it?"

"Yes. It's part of Whitney Trust. Lily inherited everything when Peter Whitney supposedly was murdered. She kept everything going—everything legitimate, that is." On his side, propped on one elbow, he pushed the hair from her face with gentle fingers. "You've got to rest, Mari. You've got three IVs in you and Lily's still running fluids. Zenith is nothing to fool around with. I should have known when you were healing so fast, but no one uses it. It didn't occur to me that Whitney would deliberately endanger your life."

Mari enjoyed the feeling of his fingers stroking across her forehead. His touch was light and gentle, and no one had ever caressed her that way. "Why are you being so nice to me, Ken?" Because she didn't want to trust him—or the strange feelings she was beginning to develop for him.

"I'm never nice to anyone, Mari," he said, a smile in his voice, although it didn't show in his gray eyes. "Don't go ruining my reputation."

She closed her eyes because she couldn't look at him

anymore without feeling the burn of tears. She told herself it was because she'd nearly died, but she knew better. Ken Norton was giving her a taste of what life could be like—and she didn't have a life, could never have a life.

"He owns us, you know. We talk about escaping, but we don't do it, because we don't know how to survive away from the compound. We've never walked a real city street. We've trained in urban warfare, in simulators, and we have mock cities we enter to face each other in battle, but we've never really been out of the facility, other than to go to a jungle or some drug lord's little kingdom. Like I said, going on missions was a kind of vacation, as silly as that sounds."

Her voice was soft and drowsy, the note hitting just the right pitch to make his body come alive. Hell. Everything she said and did, everything she was, brought out the worst in him. Ken fought to keep his mind centered on their conversation. "Were you ever in the Congo?"

"I've been in every jungle, rain forest, and desert there is," she said without opening her eyes. "And every place they have leeches, I've managed to find them. Leeches are right up there with needles and peas for me. Before Whitney's breeding program, I was a damned good soldier."

"You're still a damned good soldier."

She flashed a small, grateful smile and moved just slightly, a small shift in her position, but it brought her soft breasts right against his chest. He managed to suppress a groan, feeling more a pervert than ever. "If I put my arm around you, are you going to shove me off the bed?"

"No. Should I?"

"Do you want me to be truthful?"

Mari smiled and snuggled closer to him. "No. I hurt and I want to go to sleep. You feel safe. I need to feel safe."

"Then you're perfectly safe with me."

Ken wrapped his arm around her and tried not to feel more than the surge of sexual awareness the heat and softness of her body brought. Emotions were something he refused to deal in. She looked so young, her lashes long and thick, lying against her pale skin. Her hair gleamed with platinum and gold strands. Lily must have slipped something into the fluids to push her toward sleep, or Mari would never have made such an unguarded statement. He hoped she wouldn't remember it when she woke.

"I'm here, baby. Just go to sleep and I'll keep watch," he murmured, his lips against her temple. She should have smelled of death—not life—but when he inhaled her scent, he could taste her in his mouth, feel his heart beating in time with hers, strong and steady with a perfect rhythm.

"I can't go to sleep; it's too quiet in here."

He groaned softly. "You're going to make me turn into a fool, aren't you?" He glanced toward the door. "You'd better never tell anyone I did this." Ken wrapped his arm around her head, his arm blocking the light from the window, wishing he had his guitar.

Jack had turned to books in the long years of their childhood and Ken had turned to music. He could play nearly any instrument, but he preferred the guitar. The feel of it in his hands and against his body was the same he felt when he held his rifle—an extension of himself. It was calming and took him away from the world, just as the rifle did. He couldn't play for her, so he sang softly, filling the room with his rich voice, using his own creations, songs he'd written over the years—songs of loneliness and heartache, of rage and death, and songs about the beauty of the earth and sea. He kept watch while her breathing evened out and she slept lightly. Whenever he stopped, her body jerked and a slight frown crossed her face, urging him on.

He glanced at his watch when Lily entered the room; he was shocked that several hours had passed. Embarrassed to be caught singing, he busied himself smoothing out Mari's hair while Lily checked her pulse and heart rate.

"How's she doing?" he finally asked.

"Much better. You saved her life, Ken, getting her here so fast. Another few minutes and I couldn't have done anything." Lily began removing the IVs from Mari's body. "Zenith is an amazing healer, but like dynamite, it's highly unstable. I've never been able to isolate what causes cell breakdown, and what the exact timing is. It always varies from patient to patient. It would be miracle drug if it stopped after healing the body. Look at her wrist."

Ken remained lying on the bed, holding Mari close to him.

She was awake; he could tell by the racing energy in her mind. She'd awakened the moment Lily entered the room, but she hadn't stirred, keeping her breath slow and even.

Lily carefully cut off the cast and gently prodded the wrist. "She's probably a remarkable healer anyway and the Zenith just pushed her body relentlessly." She placed Mari's arm back on the mattress and covered it with a sheet. "Has she mentioned my father much?"

Ken didn't reply. He wasn't going to lie to her, but Lily was fragile in her pregnant state and it wasn't her fault that her father was a madman.

She sighed. "I have to know about this breeding program he's got going, Ken." She glanced toward the door to where the others were resting, a small frown on her face. "I think he's inserting animal DNA into the soldiers. I think some of you already carry it, especially the men. Has she mentioned aggression? Anything that might indicate a few of the soldiers in his programs are showing signs of instinct rather than intellectual behavior?"

Mari's fingers touched his. He enfolded her hand in his. "I'll ask about it, Lily."

"He needs help desperately, Ken." Lily shook her head. "I should have known. I should have gotten him help. Look at this." She pushed the thin sheet from Mari's leg, running her hand along the skin there, feeling the bone. "She doesn't really even need this splint anymore either. She was shot. Her leg was broken, and yet in a few short hours her body has healed. Peter Whitney did that. He created the drug and engineered the biotic enhancements to accelerate her body's healing capabilities to phenomenal speeds. Just imagine how much the world could have benefited from his discoveries if he hadn't gone crazy."

Ken tightened his fingers around Mari's as Lily removed the splint. "But he did go crazy, Lily. No matter how brilliant he was—or is—he's become a monster. We can't allow him to continue and you know that. He's holding women captive and forcing them to get pregnant. They're prisoners, held in a remote facility somewhere, with no hope of ever getting out. And he plans to experiment on their babies."

Lily let out her breath in a long sound of distress. "I'm doing everything I can to find the women, Ken."

*Ask her if what Whitney is doing to the men can be reversed. If he's inserting animal DNA into theirs or raising their testosterone levels, can she undo what he's done?*

Ken cleared his throat and tried to look intellectual. "Lily, if Dr. Whitney is using animal DNA, or if he raised the testosterone levels in any of the soldiers, is there a way to reverse it or get rid of it?"

Lily's gaze jumped from his face to Mari's then skidded back as if she'd seen too much. "The testosterone levels might be managed with drugs. Depending on what he did and how much he raised the levels, I might be able to level the men out. But if he really is inserting animal DNA into theirs, which I'm beginning to suspect, there isn't anything I can do. With the extra pair of chromosomes he inserted, he has a lot of genetic code to work with."

She examined Mari's leg a second time, paying close attention to the wound. "She'll need more rest, Ken. Try to get her to sleep as much as possible, and she'll need to drink a lot of fluids. Really push the water. The bathroom is over there," she indicated a door to their left. "Walk with her so she can test the leg, but only to the bathroom and back until I take X-rays. It 'looks' good when I feel it, but psychic ability doesn't always catch the little nuances."

"Thanks, Lily. I'll watch over her."

Ken waited until Lily had left him alone again with Mari. "What are you thinking?"

Mari opened her eyes, and his heart reacted with a peculiar leap. She had the darkest brown eyes, large and heavily fringed. He hadn't noticed before because he had been too busy fixating on her mouth, but a man could get seriously lost in her eyes. He was in trouble and getting in deeper by the moment.

"Brett acts more like an animal than a man. He doesn't care at all what I want or don't want. It really doesn't matter to him, other than that I cooperate with him. When I don't, he's furious. He wasn't always like that. Not to say he didn't have brutish behavior. I think he liked being strong and he picked fights, and none of us liked him all that much, but his behavior is even worse now."

Ken took a deep breath and let it out. Jack and he had always had better than average eyesight, but now both of them could see not only at night, but at distances more like those an eagle could see than a man. They had assumed it was due to genetic enhancement of vision and hearing, simply increasing their own capabilities, but they could both see heat sources as well. They could change skin color and hold the outside temperature of their skin at a different temperature than their internal body heat, which negated anyone else's ability to see their heat images. Did that mean Whitney had inserted animal DNA into each of them? Was that part of the reason he had been so adamant that Briony have Jack's baby?

"What is it?" Mari turned her head to look him directly in the eye. Her fingertip traced the frown on his lips.

"Jack and I have always had dominant personalities," Ken said. *Whitney couldn't have added animal DNA to our genetic code, could he, Jack? Is it possible he made us even more aggressive, knowing our history?* "We're both aggressive and neither has much backup in him. We had certain traits, both physical and mental, far before we volunteered for Whitney's psychic program."

*Ken, there is every possibility. I didn't want to consider it, but our vision is unlike human vision. And we've both become a little too much like shaggy bears growling in the woods.* There was a hint of humor in Jack's voice, and the hard knots in Ken's belly relaxed a little. *Even if the bastard did insert animal DNA, we've been living with it for a few years now and we haven't eaten anybody.*

*He would have given us something difficult to control— something that would mix with jealousy and aggression and heighten those traits.*

*Probably.*

Jack sounded complacent. He could be complacent. He had Briony tied to him, and she was pregnant with twins. She was totally committed to him. Jack was a handsome man with a physique any woman would be attracted to.

Mari, on the other hand, was sexually attracted because

Whitney had paired them. He had the face of a monster, and his body was a patchwork quilt sewn rather haphazardly together. Mari wouldn't want to be seen walking down the street with him, let alone dancing with him, if Whitney hadn't intervened.

Jack had managed to escape the legacy of violence and jealousy and disgusting behavior their father had bequeathed to them, but Ken hadn't. He knew he hadn't, and Mari would sooner or later suffer for his baser traits if they were together.

Self-pity was a miserable and useless pastime. He refused to indulge himself.

Mari's fingertips were feather-light on his face as she traced the pattern of his scars. "You're so silly sometimes, Ken. You don't see yourself as you really are at all."

"How do you see me?" He wanted to sink his teeth into her finger, to draw it into the warmth of his mouth, but he kept himself absolutely still, not daring to really breathe, in case she stopped touching him.

"You're extraordinary. Absolutely extraordinary."

His mouth curved into a semblance of a smile, the scar stretching tightly. It amazed him how that shiny skin could be so tight and not feel at all until it stretched, and then it could be painful. There didn't seem to be a middle ground. "You're doped up."

"I know. I'm floating. But that doesn't make it untrue. If you do have animal DNA, you seem to be able to handle it a lot better than any of the others."

"You won't be saying that when you're asleep and I wake you up croaking like a frog and my tongue darts out and finds that perfect little tempting ear of yours."

"Does my ear tempt you?" She tucked strands of hair behind her ear.

"Hell yes. Everything about you tempts me."

Mari felt herself blushing. No man paid attention to her in quite the way he did. He made her feel almost shy, when she wasn't a shy woman. Heat curled through her body, and when he was close to her, she could barely breathe. Her womb clenched, and in between her legs she grew hot and moist and throbbed eagerly, as if her body had a mind of its own. She was in over her head. She knew what to do in a combat situation, and she knew how to fight off a man's unwanted attentions, but she had no clue how to entice Ken Norton into wanting her with the same feverish intensity with which she wanted him.

Swallowing hard, she changed the subject, deciding that safety was preferable when she didn't have her wits about her. "Is Jack really with my sister?"

"Coward." He trapped her hand against his lips and, this time, drew her finger seductively into the velvet heat of his mouth.

Her heart jumped and began to pound fast. He made the smallest of gestures seem so erotic. She'd had sex, hated it, and had made up her mind she would never willingly participate, yet with a simple pull of his mouth, her breasts tingled and her muscles tightened in urgent need. "Yes, I am," she agreed. "I don't have a lot of experience."

"I do."

This time her stomach somersaulted. His voice was low, a whisper of sound that slid over her skin in a devil's temptation. For a moment she couldn't look away from his mouth and the way he tugged at her finger. Her breasts reacted as if they could feel his lips and tongue and teeth sliding over creamy flesh, tugging at her nipples until she ached and ached for him.

She loved to look at his face, the shape of it, the scars only calling attention to the perfection of his bone structure and the way his lips were sensually chiseled. She couldn't help the fact that she was drawn to his wide shoulders and thickly muscled chest. She liked big-muscled arms and narrow hips. The man was built exactly the way she thought a man should be built.

Mari swallowed hard and tried not to feel the dance of his tongue or imagine the stroke of it along her skin. He was the most erotic man she'd ever encountered. Everything about him, including that edge of danger, appealed to her. "Tell me about Briony. I know Jack is being careful in case I'm a threat to her, but I need to hear about her. I've thought about her every day of my life and sort of built up a fantasy life for her. I need to know if she's happy. Does she look like me? What's she like as a person?"

His teeth scraped back and forth over the pad of her finger, his brows coming together as he thought. "Briony is like the sunshine. She's bright and cheerful and lights up a room, and when she laughs, she makes you want to laugh with her. She looks just like you, beautiful dark eyes and the same beautiful hair." He rubbed strands between his fingers. "When the sunlight shines on her, with all that gold and silver and platinum, she looks like a million bucks."

There was genuine affection for her sister in his voice, and Mari hugged that knowledge to herself. She needed to know that with everything she'd lost, her sister had been allowed to live a real life. "What about her family? Were they good to her?"

"She grew up in a circus family with four big brothers. I think performing was difficult on her because none of them were an anchor and she had to learn to cope on her own, even as a child, but she's strong, Mari, and has courage."

"What about her parents? Were they good to her?"

"She loved them very much, and yes, they were good to her. They had always wanted a daughter. One of her brothers served with us for a while. He's a good man."

"Does Jack love her?"

"What do you think?"

"I think he put a gun to my head and would have pulled the trigger if he believed for even one moment that I was a threat to her—or to you."

"She didn't know about you. Whitney erased her memory. Whenever she tried to remember, she'd feel pain. When she finally was able to push past whatever he did to block her memory, she made us promise to find you."

"And you shot me."

A faint grin touched his mouth. "Well, I might not tell her that part."

An answering ghost of a smile curved her lips. "I guess not." She swallowed and looked away from him. "I need to go to the bathroom."

Ken shifted, sliding off the bed to give her room, trying to be casual and not embarrass her. "Let me help you sit up. You're going to be a little shaky for a day or two. That cocktail Lily gave you can make you pretty sick."

Mari frowned at him, looking alarmed. "We can't stay longer than a day or two, especially not with Lily here. They'll keep coming until they find me." And why did that make her so sad? While she'd yearned for freedom, a part of her had been terrified of going out into the world without a clue what she'd face.

Ken wrapped his arm around her back and lifted her into a sitting position, steadying her when she swayed with weakness. "Why haven't you escaped? You can't tell me that you and the other women, all trained soldiers, all psychically and physically enhanced, couldn't get out in all this time."

Mari pressed a hand to her rapidly beating heart. Did one admit cowardice to a man who had been tortured so hideously? She couldn't meet his eyes.

Ken caught her chin and forced her head up. "Mari, stop that. You were raised by a madman in an environment of discipline and duty."

"At first, I didn't mind it at all. I liked the training and the discipline. There was a lot of physical activity, and I excelled at weapons training and hand-to-hand, so it was simply a way of life to me. I didn't know any other way really existed. And there was Briony. I was so afraid for her. He promised she'd have a good life if I cooperated with him. When I read about families, I just pictured Briony in the role and it was all good."

Mari swung her legs over the side of the bed, testing the strength in her injured one. Zenith healed fast, but one still had to work the muscles to get them in shape, and Ken was right—she was trembling with weakness.

"When did you begin to realize all people didn't live the way you did?"

"Whitney gave us an excellent education. He wanted intelligent soldiers capable of making quick decisions when we were cut off from our unit, but in doing that, he encouraged us to think for ourselves. It didn't take long to realize our compound was a prison, not a home."

She stepped onto the floor, acutely aware of Ken's body heat seeping into her pores as his arm circled her waist to steady her. His scent enveloped her, clouding her mind for a moment, until all she could think about was the feel of his skin against hers. She wanted to push his shirt aside so she could examine the scars on his chest and down his belly . . .

"Stop. I'm not a saint, Mari."

She kept her smile to herself. She liked the rough edge in his voice and the way his eyes, such a startling silver, darkened with such intense hunger whenever she thought about touching his body. "It doesn't take much to get you going, does it?"

Ken swallowed his answer. It hadn't taken much prior to his capture in the Congo, but he'd thought that part of his life was long gone. Mari had changed everything. His body was hard and full and one painful ache with just the slight brush of her soft skin against him. Nothing had gotten him revved up since his return from Africa, nothing and no one until Mari. Could pheromones possibly be that powerful? So powerful that he was not only sexually attracted, but emotionally drawn to her as well?

He walked her across the room without answering her. Just thinking about sex was enough to make him feel wild.

After a few minutes, Mari emerged from the bathroom pale, her body swaying. Ken didn't wait for her to try to walk back to the bed. He swept her up, cradling her against his chest. For a moment she was stiff, holding her body away from his, resistance running through her.

"Don't fight me. You're as weak as a kitten right now. You can do push-ups tomorrow, but for right now, I'm putting you back in bed."

She stared up at him with her big, dark eyes and her sinfully full lips and a look somewhere between an innocent and a temptress, and he knew he was lost. "Damn it all to hell," he muttered, stalking across the room and placing her on the bed. "You can't look at me like that, Mari."

He bent down, framing her face, thumbs sliding over her soft skin once before he took possession of her mouth. He had thought—hoped—that that first kiss had been a fluke, but the moment he touched her lips, teasing and tugging with his teeth until she opened for him, he was in instant meltdown. He kissed her over and over, stealing her breath, giving her his own, drowning in need.

She was frying his brain. He couldn't even think clearly, his head roaring, thunder in his ears, his heart pounding, and his body so hard and rigid, he rubbed his palm over the thick bulge desperate for relief. She had done that—made him come alive, feel like a man again. She'd given him back his life, and if he took what her dark gaze was offering, he might completely destroy hers.

Ken forced himself away from the edge of madness, jerking his hand away from her and stepping back to shove his fingers through his hair in agitation. His breath came in ragged gasps. He wanted her so much that for one moment he couldn't think coherently, couldn't think about anything but her soft skin and lush body. He took another step back. "This is crazy. Go back to sleep."

"I'm thirsty."

His gaze jumped to her face. "I'm doing my best to look out for you, Mari, and you're not making it easy."

"I'll be good, but I really am thirsty."

She sat up a little tentatively, and he leaned in to arrange her pillows. His arm brushed her breast, and he bit out a curse between clenched teeth. Ken poured water into a glass and shoved it at her, careful not to let their fingers touch.

She brought the glass to her lips, dragging his attention back to her mouth. He nearly groaned watching her throat work as she swallowed the water. He dragged a chair to the side of the bed and straddled it, leaning his arms on the top of the back and resting his chin on his hands. "You never wince or avert your eyes when you look at me."

Mari pressed the glass against her temple. "Do people really do that?"

"Of course they do, look at me."

"I have been looking at you." Her gaze drifted over his face and dipped lower to follow the scars disappearing into his shirt. There was blatant interest in her eyes. "People are idiots."

"God, woman, you're not safe." He took a breath, let it out, and forced his mind away from her sinful mouth. "Tell me about the compound. How could military personnel and, I'm guessing, lab techs be there and not realize what was going on?" She was too much of a temptation to him sitting there looking vulnerable and drowsy and eyeing him like he might be candy.

She shrugged, hiding her smile at his reaction to her. "The compound is multilayered and they rotate the soldiers coming in fairly often. From the outside, the place looks fairly innocuous. The ground layer has a few buildings, sheds, the airstrip, helicopter landing, that sort of thing, with high fences and a security system. The regular military guards stay aboveground and are housed in aboveground barracks. Most of the regular lab techs have their barracks above ground as well."

"You live below ground?"

"We always have. Four floors down. There are two laboratories above us. The first one is for show. That's where he takes men like Senator Freeman, and the techs on that floor sign contracts for six-month rotations. They never go below that level. We train on the fourth level and are airlifted to various outdoor sites, always under the eye of Whitney's guards. The fourth level has all kinds of workout rooms and training modules and simulators."

He listened for what she didn't say, the information between the lines—the stark, cold existence of being raised by a man who thought of using a child only for experimentation. It was no wonder she was so close to the other women. They had only had one another as they grew up.

"And Sean? Where does he fit in?" Because he felt the affection in her mind when she thought of the man, and it made him a little crazy.

"In the last couple of years we trained with several men. Sean is one of them. They're enhanced both psychically and physically. It was the first time Whitney ever allowed us to be around anyone else for prolonged periods of time. He even rotated our instructors so we wouldn't get attached to anyone. At least, at first, that's what I thought."

"But now?"

She slid down beneath the sheet, unable to sit up straight any longer. "I think he was afraid someone would get attached to us and they'd tell us what was going on or try to help us leave. At the time he brought in the men for us to work with, he also brought in his own guards. They're pretty aggressive and revved up all the time." Her fingers plucked at the sheet, the only sign of nervousness she gave.

Ken reached out and covered her hand with his. "And Sean isn't one of his guards?"

She frowned. "He wasn't. He was part of our team. We worked well together and went on several assignments. He and a man named Rob Tate were the nicest, as well as being the best at what they did. Brett worked with us for a while."

The mention of Brett made her wince inwardly. She hid it well, her face never changing expression, but he was touching her and her mind was open to his. She despised Brett.

"He's the man responsible for those marks on your back." Ken kept his face entirely expressionless, his tone neutral, but beneath his calm mask, adrenaline surged and ice-cold rage settled in the pit of his stomach.

"Everything changed when Whitney announced his breeding program. We were pulled from any assignments that took us outside the compound, and put in locked rooms. After that, life became unbearable."

Her simple statement hung in the air between them. The walls rippled, and beneath them the floor shifted. Mari gasped and tugged at her hand. Ken glanced down. He was strangling her hand, crushing the fine bones as he made a tight fist. Instantly he loosened his hold and bent to examine the damage.

"I'm sorry, Mari." He brushed little kisses over the back of her hand. "I don't know what the hell is wrong with me. I usually keep my psychic and physical abilities under wraps."

She rested her hand on the back of his neck, feeling the scars there, the beginnings of ridges that weren't so precise as the smaller cuts crisscrossing his body. He rested his head in her lap, and she stroked soothing caresses along the nape of his neck and up into his jet-black hair. "Except for the hand-crushing bit, it's nice to have someone angry on my behalf." She flashed him a small, teasing smile.

No one had ever cared enough to be angry—not even the women until Whitney had started his breeding program. Their lives had been all they knew—some of it good, some of it bad, but they didn't question how they lived or had been brought up. What was the use? She didn't know how it felt to have someone concerned about *her*, but it gave her a warm glow inside she couldn't describe.

"Ken, what happened to your back?"

There was a small silence. He started to shift out from under her hand, but she exerted pressure, holding him to her.

"Just tell me," she prodded gently.

He didn't want to tell her. The truth of it was, he couldn't think about it, think about the wrenching agony that never seemed to end. He didn't want to feel like those deer, swaying skinned on meat hooks at the senator's hunting cabin. He didn't want to hear the drone of flies, or the steady dripping of blood, or feel the hundreds of bites of insects that should have been nothing more than a nuisance in the middle of such an extreme torture, but at night, when he was alone, he remembered every vivid detail.

Her fingers tunneled in his hair and gripped as if gathering courage. "I don't cooperate with Brett and he hates me for it. Whitney won't let him mark my face, so he beats my back and legs with his belt and sometimes a cane. I still don't cooperate, so he forces me when I'm too weak." There was humiliation in her voice.

She didn't understand why she told him—only that she had to.

Ken stiffened. He could hear his own heartbeat thundering in his chest. There was a roaring of protest in his head. It had cost her pride to tell him. He wanted to smash something and go on a killing spree, taking down Whitney and Brett and anyone else who helped perpetuate such a vile crime.

She held herself very still. She had given him something important of herself, and she was waiting for his reaction. He couldn't tear down the walls and roar like a wounded animal. He had to give something equally important back.

"Ekabela had my skin peeled from my back. I guess they were a little tired of making all those nice clean cuts on my front and wanted to get it over with."

She was silent a moment, her fingers massaging his neck and scalp. He hadn't said a word about the pain or the fact that he couldn't possibly have escaped a major infection being in the jungle. It was a wonder he was alive. And it made her even more curious about how far they'd gone with that knife.

"Come up here with me," she finally said. "Sing to me. That was the most beautiful thing I've ever heard. I didn't have a single nightmare."

Ken slid onto the bed, curling his body protectively around hers, his arms holding her close. He sang softly while she drifted off to sleep, and then he lay still, tears burning behind his eyes and his heart pounding loud and desperate in his chest.

# CHAPTER 10

Mari slept on and off for the next two days, slowly gaining her strength back. Ken stayed with her most of the time, but she was free to move around the room, building up the muscles in her leg again. Ken did a workout with her, push-ups and sit-ups and rubbing her calf muscle for her. Each time she went to sleep, he was there, holding her close and singing softly to her. If anyone else entered the room, he would stop abruptly as if embarrassed, but when they were alone and she asked, he would sing. It made her feel as if there was a connection—an intimacy—between the two of them.

She woke at night, staring up at the ceiling and savoring the feeling of his body so close to hers. She knew he was awake, unable to sleep. She wished she could find a way to take away his nightmares the way he did for her. She could tell by his ragged breathing and the intense heat of his body that the memories were too close. He was sitting beside her, the sheet—and little else—separating them. She was always acutely aware of him as a man. "Bad tonight?"

He turned his head to look down at her, and she caught a glimpse of hell in his eyes before he smiled at her, covering his thoughts, his fingers coming up to tangle in the gold and silver silk of her hair. "Not too bad." He tugged at her hair, rubbing the strands between his thumb and finger as if savoring the feel of it. "I love to watch you sleep."

It should have bothered her, being so vulnerable as to sleep with a man watching her, but somehow, he made her feel safe. She wanted that for him. He was the silent sentry, standing guard over her, his nightmares close and vivid, while he made certain she was able to sleep like a baby. It hardly seemed fair. "I wish you could sleep too. We need to find something to help you with that." There was an unconscious invitation in her voice.

Ken sat beside her, feeling the warmth of her body, the rush of electricity sparking along his skin. He had every good intention, had given himself a million lectures, but being with her night and day, watching the shadows chasing across her face, knowing what her life had been—what it would be again if Whitney had his way—made him feel less of a monster than he was. And that was dangerous.

"Ken." There was an ache of longing in her voice. She reached up and touched his lips, tracing the outline with a light caress.

He shook his head. "You're tempting the devil, Mari."

"I don't think of you as a devil."

Ken framed her face with his hands, his fingers exploring, tracing the fine bone structure of her face and sliding down her chin to her neck. "You're so delicate. How can you have so much strength packed into such a delicate little body?"

"No one's ever called me that before." She turned her face into his palm and rubbed like a cat. "You just have big hands."

Ken found the way her face moved over his hand far too sensual for his liking. Her tongue darted out to taste his skin, a soft, heart-stopping curl along his thumb, sending erotic images into his head before he could censor. He needed Mari to feel safe with him, but she was naturally sexy, responding to their potent chemistry with little inhibition due to the drugs in her system. Her soft breasts pushed against his chest, sending an electric current through his body. "Maybe you should go back to sleep."

"Why?"

"It's just safer for you."

"You mean safer for you," she said, mocking him. "You're such a baby." She nuzzled his hand again, her tongue and teeth this time sliding up his wrist. Her lips were featherlight against his scars, tiny kisses designed to drive him crazy.

Ken cleared his throat, his heart racing. "I have no idea what kind of drugs Lily is giving you, but I'm sure it's a potent combination."

"It's the drugs? I want you because Lily gave me drugs?" Her mouth engulfed his thumb and sucked hard, tongue fluttering suggestively. All the while her chocolate eyes remained locked with his.

His heart nearly stopped. His body reacted, blood pounding, filling his groin to bursting, centering awareness in one pulsing, throbbing ache. "Sweetheart, you just can't do things like that. You're playing with fire."

Teeth scraped and teased the pad of his thumb. His cock jerked in response, anticipating the pleasure of teeth scraping along his scars, tongue and mouth tight and hot and oh so moist.

He slid his hand beneath her shirt, sliding over her bare stomach and up along her ribs to cover her breast. He took his time, giving her plenty of time to pull back, to stop him. She arced into him, pushing her nipple into his palm. It was already tight and erect, begging for attention.

"Tell me what your home is like. I've never been in a home."

Ken laid his head on the pillow beside hers, fingers stroking gently. "Jack and I built a house in Montana. We have quite a few acres and the national forest surrounds our property on three sides, so we're fairly isolated. We're entirely self-sufficient. Jack made most of the furniture. We have a gold mine—never worked it, but there's a vein there for certain."

"Is it beautiful?"

He edged her shirt up, bunching the material little by little to reveal the smooth skin from her tummy and her tucked-in waist to her narrow rib cage, until he'd exposed the underside of her breasts. "I never thought a lot about it, but yes, the country is beautiful and the house is wide open with plenty of space for two families. The view from nearly every room is amazing." His knuckles rubbed back and forth under her breast, savoring the soft, satiny skin. No one had her amazing skin.

Mari relaxed more, her body soft and pliant from the mesmerizing movement of his hand. The heat of his body warmed hers. "Do you have a fireplace? I always thought pictures of fireplaces were romantic and homey at the same time."

"We have a fireplace in the great room, a common room shared by Jack and me. We both have our own wing of the house. He has two bedrooms and a couple of bathrooms and an office. We both have fireplaces in the bedroom. The house is large and very spread out, and we heat mainly with wood. It snows there, so it can get very cold at night."

Her skin fascinated him. It was softer than anything he'd ever felt before. He had to admit, when it came down to sex, he liked rough and fast and plenty of it, but there was something magical in lying beside her simply savoring the feel of her skin. He enjoyed his rising temperature, the pounding of blood through his swollen cock. He felt alive and he felt— happy. He almost didn't recognize the emotion.

"I grew up in the barracks. I have my own room now, but there's nothing in it. Just the bunk and my locker. We aren't really allowed personal items. There's a television in the game room, but we're watched all the time, and everything we do is recorded. Mostly we train and work on education and strengthening our psychic talents to make us better soldiers. Well, at least we did, until Whitney came up with his latest brilliant program."

"What do you do when you have time off?"

"In the evenings? I like to read and listen to music. I love music."

"What about vacation time? Did you travel?"

"We didn't have vacation time. And the only traveling we're allowed is when we're on a mission." Mari pressed against his hand. The sensations drifted through her like lazy smoke, until sexual awareness smoldered throughout her entire body. His fingers took the aches and pains and turned them into something altogether different. "Of course now, since he started his breeding program, all the women are virtually prisoners."

"You grew up with these women? You were all raised in the barracks by Whitney since you were infants?"

"Yes. They're my family. I consider them sisters. Cami's tough, she'll get out no problem, and the others will follow our lead, but I have one sister who suspects she is already pregnant. We have to get her out of there before he runs his weekly tests on us and actually gets the results. She's terrified Whitney will find out."

"We'll get her out." Ken didn't ask which one of the women was pregnant. Mari was already regretting telling him that much information; he could see it on her face and he didn't blame her. He slid his body down, just a little bit, just enough that she could rest her chin on the top of his head and his face was opposite her beautiful breasts. Her breath hitched.

Moonbeams from the skylight overhead spilled across her body, illuminating her skin, turning it to cream. He pushed her shirt up further, slowly exposing her breasts to the cool night air—and his hot gaze. His own breath left his lungs in a heated rush. This woman brought him something no one else had ever done. It wasn't the combination of lust and need, or even his body springing back to hard, vivid life; it was simple happiness. He felt different when he was with her. Lighter. The memories of the scent and sight of blood, of dark sweat, the sound of his own screams, the rage that never left him, that consumed him until he thought his world was only one of complete darkness, devoid of anything good—she forced it all to retreat, just by her presence. Whitney—the son of a bitch—couldn't have made that happen with his meddling—it was all too real.

Mari brought up her hands, brushing her fingers through his thick wavy hair. Her body nearly vibrated with the need to feel his hands—and mouth—on her. Her body felt as if it was melting, so soft and pliant he could shape her into anything. Her breasts tingled when the cool air hit her nipples like the flick of a tongue, teasing them into twin, upright peaks.

Her fingers fisted in his hair when he shifted again, and she felt the dark five o'clock shadow rasp across her nipples, sending little jagged streaks of lightning through her bloodstream. "Ken."

She said his name in a breathy little voice that threatened to shatter his rigid control. Ken thought he had his desire well in hand, but he hadn't counted on the way her body responded to his. Her bare breasts were laid out in front of him like a feast, and he drank in the sight of her lush flesh, swollen and flushed with desire, rising and falling with every breath, luring him closer to the tight, pink buds that stood up to beckon him. She wanted him—no, *needed* him—and that was the biggest aphrodisiac of all.

She didn't seem to see the scars on his face or body. She touched him, skimmed her mouth down his scarred flesh, as if he was whole. She seemed as ravenous for him as he was for her.

"You're incredibly beautiful, Mari," he whispered. "This isn't Whitney's pheromones talking. This is me, wanting you so bad I'm almost afraid to touch you."

"Almost" wasn't true—he *was* afraid. If he knew what paradise felt like, could he go back to the barren world of the desert? He stroked his hand between her breasts, back down her body to her flat belly. Firm muscles played beneath soft skin. He rested his hand over her stomach possessively, fingers splayed wide to take in every inch of her that he could. Beneath his palm, the muscles of her stomach clenched.

She didn't know home or family. He'd had foster homes and Jack. Hell, they'd been kicked out of a dozen places, run away from more, and yet he was fairly certain he'd had it better than Mari. Briony had been taken from her when they were been small children, and she'd been raised in a brutal, disciplined world. His world had been brutal and disciplined, but he'd had Jack. He'd always had his brother.

He moved the pads of his fingers over her skin, tracing her sexy little belly button. No piercings for Mari. No jewels or fancy clothes. She didn't have evening gowns or expensive perfume. She had soldier-issue boots and routine camouflage clothing.

With every stroke of his finger, he felt the ripple of response in her stomach, her muscles clenching beneath the small caresses. He could barely breathe with the intensity of his desire. The roar in his ears grew louder. He shuddered with the effort to keep his mind away from the thought of her naked under him. He might need it, and he sure as hell could make her need it as well, but hot sex wasn't what was best for her, not right at that moment.

There was a part of him that detested the way lust intruded, so sharp and terrible that he could taste her on his tongue. He was beginning to crave her like a drug he was addicted to. He wanted to comfort and soothe her, to talk about things that mattered to her, but his cock throbbed and burned for her, stretched to the bursting point, an urgent reminder that he was alive and was more than an infinitely normal man.

Maybe it was the need to show her that beneath the mask he wasn't all monster—that for her he could push aside his baser animalistic instincts and be a better man. She had nearly died. Technically, although he didn't think of her as a prisoner, she was one, and that made her vulnerable. He wanted to think about that—had to think about it, in order to keep from climbing on top of her and fucking the brains out of both of them. Once he started, he wasn't altogether certain he'd ever stop.

"Ken?" Mari's fingers moved in his hair, massaging his scalp and sending a shudder of awareness down his spine.

"Why is it that whenever a man is doing his best to be noble, his body goes into overdrive and he can't think with his brains?"

"Has it occurred to you that I might not want you to be noble? I almost died. I have to go back to an existence I don't even want to think about. This might be my one chance—my only chance—to be with a man I choose."

"Here? In this lock-down laboratory that is a constant reminder of everything you've never had? In this narrow, hard bed? I want you someplace where I can spend hours—days— exploring every inch of your body. Somewhere beautiful with the fire roaring in the fireplace and waterfalls out the window."

Her breath hitched again, the smallest of reactions, but he caught it. She didn't believe she would ever have those things, and in that moment, he resolved to make certain she did—that she would have everything he could give her.

Mari shifted again, her breasts brushing his shadowed jaw. Ken's body nearly went rigid, every muscle tight and hot, contracting into hard knots. His breath fanned the temptation of her nipples. He needed her more than he needed the air in his lungs, but once he touched her, once he claimed her, there would be no walking away.

"Mari . . . ," he tried again, his face, of its own accord, moving that scant inch so that his tongue could dip lower and take one delicious lick along her nipple.

Mari jumped beneath him, her hips moving restlessly, her breasts rising sharply with her indrawn breath, arching into him, into the dark, hot cavern of his mouth. His hand cupped her breast, kneading, as he suckled, using his teeth to sharpen her desire, his tongue to tease and draw out her pleasure.

She made a single sound, a gasp of shock, her hips bucking, her hot mound sliding over his thigh in an effort to get some relief. At once, he dipped his fingers lower, to find a furnace of heat. His teeth closed on her nipple with a small bite of pain, as his fingers found her slick entrance, testing her response to his need for a little rougher play. A fresh wave of her heady scent rose and his fingers were damp with her welcome.

Mari's moan was so soft he barely heard it—but he felt it vibrate through his entire body. His cock jerked, rubbing against the material of his jeans, swelling to a breaking point. He had to have some relief before he shattered. He switched to her other breast, suckling strongly as his hand slid to his jeans, working them open, sliding them over his hips so his enormous erection could spring free. He couldn't stop himself— his hand sliding over the thick, hard pole, feeling the ridges, squeezing tightly in an effort to create sensation. Hell, he didn't even know if his equipment really worked anymore.

Teeth teasing the nipple, keeping her pleasure sharp and edgy, he dragged his jeans from his hips. He shifted back, lifting his head from her soft, perfect breasts, to look at her. Mari lay on the cot, her eyes glazed with desire, lips parted, with her breath rising and falling rapidly. Her breasts thrust up from the open shirt, her legs bare and sprawled apart, her body open to him. She was the most beautiful sight he'd ever seen. Her gaze dropped to his fist curled around his thick erection. There was a drop glistening like a pearl on the large, swollen head. Her gaze locked with his, Mari leaned forward and licked it off.

His entire body locked up, a firestorm raging hot and wild, a fever building so fast, so intense, he shuddered, his heart thudding loudly in his ears. Sweat broke out, beading on his brow. She was killing him. *Killing* him.

He caught her face in his hands and forced her dark eyes to meet his smoldering gaze. "Mari, honey, you have to be sure." His voice was hoarse. "I'm not going to be able to stop in another minute. I don't have a damn thing to use as protection and this is bullshit, taking you here. I'm not going to be gentle and loving like you deserve. And I don't want to hurt you. I'm so damned afraid of hurting you, but I swear I'll give you more pleasure than you've ever had in your life. If you can't do this with me, go all the way, take everything I need to give you, you've got to tell me to stop now and I swear to you, I'll find the strength to leave you alone."

"Ken, please," she whispered, her dark eyes pleading. "I want you so much I can't think straight. This is our moment. We have to take it or it may never come again. Give me this, give me a memory, something real, to last me forever."

He took her lips. He tried for gentle, but the moment he slid his tongue into the velvet darkness of her mouth, he was lost in a haze of madness. Lust rose, so sharp and terrible it consumed him, ate him alive. He took her mouth, giving in to the demons riding him so hard.

Hard hands held her still. Mari was shocked at his enormous strength, at her own sudden arousal at his aggression, so hot and fast and hard, shaking her body before she was ready, almost pushing her into an orgasm before he'd really touched her. His ragged breath was harsh as he bit at her lip, his teeth and tongue doing wild things to her mouth until she couldn't see, let alone think.

His lips moved down her neck, tiny stinging kisses that left fire dancing over her nerve endings. His thumb and finger caught her nipple, rolling and tugging until her head thrashed back and forth over the pillow and she sobbed out his name. She hadn't known she could feel this way, hadn't known that a small burst of pain could bring heat flaring and his tongue could feel like velvet over smarting hypersensitive skin.

He kissed his way down to her breasts, stopping there to feast, wanting her in a frenzy of desire, needing her compliance, afraid that if she fought him, he'd go wild. His hand moved lower, savoring the shape and texture of her, cupping her hot, damp mound, feeling satisfaction as her hips bucked and another soft sob escaped. He slid a finger into the deep recesses, searching for honey and spice and a way to make her his for eternity.

"Spread your legs for me, Mari." His voice was harsh,

hands rough on her thighs, forcing her obedience before she could give it to him, positioning her so he could kiss his way down her belly button, pausing to nibble the underside of her breasts, trace each rib, and lavish attention on her abdomen with hot licks as if she were an ice cream cone.

"Ken." Desperate, she fisted her hands in his hair, trying to drag him over her, to blanket her.

He caught her wrists and jerked them down. "Behave," he ordered. "We do this my way. I warned you, it has to be my way." Because watching her lose control, watching the lust build into mindless need, fed his violent instincts and increased his pleasure. The more she came apart for him, the better it was for him.

"I can't take it. You're too slow."

"Stay still," he repeated, his voice roughening. His tongue followed his finger in a long, slow sweep searching for the nectar he was craving.

She nearly came off the cot, her sobs real, her hips thrashing wildly. He smacked the side of her bottom in warning and watched the answering flare of arousal in her eyes. Ken clamped one arm down tight across her hips, pinning her down. His need raged white-hot now, coursing through his body with the force of a tidal wave, a storm of fire so out of control it was crowning. He didn't just need her body; he wanted her soul. He wanted her so tied to him she would do anything he asked, anything he demanded of her.

Mari raised her head to look at him, the dark sensuality on his face, the intensity of his desire that shuddered through his body. His eyes were pure silver, twin slashes of light that focused solely on her. His hands were hard and terribly strong. His scars traveled down his belly right over his enormous cock. The knife cuts had been made with surgical precision, each slice designed to cause the maximum amount of pain without killing him. His balls were cut, as were his belly and hips and down across his thighs, until the scars disappeared into the legs of his jeans.

She would have thought no one could recover from such an ordeal, but he was hard and thick and long enough to be intimidating—and she wanted to touch and taste and soothe, make it all better for him. Mostly she wanted to drive him past all sanity, the way he was driving her. She licked her lips to moisten them, parting them as she stared at the long, daunting length of him. She was coming apart, her body coiling tighter and tighter until she was afraid she would be screaming, throwing herself at him, begging for release.

He whispered something guttural and faintly obscene, his voice so rough she found it sexy. His silver eyes branded his name into her flesh and bone as he clamped down on her thighs and lowered his head, his mouth on her most intimate lips, his tongue thrusting deep into her. Everything around her seemed to explode. She shattered, utterly and completely shattered, breaking into a million pieces, her mind fragmenting until there was no conscious thought, only wave after wave of sensation, tidal waves swamping her, carrying her far out to sea, where she had no anchor and no way back.

She fought to get away, using her strength, terrified of losing herself for all time, afraid if he didn't stop she might die from the crashing pleasure. Her vision narrowed, and she saw dark streaks covered in blue-hot stars as her breasts tightened and her womb spasmed and every muscle in her body clenched and coiled, winding tighter and tighter. He held her still, as no one else could have, his enhanced strength impossible to fight while he drove his tongue relentlessly into her feminine channel, spearing deep, over and over. She couldn't stand it. He had to stop. He *had* to.

The tongue went from stabbing to fluttering; teeth found her most sensitive spot and began a slow, torturous assault. His finger added to the insanity, pushing deep and pulling out to spread hot liquid over her most intimate parts. His mouth went to her sensitive bud, tongue flicking back and forth ruthlessly, throwing her into a wild, never-ending orgasm. The more sensitive she grew, the more he persisted, holding her down while he sucked at her, before once more taking her bud between his teeth and stroking with his tongue. She lost her ability to breathe, thrashing back and forth wildly in an effort to get away from his mouth.

Her breath came out in ragged sobs. "I can't take any more. No more." The sensations were building continually. She'd lost count of how many times she'd come apart, each orgasm stronger than the last, until she felt it through her stomach and up into her breasts, until every part of her was stimulated beyond her imagination.

"Yes, more. You'll come for me, Mari, over and over." His voice was guttural as he sucked ravenously at her, throwing her into another climax.

It was too much; she had never had anyone give her so much, demand so much, take so much. She dug her fingers into his shoulders, desperate to hold on when the world was gone. Their combined scents were potent and heady, so sexy she couldn't think. His hands were everywhere, making her body his, taking possession of each separate part of her.

When she stiffened in protest—afraid—his mouth devoured her, eating her like the candy he'd called her earlier, devouring everything until she was certain there was nothing left of Mari. He lifted his head to look at her, his face pure carnal sensuality.

"You belong to me," he whispered roughly. Body and soul. Whatever he wanted or needed, she was going to be the one to supply it. The dark violence in him could be harnessed and used for much more pleasurable purposes, the demons caged by one woman—Mari. She made his cock ache and his balls burn and his control slip away, until all he could think about was having her. He was a man who could ride a woman all night and never feel completely sated, yet just looking at her sprawled out beneath him at the mercy of his body, hearing her pleas and sobs for him to take her, he knew everything was different with her. His life would always be different.

She clutched him tightly, her body writhing beneath his tongue and teeth, her breath coming in sobs as she pleaded with him to possess her. Her breathless cries added to the intensity of his pleasure. The nails biting deep into his skin, the scratches on his back he knew she didn't realize she was putting there, all added to the building fire.

Retaining his hold on her hips, Ken slid off the bed, pulling her bottom to the edge to lift her legs over his shoulders. Fingers digging into her bottom, he pressed against her damp heat. Although she was slick and wet, and hungry for him, it seemed an impossible task to stretch her tight channel enough to accommodate his size.

And then he moved, ramming into her hard and deep, driving through her tight muscles to bury himself balls deep. A soft scream escaped from her throat, hastily muffled by the back of her hand. She stared up at him, eyes wide with shock and glazed over with feverish desire. The hard ridges on his cock rasped over her velvet-soft inner muscles, adding to the pleasure-pain of his deep penetration. He needed this, needed her and her acceptance of his control of her. She didn't wince away from his appearance, and every hard, rough stroke took her pleasure higher. He made absolutely certain of that.

He controlled the rhythm, hard and fast, and then slow and deep, dragging her hips into him to double the impact, or holding her still so she could only accept his deep invasion. She was tight, tighter than he expected, and fiery hot, engulfing him in a velvet inferno. He rode her hard, pounding roughly to stimulate his cock—the glorious erotic bite of pleasure and pain as he stretched and thickened, as he forced her to take every inch of him, stretching her impossibly.

She went wild beneath him, ripping at his arms with her nails, slashing his chest, long, deep scratches as he drove her higher and higher, compelling her into a level of sexuality she'd never imagined. He held her thighs apart, yanking her legs higher, wider, refusing to give an inch, refusing to allow her to catch her breath. The pleasure was mushrooming out of control, turning into a whirling tornado spinning through both of them, taking them away from all reality.

He caught her hands, slammed both to the cot on either side of her head, ramming into her body in a frenzy of raging need, driving his cock so deep he thought he might lock them together forever. The lines in his face were etched deeper, his scars standing out starkly against his skin as her muscles gripped tighter and tighter, adding more and more friction and heat. Sweat beaded on his body, darkened his hair, but he kept thrusting, over and over, while his balls grew hard and his cock screamed for mercy.

He felt the explosion tear through her body, a dark tidal wave that rose and rose, refusing to be stopped. She sobbed, as he drove into her, the hot wash of her cream sending him over the edge, his own ejaculation ripping through him so forcefully his body shook. He was elated, ecstatic, more alive than he'd ever been. Maybe it was because he thought he'd lost his ability since the torture in the Congo, but he suspected the pleasure was so intense because he finally was with the right woman. His breath coming in ragged gasps, he collapsed over her.

"Son of a bitch, Mari, you nearly killed me."

Her arm slid around his neck, her fingers tunneling in his thick hair. "I can't think. And I'll never walk again."

She touched her tongue to her lips. Her breasts ached, her thighs; she throbbed between her legs. There was a burning sensation as if he'd stretched her and left her with skid marks. "I think I have road rash." Her heart was never going to beat normally, and no one—*no one*—was ever going to satisfy her again.

Ken lifted his head to look at her. Her bone structure was so delicate, yet there was steel in her. She'd been afraid, but she'd put herself in his hands. Her fingertips skimmed over his face, over the scars, traced them down his neck to his chest. She leaned forward to press kisses where his skin was exposed. His heart turned over. She'd seen the monster and it hadn't frightened her. He couldn't help the possessive feeling rising to choke him. She wasn't going back and he wasn't doing the right thing. He could no more give her up now than he could shoot his brother.

"I'll clean us both up in a minute, honey. Just give me a minute." He had never felt like that, such an explosive orgasm, so complete and so unexpected when his body was so damaged. He knew the pressure it took against his skin to feel sensation, and her tight channel had given him more than he'd ever thought possible. It shook him that he could need this woman so much.

It wasn't that he was totaled—on the contrary, he wanted to take a few minutes' rest and start over again, a marathon this time—but she looked exhausted and a little freaked out that she'd given him so much of herself. He'd taken her cooperation, giving her little choice in the matter, but she had only fought him when the pleasure was skidding into pain and it had frightened her.

He hadn't wanted to lie to her, to be something he wasn't—something he couldn't be. His body was ruined for anything but a certain kind of stimulation and she had to accept that. Hell. It had taken him months to get around the idea that he couldn't perform, and then a few more weeks to acknowledge what might get him off.

"Did I hurt you?" His hands framed her face, thumbs sliding over her smooth, soft skin. She was so beautiful he ached.

"I don't know." She leaned forward and dragged her lips, feather-light, over his. "It was wild and amazing and somewhat frightening. I didn't know sex could feel like that." Her gaze slid away from his. "I'm not a virgin or anything, but I've never had an orgasm." She touched a long scratch on his chest. "I was scared, but I wanted it so much. I didn't want you to ever stop, not even when I said stop."

He tipped her chin up. "Did you say stop? Because if you did, I didn't hear you."

"Not out loud. No one's ever done that before."

He frowned. "Done what?"

Color crept under her skin, flushing her face and her breasts, drawing his attention to the marks on the creamy flesh. His marks. His fingerprints. The faint teeth marks and numerous strawberries standing out starkly against her pale skin. She had them on the inside of her thighs as well. He touched one—pleased.

Her color deepened, turning an interesting shade of crimson. "Oral sex."

His eyebrow shot up. She looked innocent and almost shy, so much so that he couldn't help but bend down to kiss her. "Oral sex? Is that what you thought that was?" He rubbed the scar splitting his lip with the pad of his thumb. "I don't think so, honey. That was more like gobbling you up. Eating you alive. And just talking about it is making me hard all over again."

The color spread through her body. "Well, regardless, no one's ever done that."

The smile on his face faded. "Never?"

She shook her head.

He scowled at her. "What the hell did this idiot Brett do to prepare you?"

"He didn't care if my body accepted his or not. He used a lubricant for his own convenience, not mine."

Ken swore out loud. "Someone needs to tear his heart out."

A small smile curved her mouth. "Jack likes to shoot people. Maybe we just ought to introduce them."

Ken slid off the bed, pulling up his jeans before finding a cloth. Dipping it in water, he carefully washed her body, deliberately stroking caresses between her legs. "What other things have you managed to miss?"

"Why? I shouldn't have told you that."

"If I don't know what you've missed, I won't know all the things I get to introduce you to." He dried her body with careful strokes.

"I've never celebrated a birthday or holiday."

"When do you get presents?"

She laughed. "What kind of presents? Sean gave me a knife once, but he took it back when I was put in the breeding program. I think they were afraid I'd remove certain portions of Brett's anatomy."

It bothered him. Okay—it bothered him a lot—that she didn't have holidays and fireplaces and presents. At the worst home he'd been in, they still celebrated birthdays. "When is your birthday?"

Once again her gaze slid from his, and she shrugged with exaggerated casualness. "I have no idea. Whitney found me in an orphanage somewhere and he didn't exactly think that date was important, so why would you think he'd celebrate our birthdays?"

Ken's belly knotted up again, but he kept his voice and face expressionless. He cupped her face and leaned in for another heart-stopping kiss. The woman tasted like honey and exotic spice, so addicting he thought about just kissing her until neither of them knew their own names anymore. "He's a scientist. Isn't the age of his guinea pigs important? Let's break into his files and get the information. I'll bet he has it."

She laughed. Really laughed. The sound was very soft, but it made him want to smile. He pulled a chain from around his neck. Made of braided gold, it held a small golden cross. He slipped it over her head, lifting her hair out of the way so that the chain slid along the back of her neck and the medal nestled between her breasts.

"Your first present, one of many. I'm not very religious, but

I always like to keep my options open. It will keep you safe when I'm not right beside you."

She inhaled sharply and blinked hard several times.

Ken touched her long lashes and found them wet. She suddenly looked sad, shadows replacing the laughter in her eyes. "Presents are supposed to make you happy. I don't think you're getting the concept here."

Mari slid her arms around his neck. "Surprisingly, this has been the best day of my life. Thank you." She lifted her mouth for his kiss, her fingers gliding over his neck. She struck hard and fast, finding the pressure point with little problem and, using her enhanced strength, digging deep. She could never have done it if she hadn't caught him completely by surprise, but he succumbed, slipping into a black void, slumping to the bed and then sliding to the floor.

# CHAPTER 11

Mari jumped off the bed, crouching down to check Ken's pulse. The whisper of warning buzzed in her head like the distant sound of bees. They were here. They'd found her, and if she didn't act fast, they'd kill Ken, Jack, Logan, and Ryland. Lily would be taken prisoner.

She took a deep breath and opened her mind to the team leader. *Pull back. There are civilians and innocents here. This team was protecting the senator, not there to assassinate him. Until we know how the wires got crossed, we can't risk killing innocents.* She prayed Sean listened to her. She was not going to be responsible for bloodshed, and no one was going to hurt Ken Norton, not if she could help it. If he was conscious, he'd fight to the death to keep her; she knew that much about him.

She had to keep Sean and her team away from this room and away from the others. But how? She had only seconds before someone triggered an alarm or set off one of the other GhostWalker's highly tuned senses. Quickly pulling on a pair of jeans, she laid her hand on the wall as she leaned against the door to listen, hoping to hear if Jack Norton had already been alerted to the danger descending on them.

Silence. Complete and utter silence. That made no sense.

She caught the whiff of a peculiar odor, faint, but disgusting, much like rotten eggs. Cautiously, Mari pushed open the door. Bodies were strewn all over the floor. Her heart nearly stopped beating. This couldn't be happening. Were they all dead? Jack, Ken's brother? Ken would go berserk and hunt down every single member of her team and execute them.

*What have you done, Sean? My God, the woman is pregnant. You killed them all?* She tasted fear and anger. Tears burned her eyes and clogged her throat. She inhaled sharply and knew the smell was a mixture of gases.

*What are you talking about?*

She could hear a soft hiss as the gas entered through a pipe in the wall. Her heart nearly stopped beating and she ran to the windows, forcing several open before she caught Lily's arm and dragged her into the room with Ken before rushing back for Jack.

*Stop the gas, goddammit. I mean it, Sean, stop the fucking gas.*

*Gas? I didn't*—His voice broke off then resumed sharply. *Get the hell out of there now. That's an order, Mari.*

She ignored the coordinates of the rendezvous point he sent her, and dragged Jack's limp body into the room with Ken and Lily. Ryland was next and then Logan. As soon as she had all of them in the small medical room, she shut the door and sealed the crack using towels and clothing, anything she could find.

Tears streamed down her face, from the gas or because she was so afraid for them all, she wasn't certain, but it blurred her vision. She put a wet cloth on the back of Ken's neck in the hopes of bringing him around faster.

*Damn it, Mari, we can't get farther into the building without raising the alarm. You're supposed to be making your way toward us. Get moving fast.*

She put an oxygen mask on Lily. *If you didn't do this, who did?*

Sean swore at her, a long burst of eloquent and dirty curses. *Haul your ass out of there, soldier.*

*I'm not leaving them to die.*

*We had nothing to do with killing anyone.* Sean's voice changed, dropped an octave, held a low plea. *Whitney has someone there on the inside. We came to get you out, but he wanted us to kill them all and pull out his daughter, Lily. The orders came through as we were entering the compound. I pretended to be out of range, but he has someone inside supposedly helping us.*

Mari crouched down beside Ken again and shook him, wiping his face with a cold cloth to bring him around. He was limp and completely out one moment, and the next he exploded into action, swinging a fist, connecting with the side of her face as she tried to scramble out of the way. She fell back, one hand stretched out in placation. "Stop! Stop, Ken. We're in trouble."

Ken's head was pounding, his vision swimming. He shook his head, saw Mari, clutching her jaw. Realizing what he'd done, he scrambled to his knees and reached for her, catching her face between his hands, his thumb sliding over the bright red spot. "My God, Mari, I could have killed you."

"I didn't have time to stand across the room. Someone is trying to kill them. The room next door is filled with gas and I'm afraid someone is going to toss a match. You have to help me get everyone out of here now. Hurry—we don't have much time."

The headache would last a long time, but his vision was clearing. He didn't reprimand her for knocking him out, or ask questions. He shrugged out of his shirt and handed it to her, hurrying first to Jack.

Mari was a little shocked by the fact that he'd choose his brother over Lily, by the gentle way he lifted Jack onto his back and took him to the window. Mari scrambled out and held out her arms. Ken passed Jack's body to her. With the clean air, he was already beginning to stir, and she hurried to put him some distance from the building before she ran back. She didn't want Jack waking up and attacking her.

*Mari!* Sean's voice sounded insistent and worried. *I'm coming in after you. The others will cover me.*

*No! Give me two minutes, Sean. I can't let them die. I don't know why anyone would order them killed, but that's not what we do and you know it. If Whitney wants to commit murder, he can send his goons.*

She ran with Lily's limp body in her arms, to lay her beside

Jack. He was already sitting up, squeezing the back of his neck, coughing and looking around him. She put a hand on his shoulder. "Conserve your strength; you're going to have to run in another minute."

She had to get away before anyone suspected her team was nearby. If Ken or Jack suspected the men were there, they'd blame her guys for the attack. And if one of their friends died, every member of her team would be living under a death sentence. She knew what men like Ken and Jack were capable of. She knew they would keep coming until their sense of justice was satisfied. She went back to the window and pulled Logan out, dragging him as far as she could.

*I told you, they have someone on the inside. He's going to blow the place. You're out of time. We're holding them off to get you clear, but they're balking.*

Mari's heart thudded. Jack was stumbling toward the building to help with Ryland, but Ken hadn't come out. *Ken! What are you doing? They're going to blow the building.*

Jack had Ryland slung over his shoulder, his face set in grim lines. Ken was talking to him, she was certain. Ken knew they were going to blow the building and he'd told his brother to run. Jack jerked Logan to his feet, yelled something to him and reached for Lily. "Come on, Mari! We have to go now."

"What's Ken doing?"

"There are other people working in the building. He's setting off the alarms." Jack was already running as he gave her the information, Ryland across his back. Logan stumbled after him with Lily in his arms.

Mari hesitated, torn between running to join her team and getting them all away safely, or going after Ken. Ken won. She dove back into the building, landing in a roll and getting up on her feet, sprinting through the room to the hall. She heard shouting and the sound of people running. Lab techs and researchers hurried to get outside. She couldn't see Ken anywhere, and she started down the hall, ignoring a man who caught at her shirt and tried to tug her toward a door.

The shriek of a siren cut through the air, a loud alarm that drove the tension up significantly. Doors opened and more people spilled into the hall, rushing toward the nearest exit. *Ken! Where are you?* What if he was still groggy and he'd passed out? What if Whitney's man on the inside had already found him and stuck a knife in his back? For a moment she couldn't breathe, utter terror consuming her, the sensation one she'd never known before.

*Mari, are you clear? Get the hell out of the building. Where are you?* Ken's voice penetrated her mind.

Relief was instantaneous, sweeping through her so that for a moment her legs went rubbery. She leaned against the wall for support, feeling sick, her fist closing around the cross Ken had given her, holding it tightly, as if she could thus somehow keep him close to her.

"Mari!" Sean's voice startled her. She turned to see him running toward her, gesturing toward the exit a few yards ahead of her. "Run."

She whirled around and ran right into someone, bounced off and slid to the floor. Sean reached her. Without breaking stride, he grabbed her by the shirt and yanked her after him. "Run! Come on, Mari, run."

They sprinted for the exit, using blurring enhanced speed, diving out the door and racing across the ground. She knew she was on the opposite side of the laboratory from the other GhostWalker team. She still didn't know where Ken was, but her people were covering them and anyone trying to stop them was going to be shot. She had to go back with them to the compound. No matter what, she had to go. It was the only way to protect her sisters—and Ken. Nothing could happen to Ken.

She kept pace beside Sean, staying to the hedges for as much cover as possible. Sean handed her a gun as they ran, signaling her to go up and over the security fence. She shoved the gun in the waistband of her jeans and leapt to catch the top of the high fence, flip over, and drop to the other side.

Ken would try to follow them. The moment he knew they were gone, he would come after her. And he'd remember that she'd knocked him out. Ken Norton wasn't a man to forget such things. Her breath came out in a little sob, and Sean shot her a sharp glance and fell back to protect her.

The blast was thunderous, debris shooting up and out as the building exploded. The fence burst outward toward them. The concussion blew both of them into the air and sent them flying across a small open expanse of grass to land hard on the ground. The air left her lungs in one awful rush, leaving Mari gasping and wheezing.

Sean crawled to her side. "Can you move? We've got to keep going."

She nodded. Everything hurt. She couldn't hear very well, but it didn't matter. She had to get out of there and she had to get out fast. She climbed unsteadily to her feet, using Sean as a crutch. Her arm was bleeding.

Instead of running, Sean retained his hold on her, inspecting her for damage. He took in the bruises on her wrists and face, the marks on her neck, and the too-big pair of jeans. He stepped closer and inhaled. "Some son of a bitch fucked you. I can smell his stench all over you," he snarled.

It was the last thing she'd expected him to say. "What? No sympathy? No how did they treat you? No wow, you were shot, it's a miracle you're alive?" Mari scowled at him. "Nice of you to get so upset on my behalf, Sean. Too bad you don't feel the same way when Brett comes to my room and you let him in. You're a hypocrite."

"That's bullshit. It isn't the same."

"Why? Because you didn't get to have your usual vicarious experience? What do you do? Stand there and listen while he beats the crap out of me and then gets what he wants? Don't pretend to get all bent because some man touched me. You give the key to Brett whenever he gets a little horny."

"I do my job. You're in a special program. Get pregnant and the visits will stop. I know you're doing something to prevent it. Whitney knows your cycle. You should be knocked up by now, and then he wouldn't let Brett near you again."

Sean slapped her across the face. Without hesitation, Mari punched him hard, turning into it, pushing off with her right foot to use every bit of strength she possessed. Sean dropped like a stone when her fist smashed into his cheekbone. Simultaneously, a bullet whined just over him, right where his head had been.

*Don't you dare shoot him, Ken.* She should have known the man would never let anyone walk away with her. *I have to go back.*

*Bullshit.*

She detested the implacable resolve in his voice—in his

mind. *You know the way you feel about Jack? That's the way I feel about my sisters. I'm not taking a chance with their lives. So you're not shooting him.*

Sean climbed unsteadily to his feet. Mari didn't back up or even flinch, staring him straight in the eye. "I can see you're very torn up about my appearance. The gunshot wound, the broken leg and hand, and by the way, Zenith kills if it's in your system too long—but maybe you knew that already. I died and had to be revived."

"Zenith saved your life." Sean rubbed his face, glaring at her. He inhaled her scent and scowled, still obviously furious over the idea that she'd been with a man. "Some man treated you like a camp whore and you're thinking you might give birth to his baby? No chance, Mari. When you get back, you're going to make damn sure you're not pregnant."

"How do you know how he treated me, Sean? Maybe I jumped him. You just never know with me. After Brett, a monkey might look good."

"I've known you for years, Mari. Why do you think I stay in that hellhole and put up with Whitney's insanity?"

"Because you care? Is that what you're going to say? Save it. You pimp me out to that jerk and then have the gall to pretend we're still friends. No thanks, Sean. You killed that a long time ago. You've been brainwashed by Whitney's 'take one for the good of mankind' speech, but you know, it seems I'm always the one taking it, not you." She stepped close to him, her fingers balled into two tight fists. "And if you ever hit me again, you'd better make damn certain I can't ever get up, because I'll kill you."

She turned away from him and began to jog toward the treeline, head up, shaking with fury. Sean had been her friend, someone she cared a great deal about. Whatever had gotten into him sickened her. Her vision blurred and she stumbled, realized she was crying, and wiped the tears with the back of her hand.

*Ken. Can you hear me?* She reached out to him, needing someone. She never needed anyone, but she was shaken and angry and terrified that something could have happened to him.

Sean fell into step with her, sneaking quick, hard glances at her, but she refused to acknowledge him.

*I hear you and I've got a rifle trained on your friend, Mari.*

She heard the sound of her heart pounding in her ears. Her hand went once again to the cross nestled between her breasts. "Sean. You ever hear of a couple of snipers named Norton?"

"Hell yes. Everyone's heard of them."

"One of them has you in his scope right now. He nearly killed you before. Didn't you hear the bullet when you hit the ground?" *You can't shoot him, Ken. If you do that, how are you going to follow me back to the compound?*

*I'm feeling a little mean right about now, Mari.*

Sean's breath sounded like one long wheeze. He looked wildly around. "Are you certain, Mari?"

*I suppose you have reason to feel that way,* she conceded to Ken. *I had to think of something to keep everyone from getting killed, and after all, you did it to me first. I was saving your life, just like you saved mine.*

*Is that what you call it?*

"Oh, yeah. I'm certain," she told Sean. *That's what you called it,* she reminded Ken. *And just so you know, I didn't know about the gas or the building blowing up at the time. It wasn't my team. Someone on the inside working for Whitney did all that.*

*I have one hell of a headache, thanks to you. Veer to the left. I like seeing him sweat. If you go left it gives me more of an opportunity to wing him.*

She glanced sideways. Sean was sweating. Droplets ran down his face and his shirt had damp spots on it. *You are feeling mean. You don't need to wing him. And I'd have more sympathy for the headache, except you gave me one first and I think you sort of deserve it.*

*I'm going to shoot the bastard, Mari.*

*Fine. I have sympathy. Loads of sympathy.*

*The son of a bitch didn't need to slap you.*

Her heart jumped again. Ken sounded lethal, all playfulness gone. *I need him to help me get the others out.*

*You really think I'm going to let you go?*

*You have to, Ken. I mean it.* Her heart thundered in her ears. It was only a few more steps. Once they made it into the trees, Sean would be safe from a bullet and she could figure out what was going on with him. *I couldn't live with myself if something happened to one of the other women.*

There was a small silence. She was counting steps now, trying to judge how many more to reach the safety of the trees.

*Mari, if he touches you, he's a dead man. You'd better know that. And I'm going to be with you every step of the way. Don't try to throw us off the trail. That's just going to piss me off, and you don't want to see that side of me.*

No, she didn't. She knew men like Ken, and they didn't have that glacier-cold burn in their eyes because they were nice. *I'm counting on you following me. I don't want to get trapped there ever again.*

*Then you're both clear.*

Relief swept through her. Sean put on a burst of speed, seeing the trees close, and she fell back a couple of steps to help block his body just in case Ken changed his mind. With every step she took, relief turned to dread. Even though it was her choice to go back, and she knew Ken had her back, the idea of being trapped again in Whitney's nightmare world sickened her. The other women were as desperate to escape as she was, going so far as to plan it, but even their allies within the compound were afraid of Whitney and his bodyguards. The men were cruel and brutal. Brett had been one of them. All had seen plenty of combat and all were enhanced.

*You think I'd let you go there alone, honey? Jack and I are right on your hot little tail. We can follow a ghost.*

His voice brushed along the walls of her mind like a physical caress, steadying her. She could go back and get the others out. Whitney seemed invincible, but that was only because he'd been the authority figure from her childhood. He had stood watching them all with that dispassionate look on his face, so unemotional no matter what happened, his terrible half smile on his face as he forced obedience.

*Ken, most of the people at the compound are good people, following orders and struggling to make sense of it all.*

*I'm not the devil.* But maybe he was. Ken watched Mari disappear into the trees with Sean and reluctantly dropped the rifle from his shoulder. He wanted to pull the trigger. The moment he saw Sean—and he knew the big man was Mari's Sean—Ken had wanted him dead. The shot he'd taken had been a kill shot, and Mari had to have known that. If she hadn't punched the bastard and dropped him to the ground, the son of a bitch would be dead.

And why the hell did they need him alive? Mari needed to return to Whitney's secret compound, and that went against every instinct Ken had, but hell—he was in her head and knew she wouldn't stop trying until she'd done this. Short of locking her up—and he'd contemplated that very thing—he had to let her go back.

He rolled over, wiping his brow on his sleeve. Jack came up behind him. "How the hell do men do this? Because, let me tell you, bro, it's fucked. She's asking for something I don't think I can give her."

"Let's go," Jack said, his face grim. "You made the decision to let her go and we've got it to do now. We can't lose her."

"Lily make certain the tracking device is in her bloodstream?"

"Yes. She didn't like it, but she did it."

"How is she?"

"Ryland took her to the hospital to make sure the baby is okay. Everyone's in place. Let's do this and get Mari out of there as fast as we can," Jack insisted.

Ken rose to his feet and followed Jack from their vantage point. "No matter what, we had to put that tracking device in place. You have one in Briony and Lily has one. If Whitney takes them, we can get them back."

"They wouldn't like it if they knew, especially Mari."

"Who gives a damn?" Ken asked. "Mari can fucking well live with it. Asking me to let her do this is bullshit and she knows it."

"Women don't go for the word 'allow' anymore, bro. It's not politically correct." Jack kept his back turned as he listened to his brother spit out curses. Mari might look like Briony, but she wasn't ever going to act like her. Ken had his hands full.

"I am surprised you didn't chain her up inside a cave somewhere."

"Like you've done with Briony? Bri has the brains to listen to you. Mari would fight me every inch of the way."

The tension in Ken's voice made Jack glance at him sharply. "Ken, I know you're struggling here . . ."

Ken shook his head. "Don't even go there. I wanted to kill that man for just being near her. It wasn't that he hit her. He was a dead man the moment he did that, we both know that, but I wanted it *before* he was that stupid."

Jack sent a small, tight smile in his brother's general direction. "I wanted to kill him too, Ken. That doesn't mean either of us is like our father. It means we might need psychiatric help, but it doesn't mean what you think it does."

"She makes me crazy."

"She's supposed to make you crazy."

Ken shook his head in disgust. "You don't know, Jack. I have this driving need to keep her in a little cocoon, wrap her up in bubble wrap and force her to do every single thing I say. What the hell kind of man thinks that way?"

Jack snorted. "Pretty much all of them. We aren't that far from swinging in the trees, Ken." One eyebrow rose in inquiry. "So, if you want to force her to do what you say, why don't you?"

Ken shrugged, muttering under his breath as they reached their vehicle. "Mari's smart, you know. She's fast and she's efficient and she doesn't fuck around. Man, she put me out so fast I didn't know what she was doing until it was too late." He rubbed the back of his neck, but there was admiration in his voice. "Trying to control someone like that is like trying to hold water in your hand. It just makes a man insane."

"So, basically, if you locked her up, she might kick your balls right up into your stomach and then smile at you as you're lying on the floor."

"Basically."

Jack shot him a grin. "Good for her."

"Yeah, you can say that. She's not your woman. She was going back to that compound no matter what anyone said, but Jack, she doesn't know me. She only thinks she does. If they hurt her—if they touch her—they're dead men. I won't be able to stop myself. It won't matter if she thinks the women are in danger. Nothing is going to matter."

"That's not a big surprise, Ken," Jack said. "We both are fairly one dimensional in our approach to solving problems. Freud would have a field day with us."

Ken sighed. Mari was smart and sexy, far too independent,

and as tough as they came. She was highly skilled, well trained, and unflinching in battle. She hadn't even hesitated to punch Sean, dropping him like a stone. And she'd known her team was there before he had, even though he'd fucked her brains out and he lay like a limp dishrag, unable to hear anything but his own heartbeat.

Soft laughter touched his mind. *You're just being silly now.*

He had inadvertently connected with her and shared his thoughts. *Well, you recovered first when you should have been fainting or something. That's a challenge, Mari. You've challenged me. I can't have you able to think and act after sex if I'm incapacitated. I'll take my time next time. Slow torture. Make you want me so bad you're screaming for me again.*

*You have such an ego.*

*With good cause.* Deliberately he sounded smug. *What's your plan? You do have a plan, right?*

*We've been working on one.* She broke off abruptly.

Alarm spread through him. *Mari?* He swore. "I think someone heard us. I kept the energy spillage to a minimum, but Mari isn't as experienced at it. Sean is close to her. He may have caught the energy surge. Damn it. Have Logan give us a report."

"Ken," Jack cautioned. "We don't want to chance Sean spotting Logan. We've got men all over. Ryland's crew is helping us out. She's got a tracking device they don't know about and can't find on her, even with good electronic equipment. Whitney doesn't have this or access to it. Relax a little. She's not getting away from us."

"I don't care if the entire navy is watching. I want one of ours to eyeball her and let me know she's alive and well and we're staying right on her."

The edge to his voice made Jack shoot him another quick glance, as if assessing his mood. He started to protest, met Ken's glittering glare, and shrugged. "I'll let them know. But if they blow it, we're in trouble."

"We're already in trouble." At least Ken was. His gut was a series of hard knots that wouldn't relax. He'd never had a problem carrying out a mission, but he'd never *felt* anything before when he did. He was always—always—emotionally detached. Right now he was afraid that if anyone said or did the wrong thing near him, he wouldn't be able to control the violence pounding to break free.

He had awakened from nightmares with his heart slamming against his chest and his body drenched in sweat. He'd awakened with a gun in his hand. He'd even stabbed the mattress a few times, and once, when the flashbacks had been particularly bad, he'd shredded his down comforter so badly he'd been plucking feathers off the floor for weeks afterward. None of those times had felt like this.

His mouth was dry, his lungs burned, his palms felt sweaty. He was burning in hell for his sins and he had too damn many to count. None of the others would know, but Jack did. Jack always knew. He'd cover for him, they always covered for each other, but it was harrowing to suddenly have to contend with the terrifying realization that someone you didn't have in your control could change your life forever.

"Logan's got a visual on Mari," Jack reported. "Sean must have knocked her out. She's lying on the seat, buckled in, but he's cuffing her."

Ken swore, a blistering string of obscenities that would have shocked a sailor. "I knew I should have capped that bastard. What the hell was Mari thinking trusting him?"

"I don't know that she did trust him, Ken. All I caught was her need to get back to the women she loves—her family."

"I should have stopped her. I could have. I just let her go right back into the enemy's camp." His gaze glittered hotly, his mouth set in a grim, implacable line. "She's the primary mission, Jack. You make certain the others understand that. They don't want to be hunting me, and that's what's going to happen if they blow this. She's primary. The other women and Whitney are secondary."

"That's understood, Ken," Jack assured. "You're letting this get to you. She's a soldier and she'll act like one. Trust her. Hell, Ken, she saved our lives and she bested you, even knocked your ass out. She acts fast, hits hard, and does the unexpected. She gave us enough information to lull us into a false security, but nothing that would trip up her team or lead us back to her base." There was respect in Jack's voice. "I put a gun to her head, Ken, and she didn't even flinch. Did you notice that? Her mind was working the entire time. She doesn't

panic and she's sorting through all the possibilities fast. There's
no backup in her."

"She must have driven Whitney crazy. He doesn't like op-
position of any kind, but he wants those very traits for his supersoldiers. He'd want to control her, but not break her
spirit," Ken said. "I'm planning on using sex. Lots and lots of
sex."

"Yeah, good luck with that." Jack quirked an eyebrow at
him as they turned onto the road leading to the small airfield
where Lily had private transportation waiting. "Am I missing
something here or didn't you already have sex with her, really
great sex, and her answer was to knock you out? Am I wrong?
Didn't that happen?"

"Shut the hell up."

Ken shouldered his pack and stalked across the tarmac to
the waiting plane. Jack followed at a more leisurely pace,
whistling off-key.

Kadan, Ryland's second in command, joined them, glancing from one to the other. "You haven't switched roles on us,
have you?" he asked. "Because, frankly, Ken's looking a little
hostile."

"Yep. I'm the easygoing Norton," Jack said, prodding his
brother with his satchel. "Isn't that right, Ken? He got beat up
by a girl and he's sulking."

"Keep it up, Jack," Ken said, "you're not going to make it
to your next birthday."

"But then Briony would be all upset and cry all the time.
She probably would never get out of bed, and you'd have to
take care of the babies."

Kadan's eyebrow shot up. "Someone must have given you
a happy pill, Jack."

Jack shrugged. "There's nothing quite like seeing a woman
wrapping my brother around her little finger. He's whipped . . ."
He grinned. "Literally."

Ken muttered a suggestion that was anatomically impossible. "If you're here, Kadan, who's watching Briony? I
wouldn't put it past Whitney to try for another grab at her."

Jack flicked him a warning look. "You can stop right there,
Ken. I've stashed her somewhere very safe, somewhere Whitney would never think to look."

"He knows where all the GhostWalkers live, Jack. He probably knows the safe houses as well. You should be home with Briony right now, protecting her."

"Whitney doesn't know about this house."

Ken was silent for a moment. "She isn't with a Ghost-Walker."

Jack shook his head. "I sent her first to Lily's place, and then she was supposed to have gone to visit with Nico and Dahlia. Lily smuggled her out and she's safe with Miss Judith. I've wanted them to meet, so Jeff escorted Briony to her home. She's promised she won't leave the house and will stay out of sight. I've got two guards on them, but Whitney will never think to look for her there."

Miss Judith was the woman who had turned their lives around and kept them both out of jail. She'd been a volunteer, working at the group home where they were placed, and she had seen the rage hidden beneath the icy and very frightening demeanor of the two boys who had been constantly shuffled from one foster home to the next. She wasn't put off by their bad reputations or the fact that they had retaliated against a couple of their foster parents for mistreatment or the fact that they refused to be separated, running away each time the system had insisted on splitting them up. She looked beyond their horrific past, the fact that they'd killed their father and refused to be separated, no matter what the system said.

It was Miss Judith who had saved them, giving them a love of music and books and education. She taught them to harness the never-ending rage in positive ways, and when they joined the military and, eventually, Special Forces and then special ops, they created a very public and heated argument in order to ensure her protection against their enemies. Miss Judith had disappeared from their lives. She moved away for a year or so before returning to Montana. No one would ever find a single contact between them again.

Ken looked out the window, his mind once more reaching for Mari's. How had it happened? He'd been so certain he was going to walk away from her, yet now that she was gone, he knew he couldn't be without her. He had to find a way to control his baser traits. He wouldn't be jealous and domineering.

He'd be one of those men women were always talking about, sensitive and socially correct.

He looked at his reflection in the window. What a crock. Who was he trying to kid? He looked the monster he was. Truthfully, he had every intention of controlling her. He wanted her completely under his thumb. He was no saint—not even close—and he wasn't going to pretend. She was going to have to learn to love the real man. He'd given her a choice. He'd told her to be sure. He'd warned her. Over and over.

His fist hit his thigh in a frustrated protest. *Mari. Damn you. Where the hell are you?* He tunneled his fingers through his hair, betraying his agitation. *Come on, baby. You've got to answer me. Just touch my mind with yours.*

# CHAPTER 12

"Mari, come on, hon, you have to wake up."

The voice was insistent. Mari moved her head, and immediately a jackhammer began to drive on full throttle through it. She suppressed a groan and forced herself to reach out with her psychic senses to tell her where she was and what kind of trouble she was in.

Rose. She could never mistake Rose's soft feminine scent. Sean was there too. Bastard. He'd shot her full of something and knocked her out. He was going to pay for that. She heard the solid chink of a metal door closing. The sound of footsteps pacing. She was back in the compound.

Her body ached, her arms especially. She tried to relieve the pain by pulling them in close to her and found that she was cuffed to the metal rail of the bed.

"Mari," Rose repeated. "Wake up."

A cold cloth was pressed to her face. Rose leaned close. "Whitney's going to be here any minute. Come on, honey. We need you alert."

Mari pried her eyelids open and stared up into Rose's concerned face. She looked like a little pixie with her too large eyes and sultry mouth and small, heart-shaped face. Rose was delicate and a little younger than the rest of them, with not quite as tough an exterior, but she had steel beneath that soft skin and delicate bone structure. She smiled at Mari.

"At last. We were getting alarmed."

"Sean handcuffed me." She jerked at her hands and turned her head toward the man standing guard. "Why?"

"You were communicating with the enemy," he said.

"I was saving your butt, and right at this very moment, I can't think why." Mari maneuvered into a sitting position, clenching her teeth against the pounding in her head.

"Just how did you do that?"

She cast Sean the best glower she was capable of, dark and filled with contempt, *withering* even. She wanted him to wither. Switching her attention to Rose, she forced a serene smile. "I'm awake, hon. My head hurts like a bear, and I'm a little worse for wear, but I didn't get a chance to talk to the senator."

The smile faded from Rose's face. "We were counting on that." She lowered her voice. "Whitney brought in his other guards. Even if some of the men help us, those men are killers." She shivered, running her hands up and down her arms. "I hate the way they leer at us when we're in the yard."

*We can't trust Sean. Something's different about him.* Mari wanted to perfect her telepathic technique. Manipulating energy directly to one individual without other psychics receiving a faint "buzz" was extremely difficult. If Ken and Jack Norton could do it, then that meant it was a level of skill. Mari was always top of her class in everything. Competition alone could drive her to succeed.

*He was freaked out when they said you were shot. And Brett went crazy. He tore up the complex like a madman. That's how Whitney found out. We were all trying to keep it quiet, hoping the team would find you and get you back here, but Brett didn't care about the rest of us. He made certain Whitney knew.*

"Stop it, Mari," Sean snapped. "If you want to say something, say it out loud."

Mari shrugged. "I was just telling Rose what a horse's ass you are. She agreed. She especially liked the part where you were so concerned about how I was treated as a prisoner and worked so hard to make certain I was healed from the bullet that nearly killed me. Well, the Zenith nearly killed me. What about that, Sean? Did you know about the time limit on the Zenith? Do all the men know, or only Whitney's chosen few?"

The door opened. Mari stiffened. Although her back was to the door, she knew the moment Peter Whitney entered the room. There was a distinct scent about him she couldn't quite identify, something "off."

"Well, well," Dr. Whitney said in greeting. "Our little Mari is stirring up trouble as usual. You've been off on an adventure."

Mari had no idea what Whitney had been told, but she wasn't going to give him anything for free. She turned, stretching lazily, striving to look bored. "I'm a soldier. Sitting around waiting for that idiot Brett is boring. I took a chance and went for a little action. It's what I'm trained for."

"You're trained to follow orders," Whitney corrected. "Rose, leave now."

Rose squeezed Mari's arm, her body blocking the gesture. Without a word she went from the room, leaving Mari alone with Whitney and Sean.

"Sean tells me you need the morning-after pill to make certain you're not pregnant. Have you been a fraternizing with the enemy?"

She lifted her head and stared him right in the eye. "Ken Norton. He's the one who shot me. It seems you made him part of your program as well." She saw the shift in his expression. Elation. Hope. Emotions played behind his superior expression. He wanted her pregnant by Ken Norton.

"So Sean is right and you could be pregnant?" Whitney knew her cycle better than she did.

Mari shrugged. "We had sex. I suppose it could happen."

Whitney studied her with the same detachment she'd observed in him studying his lab animals. "We'll give it a few days and test you."

Sean took an aggressive step forward. "No. No way. If you wait to see, it will be too late and she'll have to have an abortion."

"Norton carries a remarkable genetic code," Whitney said. "Paired with Mari's, the child could be everything we've been hoping for. No, we'll wait and see. Meanwhile, Mari, you'll need a medical examination to determine if your injuries can in anyway impair you, and of course, you'll be locked up for a few days to make certain we don't have a repeat of this incident."

If she could establish that she'd gone AWOL for reasons of inactivity, that the rebellion among the women was mostly due to boredom, he might buy it. Whitney had raised them in a military environment, and it stood to reason that after running physical exercises and learning weapons for hours every day, they would be unable to just sit around.

"I need action, Dr. Whitney. Sitting around waiting for a man to knock me up is making me crazy. I'm a soldier. At least give me some training exercises. The other women feel the same way."

He smiled at her, a cold, empty smile. "You want me to believe inactivity is the reason you've been causing so many problems lately?"

"I tried to talk to you a couple of times." She glared at Sean as if he hadn't carried messages to the doctor. "Nobody would let me near you."

"And your rejection of Brett? Was that out of boredom as well?"

Mari rubbed her pounding head. "Brett is an ass. I don't want to have his baby. I made that very clear. He's not nearly as intelligent as you seem to think he is. And it's way too easy to make him lose his temper. My child is going to be cool under fire at all times. I've never lost it during a mission, not once. I read Brett's file, and he has issues I'm not passing on to the next generation."

"Well thought out as always, Mari," Peter Whitney said. "And what are you objections to having a child by Ken Norton?"

"I have none, although I'd like to read his file if you have one on him. From what I could see, he has extraordinary psychic talents, and he's earned a reputation as one of the best snipers in the business. Sean told me."

"I did not."

"It was in your mind when I asked you about the Nortons."

"You want me to believe you left this facility in order to participate in a mission because you were bored?"

She met his gaze without flinching. "Yes. And I will do so again at the first opportunity if you make me continue to live like this. No one can live this way. We need to go running and to continue to work on our skills, both physical and mental. We're going crazy doing nothing but lying around all day."

Whitney's eyebrow shot up. "I suppose we could both pretend you haven't threatened to slit my throat the first chance you get and that the only reason you haven't done it is because I've bought your cooperation by holding a gun to the head of the other women—your bored sister soldiers."

Mari silently cursed her big mouth. She had threatened him on many occasions, meaning every single threat. Whitney wasn't going to buy into her cooperation act. She tried another course. Mari looked down at her cuffed hands, trying to look chastised. Sean grunted in disbelief and she shot him a quick glare. "There's one more thing you should know. I met Lily. I met your daughter. She saved my life." She hastily looked up to catch the expression on his face.

There was a long silence. Whitney stood without moving or speaking, blinking down at her as if confused.

"Dr. Whitney?" Sean broke the silence. "Do you need a glass of water?"

Whitney shook his head. "Lily is brilliant. I've been so proud of her work lately. She's a fast learner and very astute. Did she appear healthy?"

Mari nodded. "She looks very healthy and is obviously happy."

"And pregnant. Why weren't you going to tell me about her pregnancy?" Whitney bent down, sticking his face close to hers, eyes furious. He could get remarkably angry when someone thwarted his plans. And he was angry now.

"I didn't have a chance. I didn't know if you knew, and I wanted to break it to you gently. I know good breeding is important to you, and I was afraid . . ." She let her voice trail off and tried to look helpless and distressed. She just wasn't good at this actress crap. She'd rather be boiled in oil than pretend concern and look girly-girl nervous.

Rose assured her that turning girl worked, though, and she was feeling on the edge of desperation. They told her the soldiers always fell for it, and Whitney would become so disgusted he'd walk away. The other women had actually made her practice looking tearful. They'd all laughed at her, and right now she wished she'd paid a lot more attention to their lessons. She really, really wanted Whitney to walk away right now.

"Did you see her husband?"

Mari nodded again. The one thing she'd learned about Whitney over the years was that he had poor social skills. He rarely bothered to read other people—certainly not enough to know if they were telling the truth or not. If she could say what he wanted to hear . . . She chose her words carefully. "Yes, he's definitely a good soldier and psychically talented." She kept her tone reluctant.

"But . . ." Whitney pressed.

"I doubt he's her intellectual equal."

"Do you think that matters?"

Whitney had never really asked her opinion before. It was a trick question; she could tell by his tone and the sharp look he was giving her.

"I have no idea."

"Lily is unquestionably brilliant."

"As I said, she saved my life. She has discovered that Zenith kills if it stays in our systems too long, but you must have known that."

"Of course."

"And the risks are acceptable because . . . ?"

"I don't have to answer to you."

"No, you don't. But I figure they're acceptable because the benefits outweigh the risks. Those of us who need anchors can perform without them being too close to us. If we're wounded, we heal much faster, and if we're captured, we don't have time to give up information under torture." She kept a straight face, simply reporting, not thinking about breaking his scrawny neck. She wanted to recite the reasons in front of Sean. Sean—who often ran missions and was shot full of the drug. Sean—who had turned on the very people who had been his family.

Sean met her gaze and looked away. Good. He was getting it—finally.

"You will be taken to the medical facility and examined there, Mari. In a few days we'll test for pregnancy. I'll send Norton's file to you so you can read the data I've collected on him. I think you'll see it's a good match."

Mari nodded, keeping her head down, afraid she wouldn't be able to hide the relief she felt. The story was plausible, and Whitney was happy there was a chance she had conceived a child with Ken, so he wasn't going to delve too much further. She waited until he was gone before looking up at Sean.

"Unlock the cuffs."

"This isn't over, Mari. You're not having that man's baby."

"Better his than Brett's."

"I was taking care of Brett." He reached for her hands and unlocked the cuffs.

She rubbed her bruised wrists and sent him another glare. "You didn't have to put them on so tight."

Sean took her hand in his, thumb sliding over the bruises. "Did Norton force you?"

She jerked her hand away. "You should have asked me that question hours ago. It's too damn late to show concern now. Go to hell, Sean." She stood up, had to grab the metal railing to keep from falling, and stood swaying, gritting her teeth against the ferocious pounding in her head. "Did you hit me again?"

"No way. I wasn't about to give you an excuse to kill me. And I knew you'd wake up pissed." He reached out and captured her hand again. "I did put those things on a little too tight. You've got bruises."

She pulled her hand away again and rubbed her palm down the thigh of her jeans. "I'm really angry with you, Sean."

"I know. You scared the hell out of everyone. Damn it, Mari, they shot you."

"Everything is all mixed up. No one was there to assassinate Senator Freeman. Both teams were there to protect him. Could the threat have been a publicity stunt? And why would they send two GhostWalker special ops teams in to do the same job? There aren't that many of us. They couldn't just have made a mistake."

She took a tentative step and the room lurched. "What the hell did you do to me, anyway, Sean?"

He steadied her by taking her arm. "I drugged you. It probably reacted with whatever was already in your system."

"Well, that's all right then." She gave him her best sarcastic tone, wishing she had a knife to slit him from throat to belly.

"I'm still really angry with you. You acted like a jerk. I should have let Norton shoot you."

"You were really talking him out of killing me?"

"Yes. He doesn't like you, but I told him you had a good side. When he asked what it was, I couldn't remember. I need to go to my room before I go to the doc."

"I'm supposed to take you straight to the medical wing."

"Sean, don't make me kick you. I need to stop off in my room. It will take two minutes. I can't stand wearing these shoes a minute longer. In case you hadn't noticed, they aren't mine."

"We swept you for tracking devices."

"Did you sweep me for shoes hurting my feet and giving me blisters?"

"All right." Sean glanced at his watch. "But we have to hurry. You know how Whitney is; he wants every minute accounted for."

"You can tell him about the blisters on my feet. The first thing they teach a good soldier is to take care of his feet." She pulled away from him. "I'm fine now—well, except for the headache. I'm not forgiving you for a long, long time, in case you're interested."

"I don't know what got into me, Mari. When you started talking about having sex with Norton, I just lost my mind. I'm sorry I hit you."

Mari kept her gaze straight ahead. Anger was alive and well and living just beneath the surface of her purposely calm expression. "You would have been a lot sorrier if I hadn't retaliated. Apparently the Nortons aren't very fond of men hitting women. He would have shot you right in the head."

"You really are pissed at me, aren't you?" Sean held the door open for her.

"You think? I was taken prisoner and they treated me better than you did. I've known you for years, Sean. I thought we were friends. You've turned into a jerk." She sat on the edge of her cot and leaned down to unlace the shoes.

"Yeah, they treated you so good you slept with one of them." The edge was back in his voice.

Mari threw the shoe with deadly aim, hitting him square in the chest. "You don't know the first thing about what happened to me, so shut up." She turned her back on him, yanked her hair in frustration, and let out a hiss of anger. She brought one hand sliding down quickly to remove the braided gold chain from around her neck. The movement was fast, the chain bunching in her hand out of sight. "Do you see my slippers anywhere? I thought they were right here."

She dropped down to look under the bed, shoving her hand beneath her mattress as she leaned her weight against the cot. "Do you see them?"

Sean yanked open the doors to her locker. Mari's room was stark, not a thing out of place. He couldn't imagine her slippers being under her bed. "I don't see any slippers anywhere. Why don't you grab a pair of socks if you don't want to wear shoes?" He tossed her a pair.

Mari caught them and sank down onto the cot again. "How did all this happen, Sean? When did it all go to hell?"

"Just put the socks on."

"If Brett comes back here, I swear one of us isn't going to walk out of this room alive." She paused, the sock hovering near her toes. Her gaze met Sean's. "I mean it. I can't let him touch me ever again. I hate it that much."

"I'll take care of it. I'll find a way."

"You've been saying that for weeks now. I'm not the only one being forced into something disgusting, Sean. We talked about this and you said you'd get Whitney to listen to you, but he didn't. Would you honestly want to live this way?" She donned her socks and stood up, following him out the door.

"Is Brett the reason why you did it? Are you hoping Whitney will keep him away from you if you're pregnant with Norton's baby?" He led her down the hall to the elevator.

Mari shoved her fingers through her hair, betraying agitation. "I'm not accepting him. One way or the other, I'm not accepting him."

"Whitney told me he doesn't want the women to feel the same way over the men, because if the pairing doesn't work— if for some reason she doesn't get pregnant, or the baby isn't what he'd hoped—then he can send another partner."

She stiffened. "The baby isn't what he hoped? What exactly does he plan to do with a baby that isn't what he hoped?"

Sean frowned. "I hadn't thought about it. Maybe adopt it out?"

"Adopt it out?" She dragged her feet, slowing as they made their way down the corridor toward the laboratory.

"Well come on, Mari, you can't tell me you want to sit around with a crying kid hanging on you."

"If it was my kid, yes. Is that what you'd want? Your child sent away?"

"I don't know what I want. When Whitney talks about how genetic enhancement can save so many lives and if we just developed a group of soldiers with superior skills, so many young men and women would never have to lose their lives or have catastrophic injuries, it makes sense. I can go out and do what I've been trained to do and know that someone else, someone not nearly as skilled, might be killed—would probably be killed—if I wasn't doing my job. Doesn't it make sense to work toward finding a solution to war?"

"The babies are still our children, Sean," she pointed out. "They aren't robots; they deserve to have the same choice you as an adult have. They deserve the same rights other children have."

Sean pulled open the door to the medical laboratory and waited for her to enter first. "If you could just hear him, Mari."

"I have heard him. He raised me. He found me in an orphanage, and facilities and laboratories like this one have been my home since that day. I didn't play like normal children; I didn't even know there was a normal. Martial arts and shooting guns were normal to me. I've never been on a swing or gone down a slide, Sean. I was out in the field playing battle when I was six. I never had a holiday. No one tucked me in at night. Is that the kind of life you want for your son or daughter?"

Sean shook his head. "I'll talk to him again."

"It won't do any good. You know it won't. He'll just present his 'this is for the good of mankind' argument, and no one can get around that. He doesn't think with emotion, Sean. He discounts emotion altogether. When he pairs a couple, it's just physical attraction. Or that's what it seems to be. He doesn't want to run the risk of emotion, because then the parents might care about each other as well as their child. What would happen when he decides to experiment on the child—or he doesn't think the pairing was what he wanted after all and he wants to break the couple up?"

"He wouldn't do that."

"No? I think you're deluding yourself, and I don't understand why. We had hundreds of discussions about this and you always agreed with the rest of us. What Whitney is doing is wrong, Sean."

Mari looked around her at the cold stainless-steel counters, sinks, and gurneys. She hated this room. It was so cold, yet when they turned on the spotlights, it was glaringly hot. Surgical instruments lay like torture implements in neat little trays. She tore her gaze from the knives and forced herself to smile at the small, thin man waiting for her. "Dr. Prauder, I'm reporting for a checkup."

"So I've heard. Whitney wants a full report on you."

"I'm here to give you whatever you need," she said, forcing a cheerful tone. Her stomach knotted up at the thought of what was coming. She didn't look at Sean. He knew her well enough to know she detested the poking and prodding. Whitney even tried to extract memories. Everything, no matter how humiliating or private, was recorded.

She took the gown the doctor gave her and changed in the small alcove, counting in her head to control shivering. *Ken, where are you?* If she ever needed another human being to get her through something, now was the time. She didn't want them to give her a morning-after pill. She didn't want them touching her body or deciding she needed more shots or another tracking device.

She detested the lack of control, how vulnerable she felt when she was strapped down helplessly and the doctors were able to do whatever Whitney decided was her fate. Most of all she detested the sneaky, very personal way Prauder touched her when he was pretending to be impersonal. Whitney often came for the exams. He stood on the other side of the glass with that terrible little half smile staring at her as if she were a frog he was dissecting.

How far away were the Nortons and their team? Had they lost track of her? Had Sean managed to throw them off and now she was trapped here alone? And what if she was pregnant?

Whitney would take her baby and she'd never see it—not if he knew it was Ken Norton's. He'd looked too pleased, and it was rare for Whitney to be pleased.

"You ready, Mari?" Sean asked.

"In a minute." She folded the shirt carefully, running her hand over the material in a small caress. It was stupid and girlie and made her want to choke, but she couldn't stop herself. *They're going to examine me. Do you know what that entails? And while they examine me, they have a guard standing right there, watching the entire thing. And a camera records it and Whitney stands outside the glass staring in at me.*

There was no reason to tell him. She was stoic about it—well, usually stoic about it. Sometimes she fought and the guards ended up with broken bones and black eyes, and then they sedated her. She suppressed another shiver and held the shirt to her face, inhaling Ken's scent, hoping to keep it with her through the coming ordeal.

"What the hell is taking so long?" Sean demanded.

"I was shot, you moron. My leg was broken. Although it's mostly healed, it's still sore, so I'm being a little wimpy taking the jeans off. Do you have a date? Am I holding you up from some important appointment, because honestly, Sean, I don't mind if you want to postpone this little event."

Sean muttered an obscenity she pretended not to catch. She took a deep breath and let it out before stepping out of the jeans. Just once, one time in her life, she wanted support. It was stupid. Her entire education was about self-reliance and discipline. It was about facing pain and the impossible task and completing the mission no matter what the personal cost might be.

She'd had a small taste of freedom, ironically as a prisoner, and it was much more difficult to face the starkness of her life. Reluctantly, Mari placed Ken's shirt on the chair and wrapped herself in the gown.

She made a face at Sean as she climbed onto the table. She hated this. *Hated* it. Whitney knew it too. She'd tried various ways to distract herself over the years, pleaded for music, tried a running dialogue—nothing worked. She was the insect, pinned to the table, strapped down and stripped naked, to be examined and dissected just like the frogs and other animals and reptiles in biology classes.

The light clicked on, bright and hot and shining over her body. They were going to see every mark Ken had left behind. They would photograph and record and turn her one beautiful memory into something ugly and depraved.

She sat up before the doctor could strap her down. "I can't do this right now. I'm sorry, Sean, I can't."

"Don't go crazy on me, Mari," Sean said, holding up his hand.

The doctor backed away from her, glancing toward the glass. She followed his gaze to see Whitney standing there watching with his dead eyes.

Mari slid off the table and went to the window. "I can't. I can't do this right now. I can't tell you why, I don't know why; I just can't make myself do it."

"I'm extremely disappointed in you, Mari," Whitney said through the intercom. "You left this facility without permission and I didn't even punish you. This examination is necessary. You've had them hundreds of times and there's no reason for you to be upset about it. Get back on the table."

"My body belongs to me. I don't want to share it with science."

"You are a test subject for the laboratory and you follow orders."

"Is that what I am?" She moved away from the window, sensing Sean closing in on her. "What are you, Sean? Are you a test subject too?"

"You don't exist outside this facility, Mari," Whitney said. "Get onto the table or I will have you punished."

"Are you going to send Brett in? Drug me? Beat me? What will happen to your precious baby if you do that, Doc? Brain damage? Maybe I'll miscarry. That could happen too, couldn't it? I've never been afraid of your punishments."

Sean was close. Too close. He was very skilled, and unlike the other guards, he'd actually trained with her and knew her weaknesses. She changed her body position just slightly, enough to be able to move fast and block whatever he might throw at her.

"We don't have to do this, Mari. You can't win. Even if by some miracle you managed to put me down, ten other guards would be up here helping me out. What's the point?"

"I put you down once already. I'll take my chances."

"I let you. I had it coming and we both know it."

"How are you going to get me down, Sean? Slug me in the stomach? Knock me out with the syringe you always carry?" She beckoned him with her finger. "Come on."

"Wait!" Whitney snapped. "Mari, don't be ridiculous. No one is going to touch you." He spoke into his radio and sent her his half smile, the one she detested. "Of course we aren't going to force you. We want your full cooperation."

For a brief moment she was elated. She'd been right. Whitney didn't want to take a chance on possibly harming an unborn child of one of the Norton twins. She studied his face as he waved Sean off. Her heart jumped. He was up to something.

"Mari," Sean hissed her name, just above a whisper. "Get on the table."

She shook her head, but her defiance was already ebbing away. Whitney was the only person who terrified her. The more he smiled or looked amiable, the more frightening he became.

She backed away from Sean. If she could just have a few days, maybe the marks Ken had left behind would fade, and they wouldn't be photographed and recorded and put in a file for Whitney to show whomever he reported to. It was too intimate, too much as if he had witnessed the insanity of their passion together.

"Mari, he's bringing down one of the other women."

Mari closed her eyes against the sudden burning. "Are you certain?"

But she didn't have to ask. Cami appeared, her dark hair tumbling down her back, her one concession to being a woman. She was a fighter all the way, and Whitney detested her almost as much as he detested Mari. Cami walked with her shoulders and back straight—a soldier who had been taken prisoner and refused to yield.

"Mari, you made it back," she said in greeting. "We were worried about you. The word was, you were shot."

"My leg. Zenith fixed me right up and then nearly killed me. Apparently when it's in our systems too long the cells begin to deteriorate and we bleed to death." Mari smiled at Whitney. "Just one more piece of information that was overlooked when we were being briefed."

"So why am I here?" Cami asked Whitney.

"I'll let Mari explain it to you," Whitney said.

Cami turned her vivid blue eyes on Mari. "It's all right, Mari." Her voice was gentle, calm. "Whatever he's making you do, he can go to hell."

"I would expect that from you, Camellia." Whitney continued to smile at them in his usual cold way, his dead eyes regarding them with interest.

"It isn't worth it, Mari," Sean repeated. "In the end . . ."

"He always gets his way," Mari finished. "He's right, Cami. He'll torture you, I'll give in, and my little rebellion will be for nothing."

Cami glanced at her sharply. "It isn't for nothing, Mari. We're a team and we provide for one another. It's what we were taught and how we work."

Mari turned away to hide her sudden desire to smile. Cami was good, feeding Whitney's ego. Of course he'd love to hear how the training he'd given them all was working. They were a team, and as a team, they looked out for one another. He would feel elated by that, as if he had brainwashed them into such loyalty they would endure anything for one another. He was so vain, had such a huge ego, it was the one weapon they could use against him. They were all careful to use it sparingly, but they pulled it out when they wanted to defuse a situation.

Whitney always used their deep affection for one another against them. He tried to point out that it was a weakness, that they should be a unit without the emotional attachment to one another. He told them that they would be stronger, and he was probably right in some ways. If they had adhered to his philosophy, he wouldn't be able to use them against each other.

"Cami is ready to take your punishment, Mari," Whitney said. There was no inflection in his voice, but when he looked at her, his eyes shone with a fanatical glee. He enjoyed these moments—the decisions they had to make. It was all very interesting to him to see how far they would go for one another.

Mari's stomach rolled. She would have to find a way to endure the humiliation. It was all part of the dehumanizing process. Treat them like lab specimens, and not only the doctors and guards, but the women, would begin to view themselves as objects.

She swallowed the bile rising in her throat. She could face hand-to-hand combat, being shot, could run for miles, and be dropped in the middle of enemy territory, and not flinch—but this, this was her own personal hell. She backed up until her legs hit the table.

"It's going to be all right," Sean said softly as he caught her arm and drew it over to the strap. "You know I'm not going to let anything happen to you."

She didn't look at him. "How many times have you been stripped naked and examined in front of the world, Sean?" she asked.

"I know you two are whispering," Whitney reprimanded. "That's not permitted."

"He was calling me an idiot," Mari said. She laid back, trying not to look as hopeless as she felt. *Where are you? Do you even care?* And that's what was so utterly stupid. He probably didn't care. They'd had sex. Great sex, but still sex. It wasn't love. He didn't know her enough to love her. She didn't even know what love was. Maybe there wasn't such a thing. He was probably hundreds of miles away. She reached out anyway, because she had to find a way to get through this.

*Of course you don't care. Why would you? It isn't like we're the kind of people in the movies. It was sex. Only sex and nothing else.* She squeezed her eyes tightly closed as they locked the leather straps over her wrists and ankles. Sean pulled off the gown and left her exposed to the bright lights, Prauder's leer, and Whitney's dead eyes.

# CHAPTER 13

Mari would not cry. She would never give Peter Whitney the satisfaction. She heard Sean's swift intake of breath and knew he was looking at the marks on the insides of her thighs and breasts, virtually all over her body. Could it be any more humiliating? Cami was still in the room. They were all staring at her. She could hear the whir of the camera and the distinct click as the doctor took photographic evidence. It was like a vile pornographic film with her as the star.

"Are those teeth marks?" Sean burst out. "The bastard attacked her."

"Sean, if you cannot simply observe in silence, call in another guard," Whitney snapped. "Men display sexual passion in all sorts of ways. This is an interesting puzzle. Now stay quiet so I can process."

Cami touched Mari's hand in an effort to comfort her. A fresh flood of tears burned behind Mari's eyelids, and she struggled to hold back, to keep her face composed when she needed to go to pieces.

"I think we can dispense with Camellia's presence. Take her back to her room." There was an edge to Whitney's voice, as if his patience had worn thin.

The doctor began talking into his recorder, a slow and thorough description of every inch of her body. It was a dispassionate, clinical narrative that only served to make the situation seem worse.

She felt breath along her neck, a whisper of a touch against her throat. *Screw them, Mari. Think about me. Think about us. I can take you far away from that room and those dirty old men. It's probably the only way they can get off, having a woman tied down and exposed to them that way. You're so beautiful they're too afraid to touch you, which is a damn good thing right now. I'd have to kill them and that means blowing the big plan. Now, if I tied you down, I wouldn't be sounding like a dead reptile, I'd be so fucking hot I'd probably disgrace myself. And I probably shouldn't have used the word blow. Hell, woman, I can't even think about you without getting the hard-on from hell.*

Ken's voice slid into her mind, a teasing whisper that made her want to laugh.

She struggled to keep the energy only on one single path, away from all the others, but even if they detected it, they would suspect she was communicating with the other women. *Can you really take me away from this room while they're doing this?*

Ken rested his head on his arm. What could he give her to hang on to while Whitney and his pathetic doctor tortured her? There would be a reckoning, but it wasn't going to be today. Their team had to be in place. Now that they'd uncovered the devil's lair, they had to come up with a plan to get the women out alive. Whitney wouldn't hesitate to kill them and destroy all evidence of his research. Ken had no doubt that the entire compound was wired to blow should they be discovered.

*Ken?* Her voice was unsteady. His anger was beating at her, pounding in her head the way it was pounding in his.

*Sorry, baby, I just focused a little too much on your situation.*

They couldn't just go in there with guns blazing—but Peter Whitney, in spite of everything that Lily had said, needed to die. He couldn't be allowed to continue with his vile experiments. He could only imagine how Mari felt. This place had been her home, that man her only steady guide, and yet she was treated the way Ekabela had treated him. Stripping him naked, dehumanizing him, stripping him of pride and decency and reducing him to less than an animal.

Mari smelled the jungle, felt heat and humidity, raindrops on her skin. The sensation was vivid, so much so that she heard the cry of a monkey and the persistent call of birds. She kept her eyes closed, knowing she was seeing a memory of Ken's inadvertently triggered by what she was feeling. The smell of blood assailed her nostrils and she tasted the coppery flavor in her mouth. A face was there, a man with the same dead eyes as Peter Whitney, and the knife in his hand was covered with blood. Ken was stretched out, tied so tightly the thin wires cut into his skin.

Mari hadn't noticed if he had scars on his wrists and ankles, but with this small glimpse into his past, she was certain he had them. Why hadn't she noticed something that important?

*Baby.* He whispered the endearment like a physical caress. *You couldn't notice with all the other scars. I'm sorry I took you there. It was an accident.*

*I know that. I wish I could touch you—comfort you.* Because beside the things he'd endured, Peter Whitney's humiliating punishments were child's play. And this *was* a form of punishment even more than a collecting of documentation for Whitney. She had left the compound without permission, and this was the one thing he knew she hated. But he wasn't crouching in front of her, dispassionately slicing a razor-sharp blade through her skin while others gathered around laughing and urging him on.

*Woman, I'm supposed to be comforting you, not sharing memories.*

*The memory steadied me. I can get through this. I hated the idea of him seeing the marks you made on my body and knowing how you put them there. I thought it would turn something special to me into something altogether different, but I'm proud of the marks you put there. Screw Whitney. He isn't going to take you away from me.*

Again she felt the brush of his fingers along her neck, as if he stroked her like a kitten. *Good for you. That man can't take away anything we did or have together. He's nothing, Mari, nothing at all. I'm with you. Right here. He can't separate us now, no matter how much he wants to. I took you to the jungle, and I can take you somewhere much better. But, sweetheart, I've got to be able to picture you with clothes on. You're killing me here.*

Again she wanted to laugh and had to keep her expression exactly the same. It took discipline, but she managed. She couldn't believe that he would make her want to smile when she was exposed and vulnerable and Whitney and his doctor were dissecting her like a bug—well, maybe not dissecting her. Ken had been dissected, cut into little pieces, stripped of his dignity and then the skin on his back. She couldn't imagine the pain or the rage or the utter hopelessness. That was the worst to her—the despair one felt when totally helpless.

Whitney was a madman. It had taken her years to admit it fully—for all of them to admit it—because they were totally dependent on him for everything. They had no real contact with the outside world and nowhere to go to escape the endless demands and experiments. With the glimpse into Ken's past, she felt more connected to him, and the connection felt intimate. She clung to his mind, wanting him to keep her centered.

*Sex is a big thing to you.* She was glad it was—after all, they'd had great sex and she hoped to have even more—but on the other hand, she wanted to matter to him on more than that level.

*Yeah, sex is a big deal as long as you're my partner. I haven't exactly had a lot of any other lately. I didn't think I could.*

There was such raw honesty in his voice, she felt tears burning again and had to struggle not to betray herself. He didn't have to tell her that, but she could understand. He'd been so damaged, the slices everywhere, and when he was fully erect, it had to hurt. *Is it painful?*

There was a small silence and she found herself holding her breath. She knew he didn't want to answer, that he was weighing his words.

Ken sighed and stared up at the sky. He had known there would come a time he would have to explain it all to her—admit that it wasn't just his face revealing the monster, that Ekabela had brought that monster into every aspect of his life.

He damn well wasn't going to lie to her—not with her stretched out on a table and some son of a bitch photographing the strawberries he'd put on her inner thighs.

*You don't have to tell me.*

*It isn't that. I don't want you running away from me.*

There was the impression of laughter. *I'm tied up at the moment.*

He sent her the impression of a groan. *Don't say tied up. You know what happens to me the minute you say that. The things I could do to you—the way I could make you feel.*

The laughter in his mind was like a caress, stroking through his body until he felt it everywhere—until he felt it in his soul. Nothing—no one—ever choked him up, but he found himself doing just that. *Yes, there's pain, but in a good way. There isn't a lot of sensation as a rule, and when I'm full and ready, the skin stretches so tight pulling that it takes a lot to stimulate me. I'm rough and I have to be. The thing is, Mari . . .* He felt like a sick pervert. The last person she needed around her was him.

*Just tell me. I'm not exactly a virgin here, Ken.*

His hand knotted into a hard fist and he thumped the ground beside him. *Yes, you are. You don't know the first thing about making love. Someone should be making love to you. Gentle, tender, slow, and easy. A man should treasure every moment with you, savor it and make certain you're screaming with pleasure.* He wanted those things for her, desperately wanted them for her, and yet he would never be that man.

The impression of laughter came again. *Like you did.*

Ken frowned. She wasn't getting it. *Not exactly like I did. I was too rough, Mari. If you're with me, I would always be rough. I'd want things from you; I'd want you to learn to have the kind of sex I need, and that's not the best thing for you.*

He felt like an idiot trying out each word in his mind before he sent it to her. What the hell could he say? He wanted to make her his sex slave? He did. Ever since he'd touched her skin, he'd wanted to do everything there was to her, bind her to him so no one else would ever do for her. He wouldn't mind tying her down and having her at his mercy. He could love her for hours.

He shoved his head into the palm of his hand. She was tied

to a table, and he was thinking of how he could bring her such pleasure she'd drown in it. Maybe he was as sick as Whitney— or Ekabela.

*Don't be ridiculous. No one is as sick as either of them. And I'd fantasize about what you'd do to me if you had me tied down—or better yet let you tell me yourself—but I'd get all hot and Whitney would know you're here with me. So no sex on the table and no thinking about tying me up. You can do that another time.*

Again her soft laughter swept through him. Tears burned in his eyes and in the back of his throat. Damn her. She was killing him with her acceptance of him. He couldn't accept himself—how could she? He was going to fall in love with her. It was a long, hard fall and scary as hell. It didn't make sense and he didn't want it to happen. What the hell was she going to be getting out of the bargain?

*Mari? It wasn't just sex.*

Her heart accelerated. She knew Whitney would be puzzled over that spike, but Ken made her feel alive again in a way she hadn't in a long time. He gave her hope—and she needed hope right then.

*If it wasn't just sex, what was it? Because I don't know what to think. None of the men paired with any of the women appear to feel emotional about them, other than possessive. They could care less whether or not we derive any pleasure from them touching us. What happened between us seemed more than something Whitney did, or was I reading more into it than there was?*

She waited for his answer, her mouth suddenly dry. She barely felt the doctor's probing fingers as he poked at her. It seemed he spent more time examining the bruises and red marks on her skin than the gun wound or wrist break, but Ken's answer was more important than her modesty. She held her breath—waiting.

*You know damn well it was much more. I'm not hiding anything from you, as much as I want to. Screw Whitney. He doesn't have anything to do with us anymore.* Ken rubbed his hand over his face and sighed again. *Maybe he did at first. Maybe his manipulation allowed you to accept me sexually when you might have been afraid of me.*

Mari turned it over in her mind. Was that the truth? She'd wanted him—yes—but there was so much more to her feelings than that. The decision had definitely been hers and it hadn't been all about sex. So what was it that drew her emotionally to him? How had they connected so fast and so strong? *I don't think so, Ken. I really don't. You're right. Whatever is between us isn't about Whitney.*

He ached to hold her in his arms. *I'm not a good man—I'm never going to be. You have to know that going into this. I wouldn't give you up once you belonged to me.*

*What does that mean, Ken? You don't know if you would be happy with me. Neither of us has any idea what the future would be like. I can't conceive of being out of this place. The idea is frightening. I wouldn't know the first thing about living in the real world. How can you possibly know what you would or wouldn't do if we were together.*

*Because you represent hope, Mari. I gave up my life a long time ago and everything that entailed, including sex. You handed it all back to me and I'm just not man enough to walk away from temptation.*

Hope. Mari liked the word. And she liked the idea of being someone's hope. Maybe that's what their strange relationship was all about. Mari had never had hope—not even when she went out with her team to talk to the senator. Peter Whitney seemed so invincible. No one could ever defeat him, especially not Senator Freeman. He'd never bested Whitney in an argument. But Ken had somehow made her feel different. He'd given her a taste of freedom.

Ken swore in her ear. *I'd never give you freedom. Mari, think about this, think about what I am. I'd be possessive and jealous and want you in my sight every minute of every day. I'd be terrified of losing you. And I'd want to touch you, eat you alive, kiss you endlessly, and take you whenever I wanted, which, by the way, would be all the time.*

*I told you not to talk that way. You'll get me hot.* She tried not to flinch as the doctor touched her breast, supposedly to get a better angle with the camera, but his fingers lingered.

Ken froze, anger bursting through him like a volcano spilling lava. He could make it inside past all the security. He could make it inside and slit the doctor's throat and then go after Whitney. He was a GhostWalker and few could detect them, let alone stop them.

*No. Calm down. Seriously, Ken, it's no big deal.* Mari was lying. She hated this humiliation, but she tried to breathe through it and concentrate solely on him. As long as she was talking to him, she wasn't thinking about what they were doing to her. And if she didn't think about it, neither would he. *Keep talking to me. I don't want you cutting throats. You're so violent.*

He was a violent man. Didn't she understand that? He almost groaned in frustration. He couldn't change what or who he was—not even for her. He barely hung on to his sanity at times. His ugly childhood had shaped him, and his father had given him a dark legacy of jealousy coupled with a strong sex drive. Ekabela had added layers to the darkness and rage, so that it grew until it threatened to consume him. He had hidden it well, even from Jack, but it was there, crouching like a beast, waiting to destroy him and anyone who dared to love him.

And how could she really love him? He could tie her to him with sex, he knew he could, but how could she look at his face every day of her life and love him? How could she know what he was and still feel anything but fear and contempt for him?

*Even my children would run from me, Mari, and I couldn't blame them.* Was he actually feeling sorry for himself? Was he that pitiful when she was stretched out on an exam table? Damn him to hell for his selfishness. He wanted her with her laughter and her acceptance. He wanted her to love him in spite of the scars on his soul that showed so clearly on his body.

*Now you're just being silly. A child would love you, Ken. You only think you don't show tenderness, but I feel it every time I touch your mind. You've shown me more respect and given me so much more than I ever had, and you can't know how much that means. If I don't get out, I'll never regret being with you. Whitney can take a lot of things away from me, but he can't take what you gave me.*

Okay. He was going to hell. That's all there was to it. Because he wasn't going to be noble and give her up. No way. How could the universe hand him someone so perfect and then expect him to give her back? She had enough tolerance and compassion, and enough courage, for both of them.

She knew how to love. How had she learned to love when it was never given to her? Briefly, he'd had his mother and always he'd had Jack, but Mari's twin had been taken from her and Mari had been raised without her sister in cold, stark, laboratory conditions. She humbled him with her ability to give such unconditional acceptance.

He felt her mind jerk away from his, suddenly aware of the doctor probing her most intimate parts. He could feel the disgust and humiliation rising, the utter distaste as the man probed deeper and moved his hand inside of her. Abruptly she tried to cut Ken off, doing her best to shield him from what was happening to her. Bile rose in his throat. The one person he should be able to protect—and he had to lie still covered in leaves and twigs, and let them torture her. He gave her the only thing he could, although it cost him a great deal of what was left of his pride.

*I'm already halfway in love with you, Mari. Maybe more way more than halfway, and it's damned hard to admit. I want to do right by you, not take you out of the sun and bring you down to an entirely new level, but I'm not man enough to get you out of there and then just walk away. I'm damn well going to take you with me.*

She was weeping inside. *Weeping.* He could feel it like a knife going through his heart. He rested his head on his arm. He was a few feet from a guard, and the man hadn't moved in the last half hour. He was sitting on a rock reading a book. He hadn't looked up or around him and had no idea that Ken lay within striking distance and that right now, every emotion was slowly being driven out of Ken so he would feeling nothing at all when he went after his prey.

*I want to go with you. I'm just being a baby, so don't get upset. I can feel you pulling away from me. Women are emotional at times, that's all.*

*That's not fucking all, Mari. That bastard has his hand inside of you and he isn't going to live out the day. Who the hell does Whitney think he is, subjecting you to this kind of crap? And what kind of man is your friend Sean to allow it to go on?*

*Sean used to always stand with us. He helped me get out to see the senator, but now he seems different. I don't know how he is, or why, but he's doing and saying things that aren't him.*

*Whitney somehow got to him. Don't trust him, Mari.*

*I don't. Are you okay now?*

*Don't fucking ask me if I'm okay when that bastard is touching you. I should be asking you, but I don't have to—I know you're not.*

*He's touching me in a completely impersonal, medical way.* Mari tried to soothe him by lying, biting down on her lip, hoping the doctor would hurry his examination. Prauder was a pervert. He always took great delight in touching the women as intimately as possible, of photographing them in the worst positions, knowing there was nothing they could do about it. They all tried to pretend it was impersonal, because it was the only way they could live through it.

*Ken, you have to be close to the laboratory for us to be able to communicate and that means you're near guards. You can't get upset and blow this. I'm counting on you.*

Ken took a breath and willed a higher power to give him strength and control to hold out. If she could stand it—then so could he. There was sweat on his brow, and he allowed it to trickle down his face rather than move. Ants crawled over him. He stayed still and just let the air move in and out of his lungs. Night was falling, and always—*always*—the night belonged to the GhostWalkers.

*Ken?*

*I'm here with you, baby. I had a brief meltdown but I'm back on track. Does the doctor live in the compound?*

*Everyone here does. Most of the soldiers live in the outer barracks. Whitney's men have their own section. It's closest to the small cottages. Whitney's staff live in those houses, separate from the rest of us.*

*And where are you, Mari?*

*We used to have our own barracks, but with the new program we've been moved to the center of the laboratory underground, where he has bars on the doors. We're always on lockdown and they try to keep us apart.*

*Do all of the women have telepathy?*

*I'm strong and so is Cami. We can build and hold a bridge*

*between all the women, so we plan when we're locked in our rooms.*

*How many have to get out?*

*There are five of us, but we have a plan. We can get rid of the bars on the doors, we think. We haven't dared to test yet, but if we can, we'll go out through the south-facing doors. It's easier to move through the laboratory; there's a little less security because the cameras are angled wrong. Once we make it to the surface we can head for the electric fence that's about two miles from us. The woods are dense and there's water. They have dogs, but a couple of the women can control them. Don't do anything until we're ready. I won't leave anyone behind.*

*Well you make certain they're ready to go, because when I come to get you, you'll be coming out with me one way or another.*

Mari opened her eyes and stared up at the bright light, trying not to smile again. He had that edgy command in his voice, the one that brooked no argument, the one that said he was the boss and she'd better damn well fall in line. He made her heart beat faster and her blood rush through her veins. Her temperature went up a couple of degrees every time he pulled the caveman routine. She liked him worried and edgy and ready to tear down the laboratory to get to her—and that told how far gone she was.

"Very good, Mari," Dr. Prauder said. "We're finished." He signaled Sean, and the guard came forward and removed the straps from her arms and legs and handed her the gown.

She refused to look at him. *They're taking me back to my room. Thank you, Ken. I don't know what I would have done without you to distract me.*

Ken wiped the sweat from his face. She would have endured. She knew it and he knew it—because when you were in the hands of a madman, you resisted as little as possible and waited for that one moment to strike or run. Endurance was all you had.

*What is the doctor's name and what does he look like?* Even as he lay under cover of bushes and grass, he'd seen half a dozen men in lab coats walking in and out of the facility.

*Prauder. He's Whitney's chief doctor. The man's a worm. I'm not entirely certain he's human. He acts more like a robot.* Mari pulled her gown around her and went back toward the alcove.

"What are you doing?" Sean asked.

"Getting dressed. I don't feel like parading through the halls with this hospital gown on. I need my clothes."

Sean glanced at Whitney and then shook his head. "We need to sweep them for tracking devices."

She wanted Ken's shirt. It was stupid, but she wanted it. She didn't even glance at the alcove or at Sean. "I'm not walking down the hall in this stupid getup."

*I want a description of Prauder.* Ken's voice was insistent.

Mari was proud of herself for using telepathic communication without Whitney or Sean realizing it, both right there where they should have been able to detect it. But now that she was sitting up, facing them, she was afraid she might make a mistake. She took a breath and let it out. *He's short and skinny, balding with a small goatee.* She kept it short and succinct.

Ken could feel her nervousness and her reluctance to continue their conversation. *All right, baby, do whatever you have to do and contact me when you're alone again.*

Mari didn't reply, but she was grateful that he let her know he was going to be within her mind's reach. She snapped her fingers. "At least get me another gown, Sean. I'm not walking in front of you half-naked."

Sean muttered something under his breath, but jerked another gown from a shelf under the table and tossed it to her.

Mari caught it and shrugged into it, wrapping it around her back. She never once glanced up at Whitney, but she could feel him there, watching every move she made. She made herself walk out of the room with her shoulders straight and her chin up. Whitney hadn't broken her, thanks to Ken, not even when she'd been at her most vulnerable. She resisted throwing Whitney a triumphant smirk, because he'd retaliate with something else and she didn't have the time to devote to their usual battle. Let him put her lack of resistance down to being shot.

She would have given anything to be able to read his mind. Did he think being a prisoner had been a terrible experience? Did he think Ken had forced himself on her? The evidence on her body certainly might substantiate that theory. Whitney knew Ken was paired with her—that she would be sexually attracted to him—but that didn't mean she necessarily had given in to the temptation.

She knew Whitney. The question would eat away at him. If he even had any doubt at all, he wouldn't be able to let go of it until he knew the answer. It was one of his greatest weaknesses and she often used it against him. He needed answers. If she could pose a simple question, it would drive him insane until he figured out the answer. And he would want to know—no, *need* to know—if Ken had forced himself on her.

Sean paced along behind her and she could feel his temper smoldering. He had seen every mark on her body. She kept walking, back ramrod straight, until she reached her own room. It was small, a cell really, with a heavy steel door.

"Did he hurt you?" Sean glanced at the camera in the hallway and turned, so that when he spoke, it was impossible to see his mouth move.

"I'm not going to discuss it with you, Sean. You weren't concerned before; there's no need to be now," she said, deliberately stiff, standing in the doorway. She hoped Whitney was listening or watching. If he'd primed Sean to get information, she wasn't giving anything away.

"I know you're angry with me . . ."

"You think? You've been an ass. What's wrong with you anyway?"

A buzzer sounded and Sean grimaced. "We'll have to talk about this later. You need to get in your room. It's lockdown."

She stood there, hating that he had turned on them all. He'd been one of them, trained with them, been a good friend. "What did Whitney do to you? What's he doing to the other men? It's him, isn't it? He's still experimenting and using you all as guinea pigs too."

"Move back, Mari," Sean insisted, raising his gun slightly, the smallest of warnings, but it was there. He kept a safe distance from her, watching her with wary eyes that would never miss so much as a twitch of her body.

Marigold took a step back, deliberately reluctant, never taking her gaze from Sean. He had always been one of the best at everything. There were no mistakes with Sean, none of the small breaches that would allow the possibility of exploiting weakness. Sean never let down his guard, and he was enhanced, every bit as strong and well trained as she was. More important, he was psychically enhanced. She'd tested his mind repeatedly and his shields were strong—impossible to penetrate. Going up against Sean was a losing proposition, but she didn't mind taunting him. Again she stopped, just out of the doorway, daring him to take action.

She was so angry with him for giving in, for allowing Whitney to use him when he saw what it did to the others—and she was certain she was right. Whitney had to be raising the testosterone levels in the men, doing something to make them more aggressive.

Sean shook his head. "You always have to push it, don't you?"

"Would you want to live like a prisoner your entire life?" She waved her hand to encompass the entire compound, watching the way his gaze jumped to the graceful movement. "I'll bet no one tells you when to go to bed at night, or what books you can read. There's not a camera in your room, is there, Sean?"

He stepped closer. "Get in your room. Lockdown's in three minutes." Even as he moved, he inhaled deeply.

Her heart jumped. She saw the flare of heat in his eyes. Adrenaline surged and for a moment she couldn't breathe. "You let them pair us." It was an accusation, her voice strangled, a shimmering fission of fear slidding down her spine. Why hadn't she suspected? It hadn't occurred to her that Sean would ever volunteer for the breeding program—not when he knew all the women objected strenuously and were forced to cooperate.

"You're the best choice, Mari," he said, tone practical even when his eyes moved over her possessively. "You're a strong psychic and so am I. Our children would be extraordinary." He lowered his voice and turned away from the camera so there was no possibility of lipreading. "I've always been attracted to you, ever since I first saw you, and you aren't an anchor and I am. I doubt any of the other men could handle your abilities. I don't think Whitney has a clue what you can or can't do."

Her mouth went dry. She forced her suddenly damp palm to remain still when she wanted to rub it up and down her thigh in agitation. Sean saw too much. He'd always been the guard she'd most feared. They had trained in hand-to-hand, and he could always, *always*, best her. Few of the guards could, even though she was so much smaller.

"And you don't mind Whitney experimenting on your child?" she challenged.

He studied her face for a long time before answering, his gaze once again shifting toward the camera. "Our child will be born to greatness." He used his chin to indicate the room. "Get inside now."

"I won't accept you, Sean," she warned. "I'm not going to give him another child to torture."

"I know that. I knew it when I made the decision. But I'm not standing by and watching some other man father your child. You'll accept me one way or another."

She stepped back inside the small cell that had been her home for these last few months. "I had so much respect for you, Sean. You were one of the few I did respect, but you're willing to become a monster in order to please the puppet master." She shook her head, sorrow shooting through her. "What about Brett?"

A flash of disgust crossed his face. He stepped forward, one hand sliding down her face, touching the bruises there. "He didn't get the job done, did he?"

Her stomach churned, a violent protest, but she stood her ground. "So you're taking his place? You think you can force me to conceive so Whitney can have another toy to play with?" She leaned forward, lowering her voice. "What happened, Sean? I thought you were one of us."

She knew the moment her breath warmed his skin that she'd made a terrible mistake. Whitney and his experiments with pheromones, along with pushing up the testosterone levels in the males, had created a dangerous, very explosive situation. He wanted aggressive soldiers and if he succeeded, he wanted children from those soldiers.

Sean reacted instantly to her scent, to the close proximity of her body. He wrapped his fingers around the nape of her neck and dragged her the scant inches separating them, his mouth coming down hard on hers. The cold metal of the rifle dug into her flesh as his fingertips dug into her skin.

She twisted her head out of the way, hands catching the rifle and jerking as her knee came up between his legs hard. Sean yanked her backward, off balance, spinning to the side to avoid her knee, whirling her around as he did so, his arm sliding beneath her chin in a choke hold.

Mari kept going, using her weight and momentum to put pressure on his arm, bending it away from her neck to try to get leverage against him. He had been trained in the same school as she had, and he was bigger and stronger. He knew exactly what her reaction would be and he was prepared for it. He wrapped his arm tighter and exerted pressure, succeeding in getting her in a headlock. Mari turned her head and bit him hard in the ribs, at the same time driving her thumb into the pressure point at the back of his knee. His leg buckled and he swore, folding in half quickly to keep from going down, dragging her with him, refusing to let go.

They ended up sprawled on the floor, Mari breathing hard, trying to ignore the pain shooting through her at the awkward position.

"Stop it, Mari," he hissed. "I'm not turning into another Brett." He leaned his weight on her, pinning her down.

She gathered her strength and was preparing to push him off of her, when the hall filled to a choking point with dark malevolence. The floor beneath them rippled and the walls around them undulated. Mari knew that presence and went very still beneath Sean, her heart pounding so hard she was afraid it might shatter. She knew that scent. That aura. The scent of his cunning malevolence. There was only one man that could make her stomach churn with such bile. Brett was coming.

"Sean." She whispered the name in despair. Sean had been a good friend and now he had betrayed her. Brett was coming, and if he touched her, she would never be able to stop from silently screaming, from spilling out waves of energy at the revulsion she felt at his touch, and Ken would know, and he would come, and the escape she had so carefully planned with the other women would be impossible.

Sean moved fast, faster than she imagined possible, leaping to his feet, yanking her up, and thrusting her into her cell with one hand, while he slammed his palm against the lock with the other. The heavy metal door slid closed with a terrible clang, leaving her in shock, helpless to do anything but watch as the two men circled each other.

# CHAPTER 14

Ken moved back into deeper shadow, his gaze steady on the guard. The man was certainly engrossed in his book, and that told Ken a lot about the situation at the compound. Working at a secret laboratory was slow, tedious work. No one really considered that they come under attack or that anyone might try to break in. Most of the compound was underground, so any lost or stray hunter would find the fence, a small airstrip, and a few outbuildings. No one had come near the place for years, and Whitney had some pretty sophisticated warning systems. Apparently, the guards had been too long without incident. They had grown lazy and bored. He watched as the guard put his book down, but not once did he do more than give a cursory look around before walking along the fence line.

Ken waited until he was gone before consulting with his brother. "I'm not going to be able to hold off much longer before going in after Mari, Jack. We have to get this done and fast."

"You know we need better intel," Jack said. "I've asked for satellite views of the entire compound as well as infrared camera images to time the movement of the men. We have to have exact schematics of the entire compound—the layout, the height of the fence, and Lily will need to find someone who put the underground buildings together, so we know what we're facing before we expose the team to danger. This base is very deceptive."

"It's layers. The top layer is what the outside world sees."

"Yes, a guarded facility with a few outbuildings and a landing strip. You've got to get Mari to tell you what's belowground."

"I already gave you what she told me. Four levels, Jack. It's made of concrete, so we know there are going to be a few hollow places like we've found in the military bases. It isn't as impregnable as Whitney would like."

"Look, Ken, we can't just storm in guns blazing. Clearly there are civilians working here, and Whitney has regular military soldiers mixed with his own personal army. I'd like to get the women and get out without anyone spotting us. The last thing we need to do is hit or get hit by a friendly."

"As far as I'm concerned, anyone working at this place is fair game."

"They're soldiers obeying orders. They don't have a clue Whitney is a madman. My guess is most of them have never seen him, talked to him, or even know he's here. Their assignment is top secret, the location is, and they do their rotation and get the hell out when the opportunity presents itself."

"You know, Jack, I really don't give a damn. You know as well as I do that when you've spent time somewhere, you know what's going on—and if you don't, you hear the rumors and you guess. That guard didn't give a damn if innocent women were being used for experimentation. And where the hell is the loyalty of the team Mari and the others trained with?"

Ken's voice was turning to ice. His gray eyes were glacier cold. Jack chose his words carefully. "I agree these are all questions we need to answer, Ken, but not here. Our primary mission is a rescue. That's why we're here."

"Someone has to take out Whitney. You know it's got to be done, Jack."

"Yeah, I know. I don't want to be the one explaining it to Lily, though." Jack took a slow swig of water and let it trickle down his throat, giving his brother a little more time. Jack had always been the one pushing for a quick answer, and the role reversal wasn't comfortable. "We have a lot of work to do before we bring in the team. They're standing by, Ken, so if we want to pull her out, we have to get to work. It'll be completely dark in another half hour or so."

"I can feel her. She's very upset. I've tried to reach out to her mind, but she isn't answering me. Whatever is happening, she doesn't want me to know about it." Ken's voice was strained. "And if she doesn't want me to know about it, something bad is going on."

Jack automatically touched his mind, as he'd been doing since they were toddlers, just as Ken knew he would. Ken was prepared and kept his shields high. It wasn't easy keeping Jack at bay; they'd been shadows in each other's mind for as long as either could remember, but both had worked hard to build shields once they became aware others had psychic power as well—and the practice paid off.

Jack didn't need to know just how close to cracking he was. In that moment, Ken didn't care about the other women, or even any innocents working as techs, researchers, or guards. If Mari didn't let him know she was all right very soon, he was going in after her, and God help anyone who got in his way. He felt murderous, not cold and unemotional. Discipline was going out the window fast.

"Ken, you think I don't know how you're feeling with her locked up with madmen?" Jack crawled into a better position, his gaze sweeping the route the guard had taken.

"Whitney went after Briony because she was pregnant; he wasn't stripping her naked and laying her out on an exam table for some perverted doctor to photograph. Damn it, Jack, I could feel him touching Mari. He wasn't acting like any doctor I've ever met. And Whitney has men in there willing to rape a woman if she isn't cooperative." The knots in his belly tightened into hard lumps that threatened to climb higher and choke him.

"You have to step back, bro," Jack said, keeping his voice steady. "We'll get the intel and get the women out as soon as possible." Ken didn't answer, and Jack sighed and glanced over at him. "You know I'll go in with you and pull her out if anything goes wrong. Tell her that, give her something to hang on to."

"If I told her that, she'd freak on me. She's willing to sac-rifice herself for the other women. She considers them family and she's not going to willing come without them."

"Then we make it work," Jack said. "I wouldn't leave you behind. We can't ask her to do something we wouldn't be will-ing to do ourselves. She wouldn't be able to live with herself."

Ken bit back a retort. He hated it, but he knew Jack was right. He wanted to go in and haul Mari out over his shoulder and lock her somewhere safe, but he couldn't do that to her—at least not right now. She wouldn't be able to live with herself if something happened to the other women, so that meant get-ting them all out before he went off the deep end and took her out without her consent—which would make him nearly as bad as everyone else who had taken her life away from her. He had to give her time and the opportunity to get those she con-sidered family safely away.

Mari was a woman who wanted control of her life—deserved control of her life. He was a man whose entire being demanded that he be the one in utter and complete control of those around him. He knew it appeared to people that Jack seemed the dominant twin, always in the lead, but Ken had re-alized early on that Jack needed to feel in control, in much the same way Mari did, and he had stepped back, watching over his brother carefully, always protecting him, providing the en-vironment Jack needed.

Ken tried to remember when he'd first made the decision to be Jack's front man in social situations—it had to be right after their father had been killed. He had cultivated a smooth smile and quick intervention. Jack, like Ken, was a dead-on accurate shot. It was a gift both had been born with. They worked well as a team, each looking out for the other, Ken al-lowing Jack whatever he needed to be able to survive. But to do the same for Mari was impossible. He needed her to be safe. *He* needed that.

"We came in using the river to avoid detection, but our team will need to use high altitude, low opening parachutists," Ken said. "You know they aren't going to look up unless they hear something, and they won't hear a thing if our boys come in using HALO. Our team is trained, and I'd rather use them then people we're not as familiar working with. We can pull a few strings and cancel a commercial flight at the last moment. There's enough regular air traffic over the area that no one's going to perceive a threat if we take the commercial flight path and altitude. Whoever is doing the monitoring will never suspect a thing."

Jack nodded. "Definitely the best plan. The guards are not alert. Nothing's shaken them up in the last couple of years."

"Ryland's men can back us up, but call in Logan and tell him we want our unit for this one."

Jack nodded in agreement. "That's a given, Ken, and already done. The men know it's personal to you, and they're already assembled and waiting for the intel. They're not going to let you down."

Ken knew Jack was right, but it didn't unravel the knots in his belly. "I'm checking the doctor's house. He just went in." He indicated the small bluff overlooking the cottages. "I'll work my way down to that point and go in from there. You cover me."

"Checking the doctor's house for what?" Jack asked. "You can't just go in there and blow this for us."

"He took pictures of her."

"That's his job. He had to have left them in the laboratory."

"I'm making certain. And I'm going to find out where in the laboratory he left them."

"Damn it, Ken. You can't take a chance on tipping anyone off to the fact that we're here. Just stay put."

"He's got pictures and he knows where the other pictures are. He touched her, Jack—when she was helpless and he was supposed to be examining her impersonally—he touched her."

Mari had toned her emotions down, had even pulled away from him, but not before he'd caught the distaste, the feeling of utter helplessness, the mixture of sorrow, despair, and impotent rage that he knew intimately. He couldn't get Mari out of there and away to somewhere safe in that moment, but he sure as hell could pay the doctor a little visit. He might never be able to give Mari all the things she deserved—like a stable, easygoing partner—but he could hand the pictures—and her dignity—back to her.

Jack rubbed his mouth to keep from protesting. Nothing was going to stop Ken and Jack couldn't blame him. If it was

Briony, the man would already be dead. For the first time in his life, Jack feared for his brother's sanity. Mari was an unknown, but she was his wife's twin sister and his brother's chosen woman and that made her both important and a threat to his family's well-being.

Ken was, and always had been, a dangerous man. He was, by turns, controlled and deliberate, cold and efficient, and always capable of swift and brutal violence if the situation called for it. Where Jack was easy for those around him to read, Ken appeared easygoing and affable. The men in their unit found him much more approachable. Jack had always known on some level that Ken had forced himself to be the "front" man in an effort to protect his twin. He hadn't realized, until now, how foreign that behavior had been to Ken's nature.

Ken had the same hidden demons—the same nightmares and fears—and he had an even stronger dose of their father's legacy—the dark jealousies and need for swift and violent retribution. Ken had worn a mask all those years, hiding—even from his twin—the rage seething just below the surface. Between the trauma of his recent capture and torture and meeting Mari, Ken's way of life had been turned upside down. The smooth, easygoing façade was gone.

Jack sighed and glanced at his watch. "Don't get caught. I'd hate to have to kill anyone before we even get started."

Ken reached out to tap his brother's knuckles with his own in their familiar silent ritual. He scooted back into the foliage, careful to keep the thin branches from swaying as he passed through. Moving at a snail's pace, Ken inched his way down the hillside until he was within a few yards of the cottage he was fairly certain was the doctor's. The small house was set just a little apart from the other houses, and security was tighter. The guards walked the perimeter every ten minutes, two of them, switching their routine continually. The doctor had something to hide.

Ken slipped into the scraggly hedges surrounding the small community of houses just as a guard came around the side of the house and stopped, the heels of his boots within a foot of Ken's elbow. Ken's breath caught in his lungs—he stayed absolutely still, allowing ants and beetles to crawl over him. A lizard tickled his arm as it raced up it in little starts and stops, until it perched on his shoulder, pumping up and down, scenting the air.

The guard took three steps forward and halted again, turning fast as if he was trying to spot something—or someone. Ken's brows drew together. Had he made a sound? The whisper of clothes along the ground? He took care that his skin reflected the foliage around him. His specially designed clothes reflected the colors of his surroundings.

What had tipped off the guard? Ken slid his hand inch by inch along his jacket until he reached the knife strapped to the front. His fingers wrapped around the hilt, but he left it in the scabbard. He could draw and throw almost before others could squeeze a trigger. The move had been practiced hundreds of hours over the last few years, and he was every bit as accurate at throwing as he was with a rifle.

*I've got him.*

Jack's voice was without emotion, a statement of fact. If the guard twitched wrong, he was a dead man, and then all hell would break loose fast.

*I'll take him out and hide the body.* Ken was beginning to sweat. He could hear the man breathing, smell his fear, see the nerves as he searched the hillsides carefully. *He's got to be enhanced, Jack. He's using either vision or hearing, but he hasn't locked on to you.* They couldn't afford for the guard to raise the alarm. Something was making him nervous, but Ken couldn't figure it out. There was no telltale tree cancer where a part of Jack's weapon might be showing along the side of the tree trunk. No shiny objects. Jack had the same ability to camouflage his skin, the same reflective clothing. He disappeared into his surroundings until he was invisible. Ken knew exactly where Jack was, yet he couldn't spot him, and if he couldn't with his eagle sight, he was damned certain the guard couldn't either.

*He's psychic. He's not feeling our energy when we're talking, but he's catching something else,* he warned his brother. *Don't move a muscle.*

They both watched as the guard quartered the area with a slow, careful search. He didn't reach for his field glasses, and that told both of them he had enhanced sight. Ken tried to draw into himself, careful to keep his breath smooth and even and silent. All the while he kept his attention on the guard, not daring to risk another look at his brother. If the guard spotted Jack, Ken would have to kill him swiftly and in utter silence, before the man had a chance to either raise the alarm or turn a weapon on Jack.

Without warning Mari's fear filled his mind. It poured into him as if he were wide open with no careful shields built to protect him. His body shook with the overload. Air left his lungs in a rush, his mouth went dry, and his heart seemed to stop, then began to pound so loud he was afraid the guard would overhear. Sweat broke out on his brow—none of it was good when he was feet from an enhanced soldier.

He drew air into his lungs, pushed past Mari's fear, and stayed focused on his enemy. He was so close to the man, he knew he could get to his feet and wrap his arm around the soldier and plunge the knife in a kill zone, all in a few seconds, but the man would still have time to react. Physical enhancement made them abnormally strong, and GhostWalkers were taught to fight to their last breath. The guard might just be tough enough to have time to raise an alarm. Desperation was beginning to settle in. Ken forced his body under control and remained waiting, but all the while a growing terror for Mari's safety spread.

*She'll be all right. You've got to trust her.*

Jack's calm voice helped to keep Ken from rising up and taking a chance on disposing of the guard just so he could get to Mari as fast as possible. He waited, willing the man to move on. If he used mind control to get the man off of him, the outpouring of energy might very will tip off every other psychic in the compound. He breathed deep and felt for her. Mari. Her fear was for someone else. He could live with that.

The guard relaxed after another long, slow look around, and ambled off around the corner of the small house. Ken waited another three minutes to make certain the man wasn't doubling back.

*You're clear,* Jack said.

Ken crawled forward, sliding through the neat flower garden, a rather strange and prissy bed of color out in the middle of nowhere. The windows of the house were painted black, and where there was a small bit of streaking, he could see heavy drapes blocking any view of the interior.

*The doctor doesn't want anyone prying into his business. Why else would his windows be all blacked out?*

*He's probably paranoid. Wouldn't you be, living here with Whitney for a boss?*

Ken didn't answer. The window appeared to be clear of an alarm, but he wasn't buying it. The doctor had something to hide, and he was going to find out what. He listened for the low hum of an electronic alarm. His fingers swept the sill, searching for hidden trip wires. Oh, yeah, the place was locked down tight.

Ken placed his hand just over the glass. It was much more difficult detecting currents of energy with his body so scarred, particularly his hands. Sometimes he failed to feel things the way he should. He waited, counting the seconds, concentrating, willing himself to sense the current if it was there. If he didn't find one, he would put it down to the lack of ability in his fingertips and proceed on the premise that one was there, but if he could just spot the current running through the foil wire in the glass, things would go a lot faster.

Ken cursed the scars that left him with so little feeling. He couldn't detect the faint current, but when he listened, he was fairly certain that the doctor had an outside perimeter alarm. But the doc wouldn't just rely on that. He'd have something more sophisticated inside. A sensor system would detect infrared energy. The sensor was sensitive to the temperature of the human body. In front of each door was a harmless-looking floor mat, one Ken was certain had a pressure trigger.

*The doc is protecting something. I'm going to look for the control box. He has to have one hidden around here somewhere.*

*Maybe this isn't such a good idea,* Jack said uneasily. *You go in there and you're probably going to kill the bastard, and how do we hide that?*

Of course he was going to kill the doctor. The man had touched Mari. He had humiliated and embarrassed her and he'd enjoyed it. Maybe Ken shouldn't have shared her thoughts, but it was too late, the information had been exchanged and *he'd let it happen.* He hated himself for that. She deserved so much better. He should have gone in, guns blazing, and pulled her out, but he hadn't. He'd stood by and let them torment her. What the hell kind of man was he?

*Ken. Are you even listening to me? We've got a team coming in. We're going to pull the women out of there.*

*What the hell would you do if it was Briony?* Ken demanded. There was a small silence. *You know what I'd do.*

*Then shut the hell up and keep them off my back.*

Ken found the control box neatly tucked away under the eaves up near the attic. He'd spotted a small cable hidden along a pipe and followed it up until he spotted the box. The controls had to be set from someone leaning out the attic window or from the roof itself. The doctor thought he was clever, but unless the roof was wired as well, it simply made things easier.

*I'm going up.*

*You're clear now, but you have two guards circling around toward your position.*

Ken went up the side of the house as silently as possible, sliding onto the roof as one of the guards strode into view. The second guard joined him, and they spoke briefly before they each went their separate ways. Ken remained still as the footsteps faded.

*You're clear.*

The control box was hooked up to several alarm circuits but had its own power supply. It wasn't all that difficult to disarm it and deactivate the numerous alarms the doctor had set.

Ken gained entrance through the grate in the attic. At once he could hear classical music blaring through the house. The scent of candles, sweat, and semen assailed him the moment he entered. Although the doctor had his music up loud, Ken kept his weight evenly distributed as he crept across the floor to the stairs, to prevent any creaks from alerting the man to the danger threatening him. He removed the small door leading below and peered down. The house was dark, with only a few candles flickering, casting eerie shadows on the walls. Ken's jaw tightened and adrenaline surged once again. The lights from the candles illuminated the wallpaper, throwing faces and female body parts into sharp relief.

Ken inverted as he dropped through the floor, and then

righted himself, landing on his feet as silently as a cat. Floor-to-ceiling collages on every wall were of naked women stretched out on tables in a disgusting depiction of medical art. He recognized Mari, all ages, from young girl, teen, to woman. The light spilled across her face, and he could see every emotion in the various pictures, from fear to defiance and anger.

The entire room was dedicated to Mari. There were pictures of her back striped with cane marks, of her legs and bare buttocks, all naked. There were close-ups of her mouth, eyes, breasts, and vaginal area. He stopped at the edge of the wall where the doctor had been busy putting up the latest pictures. Close-ups of the inside of Mari's thighs revealed strawberries and faint teeth marks, marks Ken had put there when he was making love to her. The pictures were raw, almost sexual in nature, an obscene portrayal of what had been the most important moments of his life.

Holding Mari in his arms, taking her with wild abandon, her body willing and receptive in spite of his roughness, in spite of his scars and appearance, had given him back his life. She had given him hope, and the doctor had reduced what they had together to something vile for a sick mind. Bile rose in his throat and he fought a churning stomach as he looked into Mari's eyes. This time he saw humiliation and degradation. She hated what Whitney and the doctor had done with their lovemaking every bit as much as Ken did.

Rage had gone from shaking him to ice-cold, and that was always a bad sign. He moved to the next room and found the walls similarly covered, this time with a woman with an abundance of dark hair and light eyes. Floor to ceiling, in every room of the cottage, the walls held pictures of the same seven naked women. He recognized one as Violet, the senator's wife. Ken had never felt so dirty or sick.

He found the doctor in his bedroom, lying on his bed naked, staring up at the ceiling and the collage of all seven women. The music was loud and the man hummed as he writhed on the bed. He never saw Ken at all, only felt the sting of the knife cutting into his flesh.

"I'd be very still if I were you," Ken hissed.

The doctor froze, lying rigid in his bed with the razor-sharp edge of the knife pressed against his throat. "What do you want?"

"You're a sick son of a bitch," Ken said. "Does Whitney know what a sick fuck you really are?"

"He said it was all right, that I could have my girls with me all the time." The man's voice was high-pitched and whiny. "He knows. Ask him. He'll tell you. He comes in sometimes to see what I've done with them."

"Where are the original pictures kept?"

"Whitney has them all. He has places we can't go and keeps the pictures and files with him." The voice turned sly. "He only shares with me."

"Where does Whitney stay?"

"If I tell you, he'll kill me."

"I'm going to kill you right now if you don't tell me."

"He has rooms that no one can get into on the fourth level, down near the tunnels." He looked up at the staring faces of the women. "Aren't they beautiful? They like me to touch them and take their pictures."

Ken's stomach lurched, threatening to spill the contents. He slid the knife away and caught the man's head in both hands, wrenching hard, hearing the satisfying crack. Whatever legitimacy Whitney had once had, this house and this man were a testament to his growing lunacy.

*I'm going to torch the house.*

*Damn it, Ken, don't do anything crazy.*

*It's got to come down. I'll make certain it looks like the doc had a little accident with the gas, but this house has to burn.* Because no one else was ever going to see what this perverted excuse for a man had done to those women. He was going to blow the son of a bitch into the sky, and when they investigated, they would find the doctor with his candles and matches and a loose gas hose.

He couldn't look at the walls as he worked, feeling slimy surrounded by the images of the women Whitney had experimented on and allowed a very sick man to abuse. Who had stood up for Mari as a child? As a teenager? Jack and he had been in and out of a lot of foster homes and their father had been a rotten, jealous drunk who thrived on beating them, but they'd had their mother and then each other and finally a kind woman who had stood up for them when no one else would. His heart ached for Mari. He was going to be sick if he didn't get the hell out of there, his stomach churning and knotting in revulsion as he set the scene, careful to leave nothing that would indicate anything but an accident.

A slow leak no one caught, the house filled with gas, and the doctor, cavorting with his music and candles, naked in front of his obscene shrines, blown to pieces along with his house, quite tragically.

*Get the hell under cover, Jack. They're going to comb the countryside when this thing goes off.*

*I'll cover you.*

*I'm going in. I need to get to her.*

*Damn it, no.* Jack snarled it. *I mean it, Ken. Get your ass back here. You're not that dumb.*

*I'm exactly that dumb.* The thought of Mari locked down on that examining table, pinned like an insect while a sick pervert photographed her and touched her was more than he could bear. He had to get to her and hold her in his arms. It might be the biggest mistake he'd ever made, but he was going to her. She wouldn't be alone tonight.

Jack swore, a blistering round of curses that Ken ignored. He went out of the house and reset the alarms, leaving everything exactly the way he'd found it. Instead of making his way back up to the top of the bluff to join his brother, he began to crawl through the grass to reach the largest building. There was a way in, a duct, a conduit, a tunnel—anything left behind in the cement he could use. There was always a way.

He used sound, a lesser talent he had and one he wasn't the best at using, but he could bounce it off the cement walls searching for a hollow spot. The cement was thin on top of a spot near the south-facing wall. There were boxes and wooden pallets and crates of all sizes piled around. Obviously the supplies were dropped off nearby and unloaded. He restacked the larger crates and boxes loosely around him to help provide a small shelter while he worked.

It took a half hour to break through the thin layer, and another few minutes to dump the concrete into the hollow space he found inside. He knew there were often wide areas reinforced with rebar that were left open in between the walls of larger, mainly military compounds, and once inside, no one would hear or detect him as he moved around, hopefully making his way to the lower levels.

*I'm in.* He found a crate and slid it over the opening to hide the hole. It would have to do and probably wouldn't be noticeable with so many crates piled around the area. Just as he slipped inside, pulling the crate over him, the doctor's house blew, exploding outward, sending debris raining down and red orange flames billowing with black smoke high into the air.

Men burst out of the guardhouse and began racing in all directions, silhouetted by the raging fire. An alarm began to sound, breaking the silence of the night along with the roaring of the inferno. Ken paused to watch the house burn. Glass showered down and black spots appeared on the walls, then were consumed by the hungry flames. There was intense satisfaction in knowing no one could get near the place, even as they began to try to tame it with water. It was too late. He'd opened every door to ensure the gas had filled the house and it would look like Dr. Pervert had tried to light one of his many candles, accidentally setting off a bomb and blowing himself across the room, where he struck just right to break his neck.

Dogs burst out of cages somewhere, from a hidden tunnel to his left. They had known there were dogs, but they hadn't known the animals were kept inside. From his vantage point he could see the door swinging open to allow the dogs to escape into the space between the double fences. Whitney was taking no chances that his women might take advantage of the chaos and try to escape.

*If they have one tunnel, they'll have more,* Jack observed.

*Are you clear? Sooner or later they'll get around to sending the dogs to look for someone, just to be on the safe side. I don't think Whitney takes much for granted.*

*I'm fine,* Jack assured. *You know he has to have a couple of escape routes. When this place is taken down, he doesn't intend to be on it. You know he prepared for that. He must have a dozen more laboratories just like this one.*

*I figured as much.*

There was a small silence while they listened to flames roaring in anger, threatening the foliage and nearby trees.

*That's a hell of a beautiful fire,* Jack commented.

*I want the walls burned, inside and out. He had floor-to-ceiling pictures of them all, Jack. Even when they were children. Whitney not only knew, but encouraged him. It was one of the sickest things I've ever seen.*

*Damn good thing the son of a bitch is dead then.*

Ken took one last look at the raging flames, wishing it would take the sick feeling from his stomach, but his belly still rebelled, and he had to fight not to vomit every time he recalled the floor-to-ceiling wall of Mari's pictures. Her life chronicled by a perverted deviant. He wanted to smash something.

It was unlike him to give in to his violent emotions. When he went out on an assignment, it was always business. He was completely devoid of all feeling, uncaring of anything but getting the job done. When someone tried to kill him, he rarely took it personal; it was part of who and what he was. But this . . .

*You're falling in love with that girl.*

*Go to hell, Jack. It isn't that. She needs protection.*

*So do the other women. Are you feeling the same way about them?*

*How can I fall in love with someone I just met?*

*You're shallow. I've always told you that, but you never listened to me.*

*It isn't love. She just—* He broke off abruptly. It wasn't love. He didn't dare love. Love could turn into something really ugly with a man like him. He wanted her—wanted to take care of her and see that she had a better life.

Who was he kidding? He wanted to wake up with her in his arms, with her legs wrapped around his waist, his body grinding hard against hers, his mouth at her breasts and kissing her, hot, long kisses that never ended. *It's sex. Straight-up. I get hard just thinking about her. Straight-up sex.*

*You lying bastard.* Jack snorted in derision. *You walk away from sex. She isn't just sex to you, bro. She's the fucking Fourth of July and Christmas all wrapped up in one neat package. Kenny's in love.*

*Keep it up, Jack, I'll tell Briony you stuck a gun to her sister's head.*

*You wouldn't dare.*

Damn it. He refused to love the woman. He just wouldn't

do it. He wasn't going to take a chance that he could turn ugly on her. He'd just keep her. Tie her to him. He was very experienced at sex and she wasn't. Keep her hot for him, wanting him. That was the key. Forget love. Jack was full of it. That way was disaster. This way he could keep her forever and never feel so much as a twinge of jealousy. Keep his emotions out of it and be safe.

Ken wiped sweat from his face and began to walk in the narrow corridor of cement, finding his way through the maze with nothing but Mari's touch to guide him to her, because one way or another—he *had* to reach her.

# CHAPTER 15

Mari caught the bars of the window on her door and shook them, her gaze on the two men circling each other.

"We don't need the guns," Sean said.

"No, I can beat you to death with my bare hands," Brett answered.

*"Stop,"* Mari entreated. "Brett, stop."

"Shut up, Mari," Brett slammed a hamlike fist against the door, sending her heart into overdrive. "I'll take care of you later."

The camera in the corner made a slight whirring noise as it changed angles to better capture the fight between the two men. Mari's breath stilled in her lungs.

In that moment she suddenly understood what was happening. The entire compound was a laboratory experiment, and everyone in it was a participant. Whitney wanted emotions running out of control. He wanted to see if he could manipulate men into a killing frenzy. He wanted to see if he could indoctrinate them to murder their own children if the child didn't meet the stringent standards for supersoldiers. And he wanted to see if the mothers could have a strong enough hold on the men to keep them from doing so. He was testing human nature. Maybe whoever was funding him didn't know the extremes he was going to, but he'd already killed one of the seven women he'd begun training, and if Whitney had his way, the others could just as easily die.

Mari and her sisters were not soldiers. This had never been their home. They were lab experiments, nothing more, and if they wanted to survive with body and soul intact, they had to escape. They had to quit talking about it and make it happen—and soon. Immediately.

"Sean, don't do this. It's what they want—what *he* wants." She felt the need to save him, a fellow soldier, a man sworn to do his duty and carry out orders. She'd always respected him as a soldier, respected his abilities even when it had become clear he no longer considered her and the other women part of the unit. Whitney had done something terrible to him to change his personality, to turn him into another Brett, brutal and without the ability to decipher right from wrong.

"Back off, Mari," Sean hissed, eyes on his enemy.

"If you do this, there's no going back. He'll have you for murder. Don't you see, you'll be as much a prisoner here as I am." It was already too late for him; she had known it almost the moment he'd come for her and he'd acted so out of character. The man with a ready laugh was gone, and a stranger had taken his place.

He had made a choice; even after seeing what Whitney's experiments did to the men, Sean had still made the choice to participate.

"I already am," Sean said, clenching his teeth. "He isn't going to torture you anymore."

Mari felt tears burning behind her eyes. Knives had replaced guns and there was no way to stop what was going to happen. Somewhere, this was all being recorded as if it were a video game instead of real life. A man with dead eyes watched them all with no more compassion than he would have for insects. He played with their lives and recorded everything diligently, all in the name of science and patriotism. Sean was so wrong. Whitney was still torturing her. He'd taken another person she cared about away from her.

She knew no other life and neither did the other women. They had talked of escaping, had planned for months, but until now they'd always found a reason to wait, to hold on one more day. In spite of their training and their enhanced physical and psychic abilities, the simple truth was they were all afraid of what they would find outside the compound.

In all her life she'd never once talked to anyone not associated with the compound. The guards and fences weren't the only things keeping them prisoners. Fear held them just as efficiently as the guards. Fear for what Whitney would do to Briony. Fear for the other women. Fear of not being a good enough soldier. Fear of the outside world.

She didn't honestly know if she could survive away from this place. The brutal years of training, of discipline, weapons, and control, had been her way of life as long as she could remember. Every moment of education she'd ever received had been designed to make her a better soldier—a better weapon. It was the same for the other women. They had no family, no friends, and no one to advocate for them.

An alarm went off, shrieking insanely, and her heart nearly stopped. What if Ken had been spotted? She gripped the bars, her legs turning to rubber she was so scared. They would kill him. *Ken.* She reached out to him, careful to keep the energy low, as if she were talking to the other women as they often did in the evening. *I need to know you're alive.*

*I'm here, baby, on my way to you.*

*I hear the sirens. I touched all the girls and they're all in their rooms safe.*

*That little sick pervert of a doctor's house blew up. It's a real tragedy.*

She forced air through her lungs. *You didn't take any chances, did you? I can handle Prauder. It's all part of the job.*

*That's bullshit.* Ken's chest went tight. He didn't want her anywhere near Prauder, Whitney, Sean, or bully Brett. *Tell me what's wrong. And don't say nothing. I can feel it.*

She hesitated.

*Damn it, Mari. I'm losing my mind here. I can imagine all sorts of really unpleasant things, so just give it to me straight.*

*I'm safe. Locked up. Sean and Brett are trying to kill each other outside my door.*

She took a deep breath and let it out, focusing on the camera in the hallway. Brett was a brute of a man who enjoyed

hurting others. He had tried to break her, to the point of pushing the limit of the restraints Whitney put on him, but he
hadn't succeeded. Brett had been trained well and was physically enhanced so his strength was phenomenal. She ought to
know; he'd used it on her repeatedly. Sean was the ultimate
soldier, fast and hard and experienced in battle, able to separate emotion and slip into the fighting zone—and he was
deadly with a knife. He would kill Brett. He intended to kill
Brett, and he would do it on camera just like Whitney wanted,
and there would be no out for him ever again. Whitney would
own him body and soul.

Mari tried again. "Sean, stop!"

He didn't so much as glance at her, not flinching as Brett
feigned an attack. He shifted his weight to the balls of his feet,
eyes on his target. She turned her attention again to the camera. She had several psychic gifts, but destroying the inner
workings of a machine wasn't one of her greatest strengths.

Ken could taste fear in his mouth. Because whoever didn't
die was going to be visiting her, and Ken knew he'd better get
there first. *Baby.* His voice was soft, soothing; he needed to be
calm for both of them when he was really afraid for her. *Are
you gathering energy to protect yourself?* He could feel the
buildup in her mind as she pulled in psychic energy from
around her.

Was she coiling, readying for an attack? If he found Sean
or Brett touching her, he'd never be able to control himself.
Every muscle, every cell in his body, tensed and tightened,
waiting for an answer.

*I'm trying to melt the stupid camera. I can't stay focused.*

There was the smallest of sobs in her mind, hastily covered, but he heard—and felt—that gut-wrenching sound, and
his entire body reacted.

*Open your mind to mine.*

Most psychics developed natural shields, not wanting anyone running around in their heads. Ken was used to sharing
his thoughts with Jack, as well as sending and receiving energy. They had experimented often and practiced for years to
perfect their communication skills.

It took Mari a moment or two to overcome her natural ret-
icence and let her barriers all the way down. He poured not

only energy, but directions into her mind so that she knew exactly where to focus the surge of power to the camera and send the interruption back through the lines, blowing other cameras out as well. For good measure he included all auditory equipment too. Ken was shocked that she trusted him enough to let him inside her that far. Just as she'd given him her body, she gave him her mind. The feel was far more intimate than he had ever imagined it could be, as if his soul had rubbed up against hers.

*Sean is killing Brett, Ken. Right here in front of me. Whitney's done something to him and he's crazy, just like Brett was.*

*Are you safe?* He had found the route to the second level and was making his way down, but the crawl space in the cement walls was a maze. Rebar stuck up in spots like deadly stakes. There were dead ends and places where he had to push through a thin plug of cement. That took precious time—time he feared he might not have.

She didn't answer him right away, and for a moment he thought he might lose his mind. *Damn it, Mari, tell me the truth. Are you safe?*

*I don't know.*

She was worried and that added to his alarm. He took a deep breath and let it out, seeking to find a way to be detached. He had to quit acting like an idiot and think with his brain. *I'm on my way to you, Mari. Whatever happens with Sean and Brett, know that I'm coming.*

*Don't. This place is a fortress.*

*I'm already inside, sweetheart. I'm a GhostWalker. Don't you know we walk through walls?* He tried to tease her, gently, to reassure her that he was all right.

Mari peered through the bars of the window and saw streaks of blood on the opposite wall. Blood splatter went across the guard's station and pooled on the floor. Brett crawled toward her door, his shirt bright red, several large spots beginning to run together. His teeth were clenched together and he growled; all the while blood trickled from his mouth. Sean followed relentlessly, gripping a bloody knife, his face contorted into that of a stranger.

She backed away from the window, pressing her hand against her trembling lips. She had known Sean would kill

Brett, but the vicious look on his face, the utter satisfaction and triumph was more than she could take. There was a feral quality to his snarling expression as he stalked Brett.

The back of her legs hit her cot and she sank down, pushing her way back until she was huddled in the corner against the wall, making herself as small as possible. Her hand slid beneath the cot mattress to hold Ken's necklace for comfort.

Ken felt Mari's sudden rejection, her complete withdrawal as if she couldn't stand his mind touching hers. Violence had always been her life, but not like this, not the cold, cruel, animalistic aggression the two men were displaying. She wanted no part of it. His heart clenched, a strange sensation, gripping him with another fear—this time for what she would think of him. If there was a violent man in the world, one who could detach from all emotion, it was Ken. Worse than that, when he allowed emotion to prevail, he could be as brutally efficient as any wild predator.

*Don't push me away.* He was pleading inside, but it came out a command, and he felt her wince away from the roughness in his voice. He was blowing it before he even got started. There was a limit to what any one person could take, and Mari was at hers. She needed out of this place. She needed freedom and to be able to make her own choices.

*Someone is coming.* Mari held her breath, hearing footsteps outside her door. Hastily she checked to make certain the chain and cross were well hidden. There was the murmur of voices. Sean wasn't alone. She wanted to remain huddled against the wall, but she couldn't let them see her feeling so fragile. Lifting her chin, she stood up and faced the door. Her heart was pounding.

*I'm with you, sweetheart. I'm making my way through the second level. It's tough going, with a few roadblocks in the way, but no matter what, I'll get to you.*

*The entire compound has security cameras everywhere as well as motion and infrared triggers.*

*Thanks for the warning. And, Mari? Stay open to my mind. I need to know if you're in danger.* Not that there was a hell of a lot he could do from where he was. The high cement walls were narrow and the maze seemed endless. He didn't get claustrophobia, which was a good thing, because the longer he was inside the thick walls, the more it felt like the labyrinth was endless.

The door slid open and Sean stood framed in the doorway. There was blood on his hands, a grin on his face. Behind him stood Whitney in his immaculate suit, with his dead eyes and his frightening half smile.

"Sean has elected to be your new partner, Mari," Whitney said. "I'm certain the news pleases you as you always objected to Brett."

She forced her gaze to stay focused on the two men and away from the body slumped on the floor. Her eyes met Whitney's. She remained silent, not giving him the satisfaction of an answer.

"You wouldn't happen to know anything about an explosion in Dr. Prauder's house, would you?" There was no inflection in his voice, not even mild interest.

"I didn't hear an explosion." She shrugged. "Down four levels underground we don't often know about what goes on up top until someone tells us."

"Nor would you happen to know anything about a visitor coming, would you?" Whitney persisted.

Her heart jumped and then began to pound in alarm. Had they discovered the Nortons? "I'm afraid I have very few visitors, Dr. Whitney, as you well know. Why do you ask?"

"You left this facility without permission. Why would you join your former team unless you had an agenda? You were either planning to escape, in which case you knew one of your friends was likely to meet her demise, or, more probably, you wished to speak to Senator Freeman."

She kept her face as expressionless as possible. "Why would I want to do that?"

"Based on your past, I would say you were stirring up trouble again. That seems to be your most impressive talent to date." His eyes narrowed and he took a step toward her. "Sean is going to stay with you for a while. Let's hope if Norton didn't get the job done, Sean does, because after this, you aren't going to be very important to me."

Her stomach lurched. "I don't understand."

"Oh, you're a very smart woman, Mari. I'm sure you do understand. Senator Freeman is coming here and wants to talk to all the women, but he mentioned you specifically. Freeman has no authority here."

"I thought Freeman was a friend of yours."

His cold gaze swept over her. When she was a child, that particular look would wither all defiance instantly. Now it left her with sweaty palms and a dry mouth.

"People who ask a lot of questions about things they shouldn't have any knowledge of have a way of disappearing."

She knew he caught the sudden exhale as air left her lungs in a rush of comprehension. "You ordered the hit on Senator Freeman. You wouldn't have allowed our team to protect him if you'd been there to stop us."

"Cooperate this time, Mari, give me what I want. I've grown very tired of your tantrums."

"Why? Why would you do that? He's Violet's husband."

"Violet has forgotten where her first duty lies and so has the senator. We put him in that position, but he's growing more arrogant and ungrateful every day."

"I didn't ask him to come here. I never even got close to him. I was shot."

The dead eyes remained fixed on her face in accusation. "You found a way to get a message to him. Violet would, of course, listen to you and persuade him. She will find I make a far better ally than enemy."

Mari wanted to remain silent, afraid whatever she said would push Whitney over the edge and get someone hurt, but she couldn't let him leave without trying to save herself. She didn't dare look at Sean. The same brutish grin remained on his face throughout the conversation. She stiffened to attention, becoming the perfect soldier reporting to Whitney.

"I shouldn't have left without permission, but I was going crazy locked up. I thought if I could run a mission or two I'd feel better. You trained us as soldiers. Staying in these tiny cells is making us all crazy. I didn't speak to the senator, and when I was captured, I tried to reach out to my unit. My first priority was to escape, and as soon as the opportunity presented itself, I did so. Sean can verify that."

Whitney studied her face with his dead eyes, giving nothing away of what he was thinking.

"That is correct," Sean said.

Whitney ignored the soldier. "You left without permission."

"Yes, that's true. And I more than paid for my mistake."

"Your point, Mari?" He was suddenly impatient.

She forced her gaze to the floor in a more submissive role. "I'm tired and worn out tonight and would ask that you wait before you send Sean to me. At least wait until we know whether Norton got me pregnant."

"No!" Sean was adamant. "You gave me your word, sir."

Dr. Whitney held up his hand and Sean fell silent. "I certainly increased your chances with all the fertility shots I gave you," Whitney told Mari as he studied her face. "I don't think so. I think you have your own agenda, and as Sean pointed out, I did give him my word."

Mari stayed ramrod straight, keeping her expression blank, but she couldn't control the sudden pounding of her heart. She wanted to crumble and fall into a sobbing heap on the floor. She couldn't go through this again—not with Sean. What had possessed him to allow Whitney to include him in his insane program? They had often discussed how the men turned into brutes after taking Whitney's chemical cocktail.

Dr. Whitney glanced up at the camera. "After you're done here, you'll report to the med labs for a few more tests. I didn't realize your psychic powers had developed enough to damage not just one, but several of the cameras and the auditory equipment."

He waited, but she refused to take the bait, remaining silent.

"Ah well. I wish you a very pleasant evening," Whitney said. His smile remained firmly in place as he pushed Brett's foot aside with the toe of an immaculate shoe. "I'll have someone collect the body." He turned on his heel and left them.

The door slid shut behind him with a familiar clang. Mari shuddered at the thought of Brett's dead body lying within a foot of her door while his killer faced her, blood on his clothes and hands.

She shook her head. "Why did you do this, Sean?"

"You know why, Mari. You've always known how I felt about you." He stalked past her to the small bathroom, his shoulder brushing up against her, nearly knocking her back.

She pressed back against the wall, tears burning behind her eyelids and choking her throat. "I don't, Sean. I swear to you, I really don't."

He came out, drying his hands off. "How did you think it made me feel letting Brett in here and hearing you fight, hearing him beat you? There wasn't anything I could do about it. He didn't belong with you; he never did. You knew it, and I told Whitney he didn't. Whitney agreed with me."

"So you took his place? That doesn't make any sense."

"Better me than someone else. I've always wanted you. I didn't hide it from you. You were the one who wanted to keep if just friends."

"And that should tell you something. You let Whitney pair us knowing I didn't want to be more than friends with you. That's not saving me, Sean." For the first time she felt absolute despair. He was looking at her without comprehension, uncaring what she thought or felt. "This is about you. You wanted me, and this was your way to get me. You didn't care at all how I felt, did you?"

He shrugged. "Better me than Brett or anyone else. You should have just accepted me one of the hundred times I made the offer."

"I don't feel anything for you other than friendship."

"Whitney's right, you're stubborn. You refused to try. You gave me no other choice, Mari. This one's on you." He stepped close to her, looming over her. "I want you to get in the shower and scrub that man's scent off of you."

"Go to hell."

He shook his head. "We're not doing this, Mari. You have no choice. You belong to me, and I'm going to make certain if there's a baby, it's mine. Get into the shower and do as I say."

She scowled at him. "Did you really think it would be that easy? That you'd walk in here and take away what little personal choices I have left and I'd just go along with it? Brett was a vicious brute and I despised him. You were always special to me. I couldn't have respected you more. But this . . ." She spread her hands and shook her head. "This is a despicable act, and anything you get from me you'll just have to take. And you can live with knowing you're a sick fucking rapist like Brett."

"I gave up my life for you, Mari. You will do what I say. I sold my soul to Whitney for you."

"You don't have a soul."

"Get in there and shower before I drag you in and scrub you myself."

"You're such an asshole, Sean."

Sean grabbed her by her hair and dragged her toward the bathroom, erupting into fury when she didn't do as he ordered. He shoved her hard. "Get in there."

She kicked the door closed in his face.

*Mari. Baby. What's happening? You're scaring me, honey. Stop trying to cut yourself off from me.*

She thought she *had* cut her mind off from Ken's, not just tried. She must have reached out because she was so stressed and afraid. She didn't want him to know, to witness her utter humiliation. She stood for a moment leaning against the bathroom door and then began to strip. Once Sean heard the shower, he might calm down and she could talk reasonably with him.

Mari stepped under the cascading water and closed her eyes, turning up her face. *You can't help me now, Ken. This place is locked down and I can't escape without the others. I won't go without them. I'd never forgive myself. Please go away.*

*What the hell are you saying to me?*

She leaned up against the shower stall and let the tears leak out under the spray of hot water, pretending she wasn't giving in to the feeling of despair, but she was drowning in it. Her chest felt tight. She could barely breathe, and her throat was raw and choking her. For the first time that she could remember, she felt panicked.

*Honey.* His voice moved in her mind. Soft. So tender it brought a fresh flood of tears. *I'm here, Mari. Talk to me. Share it with me. Lean a little bit, for God's sake.*

*I can't.* She wanted to reach out. She wanted to feel the comfort of his arms, and maybe that was what was wrong. Ken had made her weak, made her feel she needed him. She'd always been able to endure—to stand alone, but now she wanted the solid rock of his body, the strength of his arms. She wanted him to shelter her close and stop the insanity before she lost her own mind. Whitney was tearing her into little pieces, just as Ekabela had cut Ken's body into tiny sections.

*You can tell me anything.*

*You get so angry.* She had had enough of angry men. She wrapped her arms around herself and huddled down, wishing she could disappear down the drain with the water.

*Not at you. I have rage in me that I've never let out, and maybe it comes boiling to the surface, but never at you, Mari. I just want to make things better for you. Tell me.*

She was going to tell him and she knew it was mistake, but she couldn't stop herself. She desperately, *desperately*, needed someone. *Whitney gave me to Sean. Sean killed Brett. The body is outside my door and Sean is waiting for me. He isn't going to take no for an answer and he's way stronger than I am. You can't get to me in time. Not if you're on the second level.*

For a moment he was gone; his mind jerked abruptly out of hers, leaving her alone and bereft and feeling sick. A loud thump on the door made her jump. Sean was coming to get her and there was no way out.

*Baby, listen to me.* There was pain in his voice, in his mind, pain and guilt mixed with the coldest rage she'd ever touched. *I can't get to you. I'm drilling through a cap to try to find a way into the wall below me. Everything dead-ends here.*

*It's okay. Really it is.* It wasn't and they both knew it.

*Stay with me. Keep your mind in mine.*

*No. I don't want you here with me when this happens. I feel unclean. I couldn't bear for you to witness this.*

She felt the sensation of lips brushing the corner of her mouth, and she touched her lips in wonder. *How did you do that?*

The door banged open and Sean ripped the shower curtain aside. Mari looked up at him with her tear-wet face, feeling total despair.

*Try to connect with him mentally. Is he a telepath?*

*Yes.* For a moment she didn't comprehend, and then a tiny hope flickered and blossomed. She didn't dare believe it could work, because it would be so terrible if he couldn't do it. *Can you use mind control on him?*

*I'm sure as hell going to try. You can't make a mistake, Mari, and accidentally give away the fact that I'm here and we're communicating.*

"Get up, Mari." Sean extended his hand.

Slowly she unfolded her legs, refusing to be intimidated because she had no clothes. *Why are you doing this, Sean? Please just talk to me so I can stop shaking. I'm afraid of you. I don't like being afraid of you.*

With a show of reluctance she put her hand in his and let him help her to her feet. He tugged until her body brushed up against his. She couldn't stop herself from going rigid, but she did manage not to fight.

*Why are we using telepathy?* Sean pushed her ahead of him into the bedroom, taking a careful survey of the walls, looking for a hidden camera.

*I'm pretty sure Whitney has audio surveillance in here. Things he's repeated to me he could only know if he heard them in my room. Sit on the bed with me, just for a minute, Sean, let me get used to the idea of this.*

*Didn't he say you blew all the audio when you took out the cameras?*

*I don't want to take a chance. You know he lies all the time.*

She felt Ken moving in her mind when she stepped back from Sean. He was studying the energy field, the traces of Sean left behind. She felt the sudden surge of energy entering her mind, gathering everything she was and tying the two of them together into one powerful unit. It frightened her so much she nearly pulled back. She wasn't Mari, standing on her own, but part of Ken, open to him, all her fears and hopes and every memory she had. It was shattering to be so close to another human being, so completely vulnerable to him.

She allowed her body to sag onto the bed, reaching for the thin blanket to try to protect her body from the lust in Sean's eyes. Why did it repulse her so much? When Ken had looked at her with a hundred times that hunger, she had melted for him, melted into him. Self-preservation demanded she pull away before her mind released every secret fantasy, every secret desire, real and imagined, and Ken's responded in kind.

A tremor ran through her. His mind was already filling hers with so much information, and along with his memories came power. Their energy fused into one steady stream, one powerful flow, a current so strong she feared she might pass out before Ken could take complete control of it.

Sean tugged at the blanket. Mari resisted, but it slipped enough to reveal the swell of her breasts. He jerked harder on the blanket, his elbow pushing her back until she was half-lying across the bed.

*I don't want to wait. You've known me for years, Mari. You belong to me, you always have. I'm just taking what's mine.* His mouth clamped hard on her breast, one hand circling her throat, fingers digging in to remind her not to struggle.

"Sean, you're hurting me." She slammed both hands against his chest, trying to push him off of her.

She expected Ken to lose it. She was aware of the rage in him, a living entity, black and vicious and brutal. *Use telepathy, make him answer you.*

*Sean, please, that hurts.*

*Don't fight me then.*

She felt Ken's instinctive reaction, the emotions pouring in, swirling together to make the rage even more powerful. But he grew as cold as ice—colder even, utterly still and focused, pushing away the rage as if it had never been, until his mind was the calm eye of a whirling hurricane.

She heard the soft cadence of his voice, mesmerizing, commanding, low and gentle but so insistent there was no denying it. The words slid by her, impossible for her to grasp, riding on the current of energy slipping from her mind into Sean's.

Sean sat up, his face shocked. He shook his head several times as if to clear it. The voice never stopped, never rose, never changed tones. It was relentless in its assault—pushing and pushing at Sean's mind, demanding obedience. Sean's face paled significantly, his eyes glazed over. She recognized the heaviness in his mind. She experienced it to a much lesser degree. Ken had gripped Sean's mind hard and refused to let go.

Sean stood up, shuffling backward, staring at her with a wild, helpless fear. She was afraid to move, afraid she would break the spell Ken was weaving with his voice. She didn't know how it worked, but the energy it took was exhausting. Sean resisted, fighting the continual murmur of that relentless command. Each step he took away from her dragged on the floor as if he resisted lifting his foot.

Mari held her breath as Sean swiped his keycard through

the lock to release the door. To her shock he tossed the card on the floor before he shuffled out. The door slammed shut behind him, but he kept moving, heading away from her. She could hear his footsteps fading.

Still, the enormous flood of energy continued. Exhausted, Mari lay back, pulling up the blanket, her entire body trembling uncontrollably. She heard the ticking of the clock and her own heartbeat. The energy crackled around her, crackled in her mind, surging with such power it frightened her to think what Ken and she could do together if they were bent on destruction.

The voice continued, and she tried to catch the commands, determined to find out what Ken was demanding of Sean. She couldn't interrupt, afraid that Sean would come back, that he would know she hadn't been alone in driving him off. She saw the keycard on the floor but couldn't find the strength to even crawl to it. Everything she was went into that river of energy.

She lay with her eyes closed, feeling the swelling surge, and realized she wasn't alone anymore with Ken. Jack had joined them, throwing his psychic energy into holding Sean in their command. Sean's mind was no longer his own, but had been wholly taken over by the Norton twins. She tried to pull her own energy back, afraid of being so exposed to Ken's brother, but the melding was too strong. She was drawn farther and farther away from her mind, walking through a maze of corridors, searching with a deadly, dark purpose.

# CHAPTER 16

Long after the sensation of energy flowing through their merged minds faded, Mari lay on her bed, staring up at the ceiling. Tears leaked out of her eyes, but she couldn't make the effort to wipe them away. She heard someone outside her door removing Brett's body, but no one spoke to her. It was just as well. She didn't think she had the ability to answer.

Once, she felt a flutter in her mind and recognized Cami's touch, but she didn't have the strength to answer, even though she knew she must be causing the other women distress. They would have felt her fears. And they certainly would have felt the swell of psychic energy—anyone psychic would have felt that. There was no way to contain that kind of power.

Her mind felt drained, her body as heavy as lead. She couldn't imagine what Ken felt like, but it had to be worse. Her head pounded with one of the worst, most disorienting headaches she'd ever experienced, and using telepathy and other psychic talents often caused them. Her heart beat too hard and fast and she was dizzy and sick.

She visualized Ken lying on the floor somewhere in the large complex, surrounded by enemies, vulnerable to attack, and sweat beaded on her body. She could barely breathe with needing to know he was alive, well and safe. She couldn't touch his mind, and she was certain that if he could have touched hers to reassure her, he would have. She could only lie there, terrified for him, imagining the worst with no way to help him.

No one could expend that amount of energy and not have tremendous physical repercussions. He had given everything he was to save her. She heard herself sob. Her chest heaved. It shocked her that she would be lying on her cot *sobbing*. Not tiny tears, but weeping out loud for everyone to hear. She never did that. *Never.* She was a soldier, trained in survival. You never, *never*, gave the enemy ammunition against you, and you certainly never gave them the satisfaction of messing with your emotions.

All of her training seemed to be gone in that instant, leaving her with no control. She needed to know he was safe. *How in the world could their connection have grown so strong that it was no longer just about sex?* She thought she could have moments in her life that would make the rest of it all bearable, but being with Ken Norton had changed everything. *She* was changed. He had shown her life could be different, that there could be hope for her, she could have dreams.

For a good two hours she lay in the dark, wondering if he was alive. For the first time in her life, she prayed. Whitney had taught them to believe only in science and that people who believed in a higher power were people who needed a crutch. There was no such thing as God, or a savior, or even a way of life that was about anything other than discipline and duty. She'd been indoctrinated since she was a baby into the belief that those who had mercy and compassion were soft— sheep, people waiting for someone with the intelligence and power to guide them.

For most of her life, she'd thought herself a failure because she didn't strictly adhere to Whitney's teachings. She loved her sisters, and most of what she did was out of a desire to protect them and stay with them—not her tremendous sense of duty. She'd never believed in anything but her sisters, but now, just in case, she prayed. And then, as if someone really had listened to her plea—there was no sound, nothing to warn her—she nearly jumped out of her skin when the door slid open and a man slipped through.

"Ken?" She croaked his name, still unable to lift her pounding head from the pillow. It was him, his shoulders wide, his arms like steel sliding around her, gathering her close. She turned her tear-wet face against his chest. He collapsed on the bed, and she realized he was trembling with weakness. "How did you manage to get here? I can't even move."

"You don't have to move; I'm just going to join you. My head feels like it's about to explode." He stretched out onto the bed beside her, hands running over her body to assure himself she was in one piece. "Your courage terrifies me." In truth she humbled him. To endure the things she'd endured her entire life, to stand there and face Sean and what he meant to do to her, to give herself up so fully to Ken, a man she knew to be every bit as dangerous—maybe more—it was almost more than he could comprehend.

He suddenly stiffened. "Oh, God, baby, you're crying. You going to break my heart. He's gone now. You're safe. You're safe with me."

He wrapped his body protectively around hers, feeling her tremors, the tear-wet face against his chest. His fingers tunneled in her thick hair as he dragged her as close as he could get her, trying to shield her from any further harm. "I'm sorry, sweetheart. I tried to get here as fast as possible. They put you through hell and I wasn't here."

He couldn't breathe with her crying. His chest felt tight, his throat raw, and panic rose. "Stop now." His hands stroked caresses in her hair. He rained kisses over her face and licked at the tears in an effort to stop them. "I tried. I swear I tried."

"You were here, Ken, you were; you saved me when I didn't think it was possible." Now that he was with her, alive and well, she should have been able to stop crying, but somehow, the floodgates opened and she was worse, alternating between hiccupping and sobbing, clinging to him like a child. Mari knew she would be ashamed in the morning, but the cover of darkness gave her the courage to be honest. "I was so afraid for you."

"Afraid for *me*?" Ken brushed more kisses over the top of her head and down her face. His teeth scraped her chin, and then he was kissing the corners of her mouth. "I was safe. You

were the one in danger. I thought I might go out of my mind."
His thumbs brushed at her tears.

Mari tried hard to regain control. He wasn't joking; he was
very shaken up by her tears. She took several deep breaths to
calm down. "Will Sean realize you used mind control on him?
Because if he does, Whitney will know I couldn't possibly
have done it and he could go berserk and kill all of us."

"No, he won't have any idea. You knew because I stopped
before I gave you the command to forget what had happened
to you. I can implant memories."

"Did you with Sean?"

"To protect you, yes. He believes the two of you had sex.
He believes you cooperated with him. I didn't want him coming back in the morning."

"How could you make him believe that?"

"It was easy enough. His desires were very powerful, and
the pictures of you naked in his mind were vivid. It wasn't difficult to manipulate them once I was wired to him. I didn't
want to, Mari, but I felt I had no choice. It was the only way I
could think of, besides killing him, to protect you. And if I
killed him, Whitney would discover we'd broken into his
stronghold. I did set Sean up and if we're lucky, he'll be taken
care of when he makes a try at Whitney."

"Are you apologizing to me?" She tilted her head enough
to look up at him, shocked that he would be upset when what
he'd done had cost him so dearly.

"I'm sorry, baby. He's a powerful enemy, and I should have
found a better way to remove him permanently, but we only had
a few seconds to make a decision and that was all that came to
mind if we wanted your family safe." And he had agonized and
cursed over that decision every moment since. He wanted Sean
dead. He needed Sean dead, but he had to live with the fact that
he'd left the bastard alive and Mari wasn't safe.

"I have no idea what I would have done if you hadn't
helped me," she said. Her nervous fingers stroked his hair, an
unconscious caress. She buried her face against the warmth of
his neck. "Whitney said the senator is coming here, that he
specifically asked to talk to me. I don't have any idea how he
would know to ask for me, but Whitney was really angry. I'm
certain that's why he had Sean come to me tonight."

It took effort not to keep the hot surge of fury from spilling over where she might feel it. He brushed a kiss against the soft strands of hair at the top of her head. He'd never been so choked up in his life. It was terrifying how this woman made him feel so much. He had been careful all of his life never to get emotionally involved, and yet she'd wrapped him up so tight he could barely breathe—and he had no idea how it happened, or even when.

"Senator Freeman is coming here?"

"That's what Whitney said. I don't think it's a good idea. Whitney seems really angry with him. Freeman isn't enhanced in any way."

"But his wife is."

"Yes. Whitney and the senator's father, Andrew Freeman, go way back. Andrew Freeman is in shipping. Violet told us she was being groomed to a be a senator's wife—that Whitney wanted Senator Freeman to run for vice president and that they would have a man in office they could control."

"So Violet is one of Whitney's GhostWalkers. He has a small army of them."

"No!" Mari pulled back her head to look at him. "Violet would never betray us, no matter what Whitney offered. I think she genuinely loves her husband, but she still wouldn't sell us out. Whitney has access to a team of genuine Ghost-Walkers. Violet was part of that group and so was I. Whitney has another unit comprised of supersoldiers. They're not quite the same. They're enhanced, but their psychic abilities aren't as strong and most of them are very violent. I know Violet isn't a part of that; she wouldn't betray us."

"Sean did."

There was a silence and he cursed himself for hurting her. His arms tightened even more, as if by crushing her to him and nuzzling the top of her head he could somehow make up for his blunder.

"Yes, he did," Mari said. "He blamed it on me."

"That's bullshit and you know it. He made his choices; we all do. He can take his own responsibility. If I screw up with you, Mari, it's on me."

She reached up to trace his lips with the pad of her finger, hearing the ache in his voice. "Why do you persist in thinking you're some kind of monster?"

"I don't want you getting the wrong idea about me." His voice sounded raw even to his own ears.

She smiled in the darkness. "I've been in your mind. I know you're bossy and you like everything your own way. You think you're jealous . . ."

"I *am* jealous. The thought of another man touching you makes me crazy." He squeezed his eyes shut. "My father was so jealous, Mari, he couldn't stand my mother talking and laughing with her own sons. He beat her every time a man glanced her way, which was often. She was a beautiful woman. I feel very possessive of you already. The idea of some man holding you in his arms, kissing you, sharing your body, just the *thought* alone, makes me feel violent. I don't honestly know what I'd do."

Ashamed, he wrapped his arm around her head, pressing her face into his chest so she couldn't look at him. He couldn't look her in the eye. "I could feel your emotions when Sean was fighting Brett. It sickened you to be the cause of that. I could do much worse, Mari, I know I'm capable. I was hoping I could hold you at arm's length and I wouldn't feel so strongly, but it happened and I can't stop it."

"You're not your father, Ken. You've led a completely different life. You've been shaped by your own experiences."

He gave a small, humorless laugh. "Exactly, Mari. Wonderful experiences. Witnessing my father kill my mother. Trying to do the old man in myself—hell, I wasn't even in my teens. I plotted a thousand ways to murder him. I beat the hell out of two of my foster dads and I have no idea how many boys and men growing up. I chose special ops, Mari, I chose to be enhanced both physically and psychically; after all, it would make me a much more efficient killer. Those are the things that shaped my life." He kept his tone absolutely emotionless, separating himself from the reality of his childhood the way he always did—the way he had to in order to survive.

Tears burned all over again. Hadn't she cried enough this night? This time the tears weren't for her, but for him, that little boy, the teenager abandoned by adults. Her life might have been stark and cold, but she hadn't known any different. She had nothing to compare it to. In some ways it had been fun even, all the physical and psychic training. She'd felt special and eventually respected. But Ken had known love. His mother had loved him; Mari could feel the echo of that long-ago love in his mind.

He hurt so bad inside and he didn't even know it. He wasn't aware of it, only of the fire of rage or the ice cold of his lack of emotions. It was all or nothing with Ken. Fury or ice. "Ken . . ."

"Don't!" he said sharply, because if she cried for him, it would be the end. No one had ever cried for him. His mother had been dead, and the rest of the world looked at Ken and Jack as if they were already the monsters their father created. Even back then, people had been right to be afraid.

His thumbs brushed at her tears. "You'll tear out what's left of my heart, Mari. Just stop. I can't change what I am. I might want to, baby, but I can't."

"If you really were the same kind of man your father was," she said gently, biting back the little sob that threatened to escape, "you would have killed Sean right there and then, while you had the chance, and to hell with my sisters. Your father wouldn't have put himself through the hell of knowing another man was touching me and denied himself the pleasure of killing that man. My feelings wouldn't have counted at all, but they do with you. You may have wanted to kill Sean—hell, I wanted to kill him—but you didn't." She squirmed out from under his arm and brushed kisses along the underside of his jaw.

He groaned softly. "Baby, you're deceiving yourself. I'm not a good man. I sure as hell want to be and wish I was whenever I'm anywhere close to you, but the truth is, I've done things in my life, and will do them again, that take me right out of that category. I wanted to kill that son of a bitch, and someday I will."

"Because he's a threat to me, Ken, not because he touched me."

"Don't kid yourself, Mari; it's both," he replied grimly. He knew the admission condemned all chance of happiness with her. She was not the kind of woman to walk behind a man. He was a man who would constantly need to protect her, to make the decisions, and there wasn't a damned thing he could do to change that. Unlike Briony, who accepted Jack's domination, Mari would chafe at the restraints. She had been too long on a leash, and exchanging one for another wasn't going to please her. Once she had a taste of real freedom, she would leave him and never look back.

The thought was crushing. It tore up his insides until he could barely think straight. He needed to focus on something else—anything else. Ken cleared his throat. "As soon as my brain heals a little bit, I can get word to Jack. Maybe he can warn the senator away if you really think Whitney might do him harm."

"Absolutely I think Whitney intends him harm," Mari said. "I think he put out the hit on him in the first place. When the command came down to protect the senator, I think it was a ploy to get us there and someone in our unit was going to assassinate him."

"Sean?"

"Maybe. Probably. He said something that bothered me, something about already being Whitney's prisoner. Sean's always been able to come and go. He had far less restrictions than a lot of us."

"He could have paid a high price for that. You have to consider the possibility that he sold his soul to the devil a long time ago."

There was another small silence. Mari chewed on her bottom lip while she turned that idea over and over in her mind. "If he did, and all this time he was reporting to Whitney, he would have told him I was going out with the team in order to try to talk to Senator Freeman and Violet."

"Which is why Whitney made certain Sean pumped you full of Zenith. It was Sean, wasn't it?"

"Whitney usually gives it to us before we go out on a mission. He was gone. Sean wanted to protect me."

"Whitney had him give a particularly strong dose. That's why you healed so fast and then crashed so hard."

"Do you think Sean knew what he was giving me?"

Ken wanted to tell her Sean was just bastard enough to make certain no other man had her if she didn't return to him, but she'd been hurt enough. "I doubt it, honey. Whitney gave

Zenith out routinely. It was more for his protection than any-thing else."

"Because dead men—or women—can't talk."

"Exactly."

"After you used mind control on me," Mari said, "I won-dered why you didn't on Ekabela's men. It isn't easy and it takes a tremendous toll."

He nodded. "It isn't easy to clear your mind and keep it fo-cused when someone is cutting you into little pieces."

"I guess not. And the aftermath is a killer. You'd have to be somewhere totally protected to use it. They would have had you at their mercy anyway."

"Like any psychic use, mind control has tremendous draw-backs, even more than most psychic talents, because you're using such powerful energy. I don't think Whitney can accept that. He wants his GhostWalkers to be flawless. That's why he's looking to the next generation. He's thinking our children won't have the repercussions of using psychic ability because they'll be born with it."

"I didn't think of that. I just think of Whitney as insane. He's gotten worse and worse over the years. He doesn't seem to have to answer to anyone, and because of that, his experi-ments have become more bizarre."

"Do you think Senator Freeman knows what goes on here?"

She shook her head. "Violet married him before Whitney started the breeding program. She couldn't know. That's why it was so important one of us speak to her. Why would Sean let me go if he planned on killing Freeman?"

"Because if Violet and Senator Freeman were dead, it wouldn't matter that you were there. And you're a sniper. They could have made you an accessory to killing a vice-presidential candidate. You wouldn't be able to go anywhere or do anything with that threat hanging over your head."

Mari pulled the cross and chain from under the mattress and slipped it over her head so that his gift settled in the valley between her breasts. She loved the feel and weight of it. Her fingers went to the edge of his shirt. "The guard won't be here until about five-thirty this morning. We have some time before you have to get out of here." She pushed up the hem, exposing the crisscrossing scars. "I've wanted to do this ever since the first time I saw you." She bent her head and kissed him, her lips satin soft against the forming ridges. "Can you feel that?"

He could—just barely. A soft shimmer of promise only, skating across his skin. He should stop her. The more he touched her, the more he possessed her, the more difficult it would be later to give her up. "Like a whisper." His voice was hoarse.

He wasn't man enough to stop her. Her wandering little mouth was just below his navel, teeth teasing scars, rasping over rigid skin, her tongue doing a little dance to ease each stinging bite.

"What about that?"

He closed his eyes, shifting onto his back, letting her work his pants open and down off his hips. It was dark in the room, but she could see the pattern of scars carrying lower and covering the thick, long erection she was building with those tiny sharp teeth, soft lips, and moist, velvet tongue. "Lower," he growled. "Lower and a little harder."

"You have no patience." Her soft laughter played over his abdomen like a feather. "I'll get there. I want to do a little exploring first, just see what feels the best."

She might kill him before the night was over. Her lips were heated silk, gliding over him like butter, a sensation almost beyond his ability to feel—almost. It was just enough to make his cock jerk and come to attention in breathless anticipation. Her teeth drove the breath from his lungs and sent fire rolling in his belly. Tiny, stinging bites covered by a stroke of her tongue.

Of its own accord his body arched toward her, his fists gripping her hair as a groan tore from his throat. His balls actually pulled up tight, so tight he feared he might explode as his cock filled, stretching the scars painfully, his erection thickening, lengthening, and bulging with urgent need. He thought to say something—maybe a protest, hopefully not a plea—but his mind and tongue couldn't get around the words when she wrapped her fingers around the base of his shaft in a tight fist.

He looked down at her, at her large chocolate eyes, so dark with hunger, her expression eager and hungry. She looked wildly beautiful, the darker shadows playing over her naked body. His gold cross swayed with her breasts, teasing along her skin, caressing her as she moved over him. He could see his marks of possession on her skin from their earlier lovemaking and that sent another rush of heat surging through his veins.

Mari didn't shrink from his vivid scars, the rigid lines crossing back and forth over his groin and scrotum. She studied him, fascinated, as if he were an ice cream cone and she couldn't wait to start, but wasn't certain where to begin. He held his breath as her head dipped forward and she licked a glistening bead from the top of the broad, lined head. She didn't just lick. There was that same faint sensation as if butterfly wings had brushed over him, and then her teeth followed, scraping along the damaged skin, dragging out a cry of pleasure from him.

The breath slammed out of him. His jaw tightened. Every muscle in his body contracted. He fought for control. One touch and she was destroying him. He tugged on her hair, tried to drag her up, but even as he did, his hips surged forward, forcing his cock against her soft, satin lips. He groaned again as her warm breath blew over him, as her mouth opened and slid over the broad head, tongue curling and teeth finding the most sensitive spot right beneath the ridge, the one his enemies had tried so hard to destroy. She bit down experimentally and fire shot through him, pulsed in waves, until he couldn't breathe, fighting for air, fighting for sanity.

The pleasure was so intense he was certain he wouldn't live through it. She was effectively destroying his belief in his own control. He couldn't allow her to take that from him—it was far too dangerous. Her teeth scraped again, right over that sweet spot, and he writhed under her, forgetting all about danger. Her nails joined in, scraping back and forth over the ridged lines on his tight sac, and he wasn't certain he knew his own name. She was killing him, stars exploding behind his eyelids, lashes of a white-hot lightning whip streaking through his bloodstream.

"More, Mari. Hard and hot." He bit the command out through clenched teeth.

Her mouth closed over the head of his shaft, tight and hot

and so exquisite, adding suction to the combination of teeth
and tongue, and he nearly came off the bed. There was no
preparation for what she was doing to him. Sweet hell, she
was burning him alive with her mouth. Her teeth found every
nerve ending he was certain had been severed, and they were
doing a fast repair.

She moaned deep in the back of her throat, and the vibration traveled straight through his cock to his balls and spread
down his thighs and up into his belly. He couldn't stop the
hard thrust of his hips. He tried, straining for control, but it
was impossible with the roaring in his head and his heart beating like thunder in his ears.

A soft curse tore from him as he slipped deeper, as her
throat constricted tightly around him, milking at him until his
seed boiled up hot and vicious. He caught her head, holding
her to him as fiery heat washed over him, flames crackling at
the base of his spine and washing over his body. Her teeth
found that one spot right under the lip of the broad head,
scraping as she took him deep again, her throat once more
constricting.

He came apart, a violent explosion of body and senses, his
life no longer his own, the pleasure consuming him, eating
him alive. He shuddered with the release, his hips almost wild,
thrusting deep helplessly, and each time her teeth or tongue
added to the hot, tight suction, he gripped her harder, anchoring
himself in the silk of her hair.

She owned him, body and soul. He might think he could
make her dependent on him sexually, tie her to him with the
way he could control her body, but she would never need him
the way he needed her. He knew it as surely as he knew his
heart and soul were forever in her hands.

She gave one last curling rasp with her tongue and released
him. He drove her back, catching her wrists, yanking her arms
above her head and slamming them to the mattress, his body
still hard and aggressive and vibrating with need. His thighs
pushed hers apart and he thrust into her, driving through tight
velvet folds, forcing his entrance as deep as possible, needing
her to take every inch of his thick, scarred cock.

There was resistance, her body slick and welcoming but far
too tight, and in spite of her breathy little pants and pleading

moans, her muscles tried to lock out his invasion. The reaction only added to his excitement and need to possess her, heightening his pleasure as he forced his shaft deeper, the muscles reluctantly, and barely, parting for him, squeezing hard against the scars, dragging across the damaged nerve endings until he felt fire sizzling up and down his spine.

"Wrap your legs around my waist." He loved looking at her, feasting on the sight of her body spread out before him like a never-ending buffet. Her eyes were glazed with need, her hair wild and spilling like strands of silk across the pillow. A sheen made her breasts seem to glow, creamy flesh with tight nipples begging attention and his cross glittering on her skin. He loved her tucked-in waist and the flare of her hips, but mostly he loved the soft little sounds of desperation that came from her throat as her body turned to liquid fire around his. "You're so fucking beautiful, Mari."

He bent forward to kiss her neck, the action deliberately producing an electrifying friction over her most sensitive spot. He sucked on the little pulse beating in her throat, dipped lower to find her breast, and did the same thing, feeling the answering wash of her hot cream make his next thrust easier. His teeth and tongue spent time worshiping there, while he waited for her tight body to accept the invasion of his.

"Please," she whispered urgently, her body thrusting up toward his, as he sank once again into her and held still, savoring the feel of her body surrounding his.

"Shh, I'll make it good for you, sweetheart. You need a little time to catch up."

"I am caught up," she protested, her voice breathy. Her body was already edgy with need. She didn't want to wait. She needed the feel of him filling her, crushing her, driving into her so high she would never come down.

Every squirm of her body sent shock waves washing over him. She was too tight, too small for his size, but that only served to increase his pleasure. He needed the feeling of a tight fist gripping and squeezing, raking at his scarred shaft with fiery heat, in order to get release. "You make me so damned hard, Mari." She did. One touch. One look. She was everything he could ever want in a woman. She wasn't afraid of his unusual needs—she met fire with fire. Even when he held her down, her body responded to his with a wild, almost desperate need.

His thigh muscles cramped with the effort to hold back. Every cell in his body screamed at him to take her fast and hard and as rough as possible, giving him maximum pleasure. His breath came in harsh, bursting gasps. He wanted this different. He wanted to be gentle. Gentle didn't work with his body, but she deserved so much more—a slow, tender lover, one coaxing her body into submission, not driving into her and taking by force what she was already willing to give.

He moved slow, testing his body, a long push through the hot, wet folds. The sensation was pleasant, but there was no real fire, no blaze of passion beyond his imagination. A groan escaped, a soft hiss of need he couldn't stop.

She locked her legs around his waist and pushed against him with frantic need. "Ken. Please."

That ragged little plea was his undoing, shattering his control and stealing his heart. He brought his hand down hard on her bottom, feeling the flare of heat rush through her, the wash of rich cream bathing his shaft in response. "You don't mind so well, Mari. We need to work on that."

"You're too slow."

"And I said I was going to make it good for you. Behave yourself." He wasn't certain he could do slow another stroke, teasing her body into compliance, but just to show her things would be done his way, he managed one more.

She cried out beneath him, locking her fingers on his shoulders, nails digging into him so that his nerve endings responded with a shock of electricity. He caught her hips and jerked her forward and up into him, angling her body to take more, take his full length. He wanted to bury every inch of himself in her, merge them so close together no one would ever be able to untangle them.

The moment he slammed his body into hers, driving deep, driving home, he forgot every good intention. His hips pistoned, his fingers dug into her firm buttocks to bring her body up to his. It was heaven to be in her narrow sheath, seemingly made just to rub over his scars and bring his cock to virile life. He could live here for hours, pushing her beyond every sexual limit she had ever conceived of, bringing her again and again to the peak of release, only to back off to hear her soft little pleas for mercy and see the lust building and building in her dark eyes.

She moaned his name, yanked at his hair, writhed under him, her legs locked in a tight grip as if she'd never let him go. She rose up to meet each stroke, crying out, driving him crazy with the way her small, hot muscles gripped him and her body was so eager for his. She had invaded every cell in his body, every bone, and his every organ, until he knew, no matter how long he lived, she would be the only woman he would ever crave.

The knowledge was alarming, terrifying, definitely dangerous, but there was no changing how he felt. His emotions were wrapped up every bit as tight and strong as his lust for her. The heat kept building, until he swore his semen was boiling in his balls, until lights flashed behind his eyelids and his mind roared with the fury of his desire. His cock swelled to bursting, pushing at the tight walls of her channel confining and constricting him, forcing the velvet heat over his scars until currents of pleasure swamped his nerve endings and ripped through his body.

Mari screamed and buried her face in his chest to muffle the cries as her body rippled and pulsed and shuddered with her orgasm, the muscles clamping down, convulsing around him, drawing out jet after jet of his hot release. Her orgasm seemed endless, her body rippling around his, at first hard and strong and then with more gentle aftershocks.

They lay together, locked in each other's arms, trying to find a way to breathe when their lungs were starved for air and their bodies were covered with a fine sheen of sweat. He kept his hand in her hair, fingers lazily massaging her scalp while his heart quieted and he felt strangely at peace.

"I could lie with you forever, Mari, just like this."

She smiled, her hands sliding possessively over his back. "I was thinking the same thing."

He shifted to take his weight from her, reluctantly leaving the haven of her body but wrapping an arm around her to bring her onto her side facing him. He loved the way her nipples were so erect and hard, an invitation lying against the sweet, swelling flesh.

"You deserve gentle, Mari," he said softly, kissing her as tenderly as he knew how. "I can't feel when I do gentle. God help me, I want to feel you when I'm deep inside you. I try to pull back, in my mind I try, but the need to feel you around me, to be that close to you, wins out and I can't do gentle."

"I didn't ask you to."

"There are marks all over you. I can't touch you without leaving behind bruises and little bite marks." He stroked a caress across her breast, tugged at her nipple, and was rewarded with her sharply drawn breath.

"I left a few scratches and bite marks on you," she reminded him, weaving her fingers together behind his neck, offering her breasts to his attention. "I'll tell you if you get too rough."

He couldn't resist the invitation and licked at one pert nipple, stroking his tongue over it and then tugging gently with his teeth. "I came here to comfort you, to hold you, not take you like this, in this horrible place. I want to take you home, baby, somewhere safe, far away from here. Come home with me. I swear, I had no intentions of doing anything but holding you in my arms."

A moan escaped when his mouth closed over her breast and he suckled, his mouth pulling strongly while his teeth teased and his tongued laved. "I want to go home with you." The words sounded strangled. His hand had slipped down her belly to rest at the junction between her legs.

"I could sneak you out of here," he tempted, his tongue flicking wickedly. Two fingers stroked along her pulsing entrance.

"All of the girls have to go." Her body jumped under the contact, his fingers pushing into her and finding her clit with lazy strokes. Each touch sent a vibration through her breasts to her nipples, where his teeth and tongue played. "And we have to make sure that Violet and her husband are safe."

He kissed her left breast and moved on to the right, this time pushing deep with his hand until she was riding him. They didn't have much time left together, and he would have to walk away and leave her locked up at Whitney's mercy. It was a terrifying thought, one that tied his belly in tight, hard knots. "After, will you come to Montana with me and see our home?" He stilled his hand, his mouth, his breath—waiting.

A heartbeat went by. She pushed against his fingers, trying for relief but he didn't move. "Is my sister there?"

"When we know it's safe, Jack will bring her there. It's their home as well, but I don't want you to come for Briony. I want you to come for me. No matter what, Briony is going to want to see you. She made us both promise to find you and bring you back to her." He suckled again, feeling the wash of her liquid response over his hand, and his fingers began their slow assault once more.

"I'm terrified of meeting her, Ken." She couldn't quite find her breath, but she never, never wanted him to stop. Lying in the dark with his hands and mouth roaming her body made her feel as if she belonged somewhere. This was for her, this slow, gentle wash of pleasure, completely for her and she knew it.

"You shouldn't be. She wants to love you, Mari. She wants her sister back. And she'll welcome the rest of your family. Briony is a generous, compassionate woman and courageous enough to take on my brother." His hand moved in earnest, thumb and fingers stroking caresses over every sensitive spot until she could feel the tension building and building all over again.

"As long as Whitney's alive, she'll be in danger."

"But not because of you. He had her adopted parents killed, and he tried to kidnap her the moment he found out she was pregnant."

"I can't believe she's going to have a baby." Her breath was coming in gasps.

"She couldn't believe it either. Whitney's team of super-soldiers did some damage to the house, but we've repaired it." Now his fingers were truly wicked, exploring and teasing and never quite giving her what she needed.

Mari tried to push harder against his hand, to trap him into giving her release. "He promised me that as long as I cooperated with him, he'd leave Briony alone."

Ken's teeth tugged at her nipple in a gentle punishment. "He never left her alone. He kept tabs on her all these years. He outlined her education and insisted on his own doctor treating her for all illnesses. Whitney lied about Briony just as he lied all those years to Lily."

"I feel so bad for Lily. It's a terrible thing to find out your entire childhood is built on a house of cards." His fingers pushed deep, withdrew, then pushed against her clit until she wanted to sob with pleasure. She closed her eyes.

Ken leaned down and kissed her belly button. It was so like Mari to be concerned for Lily. Mari who had no childhood, who had been treated like a grown soldier before she could barely walk. "Look at me, sweetheart. Open your eyes and look into mine."

His voice was low and commanding and Mari's lashes lifted. Her gaze met his, saw the absolute possession there, the stark need and the stamp of ruthless control mixed with something that could be love. She'd never seen the emotion, so she wasn't certain that was what she was seeing, but she kept her gaze locked with his when he took her over the edge and had her crying out his name.

# CHAPTER 17

*It rained parachutes last night,* Jack announced. *Our boys showed up, and a beautiful sight they were floating down from the sky.*

*Who do we have?* Ken asked.

*Logan, of course, Neil Campbell. Jesse Calhoun is coordinating and arranging backup in case anything goes wrong.*

That surprised Ken. Jesse Calhoun was a valued member of the team, but he had been seriously wounded and was in a wheelchair. Mainly he ran the investigations.

*Trace Aikens and Martin Howard are here as well.* Jack named the last two members of their GhostWalker SEAL team. *No one wanted to be left out. You're a very popular man, Ken.*

It took a moment for him to realize Jack wasn't joking, and it shocked Ken. He had trained with the men and they fought together, worked, and even at times lived together, but he had never realized their loyalties extended to him and his brother. Jack and he had always been a little apart, and often other men were leery of them.

Ken cleared his throat, thankful no one could see him.

Emotion was playing far too big a part with him these days. *They all in place?*

*Everyone's in position.*

*Has any word come down on the senator?* Ken asked.

*Senator Freeman asked to have Ryland's team guarding him when he visited "a high security facility today,"* Jack reported. *The general did initially give the order, then an hour later rescinded it and gave the assignment to another team.*

*Son of a bitch. Whitney has even more pull than we suspected. Who could go over the top of the general?*

Ken sat in the narrow corridor inside the cement wall. The fourth level was far more massive than he had ever considered it could be. It had originally been built as a secret military base before it had been closed down. Whitney had obviously discovered it and either bought it or persuaded his backers to allow him to use it for his experiments. There were very few in the know about the existence of the GhostWalkers. Whitney's front men were able to find a way to hide his work from the various committees who would have objected strenuously to his inhumane and illegal experiments.

*I don't know who could countermand one of the general's orders. The president certainly,* Jack responded. *The secretary of defense. But I can't see either of them mixed up with a nutcase like Whitney. He's too unstable, and the kinds of things he's doing would rock the nation—the world—if it came out. No president would risk being associated with him if they knew what he's done to children and women.*

That was true. Ken couldn't see anyone risking their political career. Hell, they'd face jail time, if not the death penalty, right along with Whitney. Mari alone would attest to the rape and murder of several women.

There was no sense in speculating. Ryland would have to approach the general, and if that went nowhere, then it would be up to the members of Ryland's team to find out whom they could trust.

Rear Admiral Henderson, the man responsible for the SEAL GhostWalker team, was already under investigation—of course he wasn't aware of it—and if they found no evidence against him, they'd never tell him. Jesse Calhoun was working hard to find out who had betrayed their team and sent them into the Congo.

Ken looked carefully around the walls of his tomb of cement. Ever since leaving Mari, he had been busy, marking the way so Cami could lead the other women out once Mari gave the signal to escape. He had tried to find Whitney's rooms and private tunnels so he could recover the pictures of the women, but it seemed impossible when the concrete dead-ended so often and was hazardous in most places to get through.

*Has Logan got the blueprints on this compound yet?* Ken wanted to destroy the pictures of the women Whitney had been taking for years. More, he wanted to put a bullet in Whitney's head. *Since it's a former military base, he should have been able to access them with the admiral's clearance. If not, put Lily on it. She seems to be able to get anything she wants. The Whitney name works wonders,* Ken said.

*Logan tracked them down. They're studying them now. They're set up to make the rescue when the senator is here. We're going to have to push our timetable forward. There's no doubt that Whitney is going to arrange an accident of some kind for Senator Freeman and his wife.*

*Maybe,* Ken mused. *But he wouldn't want an investigation anywhere near this place. I don't think he'll hit the senator here. I think he'll make his try either before or after he leaves. He'd be stupid to bring a firestorm down on his laboratory, and the one thing Whitney isn't—is stupid.*

*He has to make it look like an accident this time,* Jack said. *Get word to Marigold and tell her if she can warn Violet, to do it.*

*No. Absolutely not, Jack.* Ken was adamant. He crawled on his belly, careful of the sharp rebar sticking out of the walls, dragging his legs up and away from it. It was easy to lose oneself in the labyrinth, and Mari had been working on a new escape plan with the other women, as they feared they'd told Sean too much.

*We don't have a choice. Violet has to know what she's up against. We don't have a team in place to protect him. If he's really Whitney's enemy . . .*

Ken sent Jack the impression of disgust. *No. I'm not risking Mari. She's taken enough risks in this hellhole. If Violet is undercover for Whitney, then Mari's dead.*

*And if she isn't, the senator is dead,* Jack reminded him from his vantage point on the bluff. The air was cool. He wished he could send it to his brother trapped like a rat in the walls of Whitney's prison.

*That's not my problem. Frankly, I'm not risking her life for anyone connected to Senator Freeman. I don't trust him or his wife. I'm not risking Mari. I've gone as far as I'm willing to go for her family. We're getting them out today, because if Sean doesn't die today, he'll be back tonight. I'll kill him and be done with it, and Mari will know what a bastard I am. That won't be good, because she'll decide she doesn't want me and then I'll have to kidnap her and try to change her mind.*

Jack sighed. *You've gone caveman on me, bro.*

*Mari has that effect on me. And, by the way, Briony will be really upset if anything happens to Mari, and that will impact your life, so just get over having Mari warn Violet.*

*Man, you're edgy. Chill out.*

Ken frowned. He *was* edgy. He didn't want to leave Mari alone in that cell, locked up and trapped like a rabbit in a cage, when Sean might come back at any moment. He forced his mind to concentrate on the business at hand. *Speaking of the sick, twisted freak, have you caught sight of the bastard?*

Jack gave a short, expressive snort. *Um, that would a negative. I've never actually seen Sean.*

*I sent you an image.*

*Tails and horns aren't exactly the real deal, Ken. You gave me a picture of the devil.*

Ken made a rude noise, accompanying it with an even ruder gesture his brother couldn't see but would know he'd done anyhow. *I did my best to nudge Sean into making a try against Whitney. With a little luck, he'll kill the doctor, and Whitney's men will do him, and we can just write them both off. Thanks for helping out last night.*

*Sorry I didn't step in sooner. I went to higher ground and dug myself in, just in case using that much energy took its toll. You must have been completely wiped.*

Ken tried to sit up, and hit his head on rebar. He swore softly and glanced down at his hands. He hadn't felt the scrapes as he moved over the jagged, unfinished cement, leaving smears of blood behind. It didn't matter. Nothing mattered anymore but getting Mari out of there. *For a couple of hours. I couldn't get to Mari and I thought I'd lose my fucking mind. I didn't realize I had such a vivid imagination. I lay there scared shitless. The only time I've ever been that scared was when Ekabela's man was cutting my cock into tiny little pieces.* He'd never admitted it before. Never discussed it with Jack— but Jack had to know he couldn't do without Mari. He had to get her out.

There was a small silence. *She all right?*

*Sean was going to force himself on her. He'd been her friend; they trained on her GhostWalker team together. It's obvious she had genuine affection for the fuckwad, and for him to betray her like that . . .* Ken hit the cement with the flat of his hand, needing to expel his pent-up anger in some physical way. *She was pretty torn up, Jack.* Ken took a deep breath and forced his mind and body back under control. *I'm going to be taking the women out through the corridor the minute you give me the signal. I marked the way to make the run fast, but if you get a shot at Sean, take him out.*

*You're certain?*

*He'll never stop. Even if we don't get Whitney, and Whitney gives him a direct order, Sean is going to keep coming after her. In the end I'm going to have to kill the son of a bitch and she'll have a hard time forgiving me.*

*She isn't a stupid woman, Ken. You're underestimating her. Not that I mind killing him one way or the other.*

*Take him out, Jack, if you get the chance.*

Jack briefly laid his head on his arm. His brother's emotions swamped him at times; then he'd recover, pull back, and regroup. But Ken was at a boiling point. *Roger that. Is Mari organizing the women?*

Ken reached out to Mari. *Hey, baby. How you doing? It's a great day for freedom.*

There was a short silence while he counted his heartbeats. *Yes, it is.* There was a smile in her voice. *Everyone's excited. I've cautioned them about telling anyone the new escape route, and they're waiting for the word.* Her voice dropped an octave, the sound brushing like velvet on the walls of his mind and stirring his body in spite of the cramped, uncomfortable quarters. *I can't wait to be with you in your home.*

Ken closed his eyes and allowed that breathy, sexy sound to wash over and through him. He could admit, there with the walls closing in on him and the dark surrounding him, that he had fallen hard for Marigold. It had nothing to do with sex and everything to do with the emotion threatening to choke him. He would continue to deny it, but right now, in this place, with her soul brushing against his, and cement walls separating them, he admitted it. "I love you more than life, woman."

He swallowed and leaned his head against the concrete blocks. *I can't wait for us to be there together either.*

Mari's softness vanished and she got down to business. *Whitney grabbed Rose. She's the one who was afraid she might have conceived. He has us pee in a cup every morning, so if she is, he knows it. He's going to hold her over our heads while the senator is here, to keep us in line.*

Ken rubbed his throbbing temples. There were so many threads, and he had to pull off a precision escape to get all the women out. *Don't worry about her. If he knows she's pregnant, he grabbed her in case you all manage an escape. My guess is Sean tipped him off to what you're all planning, and he doesn't want to take a chance on losing her. Do you know where she's being held?*

*The man who is paired with her is named Kane. He's with her. Rose thinks he'll help, but I'm afraid for her, and I have no idea where she is.*

*Damn it. This is getting complicated. I have to get back to Jack, hon. Hang in there.* Ken swore again, rubbing his hand over his face. *You get that, Jack?*

*Yeah, I got it. I say screw waiting for the senator. The waters are getting murkier. Grab your woman and let's get the hell out of Dodge.* Jack sounded decisive.

Ken had been contemplating precisely that all morning. He had reluctantly left Mari right before the guard came with her food. She hadn't even clung to him. There was no last kiss, no protests, and no tears. She simply watched him sneak away, like a thief in the night. It shamed him to leave her there. He had made love to her and left his prints on her. The sex had been rough and wild. She had given him everything she was, and he had just left her there in that cage.

He despised himself. What kind of man would do that? None. Monsters did that. Sick, depraved men who didn't respect a woman. He hit the back of his head against the cement wall and felt a burst of pain.

*Cool it, bro, we've got company,* Jack watched the small plane circle above their heads and begin descent. *The senator is arriving. Jesse did some digging, and he thinks Whitney could have as many as twenty supersoldiers in his employ. Another psychic test was given out about six months ago.*

Ken swore softly. There was no stopping Whitney. *You know, Jack, Whitney isn't just a mad scientist conducting illegal experiments. He has too much help and he's too well covered. He's up to something far bigger than we ever imagined. And he can't be alone in this like we all thought.*

*The plane is down. I see two men getting off. Neither is familiar.* Jack crawled through the thick foliage for a better view. He adjusted the viewfinder. *Nope, I don't recognize any of them, but Violet knows them. She's acting very comfortable with them. Whoever they are, they're GhostWalkers. They're covering the senator like a blanket.*

Ken hated being trapped inside the walls, unable to see for himself what was going on. He didn't trust Violet at all. He wanted to get Mari out. His goal had narrowed to one person.

*We've got trouble, Ken. Sniper lying up in the trees about a hundred and fifty yards from me. Oh yeah. I recognize that son of a bitch. Remember Mitch? Big guy, smart mouth. Thought he could take the instructor and ended up staying in bed for a week? He's got to be one of Whitney's supersoldiers.*

Jack watched the woman walking beside the senator. She looked confident and tough. Her gaze was restless, searching the trees and bluffs, and twice she said something to one of the senator's guards and he immediately moved a step or two to further blanket her husband. Senator Freeman reached out and took Violet's hand even as he nodded and smiled, clearly feeling as though he was safe.

*There's no way the senator and Violet believe that Whitney put a hit out on him,* Jack reported. *They're walking in like they own the place. They're cautious, but not 'we're fucked' cautious.*

*And Violet thinks she's safe because she managed to get her*

*own team in place. The senator must have been the one who*
*tapped someone at the top to change the team,* Ken concluded.

*Mari's got to warn them, Ken.*

Ken rested his head in his hands. He didn't want to have
Mari get in the middle of Whitney and the senator's battle.
And she would.

There was deep affection in Mari's voice when she spoke
of Violet. She obviously thought of the woman as family.
And if Mari got in the middle of Whitney's fight with the
senator, her chances of survival took a sharp downturn. Whitney already disliked her. She was a rebel and stirred the
other women to mutiny. If he decided to eliminate one of the
women to keep the others in line, his most likely choice would
be Mari.

*If they're walking in like they own the place—maybe they
do. Maybe we have this all wrong, Jack. We know Freeman
helped Whitney lure us to the Congo. Maybe they're strutting
because they have reason. Mari trusts Violet, but that doesn't
mean Violet's not part of this whole thing. She could have
sold out for money and power. People do it all the time. Fuck
the senator and his wife, I'm not letting Mari risk her life for
them.*

Ken felt Mari stirring in his mind. *Violet says they're on
their way up.*

*Don't you tell her anything, Mari, about your escape plans,*
Ken cautioned. *Think of the other women. I'll be monitoring the
conversation, so don't worry about relaying me information.*

Senator Ed Freeman and his wife, Violet, entered the facility, flanked by the security team. *Mari, we're going to come
talk to you about things and then Ed will straighten everything
out with Dr. Whitney.* Violet's voice was calm, controlled, and
very confident.

*We want out of this facility, Violet.*

There was a slight hesitation on Violet's part, but when she
replied, her voice was even smoother. *Ed is going to try to
help. I told him about the breeding program and he thinks it's
appalling. He's ashamed he ever helped Whitney.*

Mari pulled back abruptly. On some level she had known,
but the confirmation of the senator's complicity still shocked
her. *What did he do for Whitney?*

There was a small silence. *He didn't know about us, Mari. Don't make excuses; just tell me what he did.*

Violet sighed, clearly reluctant. *He was on the appropriations committee and kept Whitney well funded.*

*And . . . ,* Mari prompted.

Violet was silent for another long moment. Ken's stomach hardened into knots. He resisted sending another warning to Mari.

*Mari, we're here to help you. This is unnecessary.*

*Maybe to you. I don't think you're all that safe, Violet. You and your husband may be the ones needing help. You've been away from Whitney a long time.*

*What does that mean? What do you know?*

Mari caught the impression of Violet striding down a narrow hall, suddenly looking around herself warily. *Answer me, Violet, or you're on your own.*

*Damn it, Mari. We came here to help you.* Violet hesitated again and then capitulated. *He helped Whitney draw a couple of GhostWalkers to the Congo for some experiment he was conducting. Ed didn't bother to ask what it was. He just was the bait to draw the men there. In return, Whitney and the others put him in a good position for the vice-presidential candidacy.*

Mari's stomach heaved. She knew Ken was listening, felt him go very still. She desperately wanted to wrap her arms around him.

*Was he aware that the man who went to rescue him was captured and tortured? That Ekabela was waiting for him? Violet, he had to have known, and he led them there anyway in order to get a better political position.*

*I know. It was a terrible thing to do, and he regrets it. I've talked to him, made him see what a monster Whitney is.*

Mari closed her eyes. Ed Freeman was directly responsible for Ken's capture and torture by Ekabela. Ken had gone to the Congo to rescue the senator. He'd literally put his life on the line to save him. And Freeman betrayed him for a place on the vice-presidential ballot. Neither Violet nor her husband could possibly conceive of the damage Ed Freeman had done to Ken—damage that would last a lifetime. It sickened Mari that Violet could love such a man.

Ken considered himself a monster. He feared the violence in himself, but Mari knew one Ken was worth a million Ed Freemans. Ken would never, under any circumstances, deliver another man to the enemy, especially knowing how bloodthirsty and brutal Ekabela was. Everyone knew his reputation for genocide, for torture, for the mass murder of opposing forces. Yet Whitney had made a deal with him, and Senator Ed Freeman had gone along with that deal to further his political career. She was suddenly very suspicious that if Freeman was capable of betraying a soldier for political gain—he just might have his own agenda coming here to this place.

Mari broke off contact with Violet. *Ken, I'm so sorry you had to hear that.*

*I'm all right, baby.*

But he wasn't. She knew he wasn't. Tears for him burned her eyes. *Ed Freeman is an asshole, Ken, and Violet's an idiot if she really could love a man like that. I'm not sure what to say to them.*

*It's a trap, Mari. I don't know what they expect to get out of this visit, but they want something, and it isn't to get you and the other women out. Warn the others not to talk to her at all, not to give out any information.*

*They won't.* Mari could feel Violet tugging at her mind, trying to open the pathway between them. Mari kept her out, but it wasn't easy. Her head pounded, and she felt the thin trickle of blood at her ear.

*Tell me what you want to do, baby.*

She made up her mind. They had to go now. Whatever was happening, they couldn't wait, they had to try to make their escape.

*Ken, get to the other women and get their cells unlocked. Do it now!*

*Roger that. I'll give Jack the word they're coming out.*

Violet shoved hard at her mind and Mari let her in. *Mari, honey, I'm afraid for you. Dr. Whitney seemed really upset with you. He didn't want Ed talking to you. He offered to allow him access to all the other women, but I convinced him to insist on speaking with you.*

Mari sank down onto her cot, slamming her mind closed again to Violet. *Ken, Violet is well aware any of the women could tell her husband what's going on here. This isn't about the superbaby program, that's for sure.*

*We're going with your instincts, sweetheart. I've got your back.*

Mari let her breath out. Of course he did. Ken could be counted on. *Get the cells open fast before Whitney pulls his ace out of the hole. Violet's playing with a cobra and she's bound to get bitten.*

The little group came around the corner, Senator Freeman and Violet surrounded by her security team, Whitney leading the way, and, to her disgust, Sean walking beside Whitney.

Whitney stopped in front of her cell, that same little half smile on his face. "The senator would like a word with you, Mari."

She stepped back away from the cell door, glancing at Sean. His gaze was on the smudge marks and strawberry on her throat and going lower below the neckline of her blouse. There was satisfaction in his expression, and she realized he believed she had cooperated with him and he had been the one to leave marks of possession on her body. For some reason, that embarrassed her and she found it much more difficult to face Violet and her husband.

Senator Freeman moved out of the circle of his security guards. "I've been hearing rumors about a breeding program. According to what I've heard, and I can hardly give it credence, Dr. Whitney is forcing psychically enhanced women to breed against their will with enhanced soldiers to produce offspring to be raised as weapons."

*Ken, he sounds like he rehearsed that over and over.* Mari moistened her lips and glanced toward Whitney.

"It's all right, Mari," Freeman assured. "I'm a United States senator. Dr. Whitney isn't going to harm you for telling the truth. You know my wife, Violet. My word is good. I'll see to it that you don't come to any harm."

She moved farther from the door, toward the back of the cell, and shook her head.

"She's afraid Dr. Whitney will hurt the other women," Violet volunteered. "We're trying to help you," she added. "Just tell him the truth."

Eyes locked on Violet, Mari said distinctly, "Yes, Senator, it's all true. There are several women here. Dr. Whitney holds one under threat in order to secure cooperation from the rest of us." *He already knows, Ken. I can see it in his eyes. He looks triumphant and so does Violet. They can't be so stupid as to think Whitney would let them walk out of here if he thought for a minute they'd expose him. What are they up to?*

"You're telling me that these women are held against their will? That the doctor sends soldiers in to force cooperation?"

"You don't need to act as if you're outraged, Ed. You know what's at stake here. You know what we're trying to achieve. Besides, you've done much worse. You helped deliver a U.S. Special Forces soldier to Ekabela to be skinned alive. And as for you, Violet, my dear, you really should have done a better job keeping your husband's attention properly focused."

"We're taking Mari with us," Freeman said, his voice unnecessarily loud and demanding.

It had all definitely been rehearsed. Whitney would never let the senator get away with this puffed-up importance. "No, you aren't. I absolutely won't go with you." *Violet, whatever deal you have with him isn't going to work you know. You can't trust Whitney. If you're selling all of us down the river to stay on the ballot . . .*

*I love my husband, Mari. I don't want him dead.*

Understanding dawned. Mari felt like a fool. *This was your idea. You made the deal with Whitney. Whatever he wants in exchange for Ed's life. You knew he was the one who put the hit out on him.* There was no other explanation. Whitney wanted something from Violet and Ed Freeman, and they were willing to do a deal. In return, Whitney would call off the hit and his friends would back Freeman for the vice presidency. *What did you have to do, Violet? Who'd you sell out?*

*You, of course, Mari. It's all about you and your sister and the Nortons.*

Ken had been running through the maze to get back to Mari. When he heard Violet's answer, his heart somersaulted. *Jack! If I don't get to her in time, they'll be bringing her out with the senator's group. Damn it. Damn it all to hell.*

Senator Freeman stepped close to the door. "You will come with us."

"When I slit your throat, Senator, I'm going to do it slow, so you can feel it, just the way Ekabela did to Ken Norton."

Freeman's eyes flicked to his guards and then to Whitney. "So you do know Ken Norton."

"Don't you say his name," she hissed. "I mean it. Don't you dare." She let the promise of death smolder in her eyes.

The senator stepped back, casting another swift look around him at his bodyguards to insure they were in position. Violet stepped protectively in front of him.

Mari reached out telepathically to her most vulnerable sister. *Rose. Are you clear? Can you get clear?*

*Kane is taking me up to the ground level. We're using the service elevators. He's helping me escape because he's afraid of what Whitney will do to the baby.*

Violet cleared her throat. "She's talking to someone."

Whitney had that same little half smile on his face. "She's talking to him. Ken Norton. You are, aren't you? He's close. I knew he wouldn't leave you, any more than Jack would leave Briony."

"Go to hell, Whitney."

He lifted his eyebrow and gestured Freeman and Violet and their bodyguards down the hall. "There is no point in trying to reason with her when she's this way," he said. "We'll let my men handle it. Would you care for coffee, Ed?" He left without a backward glance, Sean following.

"You look like his dog, Sean," she called after him, furious that both Violet and Sean could be such traitors.

Mari heard heavy footsteps approaching her cell. They wanted her to know they were coming. They wanted her to be afraid. Fear was creeping in whether she wanted it to or not. Whitney always seemed so powerful. Had he found a way to use Mari to capture Ken, Jack, and Briony? She felt sick.

The cell door was yanked opened and she faced two of Whitney's security team. She recognized them both. Don Bascomb thought he was tough, but Gerald Robard really was. The two stood shoulder to shoulder, both with somber expressions.

She forced a smile. "Haven't seen you two around. How

have you been?" She forced herself to look as nonchalant as possible. Mari tried to be the picture of complete cooperation.

There was no warning. Robard was on her before she was even aware she was in danger. He hit her with the force of a nine-hundred-pound tiger, driving her across the room, her head snapping back under the force and a thousand stars whirling, as the room spun and began to go to black. "Sorry, kid," Robard said, catching her before she hit the floor. "There's no need to make this harder on you than it already is." He laid her on her bed. "He wants you looking in bad shape. Whatever you do, Mari, don't defy him like you always do. Just cooperate and it won't be so bad."

Don Bascomb produced a needle and syringe. Mari's eyes widened and she shook her head violently in protest. As Robard bent over her, she brought up both feet and smashed him as hard as she could in the chest, driving him back. He hit the wall from the force of her blow, grunting a little, his face darkening with anger.

"I'm trying to make this easy on you, you little she-devil. Come on, Mari, it's the old man's orders. Anyone else would just take the shot and go to sleep. I can work you over while you're out, and it's done."

It amazed her how reasonable he sounded, as if knocking out a woman and beating the crap out of her while she was unconscious was perfectly okay. Robard swept the blankets from the bed and came at her again.

They wanted Ken to see her black-and-blue body. She was sure they planned to let him catch a glimpse of her as they brought her out to the plane. They were certain he'd follow them—and he would—even back to the Congo.

Bascomb stood back, grinning, as he pulled a couple of vials of clear liquid from his shirt pocket. "Have fun, Ger."

There was no sound, nothing at all to give him away. One moment Bascomb was standing there looking like an ape, taunting his partner, the next he was slumped on the floor, a needle sticking out of his neck and Ken filling the room looking the angel of vengeance. The guard at the door lay in the open doorway in a pool of blood, his throat slit.

"Let's see you hit someone your own size," Ken said softly.

Too softly. Mari winced at his tone. It was one she recognized as being lethal. Being a practical woman, she rolled off the bed and searched Bascomb's body for the other vial, quickly filled a syringe, and circled around behind Robard. He was concentrating on Ken, not thinking she was a threat at all. Ken shouldn't be there. He couldn't get caught, and no matter what, Robard had to be out cold when Whitney got there.

"Ken Norton. How the hell did you get here?" Robard asked, and feigned a right punch, only to swing around with a roundhouse kick.

Ken blocked the attack and delivered a fist with the force of his enhanced strength as well as his body weight behind it, straight to the man's face. Robard staggered under the impact, taking one step back in an effort to regain his balance. Ken ducked under his raised fists and hit hard with three consecutive blows, a left, right, and a hook that stunned Robard. Mari stepped forward and plunged the needle into the guard's buttocks, pushing the plunger to release the clear liquid.

The sound of a door slamming down the hall alerted her. Mari's heart nearly stopped beating. She grabbed Ken's arm and shoved him. "Get out of here. They're coming. I mean it, go now."

He gathered the front of her shirt in his fist and yanked her against him, his mouth coming down hard on hers. "You get into any more trouble, you call me. I mean it, Mari—you try to handle a couple of enhanced soldiers again, bent on beating the shit out of you, and I'm going to turn you over my knee." He brushed fingers down her bruised face. "This has got to stop."

"We're almost there, Ken. I swear, I'll go with you as soon as possible. Give me a little more time."

He crushed her mouth under his, teeth tugging until she opened for him, tongue sweeping in and taking over. She could taste anger and desperate fear. No one had ever cared that much about her before. She felt empowered by his concern. Mari kissed him back, a breathless moment of hot silk, sizzling electricity, and welling passion, and then she resolutely pushed him away.

"Go. They're coming now."

He still hadn't released her shirt. "You be safe, Mari. You hear me? You be safe. Whatever happens, whatever that son of a bitch Whitney manages to do, I'll get you out of here. Understand? Stay alive and know I'm coming for you."

The hot lick of desire mingling with his fears for her turned her heart into a melting pot of mush. She pushed at the wall of his chest again, feeling a little frantic. "I will. Just go. You have to go."

His thumb slid down the curve of her cheek; he pressed the bloody knife into her hand, and he was gone, slipping away just as she heard voices down the hall. Mari stepped back, away from the two bodies, straightening her clothes and waiting for Whitney with her chin up.

The doctor stopped abruptly when he saw the door to her cell open and both of his supersoldiers lying on the ground unconscious and his guard dead. His gaze flicked to the darkening bruise on her face and then to the knife in her hand.

"Marigold. You seem to have had a little trouble."

She spread her hands innocently. "The two of them came up looking to give me a shot for no apparent reason. They said something about vitamins, but you know what a phobia I have about needles."

Violet cleared her throat, looking suddenly nervous, her gaze sweeping the hall and ceiling, even the floor. "Come on, Ed, let's get out of here," Violet said, tugging at his arm. "This isn't our business." She signaled to her team and they surrounded the senator, pushing him toward the elevator.

Realizing they were reneging on their deal, Whitney called for his guards and then stepped back watching, as he always did, detached and unemotional, waiting to see what would happen as if he were in the middle of a scientific experiment and not a life-and-death drama being played out before his eyes.

Violet's team and Whitney's men went at each other, fighting viciously.

Violet shoved the senator ahead of her. "Run for the elevator!"

"There's no escape," Whitney said, complacent.

She ignored him, running behind her husband, a gun in her hand. Mari scooped up a gun and started to follow her. A downed security guard grabbed her ankle, tripping her. She went down hard.

"Stop them," Whitney ordered.

Before anyone else could move, Sean stepped forward and, in one smooth, efficient motion, swiped at Whitney's throat with a razor-sharp knife.

# CHAPTER 18

The soldier closest to Whitney yanked him back and down. The blade sliced across the back of soldier's arm. As he whipped out his gun and leveled it at Sean, Whitney yelled, "No! Don't kill him. I need him alive."

Sean didn't look at any of the security team. His gaze was solely on Whitney, as if he were a robot programmed to destroy. In spite of the men who were surrounding the doctor, he waded in, fists flying, trying to achieve his goal.

Mari struggled to her feet. Violet and the senator were already at the elevator, and they weren't waiting for her. She was left on her own, facing Whitney, his supersoldiers, and a demonic Sean. She took a deep breath and inched toward the hall. Most of the guards were watching Sean, trying to find a way to subdue him without getting hurt. He was fast and dangerous, and most of them had at one time or another been bested by him.

She couldn't use the elevator, so the stairs were her only option. She made it about six feet before Whitney turned his attention to her. "Stay where you are, Mari. You don't want Rose to get hurt, now, do you?"

*Rose? Are you out?* Mari hesitated, needing reassurance.

*Kane made me run. He fought off a couple of the guards. Someone, must be your friends, provided covering fire. I'm over the fence and running free. Someone tried to stop me; he kept shouting they could get me out, but I don't trust anyone. I'm sticking to our original plan. Scatter and evade. I can get to the stash of money and take my share.*

Mari knew she had hesitated too long. Most of Whitney's supersoldiers in the vicinity wrestled Sean to the ground. He was making animal noises and still trying to crawl, with the security force on his back, toward Whitney.

*Cami. Are all the girls safe and away?*

*We're close. We'll scatter and will meet you at the rendezvous point,* Cami confirmed. *Are you out? I'll come back and help.*

The doctor sighed. "You're a lot more talented than I ever suspected, aren't you, Mari? And to think I nearly gave the order to eliminate you. Are you pregnant with Norton's child?"

"You sent Sean to me last night. I won't know until after it's born, will I?" She took another step back, but two of Whitney's guards were locked on to her. Each step she took, they mirrored, so they were doing a macabre dance with her.

It was bizarre and very difficult to be in a deadly dance and yet hold a telepathic conversation with her sister. Of course Cami would risk her life and return to aid Mari. Mari would do it for her. *No! Keep moving. I'm going with Ken to his home in Montana.* She sent the images of its location she'd picked out his head.

"I don't understand how I could have missed your abilities all these years." Whitney frowned and rubbed at the bridge of his nose.

"I knew you were psychic. You use touch, don't you?" she guessed shrewdly, hoping to throw the guards off by talking to Whitney. She gained a few more inches, but the entrance to the stairs was still so far away. She was fast, very fast, but Whitney's team was enhanced.

*No!* Cami objected. *Don't trust any of them. Stick to our plan.*

*Go, Cami. I'm in a fight right now. Get away!*

"Very good, my dear. Of course I do. I have a superior brain as well as being psychic. There are very few true strong psychics in the world." He glanced toward Sean. The man was pinned down and secured with flex-cuffs on both his ankles and wrists. He was still fighting to get to Whitney. "You controlled his mind, Mari. You planted a suggestion, a nasty one at that. He hasn't touched you, has he? He simply thinks that he has. Yet Brett . . . ," he said thoughtfully, a small frown of concentration on his face.

Mari leapt to cover the distance, using enhanced physical ability to gain the stairway. She grasped the railing, leapt onto it, and, using it as a springboard, jumped half a flight of stairs. She raced up to the third-level landing. She heard Whitney yell to his men to go after her, and she caught the second banister and made a second jump.

*Ken. I'm on the run. Are the other women away clean?* She didn't like that *almost* Cami had given her and wanted him with her. She could hear the men, one leaping after her, the other galloping up the stairs, talking into a radio, and telling someone to cut her off. Someone was waiting on the next staircase; she heard the radio and the buzz of men's voices.

*I led them out through the corridor. Your friend Cami's taking them the rest of the way. It's up to them to get out once they're on the surface. Jack says all hell is breaking loose. I'm on my way back to you.*

*I'm on the stairs, trying to get to level two, but I'm trapped between two security teams. I don't think I can make it to you. You'll have to go without me.*

*Like hell, don't be ridiculous. I'm not leaving without you. How close are you to level two? Can you beat the team chasing you?*

*Yes, but I'm running right into the men waiting for me.* Mari paused, unable to decide what direction would be the most promising.

*Keep going, sweetheart. Fast. You want to be at the top; hit them hard and mean, buy us a couple of seconds.*

*What are you going to do?*

*I'm going to take down his house. I take it Sean didn't get him?*

*No, and Whitney realized he was under a suggestion, but he thinks I did it.* She had sprinted as fast as she could up the long staircase. Without slowing down, she hit the door and plowed into the security guard waiting there for her. They both went down, Mari kicking hard at his face.

The guard caught her left foot and twisted, rolling her over onto her stomach, but she kicked at him with her right foot, hitting him hard enough that his hold loosened. Still using the momentum of the fall, she rolled over into a crouch and sprang back to her feet. The second guard loomed over her, and she ran into his chest before she could stop her forward motion. He wrapped his arms around her smaller frame, pinning her arms against her sides. Mari used her knees, driving upward to hit him under the chin with the top of her head.

She dug both thumbs under his ribs, and when his arms loosened, she dropped lower, spreading her elbows to gain even more precious inches of room. She was able to get one arm free and drove the heel of her palm into his nose, pivoting to throw her body weight behind the blow. Breaking free, she tried to run again, knowing the two other guards who had been chasing her were only a couple of steps behind her.

*Get down!*

She dropped, both hands covering her head, as a deafening explosion knocked them all off their feet. Ken burst out of the rubble, grabbing her arm and jerking her up. As he turned, he drove the toe of his boot into one guard's head, dropping him like a stone. "Run, Mari!"

Ken tossed her a gun and a knife, then dropped back to protect her as she made her way through the dirt and debris. *Go left. Take the left passage,* he instructed as he laid down a spray of bullets, driving their pursuers back.

Mari whirled around, all business, as two lab techs popped up waving guns. She shot them both, her aim deadly. She kept moving, running along the narrow hall, twice taking out a camera as she went, her legs carrying her when her mind felt numb.

"The others, Ken, have you heard anything?" Mari asked anxiously.

Ken swept her against the partition, covering her body with his as bullets spat into the wall behind them. He returned fire, pushing her forward, urging her to run while he stepped out and sent covering fire down the long hall. Glass shattered, and guards leapt into doorways, finding whatever shelter they could. Ken ran backward, keeping up the fire until they rounded the next corner and he could turn and sprint after her.

"Jack says the women took off in different directions. My team had a hell of a time providing covering fire for them, but no one could stop them long enough to get them to the waiting helicopter. They went up and over the fence and scattered into the forest. We stopped most of their pursuers, but there's one hell of a firefight going on between Violet's men guarding the senator and Whitney's supersoldiers. It actually helped get the women out."

Ken caught her arm, bringing her to an abrupt halt as he yanked open a small maintenance door set into the wall. "The grill, get inside the shaft. Hurry."

She didn't waste time asking questions. They only had seconds. When the guards rounded the corner and saw they were gone, they would check the small maintenance room. She yanked the grill free and dove into the shaft, scrambling forward to give Ken plenty of room. He pulled the grill after him and signaled her forward.

Almost immediately bullets cut through the door and walls of the room behind them. Mari hesitated, her heart pounding, but Ken pushed her bottom, urging her to keep moving. Mari crawled as fast as she could, trying to stay quiet. The tube was surprisingly large, and getting wider as she moved down it. Ken tapped her ankle as she came up on another grill.

She pushed it out and like the other one, the grill fell open easily, the screws already removed. Mari slid through headfirst, rolling, gun up and ready, tracking the room. She found herself in another maintenance room, tools scattered everywhere and a bucket of dirty water with a mop stuck in it pulled away from the wall. The bucket seemed out of place to her with all the tools.

She looked around, breathing hard, struggling to control her fear. She'd been on several missions with bullets flying, but nothing had prepared her for this—escaping from Whitney. He had controlled her life for so long she wasn't certain she could even think for herself.

Ken's hand brushed the nape of her neck. "You've been

thinking for yourself for a very long time, honey. Stop worrying."

"You weren't touching me and you knew what I was thinking. I hate that. You scare me sometimes."

He flashed a small grin at her as he pushed past her to crack open the door enough to peer out. "You don't exactly have a poker face, darlin'," he drawled.

"I wish I could believe you, but I'm not that transparent. I spent too long fooling Whitney. You've got way more psychic talent than you let on."

The alarm was blaring through the compound now, and chaos had broken out. Lab techs hurried out into the corridor. Ken reached out and snagged a man by his coat, yanking him into the closet and smashing an elbow to his head. The tech slumped to the floor and lay there groaning. "Get his jacket off."

Mari crouched down to pull the jacket from the tech. Whitney had made it mandatory for all techs on the third level to wear a black lab coat and those on the second level a white one. The man was wearing a white coat, but she'd caught a glimpse of several third-level techs. They were swarming up the stairs along with the security teams sweeping through each of the levels.

"What was the explosion?" She kicked the man as he tried to rise, and he went down a second time. Mari donned the jacket and looked around the room for a hat.

"I set a few timed charges. They'll keep going off at odd intervals, just enough to keep Whitney and his men rattled. The women are over the fence and presumably away. Jack says unfortunately the senator is almost to the plane. Jack's waiting for us."

"They don't have my sisters?" She winced as Ken grabbed a second white-coated tech and slammed him into the wall. He bounced and Ken dragged him into the small room. "Not a single one?"

"Your sisters aren't very trusting." His vivid gaze pinned her. "You knew they wouldn't be. You all discussed it ahead of time, didn't you?"

To avoid his glacier-cold eyes, Mari bent down to pull the jacket from the tech. "Yes. I knew you wouldn't be happy."

And he'd be even less happy knowing she was supposed to get away from him and meet them as soon as possible.

"Just because my men are risking their lives to get the women out? Your sisters knew they were going to be there, with bullets flying and a helicopter waiting, and they went over the fence and scattered into the woods." He reached down and pulled her to her feet. "Are you planning to do the same thing?"

She avoided his eyes. What was she planning? She was going to see Briony. She was going to try with Ken. "I'm planning on going out with you, fighting for all I'm worth and gaining freedom. You know that word that is supposed to represent the American way? *Freedom*, Ken. We wanted the freedom to make our own decisions."

"They're psychic, most without anchors, the same as you are. How are they—or you–going to survive without aid? And do you really think Whitney is just going to let them go? He'll send every soldier he has to get them back. We could have protected them."

"And exchanged one prison for another?"

His heart felt like it was being squeezed in a vise. "Is that what you think you're doing, Mari?"

Their eyes met. He counted his heartbeats. She *had* talked with her sisters about taking off on her own. He had handed her his soul, and she was thinking of walking away from him. And why not? Life with him would be a form of prison. He couldn't deny it—not even to himself. He would want to run her life, wrap her in bubble wrap and keep her hidden from the world and any danger it might present. She desperately wanted, needed—and deserved—freedom.

Ken swallowed everything he wanted to say and took the jacket from her, shrugging into it. The coat was too small, and pulled across his arms and back, but it would do getting down the corridor. With explosives going off every few minutes, he doubted Whitney was staring into the security cameras. Ken had taken a great deal of time setting the charges for maximum chaotic effect.

Mari caught his arm before he opened the tool room door again. "I don't think I'm exchanging prisons, Ken. I'm just afraid. Terrified, in fact. I don't have a clue what to expect outside this facility. I feel as if I'm going AWOL. I need to find out who and what I am and if I can even live with the rest of the world."

She didn't add *before I can be in a relationship*, but he heard the echo of the words in his heart. Maybe he heard them in her head. And a relationship with him would not be of her choosing, once she was out in the real world where normal men, with maybe a penchant for romance and gentleness, were available to her.

*Ken.* Jack's voice intruded, sharp with command. *All hell is breaking loose up here. Can you get to the first level? Logan and Neil are making their way to you. I'm backing them up, but if I don't see your ass in the next few minutes, I'm breaking protocol and coming to get you. Get moving now.* There was urgency in Jack's voice.

Ken knew his brother would too. Jack would place his own life and anyone else's in danger to get Ken out of trouble, just as Ken would do for him. *I'm on my way. We're on the second level trying to make our way up to the first. Give me a few minutes.*

*You might not have a few minutes. Oh shit!* There was a moment of complete concentration.

Ken recognized the blank, emotionless will of iron in his brother that meant he was sending a bullet into someone. He waited, knowing something bad had happened.

*One of the security guards guiding the senator to the plane just shot him in the head. Violet took the son of a bitch out and pulled her husband into the plane, but it doesn't look good. We can't tell the bad guys from the good guys, Ken. You've got to get out of there and make it to the helicopter. They're pouring out of that building like bees.*

*Roger that.* Ken cracked open the door enough to peer into the hall. Mostly techs ran for the stairs. A few security guards and soldiers pushed through the corridor trying to see the individuals, which told him Whitney hadn't given up hope of finding them.

*Anyone spot Whitney?*

*You and I both know he's got himself a tunnel or two. He's not going to get trapped here. He's probably halfway to his next lair. He pushes a button on a computer and his data is sent to other computers and he abandons this lab.*

Ken pulled Mari close. "Stay close to me. Walk directly to the stairs. Keep the gun in your pocket and ready to use. Don't look up toward the cameras, just walk with the flow of the other techs."

"They'll recognize me. They don't have women techs here. Whitney thought it too much of a distraction."

"Your hair isn't that long. You can pull the jacket up around your neck. We've got to go now, Mari. And if I say run, take off and don't look back."

"I'm not leaving you."

"I'll be right behind you. I'm not a hero, honey. I'm not about to let Whitney hook me up to some machine for the rest of my life."

She caught the front of his jacket. "I may have been afraid and even hesitating, but I plan on going with you. See that you're right behind me. I mean it, Ken, because I'll go back for you." Doubts of the future aside, she'd never leave Ken to Whitney's mercy.

"You sound like my brother, and I'm warning you, Mari, you do anything stupid like that and I'm going to put you over my knee."

She rolled her eyes. "I've been caned, Ken. The threat of a spanking doesn't scare me much."

He gave her a little shove. "Get moving. Keep moving."

She was going with him. He had a reprieve. He had no idea how he was going to keep her, but at least she wasn't going to go over the fence and strike out on her own. The women had been planning an escape for some time, and even though Ken and his team had been there offering protection, they hadn't taken a chance on deviating from their plan. They believed in one another and no one else. Even Violet was out of their circle. It worried Ken. If the women turned on Mari for choosing to stay with him, would she eventually resent him?

He shoved all thoughts from his head and went into warrior mode the moment he stepped out of the tool closet. He dropped back several paces to better protect Mari as she pushed her way through the hall. She gave herself fighting room, he noted with approval, and she moved with confidence, but kept her face averted from the cameras. She had a woman's walk, her hips swaying, and he saw two of the soldiers react as she passed. The men were standing in a doorway, searching faces as the techs went by.

Before either man could speak into his radio, Ken shot them. He used a kill shot, taking them down fast and hard, a one-two attack that had both men sinking to the floor almost before the shots registered with the fleeing crowd. He kept moving, hiding the gun with his body, reacting with the others, nearly running.

A bullet whined past his ear and hit a tech close to him, driving the man into the wall. Blood sprayed and the tech screamed, clamping his hand on his shoulder. Immediately everyone ran, knocking into one another, pushing and shoving as they raced for the stairs.

Ken lost sight of Mari as he crouched low, letting the crowd hide him, while he searched for the enemy. A barrage of bullets swept low through the running mass, knocking people off their feet so that they sprawled on the floor and others trampled them. Blood ran down the corridor. Ken slipped back into the shadow of a doorway and fired rapidly at the lights, plunging the hall into darkness. Instantly he went up the wall, climbing like a spider until he gained the beams running along the ceiling support.

*Ken!* Mari sounded slightly panicked.

*I'm alive. Get the hell out. Jack will cover you. You can trust Neil and Logan. They'll get you to the helicopter.*

*I'm not going without you.*

Bullets swept the entire area where he'd been, the enemy systematically sweeping low and going high, ruthlessly cutting down anyone who ran into the kill zone. Ken fired at the flash, concentrating a tight four-point target where the heart should be.

*Mari, I swear, I'll kick your stubborn little ass if you don't do what I say. Go!*

He dropped to the floor and lay flat, waiting for a return, but there was only the sound of the dying and the frightened cries of the techs wanting out but unable to gather the courage to move again. He took a careful look around, using his enhanced night vision. A man was down several feet to his left, gun still in hand, a pool of blood spreading under him. Ken leapt up and sprinted for the stairs, leaping over fallen men, ignoring their cries for help.

He jumped halfway up the stairs, ran up the rest, and burst out into the first-level hallway.

*Down! Down!*

Mari's frantic cry had him diving for the floor, rolling as close to a doorway as possible while his gun was out and tracking. A barrage of bullets kept him rolling, the sound deafening in the narrow confines of the corridor. He managed to crawl into an open door and scramble up the side of the wall to position his body directly over the door. The jacket tore as his muscles bulged, holding his weight spread-eagled across the entryway. He could see where a bullet had pierced the material, leaving a hole through the fabric.

*They're coming in. Standard two-man drill. Watch yourself.* There was fear in her voice.

*You all right, honey?* He was calm, soothing. This was what he lived for. She may as well know it. He'd been born a warrior, and anyone stupid enough to come after him simply had a death wish.

*I've got a knife. Idiot didn't do a righteous search. Signal when you're clear.*

He ignored the anxiety in her voice, keeping his tone the same calm note. *You'll know. How many guards have you got on you?*

*Two. I can take them out; just make sure you get your two.* Mari's tone matched his now, calm and sure and filled with confidence.

The two soldiers emptied their guns into the door and walls of the room before slamming new clips in and kicking open what was left of the door. It splintered and broke from the hinges, and the two came into the room, back to back, spraying bullets in a semicircle to cover every inch of the room.

*Now, Mari.*

Ken leapt from the ceiling, palming his gun and shooting the closest soldier from midair. He landed in a crouch and shot the second one up close. He ripped the tech jacket off of him, though he disliked the white color for surfacing in the dark. *You clear, baby?* He peered around the corner.

One guard lay at Mari's feet, obviously dead. The other man fought with her for the knife. Ken saw the man's shoulder twist and he punched Mari twice, going for the throat. She managed to turn her body enough for him to miss his target, but the blows rocked her. She didn't drop the knife. Ken came up behind the guard and used his own knife, shoving the blade to the hilt into the man's kidney. He slammed the flat of his hand against the guard's head, driving him away and down, and reached out to pull Mari to him.

He did a quick appraisal, making certain she wasn't bleeding as they turned to jog down the hall. "They're going to hit us with everything they have," he said. "He isn't going to want you to get away."

"He won't kill me," Mari said with absolute confidence. "He thinks I controlled Sean and planted the suggestion that we'd had sex."

Ken shot her a glance even as he continued to scan the hall. *It's too easy, Jack. He's up to something.* "He figured that out?"

"Not much gets passed Whitney. He didn't let the guards kill Sean either. He told them not to, and that means he'll send Sean after me."

"I'm counting on it," Ken said, keeping his shields firmly in place. The last thing she needed to do was feel the raw violence swirling around in his brain. He wanted to take Sean apart one piece at a time and had every intention of doing so.

"But he'll do everything he can to kill you," Mari said. "I want to cover you. You lead and I'll drop back."

Ken pointed ahead of him. "We do it the way I've always done it. We have help waiting. Just head for the helicopter. We'll get you out." As he handed her more clips, he touched her mind, not wanting insubordination in the middle of what he knew was going to be a hell of a firefight.

Mari planned to give herself up if it came down to his life or her freedom—and she wanted freedom now that she'd had a taste of it. But she was determined he wouldn't be captured and tormented by Peter Whitney. The woman could tear out his heart if he was stupid enough to let her. Ken paused, keeping to the left of the door, holding her to him. His lips brushed the back of her head.

*No matter what happens, Jack, swear to me, you tell the*

*team we get her out. I don't care if you have to hit her over the head and take her out unconscious. She's not playing the heroine and saving my ass at the cost of hers.*

Jack's amusement was soothing balm on a sore wound. *Oh, you got it bad, bro. That woman has you tied up in knots. Get the hell out here and let's go. We're not leaving anyone behind.*

Ken believed in few things, but he believed in his brother. He gave Mari the location of the helicopter. "Run. Let the team provide covering fire. You keep going and I'll be right on your heels."

*We're coming out,* he warned his team.

*You've got enemies scattered in a loose semicircle,* Jack warned. *Mitch is trying for the bluff, but he isn't going to make it.* There was a moment of silence and then a rifle shot. *Oh darn, he slipped back and isn't moving.*

Mari took off, sprinting with the blurring speed of an enhanced soldier, Ken keeping pace right behind her. She didn't run straight, but zigzagged, trying to find cover where there was little to find. Gunfire erupted all around them, but they kept running, Ken trusting Jack and the others to keep the enemy pinned.

*Incoming.*

*Down, Mari, hit the ground.* Ken leapt forward to tackle her, driving her down even as he warned her, sheltering her body with his. Angry bees stung his back and legs, but he sprawled over Mari, striving with his arms to cover her head and keep her safe from the small, deadly missiles the minibomb was ejecting.

Jack swore in his head, the curses long and eloquent. *Nails. They put nails in the damn thing. You look like a fuckin' porcupine. Can you run?*

*I have to. I can do it. Just don't let them throw one of those again.* He hurt like a son of a bitch, but he wasn't about to get shot—or captured. He rose, his back and calf muscles screaming at him. Mari obviously felt the pain in his mind, because she kept trying to turn, to see him, but he pushed her firmly forward again.

He put the pain out of his mind. Compartmentalizing was a useful tool, and Ken and Jack had learned it early in life. He ran flat-out, the nails in his body not slowing him down. Several shooters—including Neil and Logan closing in on either side of them and dropping to one knee—systematically picked off the enemy.

Mari made it to the helicopter and caught Martin's hand, allowing him to jerk her inside. Ken leapt in and caught the rifle thrown at him, picking it out of the air with one hand, swinging it to his shoulder, and dropping to cover his brother as he came out of the foliage. He heard Mari's gasp as she saw the nails in his body, but his concentration was on the enemy and covering Jack's butt.

Jack came out into the open, firing steadily. Ken caught sight of a soldier tracking his twin and he squeezed the trigger. The man went down, and Ken immediately swept the area looking for others. One rose up right in front of Jack, shooting too fast. Ken saw Jack stagger.

*Drop.* Even as Ken gave the order, he pulled the trigger. Jack hit the ground and the soldier fell almost on top of him. *How bad you hurt?*

*Just clipped me, took a little bit of muscle, but I'll live.* Jack was already up and covering ground fast, looking just as lethal as ever in spite of the blood on his right arm.

*Stop trying to look cool and get your ass in the helicopter. Everyone knows you're a tough guy.* Ken kept the worry from his voice, covering his concern with their usual jokes.

*I was hoping you'd come and carry me; I'm feeling a bit weak.* Jack fired off another round, and a soldier using a boulder as a partial shield went down.

Ken tracked two of the enemy sighting on Jack and shot them both. *Briony's going to be really pissed at you for coming home damaged.*

*I'm bringing her sister. She'll be treating me like a hero.* Jack made it the last few feet and leapt inside. Martin and Neil followed suit.

"Go, go," Neil ordered, and all of them turned their attention to any ground fire coming their way.

Logan pressed Ken down and sat beside him. "Toss me the med kit." He pointed behind Mari's head.

She snagged it and threw it to him, her gaze still on the ground, watching. Once the rifle went to her shoulder, and she pulled the trigger.

"We're clear. No birds in the air."

She noted there was no relaxing. Neil and Martin took up positions to protect the helicopter as Logan began to pull the nails from Ken's back and calves. Most were shallow; there were one or two that looked deeper. Logan ripped Ken's shirt from his body, and she caught all of the men glancing at one another.

Mari dropped down beside Ken and put her hand on the back of his head. She leaned close to him, feeling protective, knowing he wouldn't show it, but he detested the others seeing the scars and the way his back looked like a giant grater had scraped over him, turning the skin haphazardly to cottage cheese. The front of his chest had the same thin pattern of scars as his face and neck. There was no way to block the line of vision all his team members had. She despised the looks on their faces.

*Hey, baby, you doing all right?* She wanted to ask out loud, for all of them to hear the concern for him in her voice, to hear what she felt for him, but she couldn't make herself that vulnerable. She asked it softly, intimately, in his mind, trying to join them together so he could feel she was with him.

His fingers tangled with hers. There was physical pain, but he could easily bear that. It was much, much more difficult to have his friends staring at him—seeing him—seeing the terrible destruction of his body. Mari ached for him, felt tears burning in her eyes and throat for him. He had been a handsome man with an astonishing face and physique, and Ekabela had taken great care to destroy him, inch by inch.

She bent closer, her lips feathering gently over his temple in an effort to distract him. *Thanks for coming to get me. I really didn't want to stay there.*

His fingers tightened around hers and he drew her hand to his mouth.

"What the hell's going on here?" Jack demanded. "I've been shot. Does anybody give a damn, or do I have to sit here and bleed to death while you all baby my brother?"

Neil and Martin instantly turned their attention to Jack.

"Sorry. It didn't look that bad," Neil said.

"That bad?" Jack echoed. "I'm pouring blood."

Ken choked. When Mari touched his mind, he was laughing. For the first time since she'd met Jack, she actually liked him a little. She respected him as a soldier, was filled with awe and admiration for him as a sniper, but she hadn't liked him very much and wasn't altogether certain she wanted Briony with him.

With one small performance Jack had changed her opinion of him. He wasn't the type of man to call attention to himself or be bothered by a small wound. He had his own scars, evidence of his torture at the hands of the same man who had had Ken for so long. Jack Norton had the reputation of being as tough as nails. She sent him a small smile and helped his game.

"I'll be sure and tell Briony how tough you are."

"Briony's probably going to hit me with something when she sees me. I promised her I'd be careful."

"I'll tell her you were showing off."

"You do that and I'm retaliating. That sister of yours can be mean."

Ken closed his eyes, fingers tight around Mari's, and allowed himself to drift. He was physically exhausted, three days without sleep and his body on fire from the nails, but he had Marigold and that was all that mattered. He relaxed, listening to his brother banter with her while the helicopter took them far away from Peter Whitney and his insane experiments.

# CHAPTER 19

Ken's home, situated deep in the Montana wilderness and surrounded by national forest on three sides, was the most beautiful thing Mari had ever seen. Ken stood beside her as she stared up in awe at the giant log cabin. To her, the house looked like the epitome of the wonderful homes she'd fantasized about when she'd watched old movies the men had occasionally smuggled in for the women.

"We have twenty-four hundred acres, Mari, so you definitely have freedom." Ken covered his sudden anxiety with a small smile. "Unless you think you'd prefer to be a city girl." He could never live comfortably in the city, but he knew if she wanted that—needed at least to try—he would go with her.

Mari shook her head. "I wouldn't do well in a city. Too many people, too much traffic and noise. I prefer solitude."

Ken let out his breath. "We're completely self-sufficient here. If we ever ran short of funds, we could harvest trees. We actually have a workable gold mine too, although we've never bothered with it. The water supply to the property is gravity-fed, and we use a hydro-electric system that powers batteries." He wanted her to love the place the way he did, to feel the sense of freedom in the larger-than-life forest surrounding them and the complete self-sufficiency of their home. "Right now we're using only a very small percentage of the power available to us. Jack and I could live off the land, hunting and harvesting crops if necessary, so this is a perfect place for us."

"I didn't expect it to be so big."

"Right now the house is over three thousand square feet. Jack and Briony have the larger wing. We've been working on a nursery for them. We share a kitchen, dining room, and great room with them, and our wing is on the other side. At the moment we have a bedroom, bath, and office, but I have a second bedroom roughed in. The garage nearly doubles the space, so we have plenty of room to expand if we want to, and if Jack and Briony keep it up, we'll have to very soon." He flashed a small grin. "They're expecting twins."

"You never mentioned that."

"I like to save the best for last."

She smiled at him. "That's kind of scary. Twins run in your family, do they?"

He nodded. "Big time."

She looked away from him back to the house. "I love the logs. What are they?"

Ken didn't let his disappointment show. She wasn't ready for commitment. He had gotten her to his home in the Montana forest; he had to be happy with that and hope he could convince her to stay. "Western white pine. We fitted them together with Swedish cope and used oil to finish them off. Jack made most of the furniture in the house. He's very good at woodworking."

"It's beautiful. I love the porch."

"The roof is built for warfare, and we have an escape tunnel. We have alarms and a few traps to let us know if unwanted visitors show up. The wood shop is just down there in that meadow, and the smaller garage houses the equipment. We have a vegetable garden in that little strip of land where the sun shines the most. Briony planted the flowers everywhere."

Mari's hand gripped his. "Is she here?"

"Don't sound so scared. No, Jack will bring her tomorrow. He wanted to see her first. He's protective of her."

"He still doesn't quite trust me, does he?"

"Jack doesn't trust anything or anyone when it comes to

Briony," Ken said. "She's his world, and if anything happened to her, he'd go berserk. She'll be here, honey, trust me; she's excited to know you're alive and well. Nothing is going to keep her from coming home."

"Except Jack."

"For a night. He wants her to himself tonight, and I was hoping we'd have a few hours together."

Mari stood at the bottom of the steps looking at the wrap-around verandah. The night was falling and the wind rustled through the trees. There was a bite of cold in the air, enough to make her shiver.

"Are you afraid of me, Mari?" Ken asked.

She lifted her hand to his face. As always, in the shadow of the night, the scarring faded away, leaving masculine perfection behind. "No, Ken, it's not you." She hesitated as if searching for the right words—or the trust she needed to expose her fears. "It's me. I don't know anything about who I am or what I want. When I'm away from you, I feel as if I can't breathe without you. How can I ever learn to be complete if I go from never making a single decision on my own to being in such an intense relationship?" She looked stricken. "I'm just taking it for granted that you want a relationship. You've never said. Not once."

She retreated, stepping back away from him, away from the house. The forest, with all the gently swaying trees and thick foliage, seemed a refuge, something she knew, somewhere she could hide. She felt exposed and vulnerable and very confused.

"I'll say it now, Mari. I never want you to leave me. I want you more than I've ever wanted anything in my life. I can give you time—whatever you need." Even as he said it, he didn't know if he was telling the truth. He wanted to give her time, to give her freedom, but there were limits to his abilities and he knew them better than most people.

She traced the outline of his lips. "You're frowning."

"I was lying. I can't lie to you like that. I'm not a perfect man, Mari. I want to be everything you need, but I can't watch you with other men while you figure out whether or not this relationship is the one you want."

"Other men?" Her dark eyes glittered at him. "What do other men have to do with this?"

"I don't want you looking to other men to help you figure things out."

Her eyebrows drew together, and both hands clenched into fists. She glanced toward the forest again, then resolutely turned toward the house and stalked up the stairs to the porch to keep from hitting him. "Other men? You have got to be out of your mind. Did you already forget where I came from?"

Mari paced across the porch, furious with him and herself. She'd put herself in a vulnerable position. She didn't belong here. She stole another look at the forest. She belonged there. She belonged with her sisters. She could trust them. They'd had a plan together, and she had deviated from the plan. She pressed her fingers to her suddenly throbbing temple. What had she done?

He cleared his throat, rubbed the bridge of his nose, and then shoved his hand through his hair in agitation. How the hell did men do this kind of thing on a daily basis? It was like walking through a minefield—one wrong step and everything would blow up in his face. "You're right, that was stupid of me. I'm not doing this very well."

"Get over being worried about me and other men, Ken," she snapped.

He nodded. He'd have to find a way to curb his jealousy fast. She wasn't a woman to put up with it. There was no way to miss the clenched fist. "Most women would have trouble with the solitude up here. In the winter, the road is impassable without snowmobiles. There aren't any phones. We have a radio of course, but not too many women want to be so isolated."

Her gaze flicked to his face. "Do I seem to you the kind of woman who has to be entertained all the time? I'm used to isolation."

"Mari, I've never done this before. Never. I've never once brought a woman to this house or wanted a relationship with one. I may be making every mistake in the book here, but I'm trying to be honest, not judge you."

"Never?"

"Never what?"

"You've never brought a woman here before?"

"This is my sanctuary, sweetheart. My home. I come here when the world closes in on me and I need to regroup. It's calm and peaceful and feels like home. You belong here; no one else ever has."

"I don't really know what a home feels like." She gestured toward the forest. "I look at that and I feel like it's calling to me. I want to run free, Ken. Just run through the trees." Her eyes met his. "Could I do that?"

He tried to still his pounding heart. He knew better than to try to hold a wild bird, but he wanted to grab her with both hands. "Of course. Tomorrow we'll get you a pair of running shoes. You can go out anytime you like. I prefer mornings, but it's beautiful all the time."

She didn't reply, just stood staring at the beckoning trees.

Ken held out his hand to her. She might not be fully committed to a relationship with him, but he was with her. She looked right and felt right in his sanctuary. More than anything else, for all his uneasiness over what to say and do, he felt happy, really happy, just with her being on his property. All he had to do was find a way to make her feel the same way.

Mari put her hand in his and reluctantly followed him to the solid door, trying not to show fear. "How do you keep this house warm when it's snowing?"

"We use wood heat. We have very efficient fireplaces in the bedrooms, great room, and kitchen. We can close off each wing of the house so it's private and separate, or open them and have one large home."

"And Briony lives here year round?" She latched on to that. She wanted to see Briony—just once. One time. She had lived with memories and fantasies about her twin for so long, she wanted to see her.

"We wouldn't leave her here alone if we were gone on a mission. Jack would never allow that." The words slipped out before he could censor them.

Mari glanced at him sharply as she stepped across the threshold. "*Allow?*"

"When it comes to Briony, we're very safety conscious. I imagine you will be as well. She's carrying twins, and Whitney has made several tries to take her. His last try cost us part of the house and one outer building, but the son of a bitch didn't get her."

Mari looked around her. She could see a woman's touch in

the home, and her heart did a funny little somersault. Her sister. Briony was really alive and well and living right here, in this house. Her sister whom she hadn't seen in years, but had thought of every single day.

There were thick quilts lying across the backs of well-made furniture, the kind of quilts Mari knew were made with love, by hand. Stained glass was cut above each of the windows, the work intricate and beautiful, colors swirling together to form fantasy pictures undoubtedly chosen, or made, by her sister.

Mari walked through the empty rooms, hearing the echo of laughter, feeling the bond of love woven into the very walls. By the time she reached Ken's bedroom, tears burned in her eyes and clogged her throat. She couldn't do this. Why had she thought she could? She wasn't in the least bit feminine. She couldn't decorate a house, or be any kind of a wife or partner. She didn't know about anything but fighting a battle. She should have gone with her sisters—the ones she knew, the ones different in the way she was different. They'd never lived in a home and didn't know the first thing about living in a relationship.

Briony lived here, and Briony knew exactly how to be a wife and mother. She obviously cared for both men, not just Jack. Mari would never be able to live up to her sister. And she was happy for Briony—she really was. She was just sad for herself and feeling like a complete fool to have thought she could be someone she wasn't.

Ken's heart nearly stopped when he walked into his bedroom. Mari stood in the middle of it, weeping. "What is it, honey? What's wrong?"

She held out her arms as wide as she could. "Look at this place. I don't know what to do with all of this room. My clothes fit in a locker at the end of my cot. I don't know how to cook, or take care of a house, or even be in a relationship. What was I thinking?"

He swept her into his arms, holding her close. Her body trembled against his, and he cupped her head in the palm of his hand, pressing her face against his heart, sheltering her as best he could with his own body.

"Listen to me, honey. Neither of us has ever done this. We're bound to panic, but it doesn't matter. You hear me, Mari?

It doesn't matter. This is us. The two of us. What is normal for everyone else doesn't matter. We'll build our relationship brick by brick, and it will be so strong no one will ever tear it down. I'll never walk away from you. *Never.* If there is one thing you can count it, it's me standing by you. There aren't mistakes here. We'll just work it all out at our own pace."

"But Briony made this place a home, not only for Jack, but for you. I can see that she did. She's every bit as much your family as Jack is."

"She lights up Jack's world, Mari," he said, trying to follow her train of thought. "Don't you want me to care for her?"

"Of course I do. You should, but I can't be like her. I have no idea what to do. I don't even have clothes, Ken. I'm just here with absolutely nothing."

He lifted her chin and brushed her soft mouth with his. She sounded so distressed that he felt distressed. "You don't have to do or have anything. I want you, Mari, not clothes or a servant."

"Shouldn't I be putting flowers in a vase? Or pretending to cook dinner?" She looked totally alarmed. "I have no idea how to cook. I've never cooked. *Never.* This isn't going to work, Ken."

He realized she was totally panic-stricken. She was staring at the bookshelves and the cases of music. Ken kissed her again. "Do you think that matters? And you can't put flowers in a vase if I haven't gotten them for you, can you? Tomorrow we can go into town and get you enough clothes to fill the closet and dresser if that's what you want. And I'll buy flowers and a vase, and we'll put the damn things in it together. None of it really matters to me."

"Maybe not now, this minute, but sometime you'll want me to know how to run a household." She felt totally inadequate thinking about all the things she didn't know how to do—but that her sister did. Her sister was a stranger to her, had lived in a loving family, not a military barracks. *Cami! I need you. Oh, God, what have I done?* Panic was new to her. She hadn't panicked when she was captured. She hadn't panicked when she was shot, but standing in a real home surrounded by everything unfamiliar to her . . .

"If you want to run it, you'll figure it out; if not, well, it's been just fine for years now."

She clung to him, her confidence shaken. "I've never decided when to go to bed at night. Lights out at eleven, unless I've caused trouble, and then it's nine or ten."

"You can stay up all night, sweetheart."

"I've never been allowed out of my room after nine."

"If you feel like driving to California, we'll hop in the car and go. Or if you just want to go into the kitchen and get a piece of fresh fruit, do it."

"And sit outside on the front porch?" She clenched her teeth together to keep them from chattering. She couldn't bear the thought of leaving Ken, but she couldn't stay. This wasn't her. It would never be her. She belonged with her sisters—the women who knew what life with Whitney was all about.

"All night, Mari. Briony likes the roof, although Jack gets a little bent now that she's really showing. But if it's the roof, I'm up there with you. It's one of my favorite spots. And there are trees to climb and trails to hike. Have you ever ridden a bike?"

She shook her head, a fresh flood of tears filling her eyes. "Little children ride bikes and I can't even do that. I've never been on a horse either."

"We've got mountain bikes. I'll teach you."

"It's frightening. I keep thinking about the others, my sisters out there right now, wondering how to make a decision like these. Whitney even maintained our diets for us. I detest taking vitamins." She watched him closely for a reaction.

"I mix mine in the blender with a killer recipe of fruit and juice your sister told me about, but if you don't want to take vitamins, then don't. More than half the population of the world doesn't. You have the right to make your own decisions on everything, honey." Ken rested his chin on top of her head. "Unless it comes to personal safety; then my instincts are going to take over and I'm going to be calling the shots."

"Or other men." She had to find a way to cope. She had to or she was going to run as fast and as far as she could.

He nearly choked. "We're not even going there. My heart can't take it. Our relationship is exclusive to the two of us. Marriage. Husband and wife. Partnership. Team. I can deal with all of the above, but not another man."

"So there are rules," she persisted, her stomach settling as she deliberately provoked him.

"Well, sure. Even Jack and I have rules with living on the same property. It's a matter of respect."

"So no relationship has two men and one woman."

"Not ours." He was decisive.

"But there are some," she persisted. "Because, you know, there might be some advantages . . ."

He held her at arm's length, looking down at her upturned face. There was laughter in her dark eyes, the distress fading as she teased him. "That isn't funny." But it was impossible not to smile when she was smiling.

"You deserved it. You're an idiot, you know that? Why do you keep thinking I want other men in my life? I don't even like men. Well," she corrected, "most men."

"So you were teasing me just to get a rise out of me."

"It was easy. You're too easy."

"That's just wrong, Mari," he said and bent to take possession of her mouth. She tasted of freedom, sweet and fresh like a summer rain. His arms locked her to him, and his mouth moved over hers, tugging at her lower lip, the one that was so full and sexy and drove him wild whenever he looked at her.

"I love looking at you." He whispered it, but then switched to a much more intimate form of communication, his mind sliding against hers like the melding of one soul into the other. *And touching your skin. You're so soft, baby, and warm.*

She couldn't respond, because he was taking her breath right into his lungs, bringing her body to life with just his mouth and teeth and tongue. He could create a whirlwind that swept her away from her life and into another one filled with love and passion and family. All with a kiss. Ken, with his scars and hidden demons, with his vulnerability and intense heat, was an exciting blend of gentle and rough. How could she ever think to want another man?

Her arms slipped around his neck, and she pressed her body into his, wanting to share his skin, to relieve the fierce tension that always was beneath the calm surface. He made her feel as if she were the only woman in the world, the only one he ever saw or wanted or needed. She returned his kisses, letting his mouth guide hers.

She'd had many sexual encounters—but none of them good until Ken had come into her life, and she had no idea how to really kiss or love someone. She knew the mechanics better than most, but not how to love a man—and she wanted to love this man with everything in her. It was the only thing she had to give him—before she said good-bye.

"What's wrong?" Ken's hands framed her face. "Tell me."

She couldn't meet his concerned gaze. He'd just been driving her wild with kisses, and she was thinking that she wanted to make this the best time of his life, and yet—for her it would be the worst, knowing she couldn't stay.

He bent to kiss her again, this time gently, feather-light, a mere brush of his lips against hers. That little rasp of his scar mixing with the softness of his mouth sent wings fluttering in the pit of her stomach. He hadn't meant it as a sexual overture, she could tell, but whatever his intentions, he'd sent a surge of heat spreading through her body.

"Mari." He gave her a little shake. "We have to do this together. I don't want you hiding from me."

"That's impossible when you seem to know what I'm thinking all the time."

"You need to talk to me."

Mari pulled out of his arms and crossed to the window. "How am I supposed to tell you I feel completely inadequate at this? Especially when you're kissing the sense out of me."

To her shock he burst out laughing as he followed her, coming up behind her and wrapping his arms around her, drawing her back against him. His hands locked over her ribs, the backs of his hands brushing the undersides of her breasts. She was immediately aware of his erection, thick and hard pressed tightly against her buttocks.

"Then we're both feeling inadequate. I don't have a clue what I'm doing, other than trying my best to seduce you into wanting to stay with me. I don't know any other way. I want to be good at a relationship, but look how I live." He nodded toward the window. "I'm a loner. I always have been. Maybe my life was shaped that way out of necessity. I react violently when things go wrong, and it was always better to be in control of my environment. In point of fact, I'm not good at relationships." He kissed the side of her neck, his mouth lingering there. "But it's nice to know I can kiss the sense out of you."

"That's not true at all, Ken," she protested. "You're really good at this."

"I'm good at sex, Mari—or I used to be—but I've never had sex when it really mattered. Not like this. I never knew a man could feel this way about a woman. I can't imagine ever touching anyone else—or wanting them to touch me. But I'm *not* any better at relationships than you are. We'll find our way together, even if we're fumbling around in the dark for a while."

"How could I have stayed there so long? There must have been ways for me to find out if Briony was safe."

"Whitney controlled her just as he controlled you. He just gave her the illusion of freedom. In the end, when her parents stopped cooperating with his plans for her, he sent a couple of his supersoldiers to murder them. At any time during her childhood he could have snatched her back, and probably would have if you had managed to escape. You kept her safe."

She leaned her head back against his chest. "At least I did that right."

"Don't stay for her, Mari. Stay for me."

His tone was utterly without expression, but the words conveyed pain. There were so many nuances and she knew most people would never understand Ken. He presented one image to the world and dealt with his monsters alone. She knew what that was like and she didn't want him to be alone any more than she wanted to be alone.

"I'm not going to lie and say I don't want to see her desperately. She kept me going all those years. Everything I ever wanted, I dreamed she had. I want to get to know her and look into her eyes and *know*, not just hope, that's she's happy, but I came here for you." She had. That much was true, but the thought of staying terrified her. She had skills, but none of them were needed here.

Ken wanted to believe her, and he wanted to believe she would stay for him as well, but he was beginning to know her and he could tell she was torn. He couldn't blame her. He would never be able to step aside the way he did with Jack. He would stand in front of her, and she wanted him beside her.

She wanted complete freedom, and he would never be able to give that to her.

At that moment she turned her head to look up at him. "You have shadows in your eyes, Ken. Isn't it strange how Whitney thinks he's controlling us with his pheromones, but neither of us would feel so vulnerable if it was just that? Somehow our emotions are involved, as if there really is destiny or a higher power and we were made for one another. No matter what he does with his experiments, he can't factor that in."

His hand slipped over her hair. "No, he can't. He's a very sad, lonely man. He's driven by his madness, and his inability to figure out why humans react the way they do. He wants robots able to make decisions, but decisions he deems best. No matter how he inserts animal DNA and genetic capabilities, he'll never find the perfection he seeks."

"He thinks he's perfect."

"He wants to think that," Ken corrected, "but he knows it isn't true. The only decent thing he's ever done in his life is to stay away from Lily. I hope he continues to do so, but he's broken her heart."

"He monitors her all the time. He does everyone. He has a file on you, on me, on your brother and Briony."

"The one thing we have going for us with Whitney," Ken said, "is that he wants you to have my baby and he wants Briony to have Jack's. After the children are born, they'll be high-risk, but until then, he may leave us alone to see what happens."

She turned around and began to push up his shirt so she could burrow close to his skin. "I wouldn't know any more about taking care of a baby than I would a husband."

"Fortunately, we're both fast learners."

"Speak for yourself."

"I don't know, honey, you got the hang of making love very fast."

Mari wanted him again, with every nerve ending suddenly alive and screaming for his body, but she pulled back to look at him—really look at him. Ken Norton could break her heart. Ken had somehow managed to creep into her heart—worse, he'd managed to find a way into her soul. Had her reaction to him stayed physical, she would have been all right, but he threatened her on an emotional level that was frightening.

Ken groaned softly. "I can't let you think for very long or you lose your mind." Without preamble he dragged her shirt over her head and tossed it aside, leaving her upper body bare to him. His mouth came down on hers, teeth forcing her to open to him, tongue sliding in to dominate and spread a now familiar heat. He didn't give her a chance to think, but kissed her hungrily, demanding her response and receiving it.

Mari couldn't prevent the moan of pleasure escaping as his hands cupped her breasts, thumbs teasing her nipples into hard peaks of desire. It amazed her how fast her body responded to him. He bent her backward, his mouth greedy as he kissed her over and over.

The taste of him filled her senses and set her on fire. His mouth teased hers, teeth tugging at her lower lip, tongue licking the ache away. Every flaming kiss added to the building of heat in her center, so that she became uncomfortable with the intensity of her arousal. Need built too fast, her muscles contracting painfully, her womb seizing with need. Each time she suckled his tongue, or his danced around hers, she felt the rush of heat spreading, growing, building, until she felt almost wild with need.

His hands tightened possessively on her breasts, his restrained strength apparent as he massaged the creamy, aching flesh. He pushed her back until she was against the wall, trapped between his body and the hard surface, his thigh sliding between her legs to open her to him. The material of her jeans was too tight and heavy on her body. She wanted it gone.

At once his hands dropped to the zipper and tore it open. He dragged the offending material away from her body, allowing her to kick it aside, taking her panties as well, leaving her naked while he was still dressed. She realized they had somehow connected, mind to mind. She was feeling his rising lust as strongly as he was feeling hers. They heightened each other's arousal.

It was an amazingly intimate thing to be able to feel his desperate desire for her. Her body flushed at the things he was thinking, the erotic images in his mind. He pushed her against the wall again, his thigh sliding between her legs, the material rough on her spread thighs. She rubbed against him, the friction sending electrical currents through her womb, up to her breasts. The heat was vicious, shocking her with its intensity.

"Take your clothes off, Ken." His thumbs sent lightning streaking through her nipples. She was going to see to it that this time together was as perfect as she could make it. She shoved aside her doubts and her sorrow and slid her hands under his shirt.

"Not yet. I want to see you this way, naked and wanting me." His voice was rough with raw desire. He *needed* to see her this way, so beautiful in her craving for him, her body soft and pliant, flushed with heat, nipples erect, mouth swollen, and eyes glazed.

He held her helpless against the wall, his mouth sliding down her throat, his hands exploring her body. Pinned there, her body completely his, she made him feel invincible. Heady with lust and love for her, he was humbled and excited that she trusted him enough after everything that she'd been through to leave herself so vulnerable to him.

Ken caught her wrists and stretched her arms over her head, holding them pinned together as he bent his head toward her breasts. Her breath caught in her throat. She couldn't stop riding his knee, nearly crying when he pushed his thigh up, pressing against her aching body. He stared at her breasts, the gentle swaying as she breathed in and out, his gaze hot. Through their linked senses he felt the quick hot spasm of lust that clenched her womb when he licked his lips. She arched toward him, but he held her pinned in place, forcing her to wait for him. The ache grew hotter, more concentrated.

His tongue flicked out and curled over one highly sensitized nipple. Deep inside, her temperature shot up, turning her body to molten lava. A cry tore from her throat and pushed her body harder against his, struggling to relieve the terrible pressure. His thigh dropped away even as his tongue licked her like an ice cream cone, savoring each long stroke. Mari thought she might explode with heat.

His free hand slid over her belly, easing the tight muscles with a caressing massage. She was acutely aware of the fingers sliding so close to her aching mound. His mouth closed over the hard nipple, so hot and moist, his tongue flicking at the tight bud, so that her attention instantly was centered there, to the lightning streaking from breast to belly to her feminine channel. Her muscles clenched hard, the spasm whipping endlessly through her as he suckled, yet never relieving the pressure. It continued to build, higher and hotter, until she writhed against him.

"I can't take any more. I can't, Ken. It's too much."

"Yes, you can."

His fingers stroked her tummy again, a gentle caress, tender almost, and then his teeth tugged at her nipple and his fingers plunged deep into her melting core. She screamed as fire flashed through her, her head lolling back, pressing her breasts deeper into the inferno of his mouth.

"I'm going to watch you come apart in my arms."

The wicked, sinful fingers stroked deep inside; his mouth moved to her other breast, and she nearly exploded again. Nearly. But didn't. The release she needed—craved—never quite came. Only more pressure, more sensation, until every nerve ending was screaming for release.

He suddenly lifted her, taking her by surprise. Her body was so pliant, so shaky, she couldn't have done anything but hold on anyway. He spread her on the bed, arms out and above her head, legs wide. He tugged at his shirt, dropped it on the floor, all the while drinking in the richness of her body. "You're so damn beautiful."

"I ache." Her hand slid down the side of her breast, her belly, brushed her mound. He caught it, licked her fingers, still never taking his gaze from her, and repositioned her arm, but his gaze was hotter, burning with so much lust it added fuel to her already blazing body.

"Don't move." His voice was rougher than ever.

She waited there, her body pulsing with arousal, the rough commands and demands he made on her only adding to the building inferno in her body. She could barely breathe as she watched him shed his jeans with deliberate laziness, heightening her urgency even more. He was breathtaking, his body hard and hot, his hand circling his thick shaft, his fist tight as he approached her. He knelt on the bed between her legs.

Mari raised her hips in a silent plea. He shook his head.

"You are so bad, woman. Have a little patience." His flattened palm came down on her buttocks, sending a flare of heat shooting through her womb.

He lowered his head to her stomach. The muscles rippled and clenched. He kissed her belly button, circled it with his tongue. "I love your scent when you're aroused. I could live on you, I really could."

"Don't." Her fingers twisted in his hair in an attempt to stop him. She had thought he would take her, relieve the terrible craving, but he was already dipping his head, inhaling her scent, his warm breath blowing over her very core. He moved with deliberate slowness, so that the room itself expanded with the building heat, so that her skin was so sensitive just a slight breeze from the window across her nipples sent flames streaking over her, burning her from the inside out. "You can't." She was nearly sobbing, pleading. Terrified he would kill her with pleasure.

"I can," he murmured, his mouth against her damp heat.

He stroked a sensual lick over her swollen clit, and another strangled scream escaped. His mouth closed around the bud, suckling, his arms pinning her thrashing hips, holding her still while his tongue continued to torment her.

Mari couldn't think, couldn't breathe, could only feel the streaks of fire burning her alive. His hands were hard on her thighs, holding her open for his pleasure. He made little circles with his tongue, and his teeth rasped over sensitive nerve endings; he licked and sucked, and she went mindless with ecstasy. All the while he controlled her bucking hips, holding her firm against his mouth, taking what he wanted, driving her higher and higher but never allowing her release.

Only when she was pleading helplessly, her small muscles rippling and contracting, did he lift his head, lust etched deep in the lines of his face. He moved over her, trapping her slender body beneath his, the head of his shaft at her entrance, pushing just inside, insisting she accommodate his length and thickness. "Look at me, Mari. Keep looking at me."

Mari opened her eyes and stared into his. He thrust hard, driving through tight, swollen muscles, burying himself deep, stretching her, filling her, sending her rocketing over the edge with that one stroke. She heard herself scream, but she couldn't

catch her breath, couldn't find her voice, could only flail helplessly beneath him, trying to dig her fingers into the mattress for
an anchor.

He rose above her, his face settling into harsh lines as he
began to ride her. Each stroke was brutally hard, forcing his
shaft through the tight, slick muscles of her sheath, the friction hotter and growing more intense with every stroke.

The terrible hunger never had a chance to ease; it surged
high, building all over again, so that she was riding the edge
of pain with him. The sensation only seemed to add to the
violence of her arousal. His scars dragged over her swollen,
silken inner muscles, so that her sheath gripped and clenched
around him greedily.

She couldn't look away from him, couldn't stop the tightening of her muscles, locking down, clamping, squeezing, and
contracting around him as her pleasure began to swell to ago-
nizing proportions. It was terrifying to feel so much, to not
know where pain started and pleasure ended. She fought the
sensations, fought him, twisting and thrashing, but he never
stopped the hard, brutal thrusts taking her higher and higher.

She actually felt his shaft swelling inside of her, growing
hotter, stretching her impossibly. She gasped as her body
spasmed, the sensations erupting into a wild explosion. Her
orgasm ripped through her, ferocious and powerful, as he
jerked, his face muscles tightening, his teeth clenching. She
felt their hearts beating through his shaft, felt him swell even
more, and then his hips bucked and hot jets of his release
pounded at her rippling, quaking muscles.

"Yes, baby, that's it, milk me dry."

She couldn't stop. Her body clamped down around his,
draining him, greedy for him. A harsh groan escaped his
throat as his body pumped into hers. She actually felt faint, the
edges around her shadowing and darkening. She clung to reality, refusing to be so weak that she would faint from sheer
pleasure. There were tears in her eyes, in her throat. Nothing
could be this good. Nothing could ever feel like this again.

Ken lifted his weight onto his elbows, hanging his head
while he struggled to breathe. He caught her tears with his
tongue and then kissed the corners of her mouth.

Mari touched his face. They were still locked together and

he was smiling down at her, something very close to love on his face. She swallowed hard. "I can't move."

"You don't have to move. Just lie there and look beautiful. I'm just getting started."

Her eyes widened. "Started on what?"

"You, sweetheart. I've got all night to learn what you like best."

# CHAPTER 20

Feeling drowsy and entirely satisfied, Mari woke to find herself wrapped in Ken's arms. His body was tight up against hers, his erection pressed against her buttocks. She couldn't believe he could possibly be hard again and ready, but the thought excited her. He had ridden her throughout the night, over and over, his voice growling rough orders in her ear, his hands every bit as demanding as his mouth and body, as if he could never get enough of her. She didn't want him to ever get enough. Before she could move, stroke her palm over his tempting hard-on, his soft laughter tickled her ear.

"Get the hell out of here, Briony. You're such a brat. We're sleeping."

"You've been sleeping for hours. I want to meet my sister."

Mari's heart pounded, but she couldn't look up, didn't dare. Her mouth went dry and her stomach rolled.

"Jack! Damn it. I'm naked in here and this is just wrong. Your woman has no sense of propriety."

"Stop being a baby. I'm just looking at my sister, not you, so don't flatter yourself."

Ken laughed and the sound ripped through Mari like a tidal wave, knotting her stomach with something all too close to jealousy. She recognized the emotion although she'd never experienced it before. Ken didn't laugh that often, but she could hear the easy affection in his voice. He genuinely cared for Briony, and Ken didn't care for that many people. It had never occurred to Mari that she might be jealous of another woman—especially when that woman was her pregnant sister.

Ashamed, she took a deep breath to calm herself. Life was happening too fast for her. She had wanted to see Briony her entire life, yet now, faced with the reality, she was frightened. Mari forced herself to look up, to smile, to pretend her heart wasn't thudding in her chest and that one wrong word, one look of disappointment wouldn't crush her—destroy her.

Briony was short, with platinum and gold hair. She wore it a little longer than Mari, a little softer style. It framed her face and called attention to her large, dark eyes. She had an obviously rounded tummy, but the rest of her remained slim. Mari stared at her sister, astonished at how much they looked alike, yet how different at the same time. Briony was everything she was not. Soft. Feminine. It really showed. Even her body was subtly different, and it had nothing to do with the pregnancy. She had softer curves, where Mari's muscles were small, but defined.

Briony seemed to be having trouble looking at her, keeping her concentration on Ken. "You're so lazy. Get out of bed, Ken. I waited and waited."

He threw a pillow at Briony. "You didn't wait long enough. And look at you! Your tummy is bigger than a beach ball."

Briony threw the pillow back at him. "That's not what a pregnant woman wants to hear. Get up and bring my sister out to me *now*!" Her gaze shifted to Mari, tears swimming in her eyes. She choked back a sob and turned and ran from the room.

Ken shifted Mari so she was facing him, her breasts pressed tightly against his chest, his thigh flung carelessly over hers, pinning her beneath him. "You're trembling, sweetheart. You didn't say a word to her and she said nothing to you. Talk to me."

She shook her head. "She's perfect. You know she is. She's so feminine."

Ken bit back his first reaction and bent his head to her

breasts. His teeth tugged and teased, tongue sliding over her creamy flesh. "You're the most beautiful woman I've ever seen, Mari. Surely you can't think she won't like you?"

She shivered and cradled his head to her. He made her feel beautiful and wanted. Staying in bed with him seemed her only recourse. "I've never been so scared of meeting anyone in my life."

His mouth burrowed between her breasts, blazed a trail of fire up her throat and chin to the corner of her lips. "You'll do fine. Take a quick shower and we'll go together. I'll be right there with you."

Her body was deliciously sore. She stretched languidly, sliding against him, skin to skin, loving the feel of him against her. He gave her the courage she needed to take ahold of life, and this was her most important day. Briony had been so important to her. Mari had made her into a fantasy. Everything she had ever wanted to be—everything she wanted to have, to do—Mari had imagined it all for Briony. Mari had nothing but a stark, cold, much disciplined life, and she wanted the world for Briony.

Her arms slipped around Ken and she held him to her ferociously. She felt almost desperate, wanting to fit into his world but knowing she didn't. Briony fit. Seeing her just made that clearer. Mari was a soldier. It was her way of life. Ken didn't see her as a soldier; he saw her as soft and gentle, and the reality was so very far from that image.

Ultimately, Briony was a stranger to her. If Briony couldn't accept her with all of her shortcomings, it was going to hurt, but it would be okay. Her sisters were the women who had been forged in fire, just as she had been. They knew discipline and duty and what it was like to be held prisoner, vulnerable and helpless. They knew her. They understood her, and they loved her. They were willing to risk everything with her. She belonged with them.

Choking on tears, heart aching, she kissed Ken, nibbled at his lips and licked the scar that split his mouth into two soft segments. She'd fallen in love with that scar. "Come with me to the shower."

Ken made love to her, taking his time, with the water spraying down on them, doing his best to be as gentle as he could as he held her in his arms. It didn't seem possible to have her with him in his home, that life could really be so good. In the end, no matter how he tried, the only way for him to be stimulated enough to gain relief was rough penetration. He heard the sound of their flesh meeting, like the slap of a hand, his body pounding into hers when she was already sore from a long night of his demands.

His fingers dug into her hips, taking her to the floor where there was no give, where the penetration was deep and her tight sheath gripped him the way he needed. The rougher he was, the more swollen and tight she became and the more pleasure he felt. He looked down at her, the water pouring over them, his fingerprints standing out on her soft skin, and he hated his body, hated who he was.

She wanted him, her body responded to everything he gave her, pushing her ability to accept pleasure and pain mingled together in order to accommodate his lusts, but how could she ever love him when he was so depraved and driven? When a monster lurked inside of him, one she'd caught glimpses of. Mari was not a stupid woman, and she had lived her entire lifetime with violence. She knew he was capable of making her life hell, and in spite of loving her with his body— worshiping her—he could feel her moving away from him. He turned up toward the spray, letting it pour over his face and wash away the burn of tears.

Mari said nothing as he helped her from the floor, but he noticed she looked as if she had been crying too. She pressed a kiss to his chest and stepped out of the shower to dry off. Ken stayed for a longer time, wishing the water could make him clean again. He watched it run into the drain and wished the small stream could take his sins with it.

Briony waited in the kitchen, pacing restlessly in front of Jack. He swung around as Mari and Ken entered, frowning a little in reprimand.

*About damn time. She's going to have a nervous breakdown.*

Ken flicked his brother a quick warning glance. *So is Mari. She's terrified. Don't say anything to upset her.*

Jack flashed him a small grin. *Papa bear is getting all growly over his little cub.* All the same he positioned his body so he could protect Briony should there be need.

Ken kept his hand on the nape of Mari's neck, wanting to give her support. He could feel the tremors running through her slender body. The woman had enough courage for ten people, but facing her twin for the first time in years was traumatic.

"Briony," Ken said softly. "Jack and I promised you we'd bring your sister to you and we have. This is Marigold—Mari."

Briony's eyes filled with tears. "I'm sorry. I can't stop crying. I'm sure it's the pregnancy. I'm so happy you've come at last."

Mari simply stared at her, drank her in, could barely believe they were in the same room. "Look at you. You look so happy."

"I am happy." Briony wiped at the flowing tears. "Whitney did something to my memory, and I couldn't think about my past without feeling pain. I couldn't remember anything, but as soon as I did, I tried to find you." She took two steps closer but stopped again, afraid of rejection.

Mari took a step toward her. "Whitney did that to anyone leaving the compound. He liked to tell me he knew where you were, and what he could do to you if I didn't cooperate."

Briony ducked her head. "I'm sorry. It must have been terrible for you."

"No," Mari said quickly. "It wasn't. Not really." She took another step toward her sister. "I didn't know any other way of life, and as a child, it was rather exciting. I missed you every single day."

A fresh flood of tears turned Briony's face bright red. Jack started across the room, but Mari got there first. She gathered her sister into her arms and held her. Jack stilled, halfway to his wife, his throat working convulsively. If there was one thing he couldn't take, it was Briony's tears.

Ken handed him a cup of coffee, and they sat at the kitchen table while their women went off together, arms around each other, into the great room.

Jack scrubbed his hand over his face. "Briony's killing me with her tears. I'm hoping Mari can get her to stop."

Ken flashed him a small grin. "You're looking a little pale, bro. What are you going to do when she goes into labor?"

"I'm contemplating shooting myself." He tapped the table restlessly. "What about you? How are things going?"

The grin faded, and for a moment Jack glimpsed pain sliding into the shadows in Ken's eyes. "She isn't going to stay."

"You sure?"

"Why would she? She's got everything going for her. I'm not exactly normal. And unlike Briony, she isn't going to be accepting of me telling her what to do all time."

Jack nearly snorted coffee through his nose. "Is that what you think? Briony pretty much tells me how it's going to be, except maybe in the bedroom, and even then, she likes what I do to her or she wouldn't be doing it. Don't kid yourself, bro, my woman makes up the rules and yours will too."

"Maybe." Ken couldn't very well tell his brother just what it took to feel with his skin sliced to pieces—although maybe Jack already had guessed. More than once he'd repaired damage when Ken had been unable to feel the blade of a saw slicing through his hand until it was too late. He didn't want to go there and see pity in Jack's eyes. "You hear anything about the senator?"

"He's being guarded at an undisclosed location. No one is saying how badly he's hurt. Nothing on the news. Not a single thing about him being shot and nothing in the media about Whitney's laboratory. The general sent in a team, but the place is abandoned and all data appears to be destroyed. Of course they'll take weeks to comb through everything. Whitney's moved on." Jack frowned. "Logan radioed last night to warn us that Sean was last seen getting off a plane in Montana. He's heading here. You know he is."

Ken nodded. "I was certain he'd follow her, but I didn't think he'd come so quickly. Take the women and get out of here, Jack. I'll deal with him."

Jack grunted. "Like that's going to happen. I've already called Logan. He'll be here in an hour, and he'll protect the women. I'm going to be backing you up just the way we always do it."

"Sean isn't going to stop until he has her or he's dead. Whatever Whitney does to these men makes them believe they're entitled the women. They don't care whether the woman wants them or not; she's a possession."

"We'll get him." Jack's fingers drummed against the table-top. "You realize Whitney isn't alone in this? Senator Free-man's father is involved, and Mari dropped the name of a banker. She's seen at least two of the others, and that means the other women probably have as well."

"Which increases the risk to them. Whitney and the others are going to want them back for many reasons. I should have realized when Mari didn't really talk about them or let me see what they looked like when she was thinking about them, that they planned to strike out on their own."

"You can't really blame them for not trusting anyone," Jack said.

"No, but I'm a little upset with Mari. If she'd warned me, I could have tried to persuade them that there was help out there for them." He kept his face averted from his brother. Mari was thinking of leaving him. She was going to join her sisters and follow through with their original plan. He was desperate to cage her—but how?

"She trusted you with her life, just not with the other women's."

"She did at that," Ken agreed, and stared out the window as he sipped at his coffee.

An hour later, Logan arrived, grim-faced and angry.

"I spotted Sean, or what I'm fairly sure was him," he said. "He ducked into the trees and he's too careful to make the same mistake twice. I didn't have a clear identification so I couldn't take him out."

"How close is he?"

"Close, Ken. He's moving fast. Tell me what you want and I'll get it done."

"You're going to stay and protect Mari and Briony. Jack's going to climb the mountain and let Sean get a real good look at him. Hopefully he'll think it's me. I'll try to look like Mari and go for a little walk, lead him away from the house to the spring that runs along the bluff. I'm guessing he'll make his try for Mari. If not, he'll go after Jack. Either way, Jack will be waiting or I will."

"And I babysit."

"You've got the most important job, Logan," Jack said, coming up behind them. "Anything happens to Briony and I'm no good to anyone anymore."

"I feel the same way about Mari," Ken added. "If he gets by us, you have to kill him. No matter what, he has to die."

Logan nodded and glanced at the two women as they entered the room.

"Why the grim faces?" Briony asked.

Jack took her hand and tugged until her smaller body was up against his. "You're going to have go down into the tunnel, Bri. We have a nasty visitor and we can't take any chances. Get your emergency pack and go with Mari and Logan."

Mari frowned and shook her head. "It's Sean, isn't it? He's found us."

"That's right, honey, and you've got to get moving," Ken said. "Go with your sister and Logan. We'll take care of this."

"What? You think I'm going to go hide while you and your brother put your lives on the line for me? Think again," Mari snapped, her dark eyes flashing. She looked furious. "Sean is my responsibility, not yours."

"Like hell. Get in the damned tunnel, Mari, where I don't have to worry about you while I take care of this bastard."

"I'm going to stay with you."

Strobes went off in the house. A soft alarm buzzed. Jack and Ken sent Logan a quick, hard look. "An hour?" Jack said.

"I don't have time for this," Ken snapped, his voice icy cold. "You'll do what I say. This is about safety, and when it comes to safety, you get in line, no arguments."

"No one controls me. *No one.* Whitney couldn't control me and I'll be damned if you do. I'm not hiding while you take the risks."

Ken stepped closer to her, his eyes glacier-cold. "You'll do exactly what I say when I say it, Mari. I'm not fucking around here. I'm not about to let you get shot so that you can prove a point. This isn't about freedom or whatever else you think it is. Sean wants you any way he can have you. He's got to go through me to get to you. If I fail, and Jack fails and Logan fails, you're welcome to blow him away."

Mari's face paled and she took a step back.

"Don't you dare look at me like you're afraid I'll hit you!" Ken caught her arm and jerked her toward him.

Mari's hands came up in a defensive fighting position. "Get off of me."

"That was really sensitive of you," Jack declared. "Sheesh, Ken, can you be any dumber?"

Ken ignored his brother and pulled Mari tight against his body. "Last night I was so deep inside you we were sharing the same skin. And today you're going to look at me like I'm some kind of fucking monster." He looked down at his fingers biting deep into her arm, abruptly let go, and looked to his brother for help.

Jack took great care not to glance at Briony. *Baby, you're the brains of the outfit. Do something fast.*

Without hesitation, Briony made a small sound of distress. Instantly everyone looked at her. She wrapped her arms protectively around her large stomach. "Jack. I'm so afraid. Last time . . ." She trailed off.

Instinctively Mari went to her. "Sean isn't going to get close to you. There's no way that will happen."

"They came last time, Mari, with helicopters, and we barely escaped. I can't climb the cliff now. I can't run. The doctor put me on bed rest because I've had a few contractions. I can't fight this time."

"Mari's a damn good soldier, Briony," Ken said. "She's a hell of a shot and I've seen her fight. She isn't about to allow anyone to get near you."

Mari shot him a quelling look, but smiled with reassurance at her sister. "I won't let anything happen to you or the babies. I promise. Why don't you lead the way to the tunnel?"

"Mari . . ." Ken had no idea what he was going to say, but he didn't want to leave it like this. She was wavering about her decision to stay with him, and ever since he'd brought her into the house she'd been different.

"Go. Get it done. I need another gun and a couple of clips of ammo, just to be on the safe side."

"I can show you where everything is," Briony said, slipping her hand into Mari's.

Ken shook his head and followed Jack out of the house, checking his rifle and guns automatically as they cached weapons throughout the yard.

"Keep your mind on what's going on here," Jack said. "Otherwise you're a dead man. She's not going anywhere."

"How would you know?"

"I see the way she looks at you. Any fool can see."

"She isn't like Briony, Jack. No matter how you cut it, in the bedroom or out of it, I'm going to be rough on her. Sooner or later she's going to hightail it out of here fast. I don't know what the hell I'll do then." And he didn't. He couldn't think about her leaving him because he knew she was contemplating just that. His mind went numb—blank.

"Ken." Jack put his hand on his brother's shoulder. "Sean is a trained killer. This isn't going to be easy. You have to keep your mind on what you're doing. Why don't you let me switch places with you? He won't know the difference."

Ken shook his head. "I'll be fine. This is my war, Jack. You just watch yourself up there. If he sees you climbing and thinks you're me, he could very well go after you or try to take you out with a nice, well-placed shot."

Jack shrugged. "Then you'd better be in position covering me."

Ken nodded and went into the shop, emerging a few minutes later with a blond wig on his head. He hunched, trying to make himself smaller, staying to the thicker foliage so anyone watching would only catch glimpses of him. Sean needed to see Jack, to believe it was Ken climbing the rock face. It would further the illusion that Mari was hiking in the woods by herself. Ken took up a position, sitting on a boulder near the spring, lacy fern fronds covering most of his body as he waited for Sean to spot him. All the while his gaze searched the ridges to make certain the enemy wasn't lying in wait to get a shot off at Jack.

Minutes passed. Fifteen. He could see Jack moving up the sheer face of the rock to his favorite lookout spot. To an outsider he appeared to be engaging in a little recreational rock climbing. Ken knew that once Jack was at the top, he would slide into the shadow of the cliff, right into a neat little depression where no one could spot him, and he would have a bird's-eye view of the surrounding region.

Twenty minutes. Ken bent, picked up a few small pebbles, and idly tossed them into the spring. The back of his neck prickled. He felt an itch between his shoulder blades. There was the whisper of leaves brushing against clothing. It would all be on instinct now, and Ken had survival instincts honed from his childhood, when his father entered the house drunk, intent on inflicting as much pain and damage as he could on his sons. He knew when he was in danger. He was being stalked.

Ken bent down again as though picking up more pebbles. He stayed low, sweeping the area with a casual glance around. He made a great show of selecting flat stones for throwing. A twig snapped off to his left on the narrow deer trail that criss-crossed the hills. The deer had a favorite spot to lie in the shade near the spring. Ken glanced toward the area where the grasses were perpetually trampled and saw part of a pant leg. He palmed the knife in his boot as he straightened, taking care to stay in the middle of the overgrown ferns.

"Hello Mari," Sean greeted. "If you stay very, very quiet, I might let everyone but your lover live. If you give me trouble, the first person I kill is your whoring sister."

Ken turned slowly, concealing the knife along his wrist. "Watch your mouth when you talk about my sister-in-law."

"You!" Sean scowled, anger flitting across his face; then his mouth pulled tight in a snarling grin. "Just the bastard I wanted to meet."

"You're not very smart, are you?" Ken asked, taking a step to his right to see if Sean would follow. "Did you think I wouldn't protect her?"

Sean circled Ken, eyes restlessly searching the area around them, measuring the distance separating them. "I saw you on the mountain, climbing," he said conversationally. "How the hell could you be up here?"

"My brother, Jack," Ken replied without emotion. All rage had disappeared, and he felt the inevitable ice flowing in his veins, slowing down time, tunneling so that all he saw was a man with targets painted on his body.

"You can't have her. I know you took her from me."

"She was never yours. She's her own person, Sean. You can't treat her like a possession. She has her own mind and her own will." Even as Ken said the words aloud, his heart sank. He was as bad as Sean, trying to hold her to him when he knew she needed to fly free. He couldn't change his nature any more than Sean could undo whatever he had allowed Whitney to do to him.

Sean palmed his knife. "It's going to be a pleasure to kill you."

"Do you really think it's going to be that easy? You sold out, asshole, and you didn't even do it gracefully. You must have loved her once, loved her enough to decide you could just take her—own her."

"Like you? I saw what you did to her."

Ken backed away from the spring, luring Sean toward open ground where Jack could get a clear shot at him. "You loved her so much you let those bastards strip her naked and photograph her. You let the doctor stick his fingers inside her, touch her when you knew how much she hated it. You don't deserve her."

Sean tossed the knife back and forth between his hands, all the while circling, forcing Ken to continue to give ground. His smile never wavered, a small, evil grin, his gaze hard as he compelled Ken to back a few more feet. Ken was aware that he was close to the crumbling edge of the bluff. He shifted on the balls of his feet—waiting.

Sean feigned an attack. Ken didn't respond. The smirk faded just a little. "She was always meant for me. Whitney promised her to me."

"In return for betrayal? Did you report the women's conversations? Their plans for escape? You were the one who told him Mari was going to try to talk to the senator about Whitney's disgusting baby factory. He was really angry over that one, wasn't he? He gave you the heavier dose of Zenith, and you injected it in her like the good little toad you are."

Sean hissed a breath out, feigning another attack, moving forward with incredible speed and striking with a flowing roundhouse punch. Ken just managed to jerk his head out of the way and pull in his belly enough to avoid the slice of the knife.

"I had no idea it would kill her. He said if she got hurt it would heal her. I wouldn't ever let him harm Mari."

"No, you'd just let a perverted doctor touch her and take pictures to plaster all over his wall so he could jack off at night." Ken glided forward, a blurring figure, his wrist flicking several times, as he moved on past Sean. He was now only a few feet from the edge of the bluff. "You'd just beat her bloody and rape her. You sick, twisted fuck."

Sean stared down at the blood dripping from his arm, belly, and chest. Thin lines stretched across his skin. He swore and lunged again, this time, blade up, going for the softer parts of the body. At the last second Ken pivoted, allowing Sean's forward momentum to carry him past, the wrist flicking again. This time Sean's left cheek, neck, hip, and thigh sported long wicked-looking cuts.

Sean screamed, fury burning in his eyes. He danced in, a big man, light on his feet, snapping a quick thrust and following it with a hard forward snap kick to Ken's thigh. The second kick took Ken in exactly the same spot, deadening his leg. Before Sean could retract the leg, Ken drove the point of his knife deep into the man's calf, twisted, and jumped back, precariously near the edge of the cliff.

It was a particularly brutal injury. Blood sprayed in wide arcs, and Sean yelled obscenities, desperation creeping into his eyes. "You fucking freak. You really think Mari could want a man like you? Maybe if you wear a mask to cover the horror of your face." He spat at Ken, reached down as if to pull the knife from his calf, but snapped upright, throwing his own knife at Ken's chest.

Ken moved with blurring speed, tucking his shoulder and rolling to the side to avoid the weapon. It burned across his right bicep, shaving skin. Sean followed the knife, rushing Ken, certain his heavier body would send Ken over the edge. Ken gripped Sean with two hands, one at his throat, the other on his upper arm, superhuman strength, a vise steadily closing, crushing. Sheer terror swept through Sean. He had been counting on his own enhanced strength and his hatred of this man, but he never expected the enormous strength in Ken's body.

Sean fought like a wild animal, desperately attempting to knock the legs out from under Ken, twice more finding the spot on the thigh he'd kicked. Ken seemed inhuman, a monster!

Nothing affected him, that grip relentlessly tightening. Choking, coughing, Sean flung himself backward with all his weight, his feet scraping for a purchase as the earth crumbled and gave way beneath him.

The weight of Sean's body suddenly was a deadweight on the end of Ken's arm. His grip on Sean's throat was the only thing preventing the man from falling. They stared at each other, Ken on his knees, trying to find a way to dig his toes into the soft dirt for a purchase, to prevent himself from going over the edge with his enemy. Sean gripped Ken's arm, determined that if he went crashing to the rocks below, he would take Ken with him. Blood made his grip slippery, but desperation gave him added strength. He dug his fingers into Ken's skin. The edge crumbled more, sent dirt skittering down the cliff face. Ken opened his hand to allow Sean to fall, but the man clamped on his wrist with both hands.

"I go, you go," he snarled. "Pull me up, damn you."

"Not in this lifetime, you son of bitch. You're out of her life forever."

"So are you then." Sean's teeth clenched, his grip tightening like a vise.

The edge was giving way, more dirt and rock tumbling down, Ken sliding with the weight of Sean's body pulling him. He had no leverage to fight, nothing to hang onto, and the earth around him was shifting and sliding.

*Don't move.* Jack's voice was utterly calm.

*Hell.* Ken swore at his brother, trying to stay absolutely still. He *was* moving, sliding down the cliff while Sean hung on like a terrier.

A hole blossomed suddenly in the middle of Sean's forehead, and then Ken heard the crack of the shot. The bullet had passed close to the top of his head, shaving off a few hairs as it whistled past. Sean's grip loosened abruptly, his fingers sliding away as the body fell to the rocks below.

Ken threw his body backward, rolled over, and stared up at the blue sky, his arm feeling as though it had been torn out of its socket. He was drenched in perspiration, and his leg, where Sean had landed several kicks, felt as if a sledgehammer had been taken to it. He dragged air into his lungs and waited there, knowing Jack would come.

Clouds spun across the sky, casting shadows over the ground. Ken closed his eyes and felt exhaustion roll over him. He was sick inside, his body and mind fatigued. His scars throbbed painfully, too tight for his skin, reminding him that Sean was right. He could no longer hide what he was from the world. Mari knew. Mari saw him for what he was. He couldn't hide behind a handsome face anymore.

And she would always have the contrast staring at her every morning if she did stay. How could she look at Jack and not be ashamed to be with Ken? Even so, it didn't matter. He was as pathetic as Sean. He wanted her to stay. To love him. He *needed* her, when he'd never allowed himself to need anything or anyone. Ken reached out to brush his mind against hers, needing the touch almost more than he needed the air he was fighting for.

*Mari. It's over.*

*I know. Jack sent word to Briony.* There was a small hesitation. *You know I can't stay. You know I can't.*

He had known, but he couldn't accept it. His heart nearly stopped. *Don't. Don't do this. I'm coming to you now, baby.*

*I don't want you to.* And then there was only a black void. Emptiness. No soft intimate brush, no echo of laughter or companionship. Simply emptiness. She was gone, shutting him out of her life. No more happiness. No more feeling alive. It was all gone.

His gut clenched, and he rolled to his knees, sick with the idea of losing her. He retched over and over, knowing absolutely that she left. He couldn't blame her. It was the only smart thing to do, and Mari was smart. He smashed his fist into the ground. Once. Twice.

"Ken." Jack was there, kneeling beside him. "I thought I'd lost you."

He looked up at Jack, not really seeing him. Ken realized he was lost—he'd been lost for a long time. Mari had brought him back to life. "She's gone." His gaze jumped to Jack's face; he saw a hint of guilt creep into his eyes and fade. "You knew?"

Jack sat back on his heels, his gaze watchful, wary. "Briony is crying. She told me Mari hugged her and said she couldn't stay—that she belonged with the other women."

"And you didn't tell Logan to stop her?"

"Mari is a trained soldier. I didn't want to risk Logan or Briony getting hurt. You can't keep Mari tied up for the rest of her life; you know you can't."

"You son of a bitch."

"Ken. Be reasonable."

He didn't feel reasonable. He felt like his world was crumbling around him. His mind felt fractured, his head roaring, thunder crashing in his ears. "How long ago?"

"Take it easy, Ken," Jack said to soothe him.

"Damn it." Ken's fist slammed into the dirt, although he wanted to smash it into his brother's face. "How long ago?"

"She left as soon as she knew Sean was dead."

Ken surged to his feet, a sudden cold blast spreading through his body. The knots in his belly tightened to the point of pain. His mouth went dry, the air in his lungs rushing out, to leave him gasping. He had time. He had to have time to stop her.

He shoved past Jack and began to trot down the mountain. He didn't dare run full-out; the trail was far too treacherous and his leg was on fire. His steady, ground-eating trot would get him there quickly. He tried to keep his mind a merciful blank, but her image insisted on crowding in. Her smile, her dark chocolate eyes, the way she tilted her chin. He choked back a sob, felt his heart exploding, tearing at his chest.

The mountain, the forest, his world, his sanctuary, was a hostile, unyielding place. He couldn't see its beauty, didn't want its beauty.

Nothing—no one—could take her from him. She was life. She was happiness. She was his only reason to keep going. He needed her desperately. Her sisters couldn't have her. They didn't need her the way he did. He had been so alone, so empty. Each day, he had worked, breathed, lived as an automation, and then she had come into his life and everything in him had come alive.

They couldn't take her from him. The universe couldn't be that cruel. He wanted to scream his denial, but he needed to save his strength. He ran through the trees, leapt over rocks, foliage tearing at his skin. His damaged leg throbbed and burned right along with his lungs, but the image of her rising up to taunt him kept him running. Why had he left her? Why had he allowed them to be separated when she was so uncertain about their future? He had known she was wavering—feeling uncomfortable and unsure of herself in a foreign environment. He shouldn't have been so arrogant and bossy. He could have asked—not ordered—her to go into the tunnels.

He wouldn't let anyone take her from him. She could understand his turbulent nature, his wild cravings, and he understood her need for freedom. He recognized strength in her, an iron will, the same as it was in him. He recognized her loyalty; it ran deep and pure, the same as it was in him. They fit together, two halves of the same whole. They belonged.

He burst from the forest and half ran, half slid down the trail into the yard, his chest heaving with exertion, his eyes a little wild. He ran across the uneven terrain. Dusk was falling. The house was dark, forbidding, silent. There were no lights on in the interior.

He flung open the kitchen door, his heart pounding, a raw gaping wound growing in his gut. She was gone. He knew it with such certainty he didn't need to tear through the house, running insanely from room to room, screaming her name hoarsely, but he did it anyway.

"Mari! Damn you, Mari, come back to me."

He heard his own scream of anguish, thought it should splinter the windows, but there was only silence.

Back in the kitchen he caught up the keys to the truck with a vague idea of going after her, but tears were blinding his vision. He stared, unseeing, at the tabletop, defeated, his broad shoulders slumped, his torn, dirt-streaked clothing clinging to his sweat-stained body.

It had to be her choice or he was just as bad as Sean and Whitney and his father. He refused to let his father's legacy consume him. He wasn't that man, selfish and unable to see that a woman wasn't a possession. Mari had to choose him, want to be with him. She had to accept the flaws in him just as he would have had to accept the fact that she wasn't Briony, with her much more submissive personality.

Love was a choice, and if Mari felt the need to be with her sisters, if the pull there was stronger than her feelings for him, he couldn't—and wouldn't—force her. He pressed the heel of his hand between his eyes and made no effort to stop the flow of tears because he loved her enough to let her go.

He could hear the ticking of the clock. The passage of time. He couldn't stop the sobs tearing his chest apart, the tears that had never come for his lost face and his destroyed manhood. He could hardly bear the pain this time. He had borne so much stoically, but losing Mari was losing life and hope all over again, and his throat burned raw with choking sorrow.

"Ken?" A soft inquiry, a beautiful voice.

He stiffened, not believing, not daring to believe. He passed a hand over his face, choked down the tight lump in his throat, and turned very slowly.

Mari was standing in the doorway anxious and very disheveled. Sweat beaded on her skin; leaves and twigs were caught in her hair. There were scratches on her arms and a rip in her shirt. She was the most beautiful sight he'd ever seen.

"I thought you were gone." His voice was strangled.

"I ran halfway down the road and then I couldn't run anymore. I just stopped and stood there crying. I didn't want to go any further. I don't care if I should be with my sisters. I love you. I know I do. I can't leave. I have no idea how to be anything you want me to be, but I'll try."

He took a step toward her, gray eyes moving over her hungrily. "You've never said you love me before."

She tilted her head to look up at him. "You look awful, Ken. Did you get hurt?"

He waved the subject aside, gathering her into his arms. "I don't want you to be anything but what you are, Mari."

"Well, that's a good thing because I was giving you a load of crap so you'd want me to stay." She pressed little kisses along his throat, over his rough jaw.

The adrenaline surge was gone, leaving him feeling shaky and sick. His body roared at him, calling him all kinds of names for the abuse. He didn't care. Nothing mattered but that she was in his arms and he could stroke her body, pull her closer, fit her hips to his. And that he wanted to smile again. She made him smile again. "I knew that. You're always going to be a handful."

"So true." Mari linked her hands around his neck, her body moving enticingly against his. "I'm glad you realize that."

His mouth slanted over hers, forcing her lips apart to feed hungrily.

"What about Sean?" she murmured when he lifted his head.

"He's dead." He said it tersely. "Let that be the end of it."

She nodded. "Sit down. Let me look at you." Already her hands were sliding over his body, searching for damage. She touched his face with gentle fingers. "I was afraid for you, Ken, and I needed to be with you, not stuck down in a tunnel somewhere."

"I'm sorry, baby." He brought her hands to his mouth. "I know what you're like, and I should have tried harder to see your point of view. I swear I want to see your point of view, but the thought of your life at risk . . ."

"Is how I feel when you risk yours," she said. "You have to accept what I really am, Ken. I see you with your need to keep me close, and to protect me. I love that in you. I can even accept the fact that you're going to be an idiot every time a man looks at me, but you have to accept me for who I am. I was raised practically since birth as a soldier. That's who I am and you're not going to change that. I'm not going to change that. You're going to have to take me on as a partner. Eventually, if you do, your brother will. All three of us can protect Briony and any children our two families have."

"What if I can't get there, Mari? What if I don't have that kind of courage?"

"You do," she assured him, "or I would have kept running down that mountain. Come on." She tugged at his hand. "You need a shower. Why don't you let Jack take care of all the details, and let me take care of you?"

"Say it again."

"What?" Firmly she closed their door, and began to peel the ragged shirt from his powerful shoulders.

He caught her in a hard, bruising grip, gave her a little shake. "Stop teasing me. I've waited a long time."

"We could always compromise," she offered sweetly. "You give me what I want, and I'll give you what you want."

He lifted her into his arms. "You're going to say it a hundred times before we're done here," he warned.

And she did.

Turn the page for a sneak peek at
Christine Feehan's upcoming
paranormal romance,

$\mathcal{S}$AFE

$\mathcal{H}$ARBOR

Available in July 2007 from Jove!

"You want to tell me how the hell we got into this mess?" Jackson Deveau demanded as he whipped his arm around Jonas Harrington's waist and half-dragged him toward the flimsy cover of an industrial garbage container. "We have a nice comfy job on the Mendocino coast and you decide you're bored out of your mind, which is pure bullshit by the way. You'd think getting shot once was enough for you."

If he could have answered, Jonas would have sworn at Jackson, but he only managed a glare as he forced his feet to keep moving. The pain was relentless, stabbing white-hot like a branding iron. He could feel the breath rattling in his lungs, bile rising and reality fading in and out. He had to stay on his feet. He sure as hell wasn't going to let Jackson pack him out on his back—he'd never hear the end of it. Jackson was right. They'd made new lives, lived good, found a home. What the hell had he been thinking?

Why wasn't it ever enough for him? Why did he have to keep going back, over and over, dragging Jackson and other men down into the muck and garbage of the world? He was no noble crusader, yet time and again he found himself with a gun in his hand, going after the bad guys. He was weary to death of his need to save the world. He didn't save anyone; he only got good men killed.

The alley was dark, the shadow of the surrounding buildings rising above the small lane turning the edges black. They kept the garbage container between them and the street where it seemed everyone with a gun and a knife was hunting them. Jackson propped him up against a wall that smelled of times Jonas didn't want to remember, where blood, death, and urine all mixed together into one potent brew.

Jackson checked their ammo situation. "Can you focus enough to shoot, Jonas?"

That was Jackson, all business. He wanted to get the hell out of there and was going to make it happen. The men hunting them had no way of knowing they had a tiger by the tail. When Jackson used that particular tone of voice, men died, plain and simple.

They had to get past the entrance of the alley and it was blocked by the Russian mobsters. It had been a recon mission. Nothing more. They weren't supposed to be seen—damn it, they *hadn't* been seen—but someone had tipped the Russians off and it had all gone to hell fast, turning into a bloodbath, their driver down, and Jonas taking two bullets. Neither hit was serious, but he was losing enough blood to make the wounds fatal. Jackson had two knife streaks across his belly and chest, evidence they'd gotten just a little too close to the hornet's nest. Whatever they'd managed to get on film, the mobsters wanted it back.

*No way.*

Jackson slapped a full clip into Jonas's gun and shoved it into his hand. "You're good to go." He slammed home a full magazine and shifted his weight onto the balls of his feet. "I'm going up top for a few, Jonas. You put another pressure bandage on the wound in your side and no matter what, stay on your feet. All hell's going to break loose in a few minutes and you've got to be ready to run."

Jonas nodded. Sweat dripped off his face and beaded on his body. Yeah. He was ready to run—and fall flat on his face—but he'd keep his feet and the gun and back Jackson in whatever crazy scheme he had. Because, in the end, he could always count on Jackson.

Jackson melted into the night soundlessly, the way he always did. He had come home with Jonas when they'd both been sick to death of the life of living in the shadows—when Jonas just flat-out missed the hell out of his adopted family. They'd joined the sheriff's department and lived a cushy life until Jonas had gotten himself shot on the job and became restless and edgy while recouping. His old boss, Duncan Gray—from a special ops team buried deep in the defense department—had come asking. Jackson would have given him a hard look and they would have stayed safe. But no, Duncan had known to come to Jonas, because he fell for the "we need you" line every damn time.

It was a hell of a thing he'd done, pulling Jackson into this mess. And it wasn't the way he'd planned to die, a soft recon on Nikitin's rival mob to see who was coming and going and why. Nothing special, but here they were, shot to hell, and blood leaking out all over the place. Jonas opened the packet of the pressure bandage with his teeth and spit out the wrapper, slapping the bandage in place before he could think too much about the wound.

Fire ripped through him, stabbing so deep his body shuddered in reaction. He had to hold himself up by gripping the garbage container hard—and wasn't that sanitary. Damn, he was in real trouble this time. He stood swaying; the only thing steady was his gun hand.

He reached into his shirt pocket and pulled out a photograph, the single one he carried, the one that mattered. He should have destroyed it. He could see his own face, the terrible raw truth caught on film. He was staring down at a woman and the love on his face, the stark hunger, was so evident it was a betrayal, there for everyone—even him—to see. His finger glided over the glossy paper, leaving a smear of blood. Hannah Drake. Supermodel. A woman with extraordinary, magical gifts. A woman so far out of reach he might as well try to pull the moon from the sky.

He heard footsteps and the whisper of clothing sliding against the wall. He rammed the photograph back in the pocket of his shirt, close to his heart, and shook his head to clear it. More sweat dripped into his eyes and he wiped it away. The hard-asses were coming in first, staying to the shadows but definitely advancing. The sweat stung his eyes and blood ran steadily from his side down his leg, mingling with the rain that had begun to fall in a relentless downpour. He steadied the gun and waited.

At the end of the alley, a man dropped and the first shot rang out almost simultaneously. Jackson was hell on wheels at that distance. Lying up on top of the roof, he could just pick them off if they were stupid enough to keep coming—and they were. Jonas took his time, waiting for a muzzle flash as one of them gave his position away by firing up at Jackson. Jonas squeezed and the count was two for them, but the entrance to the alley still looked a long way away when the stabbing fire was spreading through his body and his blood was leaking all over the ground.

*Don't be such a pansy-ass. You're not going to die in this dirty alley cut down by a few low-life rats. Geez.* He spoke sternly to himself, hoping the pep talk would keep him from doing a face plant in the muck. The trouble was, these weren't just low-life rats—they were the real deal, trained in tactics just as Jackson and he had been, and they were going for the rooftop too. He heard sounds in the building behind him—the building that should have been a warehouse empty of people.

Whatever was on that video tape they'd captured tonight was worth a lot of lives. Jackson fired again and another body dropped. No one returned fire, knowing Jonas was there waiting for the flash. He groaned softly as realization hit him. They knew his position *exactly*. He should have moved the moment he'd fired. He was even farther gone than he'd thought. He swallowed hard and stayed low, trying to be a part of the container, knowing he had to get out of there, but afraid his legs wouldn't hold. A wave of dizziness hit him hard, nearly putting him on the ground. He hung on grimly, breathing deeply, desperate to stay on his feet. Once he went down, he'd never be able to get back up.

Jackson came out of the shadows, blood dripping from his chest and arm, his face grim, eyes savage. He touched his knife and drew a line across his throat, indicating another kill—and that kill had come between Jackson and Jonas, which meant they were surrounded. He held up four fingers and directed Jonas's attention to two positions close and two behind them. He pointed up.

Jonas felt his heart skip a beat. No freakin' way was he going to climb a fire escape ladder three stories up. He doubted if he could have run the gauntlet, straight down the alley, but it looked a hell of a lot easier—and shorter—than three stories up. He took a breath, ignored the protest as a thousand dull knives sawed into his insides, and nodded his assent. It was their only chance to get away clean.

Jonas took a step away from the receptacle, following behind Jackson. One step and his body went ballistic on him, the pain crushing, robbing him of all ability to breathe. Shit. He was going to die in this damn alley and worse, he was going to take Jackson with him—because Jackson would never leave him.

Enemies were closing in from every direction and there was just no way he could climb that ladder. They needed a miracle and they needed it fast. There was only one miracle that he could count on, and he knew she was waiting for his call. She always knew when he was in trouble. Jonas spent a lifetime protecting her, wanting her so badly he woke up night after night, sweating, her name echoing through his bedroom, his body hard and tight and so damned uncomfortable he sometimes wasn't sure he'd live through the night. But he refused to give in and claim her when he couldn't stop himself from taking jobs like the one he was on—because he'd be damned if he got her killed.

Still, he had no choice. She was his ace in the hole and he had no other option but to use her if he wanted to survive. He reached out into the night and connected with a feminine mind. He knew her. He'd always known her. He could picture her in his mind, standing on the captain's walk overlooking the sea, her platinum and gold spiral curls cascading down her long back all the way to her luscious butt, her face serious, gaze on the sea—waiting.

*Hannah Drake.* If he inhaled he could breathe her in. She would know he was in trouble. She always knew. And, God help him, maybe that was what this was all about. Maybe he had wanted her attention—needed her attention—and this was the only way left to him. Could he be so fucking desperate that he would not only risk his life, but Jackson's as well? He didn't know what he was doing anymore.

*Hannah.* He knew he touched her mind, that she touched his. That she had known the moment the trouble had started and she had been waiting, steady as a rock. In her own way she was as reliable as Jackson; she waited only for a direction before striking. Now that she had one, all hell was really going to break lose. Hannah Drake one of seven daughters born to the seventh daughter in a line of extraordinary women. Hannah Drake. Born to be his. Every harsh breath he drew into his lungs, every promise to stay on his feet, to stay alive, he gave for Hannah.

Jackson pointed back toward the building and Jonas swore under his breath. He took a tentative step back toward the shadows, bent over, stomach heaving, tossing up every scrap of anything he'd had to eat or drink in the last few hours. The terrible wrenching sent another wave of dizziness sweeping over him and jackhammers did a macabre tap dance, ripping through his skull. Sweat dripped and blood ran and reality retreated just a little more.

Jackson got an arm under his shoulder. "You need me to pack you out?"

They'd need Jackson's gun if they were going to make it. Jonas had to find a way to dig deep and stay on his feet, crossing the distance and climbing for freedom with two bullets and a still-fresh wound from an earlier gunshot. He shook his head and took another step, leaning heavily on Jackson.

*Hannah, baby. It's now or never.* He sent the silent prayer into the night, because if there was ever a moment that he truly needed her unusual skills, it was now.

The wind answered, rising fast and furious. It blew down the alley with the force of a hurricane, howling and ripping strips of wood off the buildings. Debris swirled, rose into the air, and flew in all directions. Cardboard and other trash hurtled through the air, slamming into anything in its path as the wind made its way to the back of the alley where it curved and began to race in a horrifying circle around and around, faster and faster, building more speed and ferocity. The wind never touched either Jackson or Jonas; rather, it moved around them, creating a cocoon, building a shield where dirt and debris churned to form a barrier between them and the world.

*Be safe.* Two little words, wrapped up in silks and satin and soft colors.

"We've got to move," Jackson said.

Jonas forced his feet to keep shuffling, every step wrenching at his insides, the pain grinding through his body until he could only clench his teeth and try to breathe it away. His efforts didn't work. *Hannah. Baby. I don't think I'm going to make it home to you.*

The wind rose to a shriek of protest, throwing everything in its path into the air. Arms and legs tangled as men went down or slammed into the sides of the buildings along with the debris. Jonas could hear screams and grunts of pain as their enemies, caught out in the unnatural tornado, were tossed about in the fury of the wind.

Jonas stumbled and managed to catch himself, but pain and the waves of dizziness and nausea were his enemies now. His stomach heaved and the ground tilted. Blackness edged his vision. He stumbled again, and this time he was certain he would go down, his legs turning to rubber. But before he could fall, he felt the pressure of the wind nearly lifting him, supporting him, wrapping him up in safe arms.

He let the wind take his weight and carry him to the ladder. Jackson stepped back to allow Jonas to go up first, all the while watching the alley and surrounding buildings, squinting against the force of the wind.

Jonas reached up toward the last rung of the ladder and white-hot pain burst through him, driving him to his knees. At once the wind caressed his face, a soft fanning, as if a small hand touched him with gentle fingers. All around him raged a virtual tornado, yet tendrils broke off from the spinning mass and seemed to lift him up in strong arms.

He let Jackson help him to his feet, buoyed by the wind, and he tried again, working with the Hannah's windstorm, allowing the strong updrafts to aid him as he bent his knees and leapt to close the gap between him and the lowest rung. The metal struck the palms of his hands and he closed his fingers in a tight grip. The wind pushed and he reached for the next rung before his body could absorb the shock of taking his weight.

Somewhere far off, he heard someone's hoarse cry of agony. His throat seemed ripped raw and his side felt on fire, but he let the wind push and push until he was moving up the ladder to the roof. He crawled onto the roof, praying he wouldn't have to get up again, knowing he had no choice.

Jackson dropped a hand on his shoulder as Jonas knelt on the roof, fighting for air. "You got another run in you?"

His ears were ringing so loudly, Jonas almost missed the thin whisper. Hell no. Did it look like it? He nodded and set his jaw, struggling back to his feet. The rain was relentless, pouring down on them, driven sideways by the wind, but still they seemed wrapped in a cocoon of protection.

Below, they heard shouts as a few of the braver men tried to follow them up the ladder. The wind built in strength, slamming into the building so hard that more windows shattered and the fire escape rattled ominously. The ladder rocked with such force, the screws and bolts began to shake loose and drop toward the street below. The wind caught the small metal pieces and sent them hurtling like lethal missiles at the men attempting to scurry up the rungs.

Men screamed and let go of the ladder, jumping to the ground in an attempt to get away from the blast of bolts rocketing toward them. A few of the bolts drove deep into the wall and others into flesh and bone. The screams grew frantic.

"Damn, Hannah's royally pissed," Jackson said. "I've never seen anything like this." He got his arm around Jonas and half-lifted him to his feet.

Jonas had to agree. The wind was Hannah's favorite medium to work with and she could control it. And man, was she controlling it. He didn't want to think too much about how much of that anger might be directed toward him. He'd promised the Drake sisters he wouldn't do this kind of work anymore. They'd know he'd dragged Jackson right along with him, and telling them Jackson had insisted on coming along wouldn't do anything at all to get him off the hook.

He concentrated on his breathing, on counting steps, on anything but the pain as Jackson dragged him across the roof to the opposite edge. Jonas knew what was coming. He was going to have to jump and land on the other rooftop where they could climb down to the street and to safety. Hannah would hold off the Russian mobsters as long as she could, but only Sarah was in the country to help aid her, and Hannah's strength would eventually give out. She'd be all alone up on the captain's walk in the cold. He hated that—hated that he'd done that to her.

"Can you make it, Jonas?" Jackson asked, his voice harsh and clipped.

Jonas pictured Hannah standing on the captain's walk overlooking the sea. Tall. Beautiful. Her large blue eyes fierce as she concentrated, hands in the air, directing the wind as she chanted.

If he couldn't make it, he wouldn't get back to Hannah and he hadn't once told her he loved her. Not once. Not even when she sat by his hospital bed giving up her strength for him to recover had he actually said the words. He'd thought them, dreamt of saying them—once he'd even started to—but he didn't want to chance losing her, so he'd remained silent.

He protected people—it was what he did, who he was. Above all, he protected Hannah—even from himself. His emotions were always intense: his beserker rages, his need of her, the stark desire he felt when he thought of her. He had learned to shield his emotions from her almost from the time he was a boy, when he'd realized she was an empath and it hurt her to read people all the time. He'd been hiding his feelings for so long it was second nature to him, and no matter the opportunity, he always fell back on the old excuse that his job would put her in danger.

It seemed pretty stupid now—especially when he called on her for help. He pulled his hand away from his side and looked at the thick blood covering his palm. Not bothering to answer Jackson, Jonas took a breath and leapt, the wind behind him, pushing hard so that his body was flung onto the other roof. He couldn't keep his feet or even attempt to land gracefully. He went down hard, facefirst, the air driven from his lungs and pain burning through his body like a hot brand.

The dark closed in, fighting for supremacy, trying to drag him under. He wanted it—the peace of oblivion—but the wind whipped around him carrying a feminine voice, soft, entreating, enticing. She whispered to him as the wind ruffled his hair and caressed his nape. *Come home to me. Come home.*

His gut clenched and he fought his way to his knees, his stomach heaving again. Jackson hooked a hand under his arm. "I'll carry you."

Off the roof. Down to the street. Jackson would do it too, but Jonas wasn't going to take any more chances with his best friend's life. He shook his head and forced his body to the edge. He had nothing left but survival instinct and sheer will. He found the fire escape ladder and began his descent, every step jarring, his body screaming. The waves of dizziness and nausea began to blend together until he couldn't really tell them apart. His head felt light and the ground seemed far away, reality distancing itself farther and farther away until he simply let go and floated.

Somewhere far away he thought he heard a woman's cry. Jackson echoed it and a hand caught the back of his shirt roughly, the sudden jar sending him right over the edge into the darkness. The last thing he heard was the sound of the wind rushing at him.

Hannah Drake stood on the captain's walk overlooking the dark, churning sea, arms raised as she drew the wind to her, channeled it, and sent it racing across the night to Jonas Harrington. Fear and anger mixed together, two powerful emotions thundering through her heart, racing through her bloodstream to make a high-octane brew, adding fuel to the power of the wind. Tiny pinpoints of light lit up the sky around her fingers as she continued to gather and direct the force to her bidding.

Far below her, sea spray rose into the air as waves crashed against rocks. The ocean heaved and rocked, spawning small cyclones, twisters racing across the surface, twin columns of whirling water raging right along with her.

*Hannah.*

She heard Jonas's voice in her head, the sound a caress, a soft brushing note that both warmed her and sent a chill through her body. It sounded too close to good-bye. Sheer terror swept through her. She couldn't imagine life without Jonas. What was wrong? She'd woken up with her heart pounding and his name on her lips. She'd known something terrible was happening, that his life was in danger. Sometimes it seemed to her that his life was always in danger. "Oh, Jonas," she whispered aloud, "why do you feel the need to do these things?"

The wind snatched her question and flung it out over the sea. Her hands trembled and she bit her lip hard to maintain control. She had to get him home in one piece. Whatever he was up to, it was terrible. When he opened his mind to hers, when they connected, she only caught brief glimpses inside, as if he had compartmentalized his feelings and memories as hastily as possible. She saw pain and blood and felt his rage in a brief cataclysmic flash that he cut off abruptly.

She needed direction to keep him safe and she found and maintained it through Jackson. He was more open to a psychic connection when Jonas was too worried about her using her energy up. Jackson let her see the layout of the alley, the condition Jonas was in, the building they had to climb.

She sent a small acknowledgment, using warmth and color, knowing Jackson would understand, and once again lifted her arms. She commanded the five elements: Earth, the most physical of all elements; fire, both powerful and frightening; air, always moving, her favorite, her constant companion and guide, providing visualization, concentration, and the power of the four winds; water, the psychic mind; and of course spirit, the binding force of the universe itself.

*Hannah, baby, it's now or never.*

Hannah took a deep, cleansing breath and harnessed the power of the wind, aiming and focusing, using her mind to draw the elements to aid her. She whispered a small prayer of thanks and opened herself to the universe and all the potential force she could gather to aid Jonas. The air above her thickened and darkened, clouds beginning to boil and bubble in an angry brew. Electricity flashed and sizzled along the edges of the heaviest clouds and the wind began to pick up even more, so that the cyclones out at sea grew taller and spun faster across the water.

Terror squeezed her heart and knotted her stomach. She

couldn't imagine her life without Jonas in it. He was arrogant and bossy and always wanted his way, but he was also the most protective and caring man she'd ever met. How many years was this going to go on? How many times would he risk his life before it would be one time too many?

*Be safe.* She whispered it in her head, sent Jonas the message, wrapped it in soft, warm colors and hoped the simple request would convey so much more. The wind picked up on her fear, on her anger as she received another flash of sight from Jackson. The two men were going up a ladder and Jonas faltered. Her heart stuttered as she saw him go down.

*Hannah. Baby. I don't think I'm going to make it home to you.*

Her heart nearly stopped. For a moment there was a lull in the storm and then fury swept through her and she let it build, that terrible need for retribution that was a well inside of her, bursting open, shattering every restraint she kept so carefully on herself. She built the wind to a ferocious pitch, a shattering fury that raced through the night to crash down like a hungry tornado in that backstreet alley so far away.

The gale chased hapless men with puny weapons that were useless against the forces of nature. The violent gusts smashed windows and sent glass raining down. Boards were picked up and thrown as if an unruly child throwing a tantrum. Sweet, angelic Hannah directed it all, her flashes of fury sending Jonas's enemies crashing to the ground, helpless under the onslaught of wind and rain and icy hail.

In the midst of it all, she felt Jonas slip, move farther from her, pain knifing through him—through her, the connection beginning to tear. She sent a steady airstream to lift him, the currents carrying him higher, shoving him up the side of the building to the roof and to freedom. She teased at his face and neck with ruffles of a smaller breeze to try to keep him alert long enough for Jackson to get them both to safety.

She felt him gathering himself for one last huge effort and she sent one final blast of wind to coil around him and take him across one rooftop to the other. She felt the burst of tearing pain, an agony knocking her to her knees. She gasped, tears blurring her vision, running freely down her face. *Come home to me. Come home to me.* The plea was edged in reds and golds, blazing with light and need.

She felt his reaction, the struggle to his feet, the fight to keep dizziness from taking over—the determination that he would make it back in one piece. There was another burst of pain and he slipped even more, darkness edging her vision. Desperate, she sent the wind, a rush of air to wrap around him and then the darkness took her too.